APPLAUSE FOR CHRISTOPHER MEEKS'S LOVE AT ABSOLUTE ZERO

"Thermodynamics are nothing; it's that love thing that is so frustratingly hard to figure out. *Love at Absolute Zero* is an excellent read that is very much worth considering, highly recommended!" **- Midwest Book Review**

"It is a given, now, that Christopher Meeks is a master craftsman as a writer.... [The novel] is a gift--and one of the many that continue to emerge from the pen and mind and brilliant trait for finding the humor in life that makes him so genuinely fine a writer."
—Grady Harp, Amazon Top-Ten Reviewer

"As engaging as it is amusing, *Love at Absolute Zero* is, ultimately, a heartfelt study of the tension between the head and heart, scence and emotion, calculation and chance."
—Marc Schuster, *Small Press Reviews*

"It is impossible not to like Gunnar Gunderson. As he progresses from one disaster or near miss to the next, one views him with a mixture of compassion and laughter, but he is such a good-hearted young man that it is impossible not to root for him." **-Sam Sattler, Book Chase**

"The author hit a home run. It's a very good story, very well told." **—Jim Chambers, *Red Adept Reviews***

"A deeply resonant read that manages to be funny without sacrificing its gravity. Highly recommended!"
—Heather Figearo, Raging Bibliomania

OTHER BOOKS BY CHRISTOPHER MEEKS

THE BRIGHTEST MOON OF THE CENTURY

THE MIDDLE-AGED MAN
AND THE SEA AND OTHER STORIES

MONTHS AND SEASONS
AND OTHER STORIES

WHO LIVES? (A DRAMA)

ISBN: 978-0-9836329-1-7
Library of Congress Control Number: 2011930614

Editors, Lynn Hightower and Nomi Isak Kleinmuntz

Book Design, Daniel Will-Harris, www.will-harris.com

Typefaces: Body: PNM Caecilia, Headings: Neutra Display & Draft

Published by White Whisker Books, Los Angeles, 2011

TO MY SON,
ZACHARY MEEKS,
A TREASURE

LOVE AT ABSOLUTE ZERO

BY CHRISTOPHER MEEKS

WHITE

WHISKER

BOOKS

LOS ANGELES

CHAPTER ONE

"A BODY CONTINUES IN ITS STATE OF
CONSTANT VELOCITY (WHICH MAY BE
ZERO) UNLESS IT IS ACTED UPON BY AN
EXTERNAL FORCE."

— NEWTON'S FIRST LAW OF MOTION

The realization of what he'd done made him rush to the toilet. Gunnar just needed to throw up, but turning quickly from the bathroom mirror had made him dizzy. Before he could open the lid, he wobbled and his knees felt like mere hinges with no muscles. He desperately tried to find something to hold onto. His arms flailed. He felt himself fall back. Falling. Falling. And bang. His head must have hit the toilet, but he didn't feel any pain.

His panic evaporated for a second. He stared at the ceiling and wondered why things didn't hurt. Must be the pills.

There was a hammering at the door, and a deep male voice shouted something odd, a language he didn't understand. Gunnar tried to say something, but his voice didn't work. Got to get that fixed. Then his terror returned.

He reached to touch his head, and it was an effort. There was wetness. Blood. He was bleeding, right onto the white tile floor. Blood, Gunnar remembered, was something everyone needed. It's supposed to stay in your body. He felt so tired. Maybe this is what he deserved. She was gone. Maybe he could just get away in sleep. If only he could get some sleep. He closed his eyes.

The door crashed open and there were footsteps, *Don't step on me, don't step on me,* he thought, and he felt hands on his shoulders. His name was shouted, which he recognized. *Something's deeply wrong,* he now knew. *Am I dying?* Shouts, a male and a female voice in words he didn't understand, swirled around him, and he felt ashamed. Soon there were the sounds of an ambulance screaming as they do in those European movies, Do-Dee, Do-Dee. There was such concern in the voices, and someone was crying. *Am I dying? Don't I want to? I can't bring her back.*

-------------->

Four months earlier, Gunnar Gunderson had raced from his office on the University of Wisconsin Madison campus, late to see Wiggins, his boss, the department chair of the physics department. Gunnar always thought keeping a low-profile best — don't fraternize with your boss if you don't have to. Besides, the guy seemed like a big groundhog, a burly gray-haired man with a white mustache.

Outside of Gunnar's anxiety, if he'd been asked if he was happy then, he would have said yes. He was researching the ultracold, trying to reach Absolute Zero. He and his team were in a race to make a certain kind of matter called a Bose-Einstein condensate, which happens only near absolute zero, and his career in part depended on it.

The meeting with the department chair was on a Monday, and Gunnar hoped Wiggins was also late. Gunnar didn't know that rushing to this meeting would become the first falling domino to lead him to the bathroom floor — but there were many steps ahead and things he might do to miss the bathroom floor. Some people, strict determinists, might say that our first breath in the world sets up all that follows. Others talk about destiny. Still others argue free will. Gunnar didn't particularly like philosophy. It was too imprecise. Science was better, and he was happy with his science. He just had to see Wiggins.

He stepped out of the physics building and heard a scream. It may have emanated from under the stairs by the bushes. Was someone being mugged? He shouted, "Hey." He now heard groans. "Stop!" He ran down the stairs and around onto the lawn. "I'm calling security!" He pulled out his cell phone from his pocket.

There in the shadows under the stairs two people wrestled. As his eyes quickly adjusted, though, he realized that he'd made a mistake. A blond young woman in a short skirt and yellow blouse passionately kissed a dark-haired man in a black shirt and blue jeans, and they looked like interlocked origami, she moving up and down. Even though their clothes were on, they were having sex right there, and apparently they hadn't heard him.

A U-Haul van chugged by and backfired. The young couple turned their heads and looked at Gunnar, a tall, thin, thirty-two-year-old man with brown hair and glasses who perhaps could play the Jimmy Stewart part in a university version of *It's a Wonderful Life*.

"Oh," said Gunnar. He put away his phone. "Sorry."

They nodded, then laughed.

He stepped away, feeling like a stunned bird that had side-swiped a plate glass window. The event had startled him. How incredibly passionate these two must have been to do it outside. He'd never done it outside. Or maybe these two had roommates in their dorm rooms, and this was just practical. Yet it touched something in him made him realize he'd been subverting his needs lately. More than lately, he realized. The last year. He was damn lonely. It wasn't just sex he wanted, but more, a spiritual connection, and seeing this couple clarified what had been a hollow echo of late. Yet he had responsibilities — and he was late for his meeting. He needed to hurry to the meeting. If he only knew his first domino had just thundered down.

Remaining unsettled, he wasn't thinking about why he was meeting the chair in a library meeting room. When he found the room number and walked in, the room was dark.

He backed out to check the number again. The lights flashed on inside the room, and two dozen people yelled "Surprise!" and clapped. Gunnar saw old Wiggins grinning and holding a glass of champagne. Gunnar's good friend, Jeet Hanicker from the theatre department, husky like an old football player, bald on top, gray on the sides, raised his own glass. A banner on the wall proclaimed, "Welcome to Tenure."

Wiggins slapped him on the back. "You made it, guy. You've got this job for life."

Other people from the physics department, Carlsmith, Coppersmith, Knutson, and Lawler, shouted out their congratulations.

"How do you feel?" said Wiggins.

"Thank you," said Gunnar, and he started laughing. "Man, oh, man. I thought the committee wouldn't meet for at least another month."

"It was fast and unanimous," said Wiggins. "We didn't want you to worry anymore."

Gunnar couldn't stop smiling and looking around. "I wasn't worrying."

"Sure you weren't," said Jeet, his only non-science friend, offering Gunnar a glass with champagne. "And Jupiter is really just a big cloud with no mass."

People all around Gunnar cheered and shook his hand. His anxiety had flitted away in an instant, replaced with a sense that he could do anything. His future was his oyster. Only later would he feel the force pressing back, setting into motion a cascade of changes.

A catering crew from the university's faculty club entered and opened up steam trays with shish kabob, bratwurst, tofu something, and Swedish meatballs. And what was a Wisconsin buffet without its green Jello mold in the shape of a halo, with chunks of canned fruit cocktail? Something else was in the Jello — fish — Pepperidge Farm goldfish crackers were swimming in it.

"So is your life over now?" said Jeet, his plate full of everything.

"What?" said Gunnar, caught off balance.

"Your tenure," said Jeet. "You've nailed what you wanted. Is it all downhill from here?" Jeet popped a meatball in his mouth and ate like an astonished food reviewer. "Turkey, and I taste fennel. Wonderful."

"Tenure hasn't been my big goal," said Gunnar. "My research is bigger."

"You're still playing with the ultracold?"

"Playing? The competition's stiff. Running on my computer right now is a calculation for super-cooled strontium atoms."

"I never know what to do with my warm strontium atoms."

"Ha, ha. Strontium's a highly reactive metal like sodium. Most people don't know about it, but it's good for what I need. And I'm up against a team from MIT trying to get a condensate of strontium first."

"And it'll get you what? A prize?"

"It's more important than that. It's about understanding."

"You said once you had tenure, you'd get serious."

"What are you talking about?"

"Marrying."

Gunnar stared at Jeet, startled again. "I did not."

"You implied it."

"No, I didn't. Are you going *subtext* on me again? I'm not a subtext kind of guy."

"I read people."

"Then I don't know what I was implying."

"Well, it's been on my mind," said Jeet, "and — " Jeet turned around, looking for something or someone. His face lit up, and he raised his hand. "Sabine, I want to introduce you to my friend."

A woman with long, brown hair and square glasses, late twenties, standing taller than Gunnar who was six feet, smiled and said something to one of Gunnar's colleagues, Sylvia Drexel in the physics department. Drexel, in her fifties, taught astrophysics classes and smiled knowingly at Gunnar, as if Gunnar at last would get his comeuppance. He didn't know why Sylvia had anything against him.

As the younger woman walked over, Jeet whispered to Gunnar, "Sabine is a grad student in theatre, and you two have a lot in common."

"Hold it, I'm not prepared. You can't just — "

"Sabine! This is Gunnar, the man of the hour."

"Hello," said Sabine, holding out her hand.

Gunnar shook it and said, "Nice to meet you."

"You must be thrilled to have tenure," she said.

"I must." He grimaced hearing himself. "I mean, yes, I didn't expect it today. I didn't expect a lot of stuff today."

"Gunnar and I live close to each other," said Jeet. "I'm going to find more champagne. You two chat." With that, he left.

"So," said Gunnar. "Sabine. That's an unusual name."

"Actually, it's quite common outside the U.S."

"Even though there's the rape of the Sabine women?" She frowned.

"Rape," he said, trying to be light. "That's never a good thing, but who knows how parents name their kids, right? I'm Gunnar, after all. And the rape of the Sabine women is just a story, yes? Biblical or something?"

"Mythic, and the word 'rape' in this case has to do with abduction, not forced sex."

"Ah." He shrugged. "I guess I'm not Mr. Oxford Dictionary."

She looked at him soberly. "Romulus, cofounder of Rome, needed to provide wives for his men, so he tricked the maidens of Sabine to come to a festival, and then he kidnapped them. Once in Rome, though, he promised the women free choice."

"Free choice?" He was going to bring up what Einstein thought on the subject, that there was a lack of free will — that one could try things but not will things. Thus, we couldn't take other people too seriously. Gunnar held his tongue.

"Yes, free choice," she said. "If the women wanted to go back to Sabine, they could, but if they stayed, they'd get civic and property rights, unlike other women at the time. Their marriages would be honorable, and they'd be mothers of free men and women, quite a deal then."

"You know your Sabine women. Good. And honorable marriages are always good." He nodded and smiled, hoping he came off funny, but it didn't look like it. "So do you like science?" he tried.

"I started a fire in high school by accident with sodium," said Sabine. "I'm what you might call a science klutz."

"Yes, sodium's a highly reactive metal never found in elemental form — not unlike strontium, which I'm using now in my research."

She nodded as if pretending she knew what he said."So you like theatre?" she asked.

"Not really. Jeet drags me to a few things each year. I never quite get the thrill. After all, the actors are in front of an audience, but they pretend they aren't. And they pretend to be someone else and somewhere else. And we pretend these are people other than actors in front of us on a stage, so that's a lot of pretending, isn't it?"

"And that's why theatre's so *amazing*," she said excitedly. "The very artificiality of theatre pulls you down to the real. I like being pulled down, don't you?" She winked.

"Pulled down?" he said.

"Yes. Into a vortex. A swirl of feeling and meaning like you can just feel another person's entire nervous system."

Was she talking about love? "Okay," said Gunnar, not really knowing what he was affirming.

Her head gave the slightest shake, and she held out her hand again. "Nice meeting you," she said. Apparently that was it. Less than a minute, and it was over. She walked off.

Jeet now approached him. "What did you say to get her to walk off in a huff?"

"I wouldn't say she was huffing."

"Christ, she was perfect."

"She doesn't like science, and I know nothing of theatre."

"After all this time with me?"

"Hey, I don't get plays, okay?"

"This is going to be tougher than I thought," said Jeet.

"Please don't play matchmaker anymore. I have my own ways of doing things."

"I don't even know why I'm trying. After twenty-two years of marriage, I can't say I've seen 'happily ever after.'"

"You and Mattie are fine."

"Ha! She never agrees with me, the house is organized as if by a mad hatter, and she's PC and I'm Mac."

"Hey, Gunnar," said someone slapping him on the back. Gunnar turned to see Harry Borril, a post-doctorate member of his research team with Carl Andresen, the other member, a long-time professor in the department. They were an odd pair. Not quite thirty, Harry always had a three-day stubble of beard, but it looked great on his movie-star face. He rode his bicycle a lot, so he was in great shape. Carl, on the other hand, looked more like a silver-haired baker. He and his wife had once made a load of money starting a Weight Watchers franchise, but it didn't look as if he'd ever used his place.

"Congratulations on your tenure," Harry said. "Who was that babe you were talking to?"

"That babe was a theatre grad student."

"I love theatre."

"Her name is Sabine. Maybe you can do better than I. Don't mention the rape of the Sabine women."

"Why would I do that?"

"Go for it," said Gunnar, and Harry took off.

"See," said Jeet. "Now that's a normal guy."

"So I'm abnormal. Leave me to my own dating."

"All right, all right. I'll give you a couple of months."

Gunnar hung around the party for what seemed like a requisite time, another fifteen minutes. He hurried to the parking lot and quickly opened his ten-year-old Ford Aspire, hopping in. The various journals and books on the floor were like dirt in a vampire's coffin to him — home at last.

As he turned onto University Avenue, he noted the blue smoke he had left behind in the parking lot, and the lighter trail that he now spearheaded. He'd felt his car was well-named. It had always aspired to be a car. Its rough ride and road noise made it not the ideal car, and now this smoke. He should have reacted faster to his red light on the dash last month, the one that said "Oil." He had had too many other priorities at the time and waited a few days to add oil. Then the blue smoke began. The gas station attendant who put in more oil subsequently said, "You burned out your rings, buddy. That'll cost ya."

A lot more things would cost him soon, but he did not know that yet. He continued down University.

Stopped at a light across the street from Taco Bell, Gunnar noticed a large man in a black-and-white-striped shirt hugging his lover to the point of enveloping her completely. The guy looked like a super-sized Santa in a prison uniform, and they rocked in their hugging. What passion, what love. There was love all around him, and he was missing out. This is what he yearned for, what he needed. He wanted this more than anything. People in the world around him were pairing up like oxygen molecules — and with O2, people breathed. He wanted to breathe.

The realization made him grin like a kid. This is what today was about. Yes, he had his research, and the pressure there was high, but he needed a wife. That was the missing component in his life. A wife. And anything worth doing was worth doing quickly.

CHAPTER TWO

"OUR SITUATION ON THIS EARTH SEEMS STRANGE. EVERY ONE OF US APPEARS HERE, INVOLUNTARILY AND UNINVITED, FOR A SHORT STAY, WITHOUT KNOWING THE WHY AND THE WHEREFORE."

— ALBERT EINSTEIN

While Gunnar had a goal, he didn't yet know *how* to find his soul mate. He needed a plan. He needed to do it right and do it quickly because he also had responsibilities — his classes and his research.

Arriving home in twelve minutes, following University Avenue the entire way into the next town and passing the Gunderson Funeral Home — no relation — Gunnar turned onto his narrow road, passed a red barn, and swung into his cracked concrete driveway. Mature maple trees, an evergreen, and one tall walnut tree kept much of his front yard in shadow, and the thick lawn had lawnmower marks. Good — the lawn boy had been there. His house, white and one-story on the edge of farm country, was merely a rectangle with windows and a couple of doors.

Gunnar pressed the button to open the garage. The wooden door yawned ajar and jerked because of the warp that had begun. The warp reminded him of the small roof leak in his garage that drained on the unpainted side of the door whenever it rained. The roof leak and door warp would have to wait — perhaps until the spring. He had other priorities now — a wife.

He edged his car forward until the tennis ball that hung from the ceiling on a string gently kissed the middle of his windshield — directly at the rear-view mirror. Parking this way gave him the precise amount of room to open his car door and move around the car when the garage door shut.

While he may have had his new mission, more pressing was that he had to prepare for his first class for the semester. He needed to print out his syllabus for his *Ideas of Modern Physics I* class, which was for non-science majors.

He strode into his living room where he had a desk, on top of which were two flat nineteen-inch screens, each running from one CPU. One screen was reserved for word processing, which included his upcoming assignments for his classes as well as a paper he was writing about strontium condensates that he'd told Jeet about. The condensates were Bose-Einstein condensates, a state of matter so rare, its properties baffled many scientists. Atoms at such low temperatures lost their individuality and physical properties, going through an identity crisis. If atoms were normally like points, then near absolute zero — minus 273 Celsius or zero on the Kelvin scale — they became little squiggles of wave packets. These squiggles overlapped and behaved as a single superwave. If atoms at room temperature were like little children running around a playground, then near absolute zero, it's as if these beings turned into the surf at Waikiki. The difference was vast.

His other screen, a collection of delineated rectangles, had in the biggest window a model of strontium atoms that he was studying. He was connected by cable modem to the university's more powerful computer.

He brought up a file on his class, which held notes for each class meeting. He had planned out the entire semester so that he could spend more time on his research, which was starting to heat up — there in the ultracold. He added a note to bring to class a tennis ball, a new idea, inspired by the one hanging in the garage. He had to show his new students, his non-science majors, that physics not only could be understandable but also it related to their lives. This sensitivity to their fear of science and of physics in particular was one reason Gunnar rated high on RateMyProfessors.com.

As his file came onscreen, a horn honked — probably a boy for the girl next door. She was fifteen now, and ever since she blossomed, her doorbell hadn't stopped ringing. The biological need to mate was strong; people were just elements looking to be a compound.

The horn honked again. Couldn't people get out of their cars?

On the second screen, a calculation had stopped. It had come up with an answer to one part of an equation for his research. He was instantly energized. As Gunnar grabbed a larger notebook on his desk and was writing the answer down, he jumped at the sound of his doorbell as if lightning had cracked right next to him.

Breathing hard and still in shock, he swore. He didn't need an interruption.

He opened the door to a woman in white sandals, a bright red skirt, and an equally cheery yellow blouse. Her dark hair was shaped into a fashionable bowl like an ice skater. "Mom," he said. "You didn't tell me you were coming."

"Didn't you hear my horn?" she said, furrowing her tweezed eyebrows.

"That was you?"

"Did you forget Thomas and Lori's baby shower?"

He motioned her to come in. "I didn't say I was go — "

"You must go," she said, stepping in and looking into his office as if to find an answer to what kept him. "You can't disappoint them."

"Why didn't you call?"

"I did. Why didn't you answer?"

"So you drove all this way? And didn't she have the baby already? How can it be a shower?"

"You're going to condemn them for being bad planners?"

"You drove for over an hour to tell me this?"

"Yes, and to get you."

"I don't understand. This is so odd. Why would you do this?"

"Thomas keeps your father's hardware store going, for Christ's sake. Are you so important you can't celebrate your own friends' baby? What's happening to you lately?"

He imagined who he might run into at the party, people who would reach with their greasy fingers for another thunderous thigh of fried chicken or ask for another ice cream scoop of mashed potatoes. "It's just I'll run into my old classmates and — "

"You always think they're right out of the Diane Arbus songbook."

"What?"

"They're good people. They all respect you, Gunnar. You're a professor."

"Yes, a professor, so I seem odd to them."

"You used to be more approachable."

He glared at her. "What're you talking about?"

"When you dated that wonderful Allison."

"She left me — remember?"

"And you haven't been the same ever since."

"I'm fine. I'm busy now." He scratched his hands. "There are plenty of other Allisons. This is the right time of my life now."

"Maybe tonight," she said, smiling.

"Not in backwards Fond du Lac."

"Don't be an Eeyore. And why don't we dinner first, too? My treat."

"But their shower's a dinner."

"Who wants Tupperware Jello and buffalo wings at a bar? I said we'd make an appearance, but let's eat."

"I don't know what to do with you, Mom. This is the worst possible time."

"What's happening to you? You're becoming like Mr. Spock."

"My research can potentially bring the university millions of dollars. A lot is on the line!"

"All right, I'll go alone. You could have called me before I came down."

"I didn't know you were — "

She was already opening the door to leave.

"All right, I'll go," he said. "I always like seeing you. But do you realize what a force of nature you are?"

"And you're not? I have a gift in the car, a Diaper Genie" she said. "Wrapped with a card signed by both of us."

"Okay, I'm coming."

---------------➤

Gunnar and his mother settled on Houlihan's, not far from his house and a few blocks into the business park, tucked right next to another cornfield. Suburbia was pushing in on agriculture.

They each had the day's special, steaks with chipotle. After dinner, he trailed her Lexus to Fond du Lac in his car so his mother wouldn't have to drive him back later that night. Gunnar's younger sister, Patty, also lived in Fond du Lac, but he never saw her because he couldn't stand her redneck husband, Brad.

They took Highway 151, a four-lane divided road that was intersected, in part, by farm driveways made of gravel. Bright green cornfields, white farmhouses, red barns, and metallic silos sped past their windows like dioramas. They arrived in the middle-class city of 42,000, which stood at the southern end of Lake Winnebago. A French Canadian fur trapper, probably scratching his fur-hatted head, had come up with the name Fond du Lac, which means "bottom of lake," that is, the south end of the lake. Direction was important to fur trappers.

As they pulled into the city at twilight, passing the Holiday Inn and the Ford dealership, the sinking feeling Gunnar normally had in his stomach in this city came burrowing back. Even though he grew up here and did the whole Boy Scout and merit badge thing, much of his teenage years could be reduced to drinking with Thomas and a few friends at a limestone quarry. Thomas was a brilliant guy, getting some of the highest grades in school — even better in high school physics than Gunnar — yet Thomas had settled for the ordinary, a six-pack life, taking over his father's hardware store, which had been Gunnar's father's hardware store until Gunnar's father died.

As Gunnar passed churches and the boxy two-story wooden houses, he realized what he hated about the place. It was like the first time you saw a kindergarten classroom as an adult. The chairs were small, the sinks were low, and you were too big and awkward.

Gunnar turned left onto Main Street, the oldest part of town — still technically a part of Highway 151. Several blocks down stood the Municipal Bar. The brick Muni was the first floor of an older two-story building that had been built in 1880 and painted tan. His stomach churning now, Gunnar acutely felt how he really did not want to be there. Even so, he didn't consider how sometimes life had cars barrel through intersections or, conversely, a field of orange poppies might sway in a breeze and sing to a swarm of butterflies. He held the big-bowed and wrapped Diaper Genie under his arm and opened the door to the establishment for his mother, who immediately nodded her thanks and entered.

The first thing they saw inside through a thin veil and thick smell of cigarette smoke were the stools lined up against the long bar and an array of older people hunched over their drinks like misers over small change. Beyond that, though, younger people sat at booths or tables like groups of penguins. He could hear music, so-called "classic rock," with a man singing about going from Phoenix, Arizona, all the way to Tacoma, Philadelphia, Atlanta, L.A. "Keep on rockin' me, baby."

"Where are they supposed to be, Mom?" asked Gunnar.

"Toward the back, they said."

They plunged in further. The Muni was a simple, clean place: red leather-like seating, a gray no-wax floor, and paneled walls. Leinenkugel and Iroquois beer signs in neon added to the reddish glow and reflected on beer posters that showed beautiful-breasted women in skimpy clothes and young men who could be their Ken dolls, ready to frolic. The young people in the Muni, in contrast, were much larger, thanks to potatoes, breads, and all the free bar nuts. Keep on rockin' me, baby.

Toward the rear, against the wall with a string of tables pushed together to make one long one, sat a group of a dozen people laughing. Over their heads, a banner read, "Welcome to the World, Jules Jensen Petersen!"

Nearby, two six-year-old boys were playing tag and running around a table, fazing no one. Gunnar remembered being in a bar like this at that age with his Dad. Maybe it was this very bar.

"Lori!" shouted Gunnar's mother to Thomas's wife.

"Audrey." Lori waved back, her dark hair bouncing and more wavy than he remembered. She looked thinner and more fit than ever, too, much like a dancer, and it fit with her bubbly personality. "*Gunnar?*" said Lori in disbelief.

"*Gunnar?*" echoed Thomas next to her, turning in surprise. Thomas held their baby, swaddled in blue and asleep. Thomas, a tall, thickset man with longish blond hair that covered his wide ears, stood, then getting practical, surrendered the baby to his wife before coming around the table, which was covered in beer bottles, plastic-covered bowls of food, as well as paper plates with chicken bones, bean salad, and other partially eaten items. A pile of opened gifts, including small clothes, a collapsed stroller, and block toys were at the next table over. Gunnar handed over the large gift, and Thomas took it, leaned into Gunnar's mother, and kissed her cheek. "Audrey — always good to see you."

"I had to see your little dumpling. Open the gift from both of us."

Thomas did, and when Gunnar saw that a Diaper Genie was for holding stinky, dirty diapers, "Proven #1 in Odor Control," he grimaced. Then again, all creatures excrete, Gunnar reasoned. The alcohol everyone was drinking at this bar was nothing more than yeast piss.

"Thank you, Audrey and Gunnar! We don't have one of these yet."

"I wish I had one when Gunnar was born," said Audrey, glancing to Gunnar as if he'd made too many smells when he was young. "May I hold your little rug rat?"

"Lori will let you. Go on over."

"I will."

Before she did, though, she paused as if to take delight in Thomas and Gunnar together again. Gunnar held out his hand with a big smile. Thomas whacked the hand away and hugged his friend. Gunnar grinned. It'd been far too long since he'd talked to his oldest friend. Sure, they'd taken different paths, but Thomas was like the North Star, shining and always there. His mother was right. They needed to come here tonight.

"Gunnar, man," said Thomas, pronouncing it as everyone had in high school: "gunner" with a hard R. At the university, Gunnar's name came out with a softer R, and he felt less like a soldier in the belly of a bomber.

Gunnar said, "So you're a dad."

"I'm a dad!"

"How is it?"

"Not bad. Exciting."

"Where are all the older folks, the parents?" asked Audrey.

"Lori's folks left early because they had a barbecue to get to, and other people... well, we wore 'em out, I guess."

"That's all right," she said and went off for the baby.

Thomas turned around to point out people at the table. "Since you never come to reunions, you might not remember..." And he turned and pointed to a tall standing woman. "Ursula Nordstrom."

Ursula smiled and waved. He caught his breath as if his doorbell had startled him again. She wore a black top and black jeans over a slim but elegant figure. With high cheekbones, light skin, blue eyes, and long dark blond hair that spilled just beyond her shoulders, she reminded him of a Swedish actress from an Ingmar Bergman film.

"I remember you," she said. "Gunderson, right? We were in Spanish class together. *Como esta usted?*" she said.

"*Muy bien,*" said Gunnar smoothly. "*Y tu?*"

Ursula laughed. "That's about all I remember, sorry."

He'd had a deep crush on her in Spanish class, but he had never more than mumbled to her. He didn't feel as shy anymore — all the teaching had helped.

"So are you still living here?" he asked.

"Let me give you a hug," she said. "It's good to see you."

He scooted around the table and as she stood, gone was her lankiness, replaced by an aura of sureness. With his arms around her, something he'd wished for nearly a decade and a half earlier came to pass — they touched. She was only a little shorter than him, just the right fit. Her hair smelled like fresh apples, too.

"It's great to see you!" Was this fate that they met again? He couldn't take his eyes off of her.

"Remember how I sat in front of you in sixth grade in Mr. Prahoda's class?" she said. "You said when I ran, my ponytails were like isosceles triangles."

He remembered the thirty-degree angles her stiffened hair made, but he said, "Who knows what I thought in sixth grade?"

"You'd told me she was cute," Thomas interjected. "Remember that?"

"All the way back in sixth grade?" she said. "I never knew that."

"More than cute," said Gunnar. "In those days, I felt invisible, so I didn't think you saw me."

"I remember you," she said. "And look how handsome you've become."

He grinned. Was he glad he'd come.

Thomas pointed to a gorgeous woman with a grin sitting at the table near Ursula. "Remember Nora Miller?" Thomas said.

"Nora *Warriner*," Nora corrected, holding up her ring finger, then standing to show off the swollen abdomen of a pregnancy.

"That's right," said Thomas. "*Warriner!*"

The buzz-headed man with a day-old beard sitting next to her, who looked as equally pregnant as she, turned at the sound of his last name and then saw Gunnar.

"You might remember Ray Warriner from wood shop," said Thomas.

"Gunnar, ha," said the man. "I heard you're like some famous astronomer now or something."

"I'm at the other end of physics — physics of the very small. Atoms."

"Atoms...." said Ray as if trying to fathom the right question that goes with it for Double Jeopardy. "I don't know about those things. I just know Roto-Rooter." And he laughed. "You should go huntin' with us sometime — like the old days."

"You never know," said Gunnar.

"Hey, *Gunnar*," said the man next to Ray, completely bald and even fatter than Ray. "Remember me? Duke Needham? Your sister and my sister were friends." Duke stood, and Gunnar walked over. They shook hands. Duke's real name was Jacob. He'd been a star quarterback in high school and everyone called him Duke. Duke had never spoken to Gunnar much simply because Gunnar wasn't into sports and thus had been invisible. In fact, Gunnar couldn't believe they were talking now. "Let me get you a Heineken," said Duke.

Gunnar waved him off. "Actually, I'll hit the bar in a second, but thanks." Rather than get into the whole non-drinking thing, this was easier.

Gunnar looked back over to Ursula, who was in deep conversation with Nora, but Ursula stopped and turned as if feeling his gaze. She smiled again with such magnetism, she could slow down light. "Are you coming?" she said to Gunnar. "Let's catch up."

An arm wrapped around Gunnar's shoulder, interrupting his movement toward Ursula. "There's so much I want to tell you," said Thomas, the owner of the arm.

"You know what I'd love," said Gunnar, "is to sit down with you later when this crowd thins down a bit." Gunnar held up one finger to Ursula to say "one moment."

Thomas noticed Ursula and said, beaming to Gunnar, "Absolutely. By all means talk with Ursula."

"So, Gunnar," said Lori, coming up from the side. "Your mother tells me you've nearly reached absolute zero — a billionth of a degree from it — and if you reach it, the universe will blow up."

Gunnar burst out with a laugh. "No, that's not true. I mean, yes, I've slowed atoms within a few billionths of a degree of absolute zero, but absolute zero is a temperature that's impossible to reach. It's like trying to divide a number by two forever until you hit zero. Won't happen."

He took a step backward, toward Ursula, but Lori said, "But would the universe blow up if you did?"

"I was trying to tell my mother," said Gunnar, who glanced at his mother nearby holding the baby and cooing at it, "that molecular motion generates heat, so it's impossible to reach zero. However, she asked what if I could, and I said she had to understand Einstein's relation of mass to energy. If there was no energy, there would be no mass. Reducing an atom's energy to zero would mean no atom — and maybe no universe."

"Hey," Lori shouted, turning around. "Gunnar's been within a billionth of a degree of destroying the universe!"

"What're you doin', man?" shouted Ray.

"Be careful of scientists!" yelled Duke.

Then nearly everyone at the table and nearby was shouting things simultaneously so that Gunnar couldn't make out what was said. The only one not caught up yelling at him was Ursula, who was talking to a new guy — very handsome — wearing a bowling shirt with a name patch. Gunnar didn't recognize him. Gunnar shouldn't have spoken with Lori.

"Excuse me," he told Lori, stepping back toward Ursula and closer to his mother. Gunnar could read the name patch on the man's bowling shirt, which said "Dave," and Ursula didn't notice Gunnar standing there now. Gunnar understood how pilots must feel when their jets didn't have enough thrust at takeoff. He felt more than awkward and turned to his mother.

"Could I get you a bourbon at the bar, Mom?"

"I'm holding the baby."

"That's never stopped you before."

"Sure, a bourbon would be great."

He turned to Ursula and said, "I'm going to the bar. You want anything?"

"Ah," said Ursula, who, in seeing Gunnar again, seemed lost for a second. She smiled. "Oh, no, I'm fine."

"I have a beer," said Dave, holding up a bottle of Coors.

A fucking bowler with a Coors, thought Gunnar as he stepped toward the bar. All he wanted was to talk to Ursula, and now this. He noticed the bartender's name tag, Julie.

"How're you doing, Julie?" said Gunnar.

"Fine. What'd you like?"

"A bourbon on the rocks with a little plain water."

While he waited, two college-age women sitting to his left chatted, mugs of beer in hand. One woman wore white pants and a red tube top that accentuated her petite figure, and the other woman looked more local, in jeans and a jean jacket.

"Ever see her teeth?" said the woman in red. "How can she teach French if those of us in the front stare at her orange crooked teeth?"

"I know," said the woman in jeans. "But she's French. She probably drinks espresso coffee and smokes. I bet she doesn't shave under her arms, either. She's got dark bushes for arm pits."

"Ewww!" said the woman in red. "How're we supposed to learn from such people?"

"And how about Dr. Grossman's toupee!" Both women laughed.

"What about their *minds*?" Gunnar mumbled to himself.

"Did you say something?" said the woman in red.

"Do you know what it takes for your professors to get where they are?" he said. "Years of study, tests, low pay, politics, projects, research, and the love of trying to help students improve themselves."

"So you must be a professor," said the other.

"Yes."

"At Marian University here?" said the woman in red.

"No, at UW in Madison."

"Man, we want to go to Madison," said the woman in red.

"We go to the satellite campus up here," said the other young woman.

"I wouldn't have pegged you as a professor," said the woman in red. "Except for the jacket. It's a bit outdated."

He looked down at his coat, which he had loved — for the last ten years.

"And your shirt, buttoned to the top?" said the woman in red. "Why?"

Gunnar touched his shirt near his throat, and glancing across the way, he noticed Ursula was still talking with the guy in the bowling shirt.

The two women turned to look where he was looking.

"You're better looking than that guy," said the woman in the jean jacket. "You should take off your coat, though. Look a little more casual."

"Absolutely," said the woman in red, standing, helping Gunnar remove his coat. Were these fashion goddesses put on earth to help him? Once his coat was off, he held it, wondering what to do.

"Just hold it casually over your arm." The jeans lady stood, grinning. "And don't look so professorish," she said. "Unbutton your top two buttons. I mean, come on. It's the new millennium." She reached over to his shirt and undid his top button.

"And mess up your beautiful brown hair a little," said the lady in red. "You could use a haircut, but for now, flaunt it." She ran her fingers in his hair and it felt good. Yet rather than think about that, he thought about what'd it feel like with Ursula's fingers. That's who he wanted. Ursula seemed to hear because at that second, she glanced at him and appeared puzzled. Or was he imagining that from this far away?

"Here you go," said the bartender, placing his drink down on a coaster.

"Thanks," Gunnar said and left a ten-dollar bill. He grabbed the drink.

"Thank you, ladies," he said to the women, who smiled. He strode back to the big table, drink in one hand, his coat and self-confidence in the other.

"Here, Mom," he said when he arrived.

"Thanks, dear." She no longer had the baby. Ursula was still listening to Dave, his motor mouth running.

His mother, taking a sip, said, "The drink's a good one."

"I've never liked this place," said Gunnar.

"It's homey."

"Going to a bar is illusory thinking. You think if you go, something will happen. Never does." He glanced to Ursula, who didn't notice.

His mother laughed, and her laughter made him laugh. He didn't mean to make it so loud, but the very notion of him stuck there like an atom near absolute zero seemed funny. And his laughter caused Ursula to turn and look. Maybe it was his tousled hair or the lack of a coat, but she gazed a little longer, smiled a little brighter, and he smiled back. They both grinned as if they understood something, and what made him smile more was that this contradicted what he'd just told his mother. What are we without contradictions? Maybe Ursula could tell what he was thinking because she smiled more, too, and Dave in the bowling shirt seemed to sense Ursula was locking him out, and the guy said, "Anyway, it's nice to run into you again, Ursula."

She nodded politely and said, "You, too, Dave."

And this was Gunnar's opening. He said, "Ursula, I'd love to catch up now."

"Love to, too," she said, and as he hurried over, around his mother, Ursula glanced at her watch and said, "Whatever we can get in within two minutes. I have to get to work."

"Not ten minutes?"

"I'm sorry," she said, and a waitress swooped in to hand Ursula a coffee with a to-go top on it. After Ursula handed the waitress a five and said, "Keep the change," she looked again at Gunnar. "So give me a Reader's Digest version of the last seventeen years."

Duke shouted over, "Hey, Gunnar."

"In a little bit, Duke," and he said to Ursula, "Like a six-word biography? Let's see. 'Man gets tenure, makes atoms slow'. And you?"

"Oh, that's a challenge. Six words? Let's see. 'Woman divorces... works and studies nursing.'"

"Divorced? So you're single?"

She glanced down as if embarrassed but then turned more toward him. "I liked marriage. Maybe it was a bit old-fashioned, or I am. I don't know why the hell he needed a mistress. We're not France. Is it a male fear-of-death thing?"

She looked him in the eye as if he knew. "I don't know," Gunnar said, "I don't know why some guys need red sport cars or Jesus dangling from their mirrors or mistresses. It's a mystery."

She smiled. "You ever been married?"

"No. Not yet — but I like the idea." His heart soared in saying it, and he outright beamed. She looked pleased, and as he stared into her blue eyes, he fell into their wonderful vortex, a swirl of feeling and meaning as if he were in another person's entire nervous system. They were on the same page, compatible, sympatico — everything. She was the one.

She then looked at her watch. "Whoops. Now I'm really late."

"What's your number? Maybe I could call you?" he asked. He surged with hope. Tonight was meant to be.

"For coffee — or do you mean like a date?"

"Either would be great."

"Because I have a boyfriend right now. I met Jeff speed dating. Ever do that?"

He felt dizzy for a second. Boyfriend? So *unfair*. "No. I never met Jeff," he said.

She laughed, but his whole night had just crashed like an oil platform burning into the sea.

"Speed dating?" he said.

She waved to everyone. "See you, guys. Explain speed dating to Gunnar. I'm late." She shook Gunnar's hand. "Good seeing you again. ScurryDate's a good company."

She didn't give him her number. Then she was gone.

---- - - - - - - - - - ->

"So," said Lori to Gunnar as she casually breast-fed the baby beneath her baggy shirt. Gunnar looked at her but could not smile.

"You're speed dating?" Lori said.

"No. I know nothing about it," he said in a whisper. He'd been sure his destiny had been to find Ursula, but no — she vanished.

At the other end of the long table, his mother said, "What's going on, Gunnar? I heard something about dating." Her cigarette ash fell right on her leg. She brushed it off as if flicking a fly.

"My mother loves to do this," he said more audibly. "Loves to find my life amusing."

"Gunnar doesn't need speed dating," Duke said. "You're a full-time professor, right?"

"And I have a killer deadline in a research competition I'm in," said Gunnar.

"Too busy, eh?" said Thomas. "Maybe he does need speed dating."

"What's speed dating?" Gunnar asked.

"Take *ScurryDate*, for example," said Thomas. "For a reasonable fee, you meet eight people for eight-minutes apiece, and the next day, you fill out a form to select people for a longer date, and if they select you, too, you get her phone number to ask."

"How do you know this?" said Lori.

"Ursula told me. She went to three different evening events. She selected the men she wanted to see again — two the last time. The same two guys put her on their forms, so she nabbed two full dates."

The logic of this was brilliant, Gunnar thought. Yet he also felt low again because Ursula wasn't available. Wouldn't it have been something to tell their grandchildren about their remeeting in this bar? His grandchildren now vanished.

"What d'ya bet that guys at the eight-minute dating thing want to date every girl they see?" said Duke.

"I bet they do," said Thomas. "Heck, guys would date a horny raccoon if it showed up for eight minutes."

"I'm just glad I'm no longer young," said Audrey. "In my day, we went to dances, the theatre or the symphony to meet people."

"You're from Chicago," said Thomas. "It's not Wisconsin."

"Chicago isn't that far away or that different," said Lori.

"The hell it ain't," said Duke.

"It has the Science and Industry Museum," said Gunnar.

"The Science and Industry Museum," said Duke. "A top dating spot?"

"Did you hear that thing on National Public Radio the other day?" said Thomas. "There was a story about dating. Men end up with women who are like their mothers more often than women find men like their fathers. Men love their mothers."

Everyone turned to look at Audrey, who sipped her bourbon.

"What do you want me to say? I think I'm pretty damn good, and Gunnar'd be lucky to find someone like me."

"Damn right," said Thomas. "To Audrey!"

Everyone but Gunnar raised glasses or bottles. Gunnar was too stunned. Someone like his mother, so opinionated, was the last person he wanted.

Soon, Thomas and Lori stood to leave, and they hugged each person. "Good to see you again, Gunnar," Thomas said.

"You, too," he replied, realizing a few more years might slip by before they saw each other again. "Enjoy whatever you're doing," Gunnar said.

"Thanks."

A short time later, Gunnar left. As he drove home, he thought of how he'd been attracted to Ursula and how the world had momentarily stopped. He'd felt as if nothing, absolutely nothing, paralleled her in the universe. Logically, there had to be other people he'd get along with, people who would make great partners, but it didn't feel that way. But why get so worked up? Really — logically — there were other people, maybe even better partners. What's the point of rushing after the first attractive person? There had to be a way to find the better person.

He was reminded of the first time he and his partners created a Bose-Einstein condensate — all the work they did with evaporative cooling — and then their monitors showed the amazing moment. Their atoms had congealed into something shaped like a volcano, and their atoms acted as a single wave. Magic. If they'd been in a musical, it would have been a moment they all burst into song, and he felt the same way right now. He knew the way to find the right person. He should use the same approach that had always served him well: the scientific method. Use the scientific method for love.

CHAPTER THREE

"PREDICTION IS VERY DIFFICULT,
ESPECIALLY ABOUT THE FUTURE."

— PHYSICIST NIELS BOHR

Gunnar still needed to fill in the blanks for his scientific approach to love. His plan had to take in the scope of everything — his needs, women's needs, and all the variables that could lead to a step-by-step process. Using the scientific method, he surely could take action. When he arrived home and parked under the hanging tennis ball, he pulled out his memo book and wrote, "Observe and hypothesize."

The next morning, he did not use his computer. Rather, Gunnar wrote furiously into his memo book, putting ideas down in no particular order. The thoughts blasted down as they happened. It was a way he worked on his science problems, too. It put order into the chaos of his thoughts. He allowed himself to write randomly, a let-it-all-out list, which he could rearrange later. Finding a hypothesis was probably the most creative and random part of the scientific method. There was no one way to do it. Einstein, in coming up with a hypothesis for E=mc2, found himself in one of his famous thought experiments, thinking about running faster and faster until he was running at the speed of light and then holding up a mirror. Would he see anything if the speed of light were constant, as he assumed? What made him picture himself picture flying at the speed of light? He later wrote that the hunt for a hypothesis was about "the irrational, the inconsistent, the droll, even the insane." A hypothesis is "singled out only in the crucible of one's own mind."

In Gunnar's crucible, in order to create a hypothesis, he thought he should be clear on his goal.

He stared at his initial list of the qualities of women he'd like to date, then considered each item, crossing a few off, adding others. He had:

~~Dark hair~~
~~Blond hair~~
Hair
~~Brown eyes~~
~~Blue eyes~~
Can see well (glasses OK)
Tall — or short

He then realized he sought no particular physical qualities beyond being of average weight and height. Was that true? Not completely. He found Ursula's looks exceptional. He needed someone who gave him that kind of feeling. So what else did he want? He wanted Ursula, but because that wasn't going to happen, he wrote, "Look for people who may want to settle down right away and who like living in Madison. They should be independent but want to be with me yet can entertain themselves when I'm busy."

This seemed reasonable. But was the description too much like his mother? If so, was that bad? Instinct said yes. Logic said no because his mother was sensible. It brought up the discussion at the Muni the night before, and he started scratching his hands, which he would do when he was frustrated, so he stopped, stood, and paced. Pacing was good as it gave him a different physical outlet and allowed him to focus on his thoughts. He looked again at his list, which set in his mind his newfound goal: dating and companionship. He felt comforted.

All this planning made Gunnar late for meeting his research team. He dressed in a blue button-down shirt, pressed khaki pants, and tennis shoes, rushed to the university, and strode quickly from the parking lot across campus. As he did so, he couldn't help but notice young couples chatting or holding hands, and he felt envious. These were just kids who could barely afford a cup of Ramen noodles. They had few responsibilities, including relationships. What used to be called one-night stands were now called "hook-ups" as if people were fighter planes in an aerial refueling. How did these kids find it so easy, when he didn't? He swam amid a sense of yearning and anxiety. The last breakup didn't help. Allison. Now she was in Seattle, a vet. So what. Whatever hypothesis he came up with for love should explain these kids and how they found each other. It should explain Allison, too. He didn't act fast enough with Allison. He should be quicker.

His lab was on the bottom floor of Chamberlain Hall, the physics building, and when he walked in, the lights were low, softly lit as in a church. His two partners, Carl Andresen and the much younger scratchy-faced Harry Borril, were eating glazed donuts and drinking coffee from Greenbush Bakery paper cups. Carl glanced at his watch, and Harry pulled out his cell phone to look at the time.

"I know," said Gunnar. "I'm sorry I'm late."

"Everything's ready," said Carl, pointing to the tower of wires, glass tubes, thin silver accordion hoses, various meters, two computer screens and more, standing on a stainless steel plate on a pedestal. The plate had a grid of holes as if from an Erector set. The whole thing looked like a movie designer's idea of a mad scientist's lab, yet everything was conceived for moving a small cloud of gaseous atoms in a clear vacuum chamber to within billionths of a degree of absolute zero. The heart of the operation had two main pieces: an electromagnet to trap the atoms suspended in space, and a set of precisely tuned lasers to slow the atoms down. It was called laser cooling. The slower the atoms became, the colder they were. The atoms had to be suspended in space because no known container could be cooled so low.

"We fashioned a new vacuum chamber, and we think we solved the leak," said Harry.

"Great," said Gunnar. "Let's try her out then."

"Rubidium first," Harry mumbled, his mouth full. If they could replicate the first Bose-Einstein condensate, that of rubidium, now routinely performed all over the world, then their equipment was working again.

"I have a question — about people," said Gunnar, and his team looked at him with anticipation. "Can the Scientific Method explain love?"

Carl frowned, but Harry burst out laughing, launching several particles of doughnut into the air. Harry looked around the room and said, "Are we on camera somewhere? Are we getting punked?"

"No, I'm serious," said Gunnar.

"What the hell do you care about love for?" said Carl.

"You haven't noticed all the young couples on campus? Don't you wonder how they come to be?"

His colleagues paused. "Don't tell me you're in heat at a critical time like this," said Carl.

"I'm not a cat."

"Attraction and connection can't be explained any more than sunspots," said Harry. "It's about chaos."

"Anything can be explained by the scientific method," said Carl, disagreeing. "Even love."

"There has to be a science behind companionship," Gunnar said.

"You sound like Einstein saying that God doesn't play with dice."

"Does this have to do with your getting tenure?" said Carl. "After I earned mine, and I was forty, I just wanted to settle down. It's how I met Jolene."

"How?"

"I don't remember. She found me, I think. There's an idea of pheromones, that we put out our whiffs of desire, and women sense these things. Women sense everything, believe me."

"It's nothing like that," said Gunnar, trying to hide his feelings. "A mild curiosity is all."

"If that's settled, let's get on with our test here," said Carl. "My first class of the semester is in two hours."

"Mine, too," said Gunnar. He glanced to the clock on his wall, and his stomach lurched knowing he needed to prepare more. While eleven years of teaching gave him a lot of confidence once he was in front of a class, he still had to push himself to get himself in front of so many people. Yet he considered teaching important, unlike a number of his colleagues. If he could inspire even a handful of young people each year, they might choose science as a career and find new and important things.

And so they worked. For a few seconds, they were able to create a rubidium condensate, but something threw off the lasers. Their next challenge was to find out why.

Gunnar left for his class with only moments to spare.

-------------➤

"There are immutable laws," said Gunnar Gunderson on the stage, his very first sentence in front of his new class. The classroom was a mini-amphitheatre that could hold one hundred; the wooden seats with swing-arm desktops rose row by row. He squeezed a tennis ball while he paced in front of his black granite-topped lab bench before the class. Fifty-two sets of eyes watched him. He squeezed the ball and strolled, as if psyching himself up for the hour. When he paused, he made eye contact in a sweeping way, yet that seemed to make him as unnerved as many of the students. That brought him back to strolling and squeezing as if the ball gave him centeredness.

"There are such immutable laws as gravity," he said, pushing his voice more boldly than when he began, and he held the ball above him. "As well as immutable laws that predict acceleration and bounce." He let the ball drop. It bounced. All eyes observed. He caught the ball on the rebound. He strode to the blackboard and wrote, "V=32t," and smiled like a minister revealing a great truth. "The acceleration of a body falling where air resistance is negligible is roughly 32 feet per second per second. It's a law of physics. You will learn such things in this course."

Approximately half the students eagerly wrote down his formula. On the first day of class, all students thought of themselves as "A" students; the possibility existed, and attention was high. They wanted to know. Most wanted to know.

He quickly moved to the far side of the bench and picked up a pebble before a standing pan of water. He held the pebble between his fingers over the pan. He let the pebble drop into the water, and rings, like expanding doughnuts, grew across the water's surface.

"Wave action is immutable," said Gunnar. "The rings travel at a fixed velocity. They hit the sides of the pan and reflect back. It will always happen this way. The laws are fixed. We know how to calculate."

He looked across the room. People were writing more notes. Good. He considered the immutable laws of teaching. The students up front taking notes did well, generally — not necessarily A, but at least B. The ones in the back tended not to have notebooks open or write anything down, and they — usually young men in wrinkled T-shirts — lost their focus rather quickly. Most of them fooled themselves that they wanted to do well in college. They were already missing the boat five minutes into the class.

"The fact that you can hear my voice is another example of wave action, audio waves. The fact that you can see me is because of light waves." He moved closer to the students in front and pointed to those wearing solid blouses or shirts. "Red... Blue... Black. Colors are different wavelengths. We will learn about waves this semester. Waves are part of our immutable physical laws."

The door opened. As with every first day, there were those who could not find the right room or the right building or perhaps the right setting on an alarm clock. The students were late. It always happened and always would. Gunnar paused and let the students, a young man in a baggy shirt and shorts and a long-haired young woman with an undersized white Spandex top that displayed her bejeweled naval, find seats. He'd let the waves of their disruption subside.

As he was about to talk, the two late students turned to each other and lightly kissed, as if they were happy to have made safe passage. This caught Gunnar off-guard. Love made its own waves. He'd planned to give an example of one of Newton's laws, but inspiration now hit him.

"Some of you might ask, 'Why physics?' I realize some of you are here simply to fulfill a science requirement, and you may have heard this class is a little fun. I hope it is. But I see physics as *everything*."

He used his arms expressively, more than when the class had started as if whatever shyness he'd had earlier had diminished. He was like an actor who had found his audience. He looked at each and every face now as he spoke.

"Everything on this earth, everything you see in this room, everything about your body, can be explained with only ninety naturally occurring elements, most of which make countless compounds. Ninety elements. The air you breathe, the chair you sit in, the skin on your arm, the video projector on the ceiling — are made from just ninety things we call elements. What a simple world this is!"

Some people chuckled. Good. That meant they were listening.

"Physics can explain everything in this short blip of time we call life. We're here for, what? Maybe eighty years, if we're lucky. How old is the earth?"

"Four billion years," said someone from the front row.

"Yes. Compare your lifespan to the four billion years of earth. Your time here isn't even a sneeze. It's the first few nanoseconds on the way to a sneeze." He could see some people frown as if they'd never contemplated their lifespans before.

"So we don't have a lot of time to learn, now do we?" he said. "Physics explains things, even sex. Did you know that?"

Now he had even the attention of the guys in the back row. They sat forward, blackbirds on a tree limb.

"According to one perhaps crackpot wave theory in physics, basic matter first forms as two competing swirls." Gunnar eagerly dashed to the board and drew first one oval ring, and then a second one whose plane was perpendicular to the first. It looked like an upside down T made of ovals.

"They are tied together as if in marriage. One loop is electric — the male loop — and the other is magnetic, i.e. female. The male loop tries to be free and yet grab onto as many different female loops as possible." Laughter erupted, mostly by women. Smiling, Gunnar continued, tapping on the other loop. "The magnetic female loop is stable and holds onto the male loop, thwarting the other loop's efforts and keeping their unit whole and happy. Such is physics. The theory may be odd but I find it interesting. The universe is about duality, about sex." Everyone laughed, some boisterously.

Pleased, Gunnar noted that the one couple squeezed each other's hands and smiled. If they could find each other, he could find someone.

"This leads me back to basic physical laws. To every action force, there is an equal and opposite reaction force, said Newton." Gunnar lifted a small five-pound barbell from his bench. "Forces occur in pairs. As I lift this up, there's still the force of gravity pulling down on it." He raised the barbell above his head. "I'm pushing up on it in the opposite direction. My upward force is called the *action force*." He gently placed the barbell down and went back to his blackboard to write the term. "The downward weight of the barbell is the *reaction force*." He wrote that term, too. "In this semester, we'll be starting with Newton's laws of motion, and I'll explain them and other laws clearly with demonstrations."

He glanced at the couple who were now smiling at him like Quakers at a meeting. "Demonstrations help explain things," he said. He opened his manila folder to remind himself of all the things he wanted to cover for the rest of the hour. The top page, though, was not his lecture notes but his list of qualities in a woman he was looking for. The pages underneath were more notes on the subject.

"One second here as I get my notes," he said. He glanced to the title of his file folder. It was the wrong one. Panicked, he looked inside his briefcase. He didn't have the folder with him. He saw in his mind's eye where it was — on his desk at home. He had to fake it. He had to pretend he knew what he was going to say, but panic clouded his mind — yet he had to wipe the worry off his face for his students. They could not know that he didn't know what to do.

"How about we start with the atom?" he said, improvising. "Atoms are what my research is about and the word comes from the Greek *atomos* and means 'uncuttable,' which is in reference to its indivisibility, yet investigations since the twenties show an atom's divisibility, and the subspeciality of quantum mechanics has been formed to explain — " He stopped because a couple of hands had shot in the air.

"Yes, you in the back," said Gunnar. Keep the back row interested.

"I thought this was for non-science majors," said the young man.

"It is. Is there something you don't understand?"

"An atom's divisibility. What do you mean?"

Other people nodded. Damn. "Let me start again. Who knows what an atom is?"

A few people raised their hands, and he pointed to the young woman in the front row who looked most eager. "How about you? What's your name?"

"Svetlana," she said, "An atom has electrons whirling around and you get electricity."

"Yes, sort of, electrons are important. And what do electrons whirl around?"

He chose a young man in the second row, who said, "Electrons go around a nucleus."

"Yes, good, and what's a nucleus made of?"

"Protons and neutrons," said Svetlana, unasked.

"Exactly. The atom is the most basic form of matter. At its center are positively charged protons and electrically neutral neutrons, around which swirl negatively charged electrons."

For the next few minutes, he wrote on the board, explained the parts again, and pointed out the distance from the nucleus to the electron was huge in relation to sizes. If a hydrogen's nucleus were the size of a basketball, then its electron would be twenty miles away. "An atom is mostly empty space," he said.

Another person, the young woman who came in late with her boyfriend, raised her hand.

"Yes?" said Gunnar. In that precise moment, Gunnar pictured himself on the old TV show, *The Dating Game,* and in his own speed-of-light thought experiment, he was telling Bachelorette #1, "Einstein always tried to understand gravity by searching for what it was that actually attracted two celestial bodies together. What do you see is the key to how two people like you and me are attracted?" Bachelorette # 1, who he could not see, only hear, said in a smoky voice, "Two people are attracted because — " And then the student before him interrupted, cutting off the bachelorette's answer.

"And so what's quantum mechanics?" she asked. "I've heard that before."

Gunnar hoped the thought experiment would come back later, and he said, "I don't want to intimidate people, so I'll say quantum mechanics is a branch of physics that explains the duality of the atom. An atom is partly a particle, and partly a wave, and so quantum mechanics explains many things including photons, which we'll get into later in this course. Many things in science have been investigated using the scientific method, which we'll also get into later."

Svetlana raised her hand again. He found himself pausing for a second, fascinated by her come-hither look — or was he imagining that? *Attraction* was on his mind — that must be it. He pointed to her and said, "Yes?"

"I've heard of the scientific method before," she said in what he now detected as an accent. "And I've never understood it."

"The Scientific Method is the heart of everything. It's how in science we inquire. First you observe. Then you hypothesize."

Hands shot up in the air, but he knew what the question was and said, "To hypothesize is to make a guess." He could see many frustrated faces. This first class was always so critical because if science seemed too intimidating, students would drop the class, even if they needed it for their liberal arts degree. Worse, they would miss understanding the physical world, which was everything. In many ways, teaching was more difficult than research. As he spun back around to pretend to read his notes to get a few moments to think what to do, inspiration again hit him.

He turned back to the class. "As I said, I like to demonstrate. Let me demonstrate the scientific method. I need four people." Some of the same hands as before shot up. "Okay, Svetlana, and the person who asked the question in the back, and the couple who arrived late, you two in the middle. Come down here and you'll be part of an experiment." It was like a game show.

Once the four were on stage, he turned to the remainder of the class. "Observe well. The first part of the Scientific Method is observation." He then stood in front of Svetlana, who was much shorter than she seemed in her seat, perhaps five two. "Spin," he said. "Just turn in a circle once." She did. When he asked the other three to spin, they did, too. He turned to the class. "What did you see?"

"People spinning," said one young woman.

"Yes, but some spun right," said one guy, "and one spun left."

"Excellent observation," said Gunnar. "And why did one person spin left and the others right? This is where we make a hypothesis and come up with a possible reason why these people turned the way they did. In other words, what factors may have been at work here?"

One person said, "Gender. Male-female."

"Excellent!" Gunnar said. "The two women spun right, and half the men spun left. What other categories might we have?"

"The guy who spun left is very tall, the others, less so."

"Yes. Great. You're observing. So the short people spun right, the tall person, left." He held his fists up in victory and many of his audience smiled. "Anything else we might look at?"

One person volunteered, "We might ask them if they're right-handed or left-handed to see if that's why unconsciously they spun that way." To the group on stage, Gunnar said, "Hold your hands up if you're right-handed." The two women held their hands up as did the young man who'd spun left.

"All right," said Gunnar. "Based on this very small group, what might our hypothesis be for why one person spun left? Make it a sentence."

Many people raised their hands, some of them eagerly waving. Gunnar called on one young woman, who said, "Most people, when asked to spin, will turn to the right, and if they turn to the left, it may be because he or she is taller."

"Fabulous," said Gunnar. "Now that we have a hypothesis, we don't know if it's true. Gender or right-and-left handedness may be more important. What we'd do next, if we were to prove this hypothesis right or wrong, is to go to a whole bunch of people, young, old, tall, short, and maybe even in different ethnic groups — and maybe to different countries, both north of the equator and south of the equator, and really get a large sample. And why might the equator be important?"

Someone shouted out, "Because in Australia and South America, water spins in toilets in the opposite direction. So might people. " People burst out laughing, as did Gunnar, who said, "Exactly. That's exactly right. You see, science looks for answers, and the Scientific Method helps us." And then he grinned, quite wide, and said, "See you on Thursday. Class dismissed."

As he was wiping the chalkboard clean for the next instructor, a woman with a foreign accent said, "Will what you talked about today be on the test? For instance, the stuff about loops and sex?"

"Loops and sex?" he said, turning. It was Svetlana. The way she stood, closely and slightly turned, he couldn't help but notice her figure. In fact, she seemed to wear her body the way kids wore new mittens, innocently and delightedly. She had to know her top was straining. "Oh, no, you don't need to know that." He looked away guiltily.

"Thank you for helping me with my questions in class," she said, flirtatious.

"You're more than welcome." He kept wiping.

"If you have time, might we go out for coffee? As you may have gathered from my accent, I'm from Russia originally. I'm still getting used to things American. I have more questions."

Danger, danger, he thought, and he said, "I have to get back to my research."

"How about dinner tonight?"

"You're inviting me for dinner?"

"You're not married, are you?"

"No, but that's not the point."

"So if you were married, it still wouldn't matter?" She beamed. "That's good."

"No, you can't just go ask your professor out to dinner."

"No? Or even coffee? Is that wrong?"

"Exactly."

"In Russia we do that."

"Here in America, we don't. We want to keep this professional. After all, I'm the person who grades you."

"I just have questions is all."

"My office hours are on the syllabus."

Svetlana stared at him a moment and smiled. "I know your type. That's okay. I'm patient." And she turned, walking as if she was the hook and he was the fish following. She was damn attractive, that's for sure, but one rule he would not violate: no dating students.

As he walked back to the research lab, he wondered about that rule.

And as he approached the lab, he heard screams — from Harry and Carl.

CHAPTER FOUR

"EVERY GENERATION OF HUMANS
BELIEVED IT HAD ALL THE ANSWERS IT
NEEDED, EXCEPT FOR A FEW MYSTERIES
THEY ASSUMED WOULD BE SOLVED AT ANY
MOMENT. AND THEY ALL BELIEVED THEIR
ANCESTORS WERE SIMPLISTIC AND
DELUDED. WHAT ARE THE ODDS THAT YOU
ARE THE FIRST GENERATION OF HUMANS
WHO WILL UNDERSTAND REALITY?"

— SCOTT ADAMS (DILBERT)

"Houston, we have a problem," said Carl once Gunnar ran in. Gunnar swore the two were being attacked or something. They'd simply screamed out of frustration.

"What's going on?" Gunnar asked.

"We found out why the lasers don't hold," Carl said. "This room is too close to the road outside. We're getting too many vibrations when a truck goes by."

"So we have to move rooms?" said Gunnar.

"No way around it," said Harry.

"It's as if destiny is conspiring against us," said Carl. "MIT is probably charging ahead while our lasers aren't holding. We're going to lose for sure."

"I won't let it happen," said Gunnar. "I know there's an open lab on the other side of the building. We'll pay the phys plant people overtime to move everything this week. It should only take three days."

"Three days!" said Harry. "Should we just call up MIT and tell them we're giving up?"

"Three days isn't critical."

"It is," said Carl. "We've fallen behind. It's really more than three days."

"Come on," said Gunnar. "We should just enjoy the time off. It'll let us clear our minds." Gunnar found himself happy thinking about this. With three days, he could formulate a hypothesis on love and perhaps test it out.

"You're just going to go catting around, aren't you?" said Harry. "Three days of sex, sex, sex."

Gunnar's heart took a jolt. He wasn't that transparent, was he? "Right, that's me. Why would you even say that?"

"All that stuff about love and the scientific method you talked about earlier," said Harry.

"Yes," chimed in Carl. "Gunnar and I thought the Scientific Method could be used for love, and you didn't, Harry."

"Love is a game, not a science," said Harry.

"What if we made it a science?" said Carl. "We could help Gunnar find someone in three days."

"Cut it out," said Gunnar. "I don't want to talk about this stuff."

Carl faced Gunnar. "I'm absolutely serious. I know what I went through before Jolene, and I see you're going through it, too. Men have a biological clock."

"And it's related to tenure?" said Harry.

"It'll happen to you, too."

Harry scoffed. "You think Gunnar can find the right woman in just three days?"

Gunnar laughed and nodded. "Yes, that's implausible, don't you think, Carl?"

"If you don't find her in that time," said Carl, "then you'll just have to forget it for a long while."

"How can he forget his quest if it's on his mind all the time? He won't be able to focus."

"It'll just have to take a back seat to what we're doing here," said Gunnar.

"You can't regulate obsession," said Carl, lasering into Gunnar. "You need to be truthful with yourself. Until you find the right woman, we won't have your full concentration."

"Maybe we can get him some sort of pill," said Harry. "The kind where your sex drive just diminishes."

"I'm not going to take a pill like some criminal!"

Harry held out his hands like some savior, but Gunnar knocked them away.

"I'm serious," said Gunnar. "The person I want is not just a catalog item online. My own parents were perfect for each other. I want a relationship like that. I want someone to love me and I want to love her. So at best, I need to understand how to make myself attractive."

"Get rid of those glasses, work out until you're Adonis, dress like a reality star. That should do it."

"I want the science behind it. I'm not going to a gym for months, so there have to be easier things. We must research."

Carl nodded knowingly at Harry. "See," he said. Carl pointed Gunnar back to his screen and brought up eHarmony.com. "A lot of these dating sites now have found ways to catalogue compatibility — we need to do something like that."

Gunnar waved his hands. "We have to study how the best marriages happen. It's not just compatibility. There are other factors."

"Like meeting in a cute way accidentally," said Harry. "I'm telling you, chaos rules. You can't find someone without meeting and seeing if there's chemistry."

"That's it exactly," said Gunnar. "You meet people, converse, see if it clicks. I heard about speed dating — a company called ScurryDate."

"Speed dating is outmoded," said Harry. "These days it's 'sexting' on a cell phone."

"I don't want to even know about that," said Gunnar. "There has to be a science behind sex attraction. We need the data. We're scientists. We can do this."

The other two nodded readily. "I think we can do this," said Carl.

"We can do this," said Harry. "Three days."

"So where do we start?" said Carl.

"I know one place for answers," said Gunnar. "The humanities."

Harry loudly whispered the words "The Humanities," as if they were deep and dark, never to be mentioned.

"The theatre, specifically," said Gunnar. "That's what plays are about, right? Love?"

Both Harry and Carl shrugged their shoulders, and Harry said, "We don't know what plays are about."

-------------->

Vilas Communication Hall wasn't far away, and Gunnar headed immediately to Jeet's office, walking quickly. He didn't want to consult Jeet in particular, but Gunnar had just three days. Jeet seemed to know things Gunnar didn't, including Gunnar's desire for a wife.

Gunnar realized part of his fast pace was that he didn't particularly like going into the theatre building. The students there were odd — not only did some of them seem to have piercings and tattoos and green hair, but all the singing in the hallways was downright obnoxious — and why old Judy Garland hits such as "Somewhere Over the Rainbow," he'd never know. Maybe if he zoomed through the place, it wouldn't be so bad.

He also wasn't fond of the modern glass-and-brick building with its heavy cantilevered top floor. The physics building and most of the university had a classical look. Leave it to some hippy-dippy patron to go against tradition.

Jeet's secretary said he wasn't in but was doing auditions in a particular small theatre, and she gave him directions. He headed there. While he didn't run into many students, and they looked perfectly normal, he felt uneasy because of the dramatic black-and-white photos of past plays down one corridor, portraits of people yelling, laughing, pounding a fist, pleading, flirting, and more. It was too much emotion. As he headed to the theatre, he saw a young couple in a lobby, play scripts in hand, practicing.

"Who do you think brought the ham home?" he demanded.

"I asked you for cookies," she spat back.

"Cookies, ham, same thing!"

Sad, sad, sad, thought Gunnar, and he turned into another corridor. This is what he really hated about theatre. Everyone was so focused on things like hams and cookies, wasting time. If people just admitted they were driven by their DNA, they'd see reality. All animals had this. After all, was he really different from a salmon fish? He was in his salmon period, fighting his way upstream where he'd find his mate — but he was doing it smartly, going to Jeet to discover the currents and white water to avoid. We all carried more than ten thousand years of humanity in our DNA programming to carve our way through a survival-of-the-fittest world. The trick was to accept it and get on with it.

At the next hallway, Gunnar knew he was getting close. There were posters of upcoming plays — *South Pacific, Betrayal, Grease,* and a play called *Copenhagen* by Michael Frayn.He looked at the last more closely because the poster had scientific equations all over it, and two men argued with an older woman looking on. The caption said, "In 1941 the German physicist Werner Heisenberg made a strange trip to Copenhagen to see his Danish counterpart, Niels Bohr. What really happened?" Gunnar knew of this real-life event. Heisenberg was working for the Nazis, and his old friend Bohr was against the Nazis. Each man was brilliant, and each side was trying to create a nuclear bomb.

Gunnar found the theatre, and outside three men and three women, all in their thirties, intently read scripts. They must be auditioning next. Gunnar walked in. The lights were bright on stage. A woman with long auburn hair sat on two wooden cubes placed together and a man, well-muscled in his Polo shirt, pages in hand, stood nearby, glaring at her, saying nothing. In her hands was a book. Jeet's rotund silhouette sat in front of these people as he watched them from the fourth row.

The woman spoke. "It's not about that at all."

The man replied, "Of course, I could be thinking of the wrong book." He paused. "By the way, I went into American Express yesterday."

The woman flinched.

"Good, good," said Jeet to the woman. "This is the cat-and-mouse game he's about to start, and so much of what you don'tsay but show subtly will speak volumes." Gunnar supposed this was the subtext thing again, and he cleared his throat.

Jeet turned. "Gunnar, what're you doing here?"

"I didn't really get a chance to thank you for coming to my party."

"You came here now to thank me?"

"It's not that far."

"I'm in auditions."

"I hope I'm not disturbing you. I'm curious about what you do."

"You are?" Jeet frowned. "I don't believe it, but that's okay. Something has to be on your mind for you to come here."

"It's not that far, really," said Gunnar.

"For you it is." Jeet turned to the actors. "That's it for you two. You did well, thanks. I'll let you know in a few days. Tell the others outside I'm taking ten." He turned back to Gunnar. "I need a break anyway. Is ten minutes okay?"

"Sure," said Gunnar. "Thanks."

"Sit. Don't dance around — tell me what's on your mind."

Gunnar nodded. "You were right the other day. I didn't know it at the time, but yes, now that I have tenure, I'd like a wife, and if I could do it in my window of opportunity, three days — "

Jeet's laugh cut him off. Jeet had a deep laugh that would shake his whole body, which Gunnar normally admired but right now, it sucked.

"I know you're serious," said Jeet, "but three days. People are not shopping lists."

"I realize that," said Gunnar, "but with my other commitments, it'd be best in this time frame. Right now I'm just taking in data, so what can you tell me about love?"

"Taking in data?" Again, Jeet laughed. "I'm sorry," he said, "but you're also hoping I can tell you everything in ten minutes? What kind of data can I give you in ten minutes?"

"Or we can meet later."

"I'll tell you this. This play I'm auditioning for by Harold Pinter, you should read it — Betrayal. Stay and watch."

"Why would that subject interest me?"

"Because Pinter is amazing. No other dramatist better understands and dramatizes the power and battles that go into love than Harold Pinter. You need to find a woman that you can do battle with."

"I don't want battle. I want love. I want companionship."

"Love is a battle, my friend. My wife and I are prime examples — always fighting. If you can't believe in this truth, maybe you shouldn't get a wife."

"You're always contrary. I come for love, you tell me 'battle.' You tell me, 'Maybe don't get a wife.' If I'd have come and said, 'Hey, find me a good woman I can argue with,' you'd have said that I'd need someone peaceable, someone who listens."

"No I wouldn't."

"Even in this you disagree."

Jeet laughed again. "Maybe you're right, but really, do you really want someone who never keeps you on your toes, someone who never disagrees?"

"What's wrong with that?"

"Is that what you look for in research partners?"

Gunnar considered. If he wanted people to do everything he said, he'd have taken on new grad students. Working with Harry and Carl kept him checking and double-checking. They only agreed when the facts dictated it so.

Jeet leaned forward. "Tell me what makes you so determined today when two days ago you weren't."

Gunnar told him about the couple he saw making love, then after the surprise party and the Sabine fiasco, he realized Jeet had been right. Gunnar explained the whole thing up in Fond du Lac, too, and meeting Ursula again. She really felt like the one — but she was taken.

"Go after her anyway," said Jeet.

"No. She's not interested in me, and I've had enough of unrequited love." He didn't tell Jeet about his history. "All I'm saying," said Gunnar, "is this need is like a beep that goes off in my brain every few minutes. I try concentrating, and I'm back to thinking about women. I'm finding I'm glancing at *People* magazine at the grocery store to see which movie star is married to whom, and what their marriage is like. I feel like the culture is sucking me in and I can't do anything about it."

Gunnar didn't even know he had all that in him until he said it, but there, it must have needed saying. Jeet smiled grandly and nodded as if Gunnar had confirmed all his suspicions. "Interesting," said Jeet.

"Anyway," continued Gunnar, "I decided not to put this off any longer, and I'm a scientist. Science should be able to help me. So I thought I'd talk with you about love, formulate a plan, and find the right person for me."

"In three days," said Jeet.

"I have to. I have an intense research schedule. We're competing against MIT. I just want to meet someone nice."

Jeet stared at him a moment. "You know what I find most amusing of all? You think because I'm in theatre, I don't know science. The truth is, theatre is about every subject under the sun. The people in *Betrayal* are in publishing. The people in the play *Copenhagen* — "

"Are into physics, I know."

"At lunch," said Jeet, "I can talk with nearly any faculty member on campus about their subject, but I find most in return can't talk about the arts — certainly not about theatre directing."

"It's not like I'm going to direct ever."

"And I'm not going to write papers on sex appeal, either, but I know the science behind it. I know that beauty and handsomeness are not merely in the eye of the beholder as people have speculated, but that we're hardwired to notice a sexy walk, for instance. Why? Because a sexy walk suggests physical and genetic health. Human beings are programmed.

You're programmed. We're searching for the best genes to partner with because we have to pass on the best genes to our offspring to give them a shot at survival."

"Is that true? You learned this from theatre?"

"And why is that surprising?"

"I'm not saying theatre can't be entertaining."

"Yes, entertainingas if I'm taking up your precious time before death. What I do is as valuable as brain surgery. Now that you have a need for a wife in three days, who do you come to?"

"Nevermind then," said Gunnar standing. "Thanks for the ten minutes."

"Just listen one more moment, Gunnar. I like you, and I'm not saying your need or feelings are wrong. You're admitting to a human need. That's good. Three days — well, that may not be practical, but it's not impossible."

"It's possible?" Gunnar sat.

"I'm not saying it's probable. If finding companionship had one simple way, everyone would be doing it."

"A lot of people are speed dating."

Jeet laughed and looked at his watch. "You're right. I guess we do a lot of things in short, intense chunks. So you'll speed date — makes sense. Think up questions that will get people angry. See how they react."

Gunnar frowned. "I'm not sure I'll do that," he said standing, seeing his time was up, "But you have me thinking about what's driving me. My genes."

"Wear some good jeans to find some genes. Look genetically healthy."

And Gunnar bounced out of there, feeling particularly optimistic.

CHAPTER FIVE

"IF WE KNEW WHAT IT WAS WE WERE
DOING, IT WOULD NOT BE CALLED
RESEARCH, WOULD IT?"

— ALBERT EINSTEIN

Gunnar hurried back to the lab and as he again passed young couples, prevalent as salmon slapping themselves upstream, Gunnar realized he had his hypothesis. If the laws of attraction were about sending physical, mental, and genetic healthy signals, then to attract someone, he had to emphasize these qualities. The last two he didn't worry about, but his physical qualities needed attention. He needed a few more specifics, which Carl and Harry might help him with.

Gunnar could hear their excited voices outside the lab. Maybe the problems with the lasers were fixed without having to move the lab. Gunnar hurried in. Harry and Carl huddled around the computer screen, but on the screen, in a quick succession of photos, was the same young blond woman in stylish dresses, in a bikini on a rocky lakeshore, and in a running suit. At first, it looked like Svetlana, and he froze as if they'd read his mind and then researched.

"What the hell are you looking at?" said Gunnar.

"Hot Russian Brides dot com," said Harry.

"Russian?" said Gunnar.

"These days, Russian brides are the closest thing to mail order."

"You know Beardsley in the chemistry department?" said Carl.

"The old scarecrow-looking guy?" said Gunnar. "He hasn't retired yet?"

"Last February, he married a hot babe that he found here," said Carl. "He told me so, and…." Carl clicked on a button marked "Testimonials," and there was Beardsley, white hair and wire-rim glasses, squinting in a bright snowscape with evergreens in the background and a slightly husky young blond woman with deep blue eyes happily holding him. Carl clicked back to a screen of the young woman they'd been looking at earlier. Her code name was TenderLady P, and it gave her personal data: age 25, five-foot-four, a hundred and eight pounds, Sagittarius, Christian, from Cherkassy in the Ukraine, never been married, and under the heading "Wants Children" was the word "undecided."

"What more would you want?" said Harry. "And look what she says about herself. 'My heart leaps like a kangaroo when I think that my loneliness will exit me if I find a good and trustworthy man for me on this site.'"

"And how is this scientific?" said Gunnar. "She's pretty, probably has nothing in common with me, would be happy to get American citizenship, and then what?"

Carl said, "You have sex and you get back to research."

"And look here." Gunnar pointed to the screen. "It says she can correspond in English in email but says she struggles with live conversation. That means her Russian pimp would write me sweet nothings, but in person, she'd have nothing to say."

"What do you have to say?" said Harry.

"Yeah," said Carl with a hearty laugh.

"Man, you guys are guys," said Gunnar. "If I just want sex, I don't need to go to a foreign country. I want a companion who knows life in Wisconsin, knows how to snowmobile and cook bratwurst."

"Oh, like you snowmobile and eat brat," said Harry.

"She should speak English and like science and have an interesting mind." He was thinking of Ursula. "And maybe she went to elementary school with me and is going to nursing school."

Harry took control of the keyboard. "Oh, man, why didn't you say so?" said Harry, typing furiously: HotWisconsinNursesForPerfectWives.com.

Gunnar slapped Harry's hands off the board and said, "Jeet helped me a lot. Attraction is about physical, mental, and genetic healthiness. Assuming I'm fine in the mental and genetic departments, I have to work on the physical stuff."

"Join a gym," said Harry.

"Or is that show Extreme Makeover still on?" said Carl.

"Still on? It's more popular than ever," said Harry. "Plastic surgery is what you're saying? Impossible in just three days."

"I'm not getting plastic surgery," said Gunnar. "But what can I do if I can get into ScurryDate tonight or tomorrow?"

"Get your teeth cleaned," said Carl. "That's a simple thing."

"My teeth are dirty?" said Gunnar, covering his mouth.

"No," said Harry, "but women notice small things. Why don't you go research ScurryDate, see when you can get in, and we'll research more things you can do. How about that show," said Harry turning to Carl, "Queer Eye for the Straight Guy"?

Carl nodded briskly. "Reality TV can be good, but as you said, we have only three days."

"You're right," said Harry, returning to Gunnar. "We'll have to be your reality show. So go book ScurryDate."

Destiny seemed to be on Gunnar's side as, once back in his office, Gunnar found ScurryDate on the web, saw there was an event for the next night in Madison, and he was able to sign up and pay for it. He also found an alternate speed-dating company called Z-Dating for "Zee dates of your life," which had a event the night after the first, and he signed up for that, too — two nights of dating. He had twenty-nine hours to prepare for the first. He called his dentist's office, and the hygienist had an opening that very afternoon from a cancellation. He called Harry to tell him about everything, and Harry and Carl were pleased. They were still researching the science of attraction. Now they'd switch to studying speed dating — what works and what doesn't.

He drove into the parking garage of his dentist's office, not far from the Capitol dome. Ann, his dental hygienist, greeted him as he entered the office, smiling brightly like Vanna White on *Wheel of Fortune*. The petite woman in her mid-thirties motioned him in.

Ann led him to the windowed room that happened to overlook the state capitol building. He liked going to this part of town a couple of times of year as it made Gunnar feel he was in the center of things. She directed him to the blue reclining chair.

As he scooted in, she said, "I just checked: I saw you only two-and-a-half months ago. Janelle said you were in a hurry for a cleaning, so is something wrong?"

"I'm going on a thing called a ScurryDate and — "

"Ah, speed dating."

"Yes. You know about it — and so I should have clean teeth for it."

"Mind if I look at your mouth?"

He gave a forced smile, if that's what she wanted, and she stepped closer. "Open," she said, and he opened. She used her little round mirror on a stick. As she looked, he stared into her green eyes. He'd never noticed how beautiful they were before.

"They look good to me — maybe a little on the bottom where it's hard to floss and on the outer sides of your central incisors but — "

"That's fine. I want them clean as can be."

She stepped over to the counter to write something on his chart, and as he noticed her healthy toned arms, her straight posture, her face, and her figure with medium-sized breasts, he realized how stunning she really looked. Here she'd leaned over him at least twice a year, and why hadn't he seen? Even though she wasn't part of his scientific approach, here she was, and he felt himself stir. There. A physical reaction was certainly scientific. He wondered what kind of food she'd like on a first date. When she turned back, she caught his stare.

"What?" she said.

He quickly looked to the side, wondering if she knew what he'd been thinking and said, "Nothing. Thinking about the weather is all."

"No one thinks about the weather," she said.

"Did you grow up in Madison?" he said.

"What?"

"Okay, I admit it. I hadn't noticed the color of your eyes ever before. It surprised me."

"That's so nice. I wore glasses before."

"You wore glasses? Are you wearing green contacts? Is that it?"

"No, I had laser surgery. It really works well."

He grimaced. "I could never have anyone shoot lasers into my eyes. It gives me the creeps."

"I can see better than I ever have. It's great without glasses."

"Maybe we could go out for coffee?" he said, using Svetlana's line.

"For what?" she said, and then it clicked. She held up her hand and pointed with the other to a ring. "Did I tell you I just got engaged?"

"No, no." He tried to look happy for her, but he knew his smile was forced. "Too late for me, I guess."

"You're so sweet — you always have been. I'm sure you'll do just fine at ScurryDate."

He nodded, hoping it was true. "I'm cleaning my teeth as part of my extreme makeover," he said.

"Extreme? What else're you doing?"

"Get a haircut, maybe a new shirt. I've got some guys helping me."

She laughed. "Sorry, but that doesn't seem extreme."

"What would you recommend?"

"Laser surgery for one."

"I mean in the teeth area. Will a cleaning do it?"

"I'm just the hygienist. Let me get Dr. Marks," she said and left.

Soon Dr. Marks swept in with his cheerful smile. In his mid-fifties, Dr. Marks was short with slicked-back gray hair and was perpetually friendly and outgoing like Bill Clinton. Unlike the former president, Dr. Marks hadn't been married for the longest time and often spoke about "his new girlfriend," always someone else. He'd been a player, but even he was married now. Everyone was doing it.

"How's it going, sir?" asked the dentist.

"Fine."

"Ann tells me you're going for an extreme makeover — for ScurryDate."

"I need all the help I can get, so I thought I'd start with a cleaning, but Ann suggested it wasn't enough. Would you suggest more? Except what's more?"

"You might consider whitening your teeth. It's just bleaching. A lot of people are doing it. It's for a really bright smile."

"As if I'm super healthy, you mean?"

"Exactly."

"Do it. Let me also ask your advice since you've been, you know, experienced with women."

Dr. Marks laughed. "Hey, what gave you that idea?"

"How many girlfriends have you had? The point is you must have come to learn things."

Dr. Marks nodded, taking it seriously. "I suppose the biggest thing I learned is don't dismiss the one-armed librarian."

"What?"

The dentist told a short tale of meeting a funny and interesting woman online, discovered she was a librarian, and when they finally met, she had only one arm, which she had not mentioned. "I tried to pretend I wasn't surprised, but of course she saw it and then rather than be offended, she said something funny — such as she didn't mix up cherries and watermelons like the one-armed bandits in Las Vegas, and she was a lot softer. She was wonderful. I thought we did great until some other issues sidetracked us later. The point is, don't discount anyone just because of some surface thing."

"How about first dates?"

"I compliment them on their teeth. They worry about dating a dentist, and that puts them at ease."

"How about me? I could use your advice."

"Depends how far you want to go. I've mentioned several times that gap in your front teeth and the crowding below."

"You're talking braces? I'm needing something for tomorrow night."

"I know gaps can be closed quickly — sometimes days — but the crowding takes much longer. Caps just won't do it. That's why I'm suggesting orthodontia for you."

"At my age?"

"You said you were going for an extreme makeover."

Gunnar felt swept up by the day and by Dr. Marks' expertise, but he frowned. "I don't know."

"The best guy's in this building, upstairs. Consulting him can't hurt."

To Gunnar's own amazement, he replied, "Do you think he'll see me today?"

-------------→

In a couple of hours, Gunnar had his teeth cleaned and whitened, and he was standing in the office of the orthodontist up a few floors, Dr. Hammer. What he noticed immediately was a bookcase near the door and an oversize set of dentures acting as a bookend to a set of books on a bookshelf. He glanced at a few of the book titles: *The Teeth of the Tiger*, by Tom Clancy, *White Teeth: A Novel* by Zadie Smith, and *The Skin of Our Teeth* by Thornton Wilder. He moved up to the counter where two white-smocked women sat. One with gray hair stared at a computer screen, then typed sternly as if to erase somebody. The other, much younger, looked up from her book, *Harry Potter and the Prisoner of Azkaban,* and smiled.

Allison? he was about to say, but it wasn't her. This young woman, though, had the same long jet-black hair and big brown eyes and goofy grin — a look that said heck, let's have fun. He longed for fun again. Allison had understood him, even if she'd never understood how serious he was for her. Allison was gone and in her thirties now, not her mid-twenties as was this woman — the same age as when he last saw Allison.

"May I help you?" she said.

"A good book?" he said, pointing to what she was reading.

"Some kid left this," she said defensively. "The doctor doesn't mind."

"Have you seen the movies?"

"Are you here to pick up your teenager?"

Did he look that old? "I'm Professor Gunderson, checking in. Dr. Marks just called."

"Ah. Nice to meet you," and she introduced herself.

"*Allison?*" he said, amazed.

"Madison," she said.

"Yes, I live in Madison."

"No, that's my name. You said Allison."

"Oh."

"The doctor is running late, but he should be back by the time you fill this out." She handed him a clipboard with three pages of what seemed to be hundreds of questions. She gave him a pen. "Have a seat and read it carefully," she said, pointing to the waiting room.

Was that it? No more good conversation? He peered over to see an alcove with sofas. He walked over and sat with the form in front of him and looked again at Madison, who was back to reading. A sense of helplessness overcame him. He'd realized how he bungled something as simple as chatting. Then again, he hadn't finished his makeover. Once he was more attractive and knew all the right things to do and say — he hoped Carl and Harry were on that — things would be better.

He filled out the form. The medical history section contained over one hundred diseases and conditions, asking him if he suffered from any of them. Diabetes, tuberculosis, emphysema, seizures? Jeez, there sure were a lot of things to bring a person down. He circled no for each, feeling better seeing all the no's. Some things were on his side.

After he handed back the form, Madison looked over his pages and smiled at something. Was it his note on the side?

He'd written, "I'm in great health, physically, mentally, and genetically."

"Fine," she said and stood. "Follow me."

Anywhere, he thought. I have a house. Allison wanted a house.

Madison handed him a brochure, a biography of the doctor. "You might want to read this," she said. She brought him to an office that overlooked the Capitol building. Once she left, he glanced at the bio. Dr. Jerold Hammer was a graduate of the University of Southern California and had specialized in adult orthodontia for over four years. That long, huh?

Gunnar put down the brochure and stood to look out the window. From this height, the Capitol building was fully visible, unlike downstairs with Dr. Marks. The building looked like a wedding cake.

Gunnar now noticed his reflection in the window. His eyes seemed so serious. Hell, he was a professor — they should be serious.

Gunnar heard the phone ring in the orthodontist's office, and down the hallway, the older receptionist answered, "Hammer Orthodontia." That made Gunnar think the doctor should change his last name to something more comforting like Assured or Reliable.

He sat in the chair meant for him. An array of people's mouths and teeth on a wall-mounted light box caught his attention. With lips pulled back, full-colored examples of "malocclusions" — so said the heading — were displayed, with subheadings describing each mouth. One looked like Chiclets, well spaced, with the title, "Excessive Spacing" — his front teeth times ten. An almost all-pink-gums shot showed teeth barely descended on one side, with the title, "Submerged Primary Teeth." Then there were, "Open Bite," "Excessive Overjet," "Underbite," "Rotations," and more. It looked like all of Appalachia was up there on the box. The last shot showed part of his problem, "Crowding" — teeth jammed together and overlapping.

The door opened. A handsome man his age in a bright yellow shirt and a Hawaiian print tie walked into the room and extended his hand. "I'm Dr. Hammer. I hear Dr. Marks referred you."

Gunnar shook his hand. Gunnar noticed the man's smile, teeth straight and white.

"Yes," said Gunnar. "Dr. Marks thought it might be worth a trip up here."

"Let me see what's going on," said the man, reaching for a tongue depressor. Gunnar opened wide. The orthodontist inspected.

"Not bad," said Dr. Hammer.

"Really?"

"Most of your teeth are perfectly fine. Your problem is isolated — just your front teeth, top and bottom, the crowding and that gap. Have you noticed how the teeth next to your front teeth on top are slightly backward?"

"They are?"

"I can get them to twist around. You don't need a full set of braces, only braces in the front. You won't even need a lot of banding."

"Banding?"

"Rubber bands. Did Madison show you the different options?"

"No. How soon can you close the gap?"

"That can happen quickly, but the more important thing with all of this are your teeth's roots. Braces apply just the right forces to get the roots to move, too, so that everything is aligned up and down."

"Can the gap close overnight?"

"No, but it might happen within a week. However, the roots need time to align. To do this right, you'll need braces for at least a year."

A week for the gap? But even a narrowing would help. "Okay," he said. "It won't get done if I don't start it. Can we do it now?" said Gunnar.

"Today?" said Dr. Hammer, surprised.

"I have the time."

"I have to make an impression of your teeth and take X-rays and study it all — make a plan. It's not as simple as teeth whitening."

"It's important for me to do this now." Gunnar quickly explained his research, how he had just three days off to find a wife, and how the scientific method would help him. "You had to have a lot of science to be an orthodontist, so you know about science. And are you married?"

"Divorcing," he said. "I'm intrigued by this three-day thing."

"Dr. Marks said you're the best, and I have this ScurryDate event tomorrow night, and I simply have to be my best. Close my gap."

"It won't be closed overnight."

"It'll be better, though, won't it? And my teeth need to be better anyway if everything works out — dates and all, you know."

Dr. Hammer looked fascinated. "This is the kind of thing we had to do in dental school. I'll have you sign a contract, and we'll get started," he said. "We can do this. If you can find someone within three days, maybe you can help me." He turned to his desk, which had sets of dentures with braces on them. "You have to choose which kind of braces first." There were three kinds: standard silver braces, so-called invisible ones that use ceramic braces — only the wire shows, and Invisalign, a series of clear plastic aligners that go over one's teeth but take longer for the process to work.

"Which is the least expensive?" asked Gunnar.

The doctor gave him the three prices, and the standard was the cheapest by a thousand dollars.

"Let's go with that," said Gunnar as if choosing Door number one on *Let's Make a Deal*.

---------------➤

Carl and Harry were at the front door shortly after Gunnar arrived home, and when Gunnar saw them, pleased they were there, they laughed.

"What the hell happened in your mouth?" said Carl, holding a brown briefcase. "Are you a werewolf or something?"

"It hurts," said Gunnar. Everything had gone swiftly: X-rays, impressions with fast-drying plaster, his study, and the braces. The braces themselves were a surprisingly fast process where Dr. Hammer used some kind of superglue and a light-ray gun, and the braces adhered. When it was over, Gunnar had looked in a hand mirror. It was as if he'd chewed a chrome bumper, and the remnants stuck to his teeth. Edges were biting into his inner lip, and the doctor gave him white wax to apply to the sharp edges.

"Did I use too much wax?" asked Gunnar.

"So that's what that is," said Harry, his usual tan satchel for his notes and books strapped over his shoulder. "I don't even see the braces."

"They felt like razor blades against my inner cheeks."

"You might want to cut down on the wax," said Carl. "If not a werewolf, you look like an old man whose teeth are going."

"All right — I got the idea. So what did you find out in your research? What do I need to make speed dating best?"

"Can we come in?" said Harry.

They moved into his living room, and Carl pulled out a folder from his briefcase. "We came up with several things."

"There are studies on speed dating," said Harry. "We have some good things."

"One interesting tidbit," said Carl, "is that men should wear blue, and women should wear red."

"I shouldn't look at women except those who wear red?" said Gunnar.

"These are just subliminal things," said Harry. "What a person wears, of course, reveals who they are, but you need to talk with all colors."

"Men can increase their chances by wearing a subtle scent of black licorice," said Carl.

"You have to be kidding," said Gunnar. "They don't make deodorant in black licorice."

"Cologne," said Harry. He pulled from his satchel a small bottle labeled "Fennel Passion," which looked as if it came from Merlin's apothecary. "Try it. You'll smell like Red Vines Black."

"I never understood why they don't call them Black Vines."

"Too ominous maybe," said Carl. "Here's my favorite tip: when you walk, swagger. That's a subtle cue to fertile women that you're an alpha male, which is what their eggs want. Women need the best sperm."

"We're not just sperm and eggs," said Gunnar.

"This isn't my opinion. We're DNA — so say the studies. So swagger your shoulders to turn on the charm. Show him, Harry."

"This is how most men walk who are not dating," said Harry, and he stepped quickly and purposefully, his shoulders not moving at all. It was Gunnar's normal walk. "And this is how men on the make do it." Harry slowed down, put strut into his amble, and his shoulders moved side to side.

"That looks fakey," said Gunnar.

"You don't see men do this?" said Harry.

"Some of my male students, I suppose, but I always thought they were just from California."

"Try it," said Harry.

Gunnar did.

"Slow down," said Carl. "And your shoulders are doing nothing."

"You're sure this is science?" said Gunnar, accentuating his shoulders.

"Absolute science," said Harry. "You're doing great."

"Oh, and one other thing," said Carl. "Get rid of the glasses."

"That's what my hygienist said."

"She's right. Women know these things."

"Then I need a good laser eye surgeon."

"Why not contacts?" said Harry.

"I tried them once. It didn't work for me."

"Hans Carlsberg went to a good laser eye guy," said Carl. "You know Hans?"

"Biologist?" said Gunnar.

"Yep," said Harry.

"Eyes, teeth, a black licorice walk — you'll be in love in no time," said Carl.

"Absolutely," said Harry. "Let's meet at Indie Coffee on Regent tomorrow to celebrate — or go over your first night in case we need to refine your methods."

"Good," said Gunnar. "I'm feeling lucky."

---------------→

LASIK stands for laser-assisted in situ keratomileusis —
laser eye surgery. Gunnar called the biologist who then
recommended Dr. Anthony Wise, LASIK specialist, at the Ron
Reginald Surgery Center. Gunnar liked the doctor's name.
The man's patients would have Wise eyes. More importantly,
the doctor could see Gunnar for an initial exam late that
afternoon, and if everything was fine, he could have the
procedure the next morning. Gunnar learned the man had
performed over two thousand of these procedures.

As Gunnar drove there, his whole jaw and around his
upper lip seemed tender and sore from the braces — in fact,
his head was starting to throb and a headache was forming.
He should have taken some ibuprofen. He was also anxious.
The idea of lasers in his eyes — yikes.

The building with the laser surgeon had a pharmacy, so
Gunnar bought a travel pack of Advil, took two, and he went
up to the office. By the time an assistant directed him into a
room with a dentist-like chair and instruments around it
that made it appear they were in the belly of a nuclear
submarine, he was feeling better.

Once the assistant left, Gunnar stepped up to framed
poster marked "The Human Eye." He looked closely at the
various parts. The human eye was indeed a ball, and it had
such obtusely named features as the Ora Serrata and the
Sclera.

A sharp female scream made him freeze. He listened
closely. Did he hear crying? Maybe this eye thing was a bad
idea. Maybe he should leave. The door opened and a man in
a white lab coat and a large thick mustache whisked into the
room, smiling.

"Dr. Wise?" said Gunnar.

"Indeed. And you must be Professor Gunderson." They
shook hands and Dr. Wise pointed to the chair for Gunnar to
sit in.

"What was that scream?"

"Ah, the scream. Sorry about that. That was a nurse who
just found out her girlfriend and her husband — Let's just
say it's personal."

"So no one's eyeball was being fried by a laser?"

Dr. Wise laughed. "Heavens, no. I have an unblemished safety record. In fact, the reason I'm seeing you now is not everyone can have laser surgery. A lot depends on the severity of your — " He looked at the form Gunnar had filled out. " — Of your myopia, of the topography of your cornea, and other factors, as well as your consideration of the risks. I won't pretend there are no risks — but no frying eyeballs."

"I use lasers in my research, so I know their power."

"No worries. Please have a seat and we'll see if you're a candidate for the surgery."

Gunnar sat and soon looked into the binoculars of two machines. One tested his vision prescription and the other the topography of his corneas. The doctor also used an ophthalmoscope to examine the interior of his eye including his retina and optic nerve.

"Ah. Things are looking good."

"Am I a candidate?" asked Gunnar.

"You're a candidate."

Gunnar laughed, pleased. "I'm a candidate," he repeated, and he sensed validation, not only for his eyes, but also for his future date-ability. He was a contender for love.

"You wanted this immediately," said the doctor, "so I have you scheduled at ten tomorrow morning. Does that still work?"

"Yes," said Gunnar, standing. "See you in the morning." He pumped the doctor's hand.

Everything was falling into place.

CHAPTER SIX

"THE NET FORCE ON A BODY IS EQUAL TO
THE SUM OF THE FORCES IMPRESSED
UPON IT."

— SUPERPOSITION PRINCIPLE
OF FORCES

In the morning, Gunnar awoke to the loud chirping of a bird. He saw a blue jay on a branch outside his bedroom window. It looked so regal. How fun it must be to be a bird. The number of dreams Gunnar had had over the years of flying like a bird made him wonder if birds were the ideal creature. He smiled. Hey, today was ScurryDate day. He'd be as sure as that bird.

The blue jay sang and seemed to strut on the branch. It must have been a love song because he could see another bird swoop in. The other bird's wingspan, though, was huge, and before Gunnar could realize what was happening, the other bird, an owl, snatched the blue jay in its talons, and the blue jay, flit, was gone with barely a wiggle and no more song. Gunnar launched out of bed and flung open his window, and shouted "Hey!" He knew it was no use. The blue jay would be eaten, no doubt. It was an owl-eat-blue-jay world.

In the kitchen, Gunnar munched on Wheat Chex, which he thought of as Man Chow. The bird snatching was just not a great thing to wake up to. He realized he was really nervous about his next appointment. After all, one's eyes were everything. The doctor had told him of the risks, such as the loss of the corneal flap after surgery, an incision too deep or shallow that caused acuity problems, and of course there was infection, but Gunnar told himself the negatives seemed small considering the doctor's record. He decided things would go well. After all, he was a candidate.

Less than ninety minutes later as Gunnar sat in Dr. Wise's waiting room, a tall, grim-eyed nurse came out with a pill for him, an oral medication to relax him. She also gave him a form to sign that explained that because he was over thirty years old, the surgery couldn't give him both good distance vision and good near vision. He would need to use reading glasses. He had to write the sentence, "I will need reading glasses," and sign.

"I hope the drug's effective," said Gunnar, "because my every nerve is buzzing. The enormity of this is now getting to me."

The nurse gave him a double dose. It did the job. The nurse also gave him surgical covers to go over his shoes and his head. This made Gunnar think he was a sausage — the ends were capped, but what about the middle? Apparently the middle was fine. The nurse led him to the surgery room and had him sit on the operating table.

"Lie down," she said, "and center your head into the indentation." She could have said, "Open the window and jump out," and he may have, he felt so good.

Gunnar smiled when Dr. Wise entered the room in green surgical attire, pulling a green mask over his face and mustache. He covered Gunnar's eyebrows with a special tape. Dr. Wise then attached a speculum to Gunnar's right eye.

Gunnar couldn't blink. A film came to mind, *A Clockwork Orange*. Alex had had the same device attached to both eyes, and Alex was forced to watch violence and porn after imbibing a drug to make him nauseated. Alex then associated sex and violence with a sickening feeling. Gunnar, however, was feeling so good from the relaxant, perhaps a little porn wouldn't be bad.

The doctor spoke as he worked. "I'm now using an excimer laser to ablate part of the corneal stroma."

"Stroma?"

"Connective tissue."

The doctor asked him to stare into the red laser light. One eye at a time, the procedure was soon over.

"Look at me," said the doctor. "How do you see?"

Everything was blurry and too bright, and his eyes were watering excessively. "Yes, fine," said Gunnar.

The doctor laughed. "I know it's blurry and bright, so you need to wear these for the next four hours." He handed Gunnar a pair of thick black-framed sunglasses that Gunnar guessed were cheap knockoffs of Ray-Bans. He put them on and immediately felt better. The doctor also gave him a bag with three different types of eyedrops: a steroid, an antibiotic, and a "tube of tears."

"Use the tears as much as you want," said the doctor.

"Why use the tears if my eyes are watering?"

"The artificial tears are for when they don't water. The best thing to do is just go home and sleep. In the morning, you'll be fine. Over the next three days, your focus will improve. The eye is an amazing organ, the most resilient part of your body."

"What do you mean 'in the morning'? I have a date tonight."

"You might not be feeling up for it," he said.

"I have to feel up for it."

"Your date might be a little blurry — and you may have watery eyes or dry eyes. It's best you just rest."

"No rest for the datable."

"Call me if you have any problems. My card has my pager number."

"Good to know," said Gunnar.

"I'll check you in three months, and we may do a little post-operative enhancement if you're not at 20/20. And you may need reading glasses." He turned to his nurse, who was just reentering the room. "Is Dr. Gunderson's ride here yet?"

"No one yet," she said.

"I drove here," said Gunnar.

"You were told you needed a ride. It was in the paperwork. You can't drive," said Dr. Wise. "You can't see well."

"I knew you were just being conservative. I figured I could always call a cab if it were too bad."

"We don't allow that," said the nurse. "You can't see, and we've had cab drivers take advantage of that. You can't count your money, for one. You need a ride. I thought you understood." She seemed strident. Was she the one with the philandering husband? "You need a friend or relative. I'll call for you," said the nurse.

"But my mother's all the way in Fond du Lac."

"You'll have to wait now, won't you? Give me the number."

Gunnar did. He felt so relaxed, he fell asleep. Next thing he knew, he was being shaken awake. When he opened his eyes, he had to blink several times because everything was so blurry. His mother stood before him, but for some reason, she was so much younger, as when he was a boy. Was he hallucinating?

"Gunnar, get up," she said. He recognized the voice as from his sister, Patty, who had come instead. He cringed. His sister was going through a divorce, and he didn't want to hear about it.

He leaned forward, trying to get up. "I thought the nurse called Mom."

"She did, but her car's in the shop. And — What the hell did you do to your teeth? Are you seventeen?"

"No, I just — You know." Gunnar could feel his eyes watering excessively, and when they were closed, they felt so much better. He kept them closed.

"Aren't you ten years too early for a mid-life crisis?" his sister said, pulling him up.

She led him like a blind person. In the hallway, when she let go momentarily, he walked right into the elevator door and banged his head. "Hey!" he said.

"What? You can't even see the doors are closed?" she said.

"I can't see. Don't you get it?"

"Don't be such a wimp. As Vince Lombardi said, 'Will is character in action'."

"What's that have to do with anything?"

"You thought you could drive after an eye operation? Jesus."

"Why're you so critical?"

"I'm not critical, god damn it. You just look silly."

When they stumbled out front, Gunnar experimented by opening his eyes again. It was still painful, but there, parked in two spaces at the curb, was the Bookmobile. He could tell by its hulk. Patty was a librarian in Fond du Lac and drove the bookmobile. He guessed her husband Brad got to keep their one car.

His eyes watered anew, and he slammed them shut, saying, "You're driving me home in this?"

"What, is it too embarrassing? If you want to be embarrassed, just look in the mirror."

"How am I going to get my car back?" he now realized.

"Well, Mr. Einstein, you should have listened to the nurse. I know she told you — "

"Okay, okay."

"Since I drove all this way, you're buying me lunch, buddy. An expensive one."

"That's fine."

"A seafood place. Lobster."

"All right."

"Really?... How about a new outfit? I could use a new outfit."

"Whatever."

"God, this is great," said Patty. "I should visit you more often."

"You think I could get a haircut first? I'm on my mission."

"Mission for what?"

"I'm speed dating tonight."

His sister, of course, laughed, but she said, "I'm not taking you to your usual Supercuts. This calls for a salon."

"Be nice to me."

"You're going to be better than Brad Pitt."

CHAPTER SEVEN

"THE GREAT TRAGEDY OF SCIENCE: THE
SLAYING OF A BEAUTIFUL HYPOTHESIS
BY AN UGLY FACT."

— ENGLISH BIOLOGIST
THOMAS H. HUXLEY

Because Ursula had loved ScurryDate, the idea of it
for Gunnar loomed like a giant Exxon sign for a
car running on empty. He took a cab to the event
with hope. He needed a cab because his eyes were still
blurry, and they'd get watery for no reason whatsoever. Still,
he didn't think it'd get in his way because it was lessening,
and people may not even notice.

As he'd learned from the ScurryDate website, the evening
would be "eight dates, eight minutes each." Groups would be
set up within a limited age range, in his case, people twenty-
five to thirty-five, and the evening's meeting would be
limited to an equal number of men and women, between
twenty and one hundred people. The website explained the
meetings typically took place in a banquet room of a pub or
restaurant, and before the evening started, a computer
would randomly select eight dates for everyone. Each

participant would be given eight table numbers in a certain order, and when you would show up at each table at a specific time, so would your new date.

Each pair would have eight minutes to converse, asking questions of each other to find out if they were compatible. You were not to ask people for contact information or for a future date. Everyone's nametag would only give a first name and a registration number.

At the end of the evening, back home, Gunnar was to go online and stipulate which people he'd like to ask for a real date. If the other people asked for him, too, then it was a match. Only then would he be given their e-mail addresses and phone numbers to contact them.

"Good luck to you, my good friend," said his Pakistani cab driver when Gunnar was let off at the Great Dane Pub and Brewing Company, the site of that night's event. Gunnar had explained the whole speed-dating phenomenon to his driver, and the driver was a great listener, asking him such questions as what would be his ideal woman and where did he want to get married. He hadn't thought about "where" ever. He'd grown up a Unitarian, but hadn't been to church in years — which is okay with Unitarians. He'd like to get married by the corn field by his house, if his neighbor who owned it would let him. There was something majestic about a corn field.

He gave his driver a twenty percent tip, and then Gunnar scooted out from the back seat and stood in front of the three-story brick building where the dating would take place. He felt anxious in his brown loafers, khaki pants, and a blue dress shirt so new, the creases from the packaging were still in it. The sandblasted brick, newly painted trim, and the elegant bay windows of the old building were a contrast to the other nearby drab buildings in this oldest part of town. Perhaps this building's resurgence was a beacon of good luck. Tonight was the night.

Because he was early, maybe he'd start with a drink. He knocked on the nearest car's hood for luck. Everything was on his side. Even the ibuprofen he'd taken for the pain in his jaw had helped.

Near the restaurant's entrance, a sign said the building had originally been the Fess Hotel, built in 1858. He felt the ghosts of the long-ago hotel welcome him. Inside, he went up to the young hostess in a sleeveless summery dress. Her exposed tan shoulders held the white straps of her bra. When she looked up, she smiled and said, "One for dinner?"

"Oh, no, I'm here for — " He rechecked his watch. "I'm very early, and perhaps I should — "

"You're waiting for someone? Would you like a table, or would you prefer to wait right here — or in the bar, if you have identification." She smiled brightly, trying to be helpful.

"An I.D. to prove my age?" said Gunnar, thrown off. "I'm thirty-five. I'm a professor."

"If you say so."

"Or do you mean a nametag? Aren't I supposed to get a nametag?"

The woman looked puzzled, so Gunnar added, "For the event — is that what you meant?"

"There's an event? Another ScurryDate? No one tells me these things." Now the hostess looked annoyed as if she were always the last to know. "One sec, let me find out more from the manager." She took off before he could say anything. Was he at the wrong place? The wrong time? He grabbed the printout he made of the event from his back pocket. No, it all checked out. A minute later, the hostess walked back with a svelte woman who wore white flared pants and a silky blouse the color of a calla lily. Very sexy. He gasped when he saw her face and long dark blond hair that spilled just beyond her shoulders.

"Ursula!"

Ursula paused, looking as if she should know him. But from where?

"It's me, Gunnar. We met the other night in Fond du Lac. What're you doing down here?"

"Gunderson?" said Ursula, now smiling. "Didn't you have different hair?"

He touched his newly blond hair. "My sister insisted I go to a salon. And they made it this way. A long story."

"It's... well, it makes you look young — but still handsome. And your teeth — I didn't notice the braces the other night.

"Oh, yes, those are new, too."

"Wow."

"You really liked ScurryDate, you said, so ... you know."

"You're here for ScurryDate?" She seemed surprised.

"Yes." In that instant, he realized she might be there for ScurryDate, too. "Maybe the computer will put us both together. Then again, if — "

"I'm the manager here." The hostess, standing next to her, smiled and returned to her podium.

"You never told me you were in this business," said Gunnar.

"You never asked," replied Ursula.

"Don't you live in Fond du Lac?"

"Not for years," she said.

"Oh."

"We've hosted ScurryDate for months now — which is how I tried it. I think you'll have a good time."

"Ah," he said. His heart fell. She was still dating that guy? The world absolutely sucked at times — to paraphrase how his students would explain it. And now his vision went blurry.

"Your mom told me about your research."

His eyes started watering. "My mother?" He didn't remember telling his mother he was looking for a wife in three days.

"Your research into absolute zero." Ursula laughed and touched him on the shoulder. "That sounds odd, doesn't it, like it's absolutely nothing you research. But it's not, of course."

His eyes were watering so much, but he loved that she'd touched him so casually as if they'd been long-time friends. He could feel a drop fall on his cheek. He wiped his eyes with one of his blue short sleeves.

"Are you okay?" said Ursula. "Did I say something wrong? I didn't mean to insult what you do."

"I had eye surgery this morning. That LASIK thing. This is one of those side effects I'm learning about." He laughed. "I just wanted to make a good impression tonight — find someone as great as you did."

"You never know," she said.

"I'm only sorry you're not in the event tonight. I really like you." There, he said it. Maybe it was from the rush of seeing her, but it was also the truth.

"I like you, too."

She seemed to gaze at him wistfully — or was she admiring him? He couldn't see that well. "Once I stop leaking, I'll be okay," he said. "Glad I didn't have urinary tract surgery today."

Or was that the wrong thing to say?

"You're funny." She was laughing. He smiled.

"Thanks," he said.

"Funny how things work out," she said. "I'm sure you'll find someone as great for you as Jim is for me."

Why oh why did she have to be taken already? "Nice meeting you again, Ursula."

"You, too, Gunnar."

He watched her walk off, appreciating her form once more and thinking he should have been more alert in high school. Was it that he'd missed the opportunity then, or had it not really been there? Ever.

"So do you want to wait here or at the bar?" the young hostess asked him. "The ScurryDate E.O. should be here any minute."

"E.O.?"

"Event organizer. She'll bring you downstairs, get you your tag and all."

"Thanks," said Gunnar. He didn't feel like a drink anymore. He sat and waited.

--------------→

Later, he walked down the stairs with the E.O., a slightly chubby woman named Judy, who wore tiny high heels and a midriff-baring blouse that gave a clear view of her love handles pouring over either side of her jeans.

"What the online description doesn't explain," said Judy, "is that our computers take into account the thirty-two dimensions of our personalities — which is four more than E-Harmony promises."

"Dimensions?"

"Such as curiosity, spiritualism, romance, sexual passion."

"I don't remember anyone testing my sexual passion," said Gunnar.

"It's all in the questions. Very scientific."

"That's my approach, too."

"It's a much better approach than meeting potential mates in the wild."

They stepped down into what appeared to be a bat cave: stone floors and walls with subdued lighting. While upstairs had high ceilings and tall windows, downstairs had a low wood-planked ceiling and short windows. The bar featured a blackboard with the chalked-in offerings of the brewed ales and lagers, including Peck's Pilsner, Crop Circle Wheat, and Old Glory American Pale Ale. The event itself would be in an adjoining room. A set of windows looked out onto an ivy-covered patio filled with people sitting in wrought iron furniture.

"Has the event started already? I didn't see where — "

"Those are mere diners," said Judy as if to dine outside was like being a serf in feudal Europe. "Our event will be in a room over this way." She pointed, and they walked toward it, the room for royalty. "It'll be starting in about ten minutes," she said, "but I'm going to give everyone until 6:20 to mingle."

He looked at his watch. It was 5:50. There were three men and two women in the room when they walked in. "Am I supposed to mingle now?" he whispered to Judy.

"Sure. Absolutely. Enjoy yourself. I have a few setup things to do."

He nodded to the women first, both in dresses, then the guys next, in shorts and sandals with socks, and he stood there, his head still bobbing as he tried to relax and appear genetically attractive.

Judy came back by and handed him his nametag and a printed card of his order of tables. He'd start with table eight. All the tables were small and white-cloth covered, with burning candles and placards giving the table's number. Gunnar found the table, right near number seven. Number eight. That's where he'd sit. Right there.

People started drifting in, getting their nametags from Judy, who had made a space for herself at the bar, whose counter was painted black. The women, he soon noted, mostly came in with low-cut blouses. Cleavage. Cleavage was good. Most of the new men wore pressed pants and polo shirts. Some of the men swayed. Gunnar tried walking that way to the appetizer table. Most of the men had tan arms with bulging muscles. Apparently these guys didn't read much. They wasted their time in a gym — or maybe they were roofers. Did women really want roofers?

At the appetizer table he grabbed a small paper plate and a plastic fork and looked over the offerings, which would give him something to do for another few minutes. The steam table offered finger foods: cocktail wieners, chicken strips, fried zucchini, egg rolls. On another side was cold food: mini-cheese logs, celery sticks, carrots, and long, curled shrimp. Shrimp didn't agree with him, so he went for the vegetables and tortilla strips, giving himself a huge dollop of dip. The dip was amazing: a spicy red thick substance with threads of spinach and chunks of whitefish. He could taste horseradish.

But what did it do to his breath? He was a dragon mouth now. At such a social event, why would they make such a sauce? His instant thought was mint gum, but he didn't have any. Then he spotted the parsley garnish on the edge of the fruit plate. Parsley with its chlorophyll was a natural breath cleanser.

He grabbed a sprig and chewed. He liked it. He took two bigger sprigs and chewed them up and swished.

Another guy, clearly closer to twenty-five than thirty-five, approached the steam table.

"Shrimp. Wow," said the man.

"I wish I could eat shrimp," said Gunnar. "I'm allergic."

Gunnar could see the man's name tag: Steve 908. The young man read Gunnar's.

"So you were over in Iraq or something?" Steve pronounced the country's name "eye-rack," as did most Midwesterners.

"No," said Gunnar. "Why?"

"You're a gunner, ain't ya?"

"This isn't my job — or the spelling for the job. It's my name."

Steve 908 smiled and nodded. "Gunnar."

"Heck of a mess, though, that Iraq," said Gunnar.

"Nice tits on that girl, eh?" said Steve.

Gunnar looked up to see at the bar a very blond young woman in white jeans and a low-cut purple tank top as tight as the skin on a plum.

"I happen to know she's a physics professor specializing in high-density quark matter under stress," Gunnar said.

Steve 908 looked baffled.

Gunnar scooped into the dip and ate generously.

"Oh, I get it. You're joking!" Steve laughed, then added, "I'd like to get a hold of her high-density quark matter."

Gunnar nodded. "Maybe irradiate her with a stream of high-energy neutrons." He smiled wide. He could be a guy's guy.

"What happened to your teeth, man?" said Steve, grimacing.

"This?" he said, pointing. "Braces."

"It looks like your mouth's rotting."

"What?" Gunnar opened his mouth again for Steve, who scrunched his face, grossed out. Running his tongue over his teeth, Gunnar felt nothing. "Thanks. I'll check it out." He quickly found a restroom, and as he headed for it, an alluring woman in a yellow patterned dress exited the women's bathroom, drink in hand. She smiled at Gunnar and raised her glass. He nodded and smiled. She grimaced.

He hurried into the men's room and gazed into the mirror. His braces were covered in green dark dots of parsley and threads of spinach from the dip as if he hadn't brushed in months.

He rinsed his mouth over and over, swishing as hard as he could. Most of it came out, and he was able to pull other bits out with his fingers. Soon his silver braces appeared again. The sink was now full of green bits, and he took handfuls of water to wash them down.

He returned to the main room. Steve now stood at the bar, and the bartender in a Hawaiian shirt said to Steve, "What'll you have?" The bartender was tall and square-jawed like a movie star. He probably had no problems getting dates. Perhaps to the bartender, every guy there was a loser.

"A large Foster's malt liquor," said Steve.

"We don't have that here," said the bartender. "We're a microbrewery. Here's our list." He pointed to the blackboard.

"I'll have the Landmark Lite," said Steve.

Gunnar returned to the steam table. After all, his mission was to chat with women, but the fact was he'd never been good at party situations. Was he supposed to go up to someone who looked interesting and say something? Probably.

The blond woman in purple came over to the steam table. Gunnar could see he'd selected the right spot. She glanced cursorily at the food, then slowly looked up at Gunnar and smiled. Her tag, above her right breast but not covering it, said "Chantel 880." He smiled back.

Her smile disappeared and she returned quickly to the food. He knew he didn't still have green in his teeth. "How about that mess we have in Iraq?" he said, using a small cracker to slide into the dip.

"I'm sorry, what did you say?" She moved closer to hear.

He spoke directly into one ear. "Iraq," he said.

She looked immediately down into her breasts and then glared up at him. "My so-called 'rack' is just fine." She grabbed some carrots and celery sticks and marched directly for the bar.

He hoped the night would go better than this.

At 6:15, the room started to get crowded. A sea of heads bobbed above bright and beautiful clothing. One head rose above everyone else's, a great-looking woman with long, dark hair. She could be Rodin's exquisite sculpture of a walking man, only narrower and female. Was she a basketball player?

Judy the E.O. rattled a dinner bell. "Ten minutes until we start. If you haven't picked up your nametag yet, come over here, please. I'm Judy, the organizer for this evening, and I'll help you. Everyone else, keep mingling. Remember, if someone appeals to you, use your notepad and pencil to write down their registration number. You can select people who aren't assigned to you. Also enjoy our food and the bar."

Gunnar could see a young woman in a red dress had a man on either side of her, talking, and she was laughing. One man stared down at her breasts while the other was checking out her rear.

At last, the dinner bell rang again. When the chatter diminished, Judy said, "All right. Everyone go to your assigned seat. You have thirty seconds before the eight minutes begins. After four dates, we'll take a fifteen-minute break when you can get more food and drinks."

Everyone scurried.

Gunnar was the first at table eight. Soon the very tall woman — taller than Gunnar — sat down, and even then he was looking up at her. Her nametag said "Marshelle 702." Gunnar reached across the table to shake her hand. "Gunnar," he said.

"Mar-Shell" she said. "Like Michelle, but with a mar."

"Nice to meet you, Marshelle."

"Do you like tall women?" she said.

"Oh, do we start already?"

"I was just wondering if you liked tall women."

"Sure, tall women, short women, skinny women, fat women — well, not actually fat women."

"So you have a thing against fat women?" said Marshelle, starting to take notes.

"Oh, no," he said, seeing she had missed the humor. "I have nothing against them. I meant I'm unlikely, given probabilities and all, that a fat woman and I would become, you know, ensconced and intertwined."

"Ensconced and intertwined?"

"The numbers aren't there."

"What numbers?"

"I'm talking statistics."

"Like bust-size and waist-size? We're all parts to you?"

"What?"

"Do you know it's unnatural for women to be waifs? Do you know how much bulimia is a problem with young women today? I mean, my God." Marshelle looked upset.

"Look at the magazines in the grocery store checkout line to see what women are supposed to be in this society. Short skinny waifs with big boobs."

"But I like tall women," he said, trying to correct.

"And you like statistics. What are mine, right? I'm a 36A bra size, thirty-two-inch waist — thin enough for you? And six-feet, six inches tall. Too much for you?"

"You're attractive," he said.

"Should I get some pliers so I can extract more compliments?"

"No, you're beautiful!"

She glanced at her notes. "Question one: Let's say we're on a desert isle and it's only us but we don't know each other. I have something you want. We'll call it breadfruit. Then we go on a date and — "

"On a desert island?"

She looked at him hard. "Yes," she said.

"And am I hungry?"

"You tell me."

"I'm sorry," he said. "I'm confused. Breadfruit? Are we in Tahiti?"

If her brown eyes were photon torpedo tubes, he'd be stardust. She barked, "What are you, fifteen? You're supposed to be at least twenty-five."

"I'm thirty-five."

"Right, and I've got a dick."

"What did I say wrong?"

"I'm afraid you won't make my list," she said, and she stood and moved off. He felt deflated. Gunnar glanced at his watch. He had five more minutes to himself. Although his stomach now churned, he zipped back to the buffet table and ate bread, safe white bread.

At the sound of the next bell came Judy's voice, electrodes to his nerves. "Make sure again to write down people's registration number. You'll need the right numbers for going online, remember. You have forty seconds to get to the next table."

Gunnar sped toward his next assignment. On the way, there was another familiar face — Svetlana from his physics class. Why would she be there? She didn't see him, which was good because he didn't want to be seen by her — embarrassing. She was too busy introducing herself to Steve 908.

At his table, Chantel 880 was already sitting. She grimaced as he approached. "I don't think we're going to have much to talk about," she said.

He sat down, saying, "I think you misunderstood me. I was talking about the war in Iraq — not about 'a rack,' but 'eye-rack.'"

Chantel laughed in surprise. "That's different. I'm sorry," she said. "Let's start over. I'm Chantel."

"Gunnar," he said. They shook.

"That's an unusual name," she said. "Or is it a nickname from Iraq?"

"No, I didn't go there, I — It's just my name. Swedish. Gunnar Gunderson."

"You're not supposed to give last names."

"I'm sorry. Gunnar 1002."

"I really wonder if they've had over a thousand Gunnars here. This place must be really popular," she said.

He smiled. She now stared at his mouth. He should have splurged on the ceramic braces — less noticeable. "Should I begin?" he asked.

"I thought we're already talking."

Gunnar pulled out a list of typed questions from his pocket. "In the morning, do you like to make the bed right away?"

"Really? We had sex already, and you want to know if I'll make the bed?"

"You misunderstand."

"Your questions are like this?"

"I'm sorry. How about...." He thought quickly. "If I were a one-armed librarian — "

"You're kind of morbid, aren't you? You first talk about war, now dismemberment. Did your father beat you or something? People who were beaten as kids go on to beat their own family."

"No, I had a great father. He died when I was a teenager."

"A lot of death around you, I see. So, my turn for a question," she said, looking him straight in the eyes. "I can be direct, too. Why did you leave your last girlfriend?"

His heart sank as he thought about Allison, who'd at least understood him. "She left me, actually."

"That's because men are passive aggressive," said Chantel. "Did you know that seventy percent of all divorce petitions are by women? Guys drive their women away."

"Is that true?"

"Yeah, men are cheating jerks, for one. Did you cheat on her?"

"No, no. I — She — I mean, I — "

"Get your story straight."

"Allison was a veterinary student. I was going for a Ph.D. in physics. We had no money and little time. I had to work in the lab often and late."

"Uh huh. I heard that 'workin' late' thing before."

"No. She fell for someone else at vet school. She moved with him to Seattle. I'm a professor now. A physics professor."

She paused, nodding her head. "Like I'm supposed to be impressed. I heard how professors do it with their students. You like to teach them *physics*, do you?"

"Not the way you're implying."

"I'd put out for A's, I can tell you that, and that was just high school."

When the bell rang, neither he nor Chantel wrote the other's registration numbers down. What criteria, what analysis of dimensions, did the ScurryDate computers use to find his dates so far?

At his third table, a petite woman dressed demurely in what looked to be a long Amish dress was already sitting. She immediately stood when Gunnar approached. They shook hands formally.

"Becky 142," she said.

"Gunnar 1002."

She held onto his hand and pulled it to her nose, sniffing. "Interesting. You don't smell musky but rather like candy."

"Licorice," he said.

"So you're edible?" She looked excited, which made him yank back his hand.

"I don't know how to answer that," he said.

She pulled out a piece of paper with what he assumed were questions. "May I begin?" she asked. "Or would you like to? Let's have three questions each."

"Ladies first," he said.

She smiled softly and began. "First, let's say we're on a remote island in the Pacific and — "

"Another island?"

"Is that your first question?"

"I'm sorry," said Gunnar. "I don't know about remote islands. This is my first time."

"A newbie. Delightful. So you don't like the question?"

"No, go ahead. It was rude of me."

Becky gazed at him even more softly. He must have said something right.

She said, "So we're on this island — in separate huts, of course — and if you could put any kind of sheet on your bed, would it be flannel, satin — or nothing at all?"

He was confused. "So we're on a desert isle but we have huts with really nice sheets?" She nodded. "I've never felt satin sheets before. I don't even know where to buy them."

"Victoria's Secret. You'd love satin. Okay, now let's say we go swimming on this island, and you can have me in any swimsuit you want. In women's swimwear, do you prefer a) a tankini, b) a bikini, or c) one-piece suits like the miracle bra tortoise one-piece with a keyhole back?"

"Tankini?"

"That's your second question. It's a tank top with a bikini bottom."

"You work at Victoria's Secret?"

"Yes, sales. That's your third question, though."

"I'm sorry."

"So would you like me in a swimsuit?"

Was Becky offering? Everything was going too fast. "I — I don't swim often. The lakes are usually too cold for me."

"Tell you the truth," she said, "I've got long nipples, and they always stick out when I hit those cold lakes."

He blinked. He was trying to reconcile the way she looked with what she was saying.

"Last question before your turn," she said. "On a first date, what animal are you like the most? Turtle, kitten, tiger, or octopus?"

"A kitten is on the desert isle?"

She laughed. "I think you're a turtle."

"I'm a physicist!"

"I'm a tigress," she said, making her hands into claws, baring her teeth and moving her tongue up and down.

He must have grimaced because she said, "Never mind. You're not right for me. Forget it." She threw her questions down and looked at her watch. They sat in silence until the bell rang.

Now Gunnar was feeling that he was definitely in the wrong place. In fact, he was feeling a little nauseated, and his stomach seemed to be swirling. He moved to the next table but considered just leaving. He reminded himself that he had just a little more than a day remaining.

"Professor?" said Svetlana, sitting. "Wonderful." Her tag said, "Natasha 309." She had a martini glass in her hand with a pink beverage — a cosmopolitan, he knew. His mother loved them.

"That's not your name," he said.

"Are you sure?" she said, laughing.

"What are you doing here?" he said.

"I'm twenty-six and need a green card. Time to marry, no?"

"Surely you have a student visa."

"Then let's call it love."

"I don't understand. Did you follow me here?"

She laughed grandly. "I think it's a joke, frankly, this ScurryDating, but my girlfriend wanted to come, so I'm Natasha tonight. Really, are you taking this seriously?"

"It seemed scientific," he said.

"Well. Maybe you should meet my friend. Good Russian girls make nice wives, no? They love sex, work hard. You see the Russian girl websites?"

"I'm feeling a little uncomfortable now," said Gunnar.

"Here, have some of my drink. Are you drinking?"

"I'm fine, thanks."

"How about I buy my professor a drink?" She smiled seductively, then raised her drink to him and finished it off in a gulp. "They don't have these in Russia. Very fine drink."

"Why are you here?" he asked again.

"I'm telling you truths," she said. Her accent was getting thicker. "Olga needs green card. She's nice girl, twenty-seven, hard worker. You'd like her. She has good big hips, perfect for making babies."

"Are you drunk?"

"Not even close, but you need to loosen up a little, professor. Look at this place. Who but Americans could invent such a thing? Most people in the world are desperate to survive. They need spouses and children to live. Sons and daughters become field hands. Maybe the man works in a factory and hopes he'll keep his fingers each day, while his wife is a prostitute, servicing the young army boys in their barracks. Life is hard, but here you have videogames and Netflicks. *Survivor* is a TV show. Here, you eat Big Macs and drive big SUVs, demanding cheap gas. People here want to be famous — to sing on *American Idol* or be like Donald Trump. American women worry to have face lift or liposuction." She leaned close into Gunnar so that she was nearly at his eyeballs. He looked into her truly beautiful face. Part of him wanted to grab her and kiss her.

"Why are you here, professor?" she said. "You need a woman so you try ScurryDate? I'm a woman, no? I like you. I think you're smart, you're funny."

"But you're my student. The university has rules."

"I'm from Russia. I know about rules. Rules are for the poor."

"They're my rules, too."

"It's a crazy place, Wisconsin," said Svetlana, leaning back.

"Let me buy you a drink," said Gunnar. "It's the least I can do."

"Oh, professor. You are sweet." She handed him her glass.

"Svetlana, you're…" He was going to say sexy, but that would lead her on, and he had just one day left. He needed to break this off, and getting a drink would do it. "I'll be right back," he said.

The buzz in the room was high with all the last minute questioning and answering, which lanced into his queasiness, making him also feel lightheaded. "I'll have a cosmopolitan, please," he said to the bartender, handing him the empty glass. Gunnar reached in his pocket for his wallet, and it wasn't there. He spun around to see if some pickpocket was fleeing with it. He saw no one fleeing, and now he wanted to throw up. Maybe he left the wallet at home. No. He'd had it in the taxi. He'd paid the taxi driver and... Shit. He may have put it on the seat as he was getting change out of his pocket to make the tip exactly $3.60. Please oh please let the God of Lost Wallets come to his rescue. May the cab driver find it and return here.

"How much is this going to cost?" said Gunnar, counting his change.

"May I see your I.D.?" said the bartender.

"Are you kidding? It's not for me, anyway — it's for her." Gunnar pointed out Svetlana.

"Then let her buy it, or show me an I.D."

"My wallet's been stolen."

"I've never heard that one before," he said sarcastically.

"I'm thirty-five. In fact, I'm her professor."

"Isn't that special."

"Get your manager. She'll okay it."

"She won't care what you do with your student."

"I'm talking about my I.D. Your manager can approve me. I know her," said Gunnar, his frustrations not just about the I.D. but the whole night coming to a boil.

"I can throw you out, Blondie," said the bartender.

"I'm no kid."

"Why would you come to a bar without an I.D.? Don't you drive?"

"Call your manager."

"I will, and you'll be out." He grabbed a phone on the other side of the bar.

As the bartender was talking into the phone, Gunnar rubbed his jaw. It was starting to hurt and he felt even more nauseated.

Judy rang her dinner bell and said, "Time for a break, everyone. Fifteen minutes, then we'll begin again. Enjoy the shrimp and the shrimp dip."

Did Judy say *shrimp dip?* Is that what those white chunks were? The spices and horseradish in it had masked the shrimp. He couldn't eat shrimp. No wonder he was getting sick.

People streamed toward the bar, and the bartender hung up the phone and said, "She's coming, and now I'm busy."

"What about my cosmopolitan?"

"You'll have to wait," he said as if relishing the words.

Gunnar turned to the stairs and saw Ursula, his angel, descending from above. Queasiness aside, he smiled. He knew that it was Ursula he should be asking out, not these women here. Women like Ursula were rare.

She looked perplexed. "Are you the one causing the problem, Gunnar?"

"My wallet is gone — maybe stolen. He wants to see my I.D."

"We do have a policy that bartenders have to card if people don't look at least thirty." She turned to the bartender, who was listening while mixing a drink. "He's okay," she told him, and he glared at Gunnar. "Thank you for calling me, though," she said to the bartender. "This is exactly what I talked about the other day." The man gave her a short nod.

She turned to Gunnar with a wide, easy smile: "I'm glad you had him call me — gave me an excuse to see how things are going."

"I don't know how this worked for you," Gunnar said,. "It's not been easy — not like talking with you the other night."

"But you're so interesting," she said, maintaining eye contact. "Don't you tell them you're a professor?"

"The questions are so strange. 'If you were a kitten on a desert island, would you like to be a turtle?'"

Ursula laughed and gave him a wink. Encouraged by her friendliness, this was the time to take Jeet's advice. "I owe you," he said. "How about dinner sometime?"

"Really?" She cocked her head sideways and looked into him as if a doctor finding something unexpected. She stepped closer. "Didn't I tell you I'm involved with someone, Gunderson?" He could smell her perfume, which had a hint of jasmine.

"Yes, but... I can't help it. I didn't talk with you enough the other night. You're an interesting person, Nordstrom."

"Okay. That would be nice, *Gunnar*. I feel bad I had to rush out the other night."

"Great. And could I get your phone number?" he said.

She gave it to him, and he programmed it into his phone then and there. Tall Marshelle stepped up to the bar, and when she saw Gunnar, she said, "Asshole."

Ursula raised an eyebrow.

"Bad date," Gunnar said, nervously flexing one hand. "Would you like dinner tomorrow night?" It'd be his last night of his mission, but he'd be willing to cancel the other speed-dating event he'd reserved through another company. A flash of purple came across his periphery. Chantel stepped closer to get to the bar. As she approached, she said, "Oh, Mr. Cheater."

"I didn't cheat," he protested to Chantel, who made her way forward.

Ursula now took a slight step back, doubt painted on her face.

"I've never cheated on anyone in my life," said Gunnar, holding his stomach. It was really churning now. "I'm not clear how the computer set me up with odd, angry women."

Svetlana then stepped in, not realizing Gunnar was talking to Ursula. "So where is the drink, *Pasha*?" she said to Gunnar.

"There's been a couple problems."

"Then let's get out of here. Who cares if you're my professor?"

Ursula took a full step back, horrified as if Gunnar might be the subject of an *NBC Dateline*: charming small-town boy leads troubling sex-filled life.

"No, this isn't what it seems," Gunnar said to Ursula.

Svetlana glared at Ursula. "He's mine," she said, hugging Gunnar. "Either now or after the semester." Svetlana looked up at Gunnar. "Let's blow this popstand."

"Have a good time," said Ursula, stepping away.

"No, Ursula, you're getting the wrong impression here."

Ursula smiled, "That's okay, Gunnar. It's not like we're an item." And she moved off.

The feeling of deep nausea immediately hit him hard as his jaw throbbed and his eyes blurred again, watering. "I need to go," Gunnar said to Svetlana, pulling away.

"To the bathroom?" she said. "Are you crying?"

"I'll see you in class." He ran. He threw up on the street — luckily into a recycling container for aluminum cans — and a homeless-looking man pushing a shopping cart nearby witnessed it.

"I'm not taking those cans, I can tell you that."

Gunnar looked at him desperately.

"Go right back inside and drink some more," said the man. "You gotta get back up on that horse."

As Gunnar took another cab home — he had cash in his nightstand at home to pay — his mind spun and his stomach churned. Where had he gone wrong?

CHAPTER EIGHT

"IF THE EXPERIMENTS DO NOT BEAR OUT
THE HYPOTHESIS, THE HYPOTHESIS
MUST BE REJECTED OR MODIFIED."

— FROM THE SCIENTIFIC METHOD

As planned, Gunnar met Harry and Carl the next morning at Indie Coffee, a shop close to campus. It was all he could do to push himself there. When he shuffled in, they were eating waffles and waved him over with glee. As Gunnar approached, they both looked concerned.

"Couldn't you find a wrinklier shirt?" said Carl.

"You look terrible," said Harry. "Are you sick?"

"I'm fine."

"Didn't it go well last night?" asked Carl.

"Not really," said Gunnar.

"That's why we're here," said Harry. "A little Thursday morning quarterbacking, and we'll get you back up on the horse."

"Please no," said Gunnar. "First, a homeless alcoholic told me the same thing about the horse last night when I was puking in the street, and second, you're mixing metaphors."

"*Sorry* if I'm not an English professor," said Harry. "The point is, we're scientists, and we can figure this stuff out."

"Your hair," said Carl. "Is there something different about it?"

"You're concerned about my hair, Carl?"

"You look different," said Harry.

"My hair is shorter and blond."

"Ah," said Harry to Carl's "Okay."

"Is it too much?" asked Gunnar.

"It makes you look stupid," said Harry. "Can you recolor it today?"

"Good idea," said Carl.

"There's no point," said Gunnar. "I'm stopping here. No more dating."

"It can't be that bad," said Harry.

"Yeah, let us decide," said Carl. "Tell us about last night. Give us the blow-by-blow."

Gunnar did, and Harry and Carl laughed so much in Gunnar's telling — roaring at Ursula, Marshelle, Chantel, and especially Svetlana, punctuating often with the phrase "That's bad" — that by the end, Gunnar was nodding, feeling better. He made his vomiting seem hilarious.

"So tonight you have Z-Dating?"

"Not anymore," said Gunnar. "I'm going to cancel. I'm clearly clueless."

"You have to go," said Harry.

"Have to go," said Carl. "Do you think Einstein, when his math didn't make sense, stopped investigating relativity or condensates? Both ideas seemed preposterous, and yet they changed our whole idea of the universe. Where would we be without him?"

"This is hardly as important as Einstein. In fact, you even saying that makes me realize we have to focus on Absolute Zero. I'm forgetting about love."

"Did Einstein forget Mileva?"

"Yes, Mileva," echoed Carl. "Einstein was a player."

"Mileva was hot and smart. She understood his calculations."

"May have even helped."

"There's debate about that," said Gunnar.

The fact was with the discovery of Einstein's love letters to and from Mileva Maric, the couple gave much hope for romance to brainiacs across the world. Einstein had doggedly pursued Mileva, the only female student in physics at the Zurich Polytechnic in Switzerland, where Einstein went after high school, and after he won her over all his male rivals, he lived with her without benefit of marriage in 1901 — a scandal in those days. In fact, she had his baby out of wedlock, a child lost to history. Then Mileva became his wife.

"If Einstein could have sex, love, and physics, so can I?" said Gunnar.

"Yes," said Carl. "A wife might make you a better physicist. It did Einstein. It has me."

"Here, let's order you some waffles," said Harry.

They went over the evening a few more times, with Harry and Carl asking specific questions.

"Based on more of our research, we have a few extra things you can do," said Carl. "When the woman talks, say 'uh huh' every now and then. Sociologist Deborah Tannen, who's studied male-female communication, says that when women talk to each other, they 'uh huh' a lot or say 'Yes,' and 'I see.' Tannen calls these 'minimal encouragers,' and women feel great if they think you're listening. Try that."

"Uh huh."

"Exactly," said Harry.

"But I had some weird women last night, angry people."

"I'm finding that sometimes in dating," said Harry. "Women in their thirties have been heartbroken a few times. You have to empathize."

"And you need to go in with better questions," said Carl.

"Yes," said Harry. "And considering how the braces didn't go over, can't you get rid of them today, or at least go for something less shiny?"

"There are ceramic ones," said Carl.

"I was thinking the same thing," said Gunnar. "Even if my credit card will scream."

"Buy the ceramic braces. Time is valuable," said Carl. "Unless we throw the towel in on our research now."

"We can't," said Gunnar. "We have foundations who are supporting us. In fact, this morning, in my deepest despair, I was thinking about strontium. We're working with it because it's a heavier metal. There's a rare isotope of it, whichmay have the ideal scattering length for producing a Bose-Einstein Condensate."

"Compared to the other, more abundant isotopes?" said Harry.

"Do you know how much work it'd take to get that isotope?" said Carl. "I don't see how it could work."

"I'm going to model it tomorrow," said Gunnar.

"Then find a wife fast," said Carl. "Or just get laid. We need to get to our real work."

"To your future wife," said Harry, holding up the pump jar of maple syrup.

Carl raised the blueberry pump, and echoed, "To your future wife."

Gunnar snatched the strawberry, and they clanked in a toast. "To my future wife."

CHAPTER NINE

"TWO BODIES ATTRACT EACH OTHER WITH
EQUAL AND OPPOSITE FORCES; THE
MAGNITUDE OF THIS FORCE IS
PROPORTIONAL TO THE PRODUCT OF THE
TWO MASSES AND IS ALSO PROPORTIONAL
TO THE INVERSE SQUARE OF THE DISTANCE
BETWEEN THE CENTERS OF MASS OF THE
TWO BODIES."

— NEWTON'S UNIVERSAL LAW
OF GRAVITATION

Z-Dating was five dollars cheaper and had the slogan, "It's one minute less for more." Z-Dating offered "nine dates, seven minutes each." Gunnar nodded, liking the numbers. One more date would boost up the odds.

Early that afternoon, he went to his usual Supercuts and had his hair dyed brown, something close to what he had naturally. He was also able to convince his orthodontist to redo his braces in ceramic, though even asking made Gunnar cringe at the cost. The orthodontist did it for a fraction of the normal price, however — basically for the original difference in cost — because hearing the details about the previous night made the doctor wince and nod.

"I can help," Dr. Hammer said.

Gunnar also saw his gap was almost closed. The braces were adjusted to insure the roots would also move correctly and vertically.

The night's event was in the elegant King Royale Inn down East Washington near the airport. Gunnar again arrived early, and a sign in the lobby welcomed Z-Dating members, directing them to the Lakewinds Room upstairs. As Gunnar walked past a group of people near the downstairs lounge, the carpet had a strange lump that tripped him, then he heard in a British voice, "That man just stepped on my foot." The lump he'd felt had been someone's foot.

Gunnar whirled around. A red-haired woman around thirty years old held her white sandaled foot with one hand. She leaned against the wall and examined her foot. She wore a low-cut blue dress and had the whitest skin he'd ever seen, accented with freckles.

Her friend, a dark-haired woman with a scowl, shouted at Gunnar, "Hey, guy. You stepped on my friend's foot."

Gunnar hurried over to the red-haired woman. "I'm terribly sorry. I didn't know. Are you okay?" He kneeled to look at her foot more carefully, but she put her foot down, seemingly embarrassed.

"Yes, thanks, and my other foot is perfectly fine," she said, again in a British accent with a funny bend to it. He stood, and when they looked upon each other, she smiled and said, "I'm sorry, too. I didn't mean to cause a ruckus." She turned to her friend. "You didn't have to call him over."

"I have a meeting in a few minutes," said Gunnar, "but —"

"You're in that Z-Dating thing?" the red-headed woman said, seemingly astounded.

"Yes, in the Lakewinds room upstairs… Are you?"

She laughed. "Just heard about it. Americans are inventive folk, I'll grant you that. Nothing like this would ever be created in Europe."

"You're British?"

"Danish, actually. Danish schools hire British faculty to teach English."

"I love your accent," said Gunnar. "I wish I spoke that way."

"I'm Kara. And this is my friend Mindy." She motioned to her friend. "Thirteen years ago I was an AFS student living in Mindy's house, so I'm visiting."

Gunnar shook Mindy's hand. "Nice to meet you, Mindy. I'm Gunnar Gunderson."

"That's Scandinavian," said Kara. "Is that with an 'E-N' or an 'O-N'?" Kara asked.

"O-N."

"Swedish, then. Gunnar Gunderson," Kara said, pronouncing it *Goo-na Goon-dason*.

"My father's parents were Swedish. Mother's, Russian," said Gunnar. "Myself, I've barely stepped out of Wisconsin. Made it far as Chicago and Iowa."

"Oh, you must see the world. With this country so big, most Americans think they *are* the world."

"And your last name?" said Gunnar, reaching out his hand.

"Tornsen. Kara Tornsen — with an 'E-N'." They shook.

"May I buy you both a drink? Beer perhaps? I have a few minutes."

"No, thank you," said Kara pointing to their mugs at a nearby cocktail table. "We already have beer. It's rather too cold and tasteless, but I guess it's beer."

"Let me get you something from the region, like a Leinenkugel. All these German breweries here, and you probably have a Miller Lite."

Kara looked at Mindy, who shrugged and said, "All I know about is carbs."

Gunnar ordered two Leinenkugels for Kara and himself — Mindy was happy with her Miller — and Gunnar learned she was a kindergarten teacher in a town called Roskilde, was unmarried, and she rode her bicycle to most places. "Denmark's a healthy country," she said, "because people ride bikes. Cars and gas are just so expensive." A thousand years old, Roskilde was small, she explained, but had a

Viking ship museum, a big summer music festival, and a big brick church where all the kings and queens of Denmark were buried. She lived alone except for a cat named Frederick. When Kara learned he was a physicist, she said there was a physics research center just outside of Roskilde. "Some of the earth's best questions are answered there."

Gunnar smiled, fascinated with her.

Mindy was looking bored, so Gunnar asked where Mindy worked. She replied, "My father works for Cargill. Ever hear of it? It's the world's largest privately held company."

"They're into grains, aren't they?" said Gunnar.

"Grains, yes, and a lot of agriculture — and salt, too."

"I use their salt in my water softener," said Gunnar.

"I've never understood soft water," said Mindy.

Gunnar smiled, realizing she was just a dull, rich girl. "Hard water is ground water with a lot of dissolved minerals in it, like magnesium and calcium. You can remove the minerals, i.e. soften it, by passing it over an ion exchange resin, such as complex sodium salts."

"Gee, whiz," said Mindy who drained her beer.

"Hence, Cargill salt. You work there?"

"Not yet," said Mindy, and she went back to being bored.

Kara, on the other hand, was nodding and smiling. "You *are* a scientist," she said.

"Don't you have your meeting about now?" asked Mindy.

Gunnar looked at his watch and said, "Yes. Nice to meet you both. How long are you here for, Kara?"

"Just another two weeks."

"Ah," said Gunnar, seeing what he was going to ask dissolve like salt in water. No point in starting anything if she wasn't going to be around. It's hard meeting people in the wild. "Enjoy America," he said and held out his hand.

"Good luck on your dating," she said, shaking his hand.

"Thanks." And he waved good-bye.

The evening proved different from his last try. This time, he didn't care about impressing the people he met — just tried to listen and be friendly. He kept comparing them to Kara. One woman talked only about her cat named "Kitty," and he asked her, "Would you ever name a cat Frederick?"

"Never thought of it," she said. "Are you free for a date next week?"

"Uh huh," he said with firm gusto, though he didn't expect to choose her.

His other dates, too, treated him with much interest. There was a 34-year-old divorcee who was training to be a police officer and offered to arm-wrestle him. What the heck. He did, and she won. She asked for his phone number right then, but he said rules were rules. He said to mark him down for a date, knowing he would not select her.

Another divorcee, his same age, said how much he reminded her of her ex-husband "in the good, early years."

"He was fun?" he asked, which opened the door to a whole seven minutes of her ex-husband's affair. "He didn't even conceal it," she said. "They were having sex on the living room floor when I walked in, and when he saw me, he looked at his watch and said, 'You're early.'"

"Seventy percent of all divorce petitions are by women because of men's passive-aggressive nature."

"You know a lot," she said, smiling.

Gunnar rather liked Betsy, a twenty-nine-year-old fifth-grade teacher who loved Japanese and Italian food, riding her bicycle, hiking, skiing, and "enjoying things." Her shoulder-length blond hair parted in the middle appealed to him instantly, as did her honest smile.

"Where do you ride your bicycle?" he asked.

"Sometimes to work. Sometimes just around the lake. There's something that makes me feel like a kid when I'm on a bike."

"I just learned that most people in Denmark ride bikes."

"I'd love to go to Denmark," she said.

"I'm not a traveler," Gunnar said, "though I wonder how big Denmark is. Is it bigger than Wisconsin?"

She whipped out her cell phone, a Blackberry, and quickly typed on its keyboard. In a few seconds, she said, "It's 16,321 square miles, about twice the size of Massachusetts, it says." She typed more. "And Wisconsin is 56,153 square miles, so Wisconsin is about three and a half times bigger than Denmark."

"Wow, you're great with math and technology."

"Not really," she said. "I can't figure out how to add information about people in the database. I'm sure it's simple."

"That's easy," he said, pulling out his own Blackberry, and he showed her, pressing a button to bring up his most recent list. Ursula's name stood out. He wondered if he'd ever see her again. Probably not. To show Betsy what to do, he pressed "View Contact" and it showed Ursula's phone number. "And so you'd just hit 'Edit' if you want to add things to this entry, such as an address, a birthday, the restaurant she works at."

"That's easy enough. Gosh."

"It's a good little instrument," he said and slipped the phone back in his pocket.

"We seem to have a lot in common," she said.

He nodded.

"Would you mind if I put you down as someone I'd like to see again?" she said.

"That'd be nice. Is this your first time speed dating?" he asked.

"My seventh. I've met some nice people, but just when I think something's going to happen, well, something else happens."

"Hello? Hello?" said a high voice from his pocket.

"Your phone," said Betsy. "You must have pocket dialed."

"Oh, oh," said Gunnar, pulling out the phone. It said he was connected to Ursula. He held it to his ear and turned away from Betsy, embarrassed.

"Hey, Ursula," he said softly.

"Did you mean to dial me?" she said.

"Yes," he said, feeling instantly false. "Well, actually I meant to dial you later."

"What's that chatter?" she said. "Are you at another ScurryDate?"

"No," and he wasn't lying. "And I'm sorry about last night. You got the wrong impression of me."

"I could see you barfing outside the restaurant windows. Some customers didn't like that. But I felt bad for you."

"I'm allergic to shrimp. I ate some accidentally. Plus I couldn't believe what happened with those women."

"So you're not dating your student?"

"No. I don't date students. I don't want to hear about their problems deciding a major or that roommate Melanie is stealing tampons."

Ursula laughed.

"I'm looking for someone my age," said Gunnar, glancing guiltily at Betsy but trying to cover with a smile.

"Listen," Ursula said. "I'd still love to catch up with you sometime, but my father just had a heart attack in Arizona, where he lives. I found out this morning, and I'm at O'Hare airport now. I may be gone a couple of weeks — if I can nurse him back, that is."

"I wish your dad the best. And it's lucky you're studying to be a nurse."

"Thanks. Now that I have your number, may I call you when I get back?"

"That'd be *great*," he said, only then catching Betsy looking at him sadly. "I hope things work out for your dad. Talk to you later, then," he told Ursula. He hung up.

"A friend?"

"Yes. Just a friend," he said, wishing it were more.

"See what I mean?" said Betsy as if sensing she'd just been shut out. "Something else always happens." The seven-minute gong sounded.

"I'm so sorry," said Gunnar. "You're a nice person. It's me. In fact, I'm going to leave altogether. I'm not right for Z-Dating."

Betsy shrugged, stood, and walked to her next table, but Gunnar left the room feeling great, light as a feather. Ursula was going to call him for dinner. He still wasn't clear why, but he was hoping Jeff wasn't working out. It was a lot to base his future on, but his three days led to this phone call with Ursula. This might work out after all. He could go back to his research and he'd hear from her when she returned from Arizona.

On his way out the door, he heard, "Excuse me," behind him, and Kara was running toward him. "I just saw you coming down the stairs."

"Ah, Kara," he said. "Where's Mindy?"

"She met a friend and went off with him, but I have her car. How was your Z-Dating?" she said.

"It wasn't as fun as talking with you," he said, still feeling great from his call with Ursula. "So she abandoned you?"

"We'll do other stuff tomorrow."

"That sucks."

She shrugged, resigned. "I loved living here thirteen years ago — but Mindy and I are in different times in our lives now."

Gunnar nodded empathetically. "A few days ago, I went to a high school reunion of sorts. Everyone's married, most have kids."

"Exactly. I have no idea what I thought I could do here for so long, nearly a month — two weeks to go."

"Do you want another beer or something?" He was trying to figure out why she'd run over.

"No, that's okay. I just wanted to say hello."

"Are you hungry?"

She smiled as if he'd figured her out. "A little."

"The least I can do is show a traveler a good restaurant in Madison. Would you like that?"

"Thank you."

He smiled. "I know just the place."

Later, he'd wonder if he suggested it because he'd been feeling so good about Ursula. He felt so sure and hopeful about her. Maybe he also felt bad about Kara. She was a foreigner who needed a little kindness.

They caravanned to Monty's Steak House, Kara in Mindy's new silver BMW, Gunnar in his Ford Aspire with the blue smoke. He'd thought of the restaurant because he liked its food, even if most of its customers were old people who sat like logs in red leather booths. Walking in with Kara, though, he saw the place anew — subdued lighting, stringed music quietly enchanting in the background, and a tuxedoed gray-haired gentleman ready to show them to a table. What the heck — she could use a little elegance.

Once they were seated, a waiter whisked in, a bearded man in his forties. "Here're the menus. Could I get you anything to drink right away?"

Kara shrugged her white shoulders.

"Give us a minute," said Gunnar. "Actually, I remember this place has fried calamari as an appetizer. Do you like calamari?" he asked Kara.

"Squid. Danes love all seafood."

"May we start with that?" he asked the waiter.

"Absolutely."

When the waiter left, Kara said, "So this is where you take out-of-towners?"

"No one visits me. All my friends are in Wisconsin."

"I was wondering what places to see in Madison, tourist spots I missed as a teenager."

"There's the Frank Lloyd Wright-designed convention center on the lakefront."

"I've been there. I love Wright."

"And there's a museum of mustard someone told me about the other day."

"Nothing like a good mustard," she said.

"And there's bowling."

"Bowling," she said. "You have so many bowling alleys, and I've never noticed any in Denmark."

"Have you played before?"

"Once in high school here. It was fun."

"If Mindy abandons you again, maybe I can show you bowling."

"*Vidunderlig*," she said. "Marvelous."

"Oh, good." Except he needed to get back to research. "And what is kindergarten called in Danish?"

"Pardon?"

"Where you work, is it called Yumpingarden or something?"

She laughed. "It's called *børnehaveklasse*. You're funny."

"Thanks. Do you like teaching kindergarten?" he said.

"The little ones can be a test. Last winter as I was getting my students ready to take them for a sauna, I told them to put away their colored pencils. Then I got a call on my cell phone, so I stepped out for just a minute or so. When I came back, they were all naked, and some of the boys were marching around proudly holding their penises. Boys and their penises!"

CHRISTOPHER MEEKS • 109

Speaking of that, in the last several minutes, ever since he suggested calamari, Gunnar had become hard. He was aware of Kara's sexiness, but he did not want to let on. His arousal was embarrassing. It wasn't right to be poking up at Monty's. Also, he had Ursula to look forward to, so he shouldn't be aroused. He wasn't a player. He just wanted his life to be simple, although his body's response was making it more complicated. "Yikes," he said, referring to her story but it also could be about what was happening to him. "If your naked kids happened here, you'd be in jail for eighty years to life. So do you take saunas with the kids?"

"It's part of health."

"Naked coed saunas?"

She laughed. "Americans, I swear. You all are so uptight about bodies. Yes, naked. People take saunas naked all the time in Scandinavia, young people, old people, men, women all together. It's natural. Fat people, short people. We all come in different packages — no big thing."

"Modesty is different there. You're Danish."

"Now I know what you're thinking, and it's such a cliché. 'Danish' means liberated sex, right? Because we sauna together, you think everyone's having sex?"

"Yes, and eating pastries."

She could only shake her head and laugh. "Danes are just like Wisconsin people, conservative and concerned with work. Except Danes don't feel bad about sex. In fact, there's probably less perversion there because Denmark was the first country to do away with laws against pornography. The porn shops in Copenhagen are on the *Strøget*, the walking street for tourists. Lots of American tourists go there and to the Museum Erotica. For Danes: a yawn. So tiresome."

"Your country sounds interesting," he said.

"You really need to travel. My high school year here was the best thing I ever did for myself. Another country can open your eyes."

When the calamari arrived, the waiter pointed out the wine list, and Kara said one of the great things of America was its California red wines. Gunnar knew nothing of them — rarely drank any alcohol, so he asked the waiter for a suggestion of a good California red.

"I'd recommend Kenwood, say a pinot noir from the Russian River Valley — smooth and affordable." The waiter pointed to a bottle on the wine list. It wasn't the cheapest bottle on the list but certainly was not up there like many other wines. "A bottle of that, please," said Gunnar, feeling daring.

Kara took his hand. "Thank you," she said. "I can't believe I ran into such a wonderful person as you tonight." Gunnar's erection once again reasserted itself. His body had its own programs.

Their hands touched, going for the same ring of food. "Sorry," he said.

"Take it."

"It's yours," he said.

"I'm the visitor, and I can do what I want. It's yours."

He took the calamari, dipped it in the white sauce, and leaned over to feed it to her. Her tongue stretched out to meet the crumb-coated flesh. It was a beautiful tongue.

He then noticed the pendant on her necklace that featured a large yellow stone embedded in a gold setting with what looked like rays emanating. It was a sun. It rested on her skin above the crevasse leading down into her lacy black bra. His eyes followed the outline of her very white breasts leading into the darkness. Sun, shine a little light on thee.

"That's pretty," he said.

"Upon what are you gazing?" she replied formally with a smile.

"Your pendant," he said, stifling his urge to cough. "Is that a gemstone?"

She lifted it up for him to see better. "Actually, it's amber. See the little spider caught in it?"

"Not really."

"Amber is natural in Denmark. Bugs were trapped in sap. Later the sap became a clear yellow rock. Amber jewelry's been found in Viking graves."

"Interesting." He loved the sound of her voice.

"The spider is everything. Look closer." She lifted it.

"Oh, yes. I see a dot with protruding legs."

She winked at him. He coughed.

"You all right?" she asked.

The waiter materialized with the wine and two glasses, opened the bottle, and poured just a little in Gunnar's glass. Gunnar knew from past meals with others that he was supposed to sniff, try it, and give his approval. Gunnar brought the glass to his nose. He detected alcohol only faintly, but there was a fragrance of both fruit and — was he dreaming? — earth. He brought the glass to his lips and tasted. It was very smooth.

Kara leaned in and whispered in his ear. "How do you like the wine?"

"This is wonderful. Thank you," he said to the waiter. "Thank you," he said to Kara. The waiter poured both their wine glasses full. His erection just wouldn't go away.

"Would you like to order?" the waiter asked.

"I'm ready," said Kara.

"Me, too," he said.

They'd finished a glass of wine each before the meal arrived, and the rest of the bottle during the meal. While he didn't feel particularly high from the alcohol, he certainly felt lightheaded being with her.

When the meal was over, he walked Kara to her car, holding her hand and laughing. He didn't remember what had been funny or how he took her hand. He was just happy.

"So you had a good time?" he asked.

"Very." Later, he'd analyze this moment, too. She'd looked up, grinning, making no move to open her door, and she looked deeply interested like an art lover intrigued with an etching. As simple as a leaf falling, he leaned in and kissed her. Blazing hot javelins of lightning snapped around him. Neurotransmissions galore. He could have been the key on Franklin's kite. Take your protein pills and put your helmet on. Her mouth tasted wonderfully fruity. She embraced him as he went for a second, more passionate kiss, and she ran her tongue over his. He guessed she probably felt his erection as they embraced.

"What do you want to do now?" he asked.

"Sorry," she said, "I need to go home. But I'll go bowling with you tomorrow, if you're up for it."

He should say no, he told himself. He should explain his research and his coming busy schedule, but he said. "I'd love to. Tomorrow."

He didn't know, though, that certain forces were in motion. Dominoes were falling. Still, this was the spot where things could change. Could he change?

Forces were in motion.

CHAPTER TEN

"IT IS IMPOSSIBLE TO MOVE HEAT, BY A
CYCLICAL PROCESS, FROM SOMETHING
AT LOWER TEMPERATURE TO
SOMETHING AT HIGHER TEMPERATURE
UNLESS WORK IS ADDED TO THE
SYSTEM."

— SECOND LAW OF
THERMODYNAMICS

Gunnar stood at the open doorway of a 757 jetliner sometime after he received free peanuts but no meal. No more free meals.

He wasn't clear how the side hatch opened or why he was there, but the wind howled at five hundred miles per hour, and he stepped into the openness the way he might walk into a laundromat. And he fell. He had no parachute. He sailed through a layer of clouds, then a layer of blue sky, then a layer of clouds as if he was jumping through a parfait, and at each cloud level, a holographic sense of a naked woman waved at him in a way that said, "See you soon." Were these women about sex or about death? Considering he was plunging toward the ground, Gunnar knew he'd be joining the ranks of the dead momentarily.

He thought to himself that in peak, traumatic moments, time was supposed to slow, and it really felt as if it did. He should hit in something like thirty-six seconds, but he seemed to have minutes, and he was perfectly alive and in control. He maneuvered himself into a vertical position so he could wave back to the female ghosts — or were they angels?

The ground grew closer, and he expected a smack and then blackness, but time slowed so much, he felt the ground at his feet. His momentum was such, though, his head kept moving to the ground, and he closed his eyes just before his head hit, and he felt nothing at all, just as if he went to sleep. His head was probably caved in, but death was no more than an exhausting day.

A phone ringing woke him, and after blinking a few times, seeing that he was in his bed and it was a real phone ringing, he realized he hadn't died from a heart attack or something. Whoever theorized you'd actually die if you hit the ground in a dream was wrong. More importantly, Gunnar sensed the dream was trying to tell him something. It was a sign.

"Hello," he said into his phone.

"Hey, it's me, Carl. We're supposed to meet this morning."

Gunnar lurched up in bed, his heart racing, wondering how he could let down his colleagues. His alarm hadn't gone off. But the clock said it was only near 7:30. "We're not meeting until ten," Gunnar said.

"First you have to tell me — is someone in bed with you?"

"You woke me up for this?" said Gunnar, looking at the empty half of his bed.

"You're always up at first light."

"Not if someone's with me."

"So someone's with you?"

"No. But there almost was someone here, which might have made things more complicated."

"How so? What do you mean?"

Gunnar explained how Z-Dating was unique, starting with his stepping on Danish woman Kara's toes and ending with pocket dialing Ursula. He'd be going to dinner with Ursula after she returned from Arizona in two weeks.

"What's complicated about that? It sounds like great news."

So Gunnar described what happened after he left Z-Dating, how he'd taken Kara to dinner, drinking wine, kissing her, kissing her a lot, and she was hot.

"Oh, man," said Carl. "Some guys have all the luck."

"It's not lucky. What about Ursula? What I did was crazy. I could have made love to Kara right then and there, but she had to go. And then I had this dream just now that warned me." He went onto describe the dream in detail, then said, "It's clear, don't you see? If I see Kara more, I'll die somehow."

"First of all, that's utter nonsense," said Carl. "I've never known you to be this way. We're men of science. Dreams, tea leaves, tarot cards — none of it tells our future because the way we experience time, the future hasn't happened yet."

"It's some part of my subconscious warning me."

"No, *la petite mort*, my friend. Haven't you heard the French expression for orgasm — a little death? You had a sex dream, and it's telling you to have an orgasm with Kara. And you should, frankly, so you can get all this out of your system and we can research again."

"I told Kara I'd take her bowling today."

"And how were you going to do that if we're to start our research again today?" Carl said sternly.

"You're right — another reason I can't see Kara. My dream is right."

Carl laughed. "I'm yanking your chain, man. Actually, I'm calling to say while the lab has been moved — I'm there now — there're a lot of wires and hoses to be connected and calibrating to be done. Truthfully, I don't need you until tomorrow."

"But I don't want to ruin things with Ursula."

"You said Kara's leaving in two weeks and Ursula won't be back for two weeks. What's wrong?"

"I don't know. I worry ... But Kara's stunning."

Carl laughed. "Harry's joining me tonight for a run-through. You can see Kara if you want. Take her out. Have fun."

Gunnar called Kara, who had given him her cell number, a Madison number, the number that came with the disposable phone she'd bought upon arrival. He intended to let her down softly. She answered after the first ring. "Gunnar, *go morn*. That's Danish for Good Morning."

"Go morn."

"I'm so glad you called," she said with a sexiness in her morning British voice with a bend. "I feel I was taking *advantage* of you last night."

"Not at all. I loved our evening."

"I shouldn't have suggested bowling today. You must have so much to do."

"No, bowling sounds fun," he said.

"Besides, you're off Z-Dating and such, and I'm sure I'm just in the way. In fact, I felt terribly bad. After all, I'm just a visitor." He paused. What was she saying? Was she letting him off softly?

"You're a wonderful visitor. I wouldn't have changed a thing."

"We can bowl in a week or two before I have to go back. That way, you can go on real dates. I'm sorry I stepped in the way. It was selfish of me."

"No, I'm dropping speed dating. It's not for me."

"You make me feel so *guilty*," she said with a laugh.

"It'd be my honor to show you more sights."

"Are you sure?"

He wet his lips. "I'm absolutely sure. I planned on a whole day together. Lunch, bowling, maybe a museum, dinner. I mean, I want you to really see the city so you have some special memories when you go back."

"Last night was special for me," she said.

"Me, too. How about I pick you up in an hour?"

"*Vunderlig,*" she said.

Before he left, he worried about what they would talk about. He quickly Googled Denmark, knowing nothing of it other than its size, and he found that it's called Danmark in Danish, and it's a small low-lying country of 5.3 million people whose kingdom also included Bornholm Island in the Baltic Sea, the Faeroe Islands, and Greenland. Denmark shared a border to the south with Germany, and north of Denmark, across the Øresund Bay, lay the rest of Scandinavia, connected now by a new 7.8-kilometer bridge from Copenhagen to Malmö, Sweden.

Danish women, he discovered, had the lowest incidence of obesity in all of Europe, and according to a Cambridge University study, Danish people were the happiest people in Europe — perhaps the world. Perfect. He could use a day with one of the happiest people around.

He left with one more fact: Isak Dinesen, whose real name was Karen Blixen, was one of the country's famous writers and wrote *Out of Africa*. As Gunnar remembered the movie *Out of Africa* with Meryl Streep, Karen wasn't a particularly happy person, but she wasn't fat.

He picked Kara up at Mindy's parents' house, a Tudor mansion on the lake, and Kara came to the door alone, her long red hair spilling onto her short purple dress, and she walked confidently in high-heeled shoes — very sexy — very unbowling, and his heart swelled. Was he in a dream?

She pointed to the exquisite parquet entryway and the suit of armor against one wall and said, "People don't live like this in Denmark."

"Most people don't in Madison, either." He took her hand, and she kissed him fully on the mouth.

"Nice to see you again," she said.

"Likewise," and he knew he'd made the right decision.

Lunch at a lakeside café had him try escargot — something he swore he could never stomach, but Kara said snails tasted just like garlic, and they had special qualities.

"What kind of special qualities?"

"Haven't you been to France?"

"Traveling doesn't appeal to me. I'm comfortable here."

"Well, then, nevermind." She gave a mischievous grin. He ate the snail. He shook thinking about how gross it was, but, moments later, hey, it wasn't so bad. He smiled. She laughed.

At the University Sports Bowl, Kara rolled several gutter balls at first, until Gunnar showed her how not to twist her hand. He stood behind her and guided her hand while she held a light seven-pound ball meant for kids. "Be a pendulum," he said, and soon she had her first strike. She leaped in the air when it happened. "I rather like this bowling."

They played two games, and a few times before she rolled, she kissed him lightly on the lips "for good luck." He was thinking she was his good luck.

As they were taking off their shoes, he said, "How about a museum?"

"Are you sure? You can take me home if you have something to do."

"Don't keep saying that. I'm fine. Really." Was she teasing him? She looked at him with such sparkle, she had to be. He was going to suggest his house, but he didn't want to do so prematurely.

At the Madison Museum of Contemporary Art, he and Kara were in a side gallery when he noticed she kept glancing at him. She had that "take me" look, which emboldened him, and near a giant black-and-white photo of a man's bare feet, he drew her close and happily made out with her. She started caressing his buttocks, so he slipped his hand around to her front and felt the wonderful shape and weight of her right breast. Their kissing became even more urgent. Nearby, someone cleared her throat. A young uniformed woman, a guard, looked embarrassed and simply said, "Eucalyptus," patting her throat as if that explained everything.

"Should we leave?" whispered Kara.

"Yes. My house?"

"Love to."

His cell phone rang, and the same guard said, "No cell phones in the galleries, please."

The screen showed it was from his mother, and he answered it, saying, "Hold on, Mom. I have to walk out of the gallery." He took Kara's hand and led her out.

"Hey, Mom," he said near the men's room.

"Did you say you're in a gallery? Do my ears deceive me?"

"Yes, I'm at a museum with a friend."

"I didn't think I'd live this long."

"What's up?" he said.

"I was hoping you're on the road. It's Patty's birthday, remember? The three of us were going to have dinner."

"Oh, no. I didn't remember. Can we reschedule?"

"You can't do this to your sister two years in a row. Especially this year with the divorce."

Kara held up her hand and said, "If you have to take me home…"

He waved that off immediately and shook his head.

"No, especially with the divorce. She needs sympathy from you, Mom, not her brother in the way. Listen, I have to go, but I have something special for Patty. I'll come up later this week."

"Maybe your friend would like a birthday party. Bring him along."

"Mom, it's a woman."

"Oh — right. Patty was saying you're doing that crazy speed-dating thing."

"I didn't meet her there. She's a kindergarten teacher from Denmark. Kara — seeing America."

"We're America. Bring her."

Kara seemed to understand because she was nodding and smiling.

"Patty won't mind?" he said to his mother.

"Of course she will, but fuck it."

"Mom."

"We'll see you at six."

------------→

Gunnar's mother lived north of Fond du Lac on three acres overlooking Lake Winnebago. When he and Kara pulled up her gravel driveway in the early afternoon, blocking the garage was the large Fond du Lac Bookmobile.

The house wasn't the one he'd grown up in, which had been a small Colonial in town. After Gunnar's father died from a heart attack, Gunnar's mother had wanted something more modern where the plumbing worked, and she found a three-bedroom L-shaped home, sided in a gray stone. A huge picture window faced the lake, as did a huge garden that she had created. The house seemed big for a single person, Gunnar had always thought, but she loved to have guests.

When no one answered the doorbell, Gunnar and Kara strolled hand-in-hand around to the lakeside part of the house to find his mother kneeling in her garden. She was trimming rose bushes severely and did not notice them. His sister, barefoot, in white shorts, braless under a white T-shirt, sat on a chaise on the flagstone patio, reading.

"Hello," he said. "Happy Birthday, Patty. This is Kara."

Patty gazed at Kara as if at a bone in an archeological dig, something of interest but maybe not special. "Hello," she said and nodded but did not hold out her hand.

"Hello," Kara said back, more shyly than he'd seen her.

"Hurray!" said his mother. She stood and beamed. "Nice to see you, dear." Gunnar thought that was meant for Kara, but instead his mother hugged him.

"Mom, this is Kara."

"Oh." She turned. "Welcome, I'm Audrey." She shook Kara's hand without much of a glance and pointed inside. "I have artichokes cooked. It's Patricia's favorite vegetable."

"Mom, that was when I was five."

"Well, you hang onto tastes including pancakes, BLTs, and that husband of yours."

"If you think Brad was so bad, why did you let me marry him?"

She turned to Kara. "My children, when it comes to love, are a bit naïve."

"What's that mean, mother? " said Patty. Gunnar wondered, too; why was he included?

"That's what I adore about you two. You can be innocent."

Kara gave Gunnar a questioning look and then took his hand again.

They soon sat around his mother's modern, circular cherry wood dining table, which was by a picture window. Outside, the lake sparkled, and sailboats looked frozen against the dark water while a scattering of white clouds loomed overhead. His mother pulled a bottle of champagne out of the ice bucket sitting on the table and popped open the cork.

"I wanted to toast our visitor," said Audrey, moving around the table and pouring from the bottle.

"A treat," said Kara.

Audrey sat, her smile like the opening note of an etude. "Denmark is a quiet little country, isn't it? You export a lot of little things. Cookies, cheese … ham … sex."

Kara glanced at Gunnar as if confused. He leaped in and said, "Actually, she was telling me how Danes, after doing away with pornography laws, are not obsessed with it as Americans are."

"I'm not obsessed," said Audrey.

"Neither am I," said Gunnar.

"Hey, I'm divorced," said Patty. "I am."

That seemed to kill that line of conversation. Kara said, "The table and the view here are rather stunning. Thank you for having me."

"We're happy to accommodate," said Patty with an undertone of sarcasm. "Normally it's just us three talking about family things because, well, that's what families do." Patty glanced to her mother as if in collusion.

"Yes, I see Gunnar so rarely," said Audrey. "His research has him quite busy. In fact, I'm surprised he's been able to get out to museums and things." She said it with a smile, but Gunnar felt his mother's and Patty's disapproval.

"Yes, family things," said Gunnar. He could play this game. "Such as chatting about what Patty's ex-husband Brad's done lately. He traded in their Toyota to get himself a Corvette, making Patty drive a bookmobile," he told Kara.

"I didn't want that car."

"No, a bookmobile gets much better mileage, and it's such a man magnet."

"More wine, anyone?" said Audrey.

"A wonderful idea," said Gunnar, "Maybe it'll loosen our tongues so we won't be so shy."

She looked at her son with displeasure. "The artichokes in the kitchen are ready. Let's eat, shall we? Patty, come help."

When they were out of the room, Kara whispered, "Did I say something wrong?"

"Things are crazy with Patty's divorce, which is why I didn't want to come here."

"I'm sorry," she said.

"It's nothing you did."

"Is there anything I can do?"

"No. This family can be impossible."

Patty and Audrey returned with the artichokes on special plates that had a niche filled with a bright yellow sauce. As Patty and Audrey sat, Kara said, "I became a huge fan of artichokes in Italy. Is this béarnaise sauce?"

"Hollandaise," said Audrey, "made fresh with butter, egg yolk, and lemon juice." Audrey swept out her hands and said in Italian, "*Mangia*."

Kara replied back in Italian, "*Grazie*," pulled a leaf off the artichoke, dipped it in the sauce, and said, "*Molto bene*."

"*Bellissimo*."

Gunnar nodded, impressed.

"I don't see the point of other languages," Patty said. "English has over a hundred thousand damned words. Isn't that enough?"

"Italian is a romance language, dear," said Audrey.

"Like I'll ever see romance again," said Patty.

"You never know," said Kara. "Pardon my saying so, but you're a beautiful woman. From what Gunnar has said of Brad, this could be a blessing in disguise. This may be the best year of your life." Gunnar hadn't told Kara anything about Brad, so he understood how Kara was moving on instinct, and from Patty's nodding and growing smile, he knew Kara had said the right thing.

"Where did you get this beautiful table?" Kara asked Audrey. "I saw one like it in Denmark.

"Now that I think of it," said Audrey, "I bought it at a Danish furniture store in Madison. The Danes are smart designers."

"They are," said Kara, pleased.

"To smart Danes," said Audrey, raising her glass. Patty quickly lifted hers. Gunnar in that moment knew Kara was extraordinary.

"To Kara," said Gunnar, and they all raised their glasses higher. Kara had that gleam in her eye again. He couldn't wait to get her to his place.

------------→

When he opened his garage door and drove his car in, perfectly hitting the hanging tennis ball, Kara said, "That's interesting."

"Helps with the spatial relationship," he said.

"Special?"

"No, spatial — to do with space. Wait there," he said, and he ran around the car to open her car door.

"Thank you," she said.

He kissed her as she stood up. They fell back and kissed and clutched against the snowshoes in the garage. When they pulled apart, she said, "Someone is knocking on my door," and she reached down and pressed against his Pied Piper. He saw checkerboards, the kind he experienced when standing up too quickly from bed in the morning.

"So," he said, clearing his throat. "Shall we go in?"

"It's your country."

Once in the door, she held his belt as they kissed more. His pants fell to the floor. Gunnar started dropping backward, tripping on his own pants, and, laughing, she steadied him. He reached behind her. He unzipped her dress. She let it slip right off. Under his globed ceiling light, she stood with her skimpy lacy bra, her black panties so small that they could cover little more than a pencil. He'd never seen a real person in something that little. Her skin was so white, she was like milk.

He took her hand, and she followed. In the living room, he said, "This is where I work most of the time."

"Very interesting," she laughed.

They dashed into his bedroom, where they fell on the queen-sized bed, kissing. Only the light from the hallway spilled in.

He tried to undo her bra, but he could not find the clip in the back. His hands started searching everywhere. Were there pullover bras now? Kara wordlessly pulled away for a moment and unclipped her bra from the front. She let him slip the bra off her creamy arms, and she smiled. Motioning her onto her back, he reached for her thong and pulled it down.

She lay back, legs slightly open, and she looked comfortable in her nakedness in a way he'd only seen in paintings. Kara wasn't anorexic looking like many of his female students, nor was she the I-don't-care-I'm-out-of-shape of most people he saw at the grocery store. She was just right. Her skin glowed in the near dark as if she were a shimmering ghost.

He stared at the light red hair between her legs, trimmed into a brief Mohawk. Again, he'd never known another real woman to do such a thing. The women he'd known were bushy and preferred to make love deep in darkness. The actual act often seemed more like a favor instead of real interest. One wasn't to take too long "down there."

"Your turn," she said. "Lie down."

He rested on his side next to Kara.

She gently pushed him to his back and started to pull off his boxers. He felt extremely awkward, the way he always did at the doctor's during a physical exam in the paper gown. He didn't particularly like his body because he was thin and not well muscled, which he figured is what women really liked. He was grateful that she didn't seem repelled. In fact, as she pulled his shorts free from his feet, she smiled. *She likes me,* he thought.

He rolled onto his side. Because she was so accepting, he admitted to himself that there was something incredible about two naked bodies. The two of them were as vulnerable as two people could be.

"You okay?" asked Kara.

"More than okay."

"You look so serious."

"I guess I am."

"But isn't this fun?" she asked.

He eagerly nodded, then reached over and lightly skated the tip of his forefinger around one nipple, coaxing it to extend. The female body was so amazing. Her pink areolas were a visual stop, as was her long hair splayed on the yellow pillow. Against his white comforter, she was a study of shades, and his heart soared with her beauty. Women were so incredible. Where men were so hairy and unshapely, Kara was art, soft and serene. He felt defined by what he was not.

That was when the doorbell rang.

"Are you expecting somebody?" asked Kara.

"No."

"Maybe they'll go away."

"Yeah," said Gunnar.

But the doorbell rang rapidly three times.

"Shit. That's Carl, one of my research partners," said Gunnar. "He does that three bells thing as if it's cute."

"Should I get dressed?"

"Wait a sec. It'll only take a moment." Gunnar grabbed his robe from the closet.

When he opened the door, still tying his robe, Carl and Harry eagerly pushed in.

"Gunnar, you're wonderful; you're right," said Carl.

"About what?"

Harry grinned ear to ear. "We investigated Strontium 84, the isotope you suggested. It'll be hard to isolate, but Carl and I modeled it tonight."

"I thought you wanted me to model it," said Gunnar.

"We thought you were nuts," said Carl. "I wanted to prove you wrong."

"Great scattering qualities as you thought," said Harry.

They all stood there grinning and nodding, saying nothing, when Kara's head popped around the corner. Gunnar saw her first, then Carl gasped, and then Harry turned and saw Kara, who merely waved then disappeared. Harry's long "Oh" became a short "Ah."

"Do you think we could go over it in the morning?" said Gunnar. "Maybe we'll even start isolating Strontium 84?"

"Absolutely, man," said Harry, slapping Gunnar on the back.

"I'm so sorry for disturbing you," Carl whispered. "Is that Kara?"

Gunnar nodded.

"Enjoy tonight," he said, and they were out of there.

That was easy, Gunnar thought, closing the door. As he turned back, he saw Kara's bra and dress on the floor near the door. None of them had seemed to notice. Gunnar laughed all the way back into the bedroom.

"What?" said Kara, now under the sheet and comforter.

"Sometimes a picture is worth a thousand words," and he held up her bra and dress. He spotted her thong panties on the floor and picked those up, too.

"Are these comfortable to wear?" he asked.

"You get used to it," she said. "Do you like them?"

"Very much."

She whisked off her sheet to reveal her naked state once more.

The time away had erased his state of arousal, but as Kara opened her legs in a happy hello, he felt a rush, a surge. At the edge of his vision snapped a corona of solar flares. Was he getting too light headed? Who cared? He was happy.

He lay next to her, and her scent, her warmth, felt exactly right. With one tender hand, she massaged his back down his spine, and then her hand, her glorious, independent other hand, moved to his Happy Hunting Ground, and, oh! — it was a hand other than his own. It had been two years since he'd last had sex.

His own hands felt the smooth skin of her thighs, and as he kept edging closer to her, Kara moaned softly. He nuzzled her neck, kissed it and blew softly. Delightfully came a happy "Umm." Yum. He edged closer. Then stopped.

"Umm" — but his was a hesitation.

Kara opened her eyes. "Yes?"

"I think we should use a condom."

"Oh, yes. I'm glad you remembered because I stopped taking the pill a couple months ago. If you don't have one, we can do a lot without going all the way."

"I may have some in the bathroom, I think." Allison had bought him a box of "Beyond Seven," which she took to mean beyond seven on the ecstasy scale. It turned out they were for beyond seven inches. "That's okay, honey," she had said. "You're so big down there. You're the biggest I've ever been with." While that had made him feel good, Gunnar had found the condoms had a little extra left over when he wore one, making him wonder if Allison had simply known what to say. While the condoms worked fine, he'd nonetheless hidden them after he replaced them with normal-sized Trojans. Now he sure could use the Beyond Sevens again —

size didn't matter now, especially because whatever scale ecstasy was measured in, he was reaching new levels.

He found one. He hurried back into the bedroom.

Kara held out her hand. It took him a moment to realize she wanted to see the condom. Oh. He gave it to her, hoping she wouldn't read the name brand.

She didn't. She opened the package and indicated he should lay down next to her. He did so, and she gently, gingerly rolled on the condom. He liked that. No one had ever helped him before.

She tenderly took his hand and placed it between her legs, and he let his index finger find her form, exploring her boundaries. She hummed in his ear in an unconscious rhythm as his finger continued to go round and round an important spot. He pressed on it.

"Harder, please," she whispered.

Allison had been so sensitive there, she hardly wanted him to touch that point. Kara wasn't the same. When he pressed harder, Kara said, "Yes, oh... very good." His finger snaked around in a sensual massage. "Yes, perfect," she said. He never had had anyone talk during sex before. Kara arched her back again, and at that moment, Gunnar realized he had to hold himself back. This was delicious yet intense, so he needed to think of something else. He thought of Luigi Galvani's frog leg. In 1780, Galvani had discovered that a small current applied to a frog's leg, the sciatic nerve specifically, would cause the severed leg to jump. Muscles moved on electrical impulse. Similarly, his nerves and Kara's nerves were a freeway for electrons to zip up their bodies to their brains. "*Fantastisk*," said Kara, arching her back again.

And as she continued moving and murmuring he pictured fireworks on Lake Mendota.

"Not so fast," she now whispered, yet she guided his finger in further. God, he didn't know if he could hold out much longer.

"Yes," she said. "We are... we are... we are."

"We're what?" he whispered, thinking she was pointing out what they were doing.

"We are being," she said. "We are 'are.' Is that an idea in English?"

He didn't know. "R, R, R — that's Popeye."

She laughed. "Popeye and Olive Oyl?"

"Isn't it wonderful animation is international?"

Thankfully, she nudged her hip toward him. He moved on top and she guided him the rest of the way. Just as he thought he could hold out a little longer, she lifted her legs back so her knees nearly kissed her shoulders. Never in his life had a woman done this. Yeow.

"Oh!" she said and matched his thrusts with bounces of her own.

He was in checkerboard heaven. He came with a gasp that he didn't expect from himself.

"Oh, wow," he mumbled, and, catching him completely off-guard, tears came to his eyes.

"Are you okay?" Kara asked.

"More than okay," he said. "Like all the fly fishing rods in the world were sending out their lines at the same moment."

She smiled. "That's beautiful," and she touched a tear that escaped her own eye. "I don't know how to say this, but... that was nice."

"Really?"

"A little longer wouldn't be bad, but I loved it."

"Is that true?"

She looked at him as if wondering how to word what she meant. "It's not that I've been with many men," she said. "But most men, maybe it's Danish men, seem so concerned with their own bodies and performance. They're alone somehow. It's like I'm watching them at the Olympics — men executing an iron cross on the rings."

Gunnar laughed.

"You, though," said Kara. "You're so into the moment, like you're seeing *me,* that you're responding to me."

"I guess I feel so thankful, too," he said.

Kara smiled. "*Fantastisk,*" she said.

"Yeah. Exactly," said Gunnar. They held each other silently for perhaps ten minutes. Sometimes he wondered whether all the dedication, all the hours in the labs, the years of post-docs and poverty, had been worth it.

"What're you thinking?" Kara said.

His mind raced amid blinding-white-sun panic. He couldn't tell her about dedication — so mundane. What should he say? "I thought Meryl Streep had a great Danish accent in *Out of Africa*."

"You don't say," she said, laughing.

"It's true."

"You're a strange man, Gunnar Gunderson," she said, nudging closer, holding him to her.

CHAPTER ELEVEN

"THE RATE OF CHANGE OF MOMENTUM
OF A BODY IS PROPORTIONAL TO THE
RESULTANT FORCE ACTING ON THE
BODY AND IS IN THE SAME DIRECTION."

— NEWTON'S SECOND LAW OF MOTION

When Gunnar arrived back from the airport after he had put Kara on a plane to Denmark, a large black bat, wings spread, stared at him on his bed from his wall. It did not look ready to swoop down, but, rather, with its head cocked, it appeared to be listening to a question. Perhaps this one: why did Kara have to go now?

Gunnar knew the answer. The date of her ticket had been set when he'd met her, and that was the date she had left.

The bat was part of his wall calendar, The Cabinet of National Curiosities. Albertus Seba, an 18th century Dutch pharmacist who had passionately collected animals, plants and insects from all around the world, commissioned illustrations in 1731 for each of his specimens to create his "Cabinet of Curiosities." The calendar offered a dozen of those illustrations. The bat was curious.

Gunnar marveled at how the intervening two weeks had changed him — and Kara, too. They'd seen each other every single day. On one date, they'd gone to the Mustard Museum in Mt. Horeb and left with a Napa Valley whole-grained mustard paste. From a store down the block, they picked up bread, sausage, Jarlsberg cheese, and a knife. They had an impromptu picnic in a park where Kara built sandwiches.

"In Denmark," she said, "we use *rugbrød,* a thin, dense bread similar to pumpernickel, but not pumped up with air. We put little shrimps on it, or herring or hundreds of other things, eating our sandwiches open-faced. There's no top."

"How do you pack lunches?"

"You're so practical. We do it carefully in boxes. But I like this way, very Swiss."

Angel wings of sunlight poked through the shade of the maple tree they were under, adding a halo to her red hair. She noticed him staring, and she smiled shyly. Her teeth, exceptionally straight, made him realize she had had braces, which was perhaps why she never mentioned his.

When they were nearly done eating, he pulled out from his pocket a little white box and handed it to her. "For you."

"What is *this?* Something you picked up at the mustard museum?"

"Actually, yes, when you were in the bathroom." He smiled. "It's French."

She opened it and pulled out a necklace with little decorative white stones that splayed out on one side. "Beautiful — I love the splashes of yellow and red," she said.

"Look at them more closely."

As she did, she burst out laughing. The colors on the stones were really tiny yellow jars of French's mustard.

"*Fantastisk!* It's wonderful!" She leaned in and pecked his mouth, cheeks, and neck, laughing. To his look of bewilderment, she said, "Mustard kisses!" and then gave him a real and long kiss.

--------------→

During the two weeks, Gunnar taught his classes and worked with Carl and Harry daily on their research. At first, the three were having problems getting enough of the strontium isotope they needed, and one thing or another kept breaking down in the final cooling stage. Just as they thought they solved all the problems, news came from Austria that a team there had done what they were exactly trying to do using strontium 84. The Austrian team, whom they didn't know about, snatched the glory. "The breakthrough makes way for more precise quantum timekeeping and new studies of the quantum nature of matter," said one of the Austrian scientists to a CNN reporter.

A CNN team came to their lab to interview Gunnar, Carl, and Harry, too. Bose-Einstein condensates were interesting to the nation. Gunnar put his best face forward, calling it a photo finish and that maybe they'd start experimenting with compounds.

While disappointed, Gunnar didn't wallow in their loss. He and Kara made love nearly every day, and at times, in startling moments, he felt he needed her in order to live. He'd never felt this way for anyone. In fact, he wished he could fall into her, be of her, swim in her veins, mix his atoms with hers. In calm moments, he wondered how he could think such a thing of this stranger, and that his thoughts were a little scary.

Soon they tried different sexual positions. Once, they *knallede* with Kara lying on the kitchen counter. He'd never made love outside of the bedroom before, let alone where he prepared his morning's Cheerios. She could be so sexual one moment, and then, as they sipped coffee, naked still, she might talk about her kindergarteners and seem as innocent as Pippi Longstocking.

They ended up bowling, too, and touring Frank Lloyd Wright's studio called Taliesin. "Flat roofs," said Gunnar as they approached the Visitor Center. "Not very practical for Wisconsin winters. So why was he a genius?"

"Sometimes I can't believe how blind you are!" she said, and she looked serious.

"I'm sorry," he said. Had he upset her?

"I shouldn't say that," she said, softening. "But really. You live in an area with some samples of the world's great architecture and you don't even know. See how the roof is low and flat using the colors of the environment?" she asked. "He felt buildings should be organic and spring out of their natural surroundings."

"You're right. I should know this," he said and looked at her, impressed.

"For a while, I thought I'd be an architect," she explained. "I loved studying him. He was opposed to imposing a preconceived style. Each of his homes was site specific. Houses, he said, are always hungry for the ground. They live for nature."

"I didn't realize what a specialist you were."

"I didn't have the patience for it."

"And you have the patience for moving, screaming kids?"

"I connect more with people."

Right there on the Taliesen driveway, they kissed, and then Gunnar gazed straight upward and held out his hands. "Thank you, Lord!" he shouted. "Thank you for creating Kara."

Inside the Visitors Center, he looked out the large picture windows at the thick green landscape. Kara turned to him. "You Americans need all the art you can get. Somehow you forget that life is more than making money."

"Believe me," he said. "If I wanted to make money, I wouldn't be in physics."

"You really need to see Europe — so much art," she said.

"And you really need to stay in America."

She seemed caught off guard with that statement. She looked away, into the trees, deep in thought. "I wish I could," she pronounced. She moved closer and took Gunnar's hand. "You don't understand. I have a classroom of children waiting for me. Everything I have is there — my livelihood, my health insurance, the flat that I'm saving for. I can't abandon everything just like that."

"I didn't mean this week."

"Do you think you could come visit me soon?"

"I'd love to," he said. He left it at that for now.

Kara came with him to his next class, and his students craned their necks as they watched them enter and gazed while Kara took a seat in the back row. Who was this sexy redhead who seemed to smile the whole class period in admiration? Soon, it seemed several of the students were smiling in admiration for him, too. Their professor had a girlfriend.

After Kara's classroom visit, as they walked toward the faculty dining area, she spoke rapidly. "College is so exciting, isn't it? I'd forgotten how simulating it can be. And your subject! I'd never thought of momentum being a vector — that something keeps on going unless an outside force acts on it."

"It's a constantly fascinating subject."

"You make it so clear that physics is all around us — like your example with golf and the follow-through with the swing."

"To get maximum momentum," he said, "you have to follow through. It extends the time of contact of the golf club and the golf ball. More time means more impulse."

"Sounds like kindergarten. More time, more impulse." She laughed. "Sometimes I feel my job is to bat down kids' impulses, make them think."

He didn't like thinking about her having to teach kids again soon because it meant she'd be away. He didn't pursue that thread of conversation. Instead, he took her hand, brought it to his face, and let his lips nuzzle her skin.

"You're so romantic," she said.

He smelled lavender. She was real. They walked on.

For the last week, she had moved from her friend Mindy's house to his. They rented movies together, inevitably films with subtitles. Kara was determined to open his eyes to the world, and they saw three films: one from Italy, one from the Czech Republic, and one from Denmark. The last one let him hear Danish at length for the first time, a kind of guttural croaking not at all like the sing-song Swedish he had heard from his grandfather and others in Wisconsin. This was closer to German. The Danish film, *Babette's Feast,* was bleak. Was this what Danes were really like? Early on, one character said to his true love, Martine, as he was leaving her forever for a military career, "Life is hard and cruel, and in this world there are things that are impossible."

"Stay with her," Gunnar shouted.

"Not practical," said Kara.

The story then cut to France where Babette, a celebrated chef, had to flee the French Revolution, having lost her husband and son. Babette becomes the servant to Martine and Martine's sister Filippa. Babette lives with them and a band of Lutherans on the Jutland coast of Denmark where "food must be as plain as possible." Babette toils there for years as a cook of only plain food, saving her money, only to spend it all on creating one fabulous Parisian meal for these austere people and a visiting general — the same man who had left Martine years earlier. He now questioned his military career and whether it had been worth it.

"Of course it wasn't worth it," said Gunnar. "You should have gone for love."

"But it wasn't practical," Kara said again, this time laughing. She eagerly accepted Gunnar's kisses.

The film ended with everyone ingesting a most incredible meal: turtle soup, quail in pastry, cheeses, thin pancakes with caviar, and more, all washed down with amontillado, champagne, and the finest red French wines. Their expectations overturned, the pious now truly understood the spirituality of the artist; the artist called forth the spirit of joy.

"Hurray for art," said Kara.

Perhaps inspired by the movie, Kara two days later cooked him what she called a typical Danish breakfast, which featured a soft-boiled egg in its shell, thick pumpernickel bread that she found at the supermarket, granola, yogurt, paper-thin slices of ham and turkey, good rich coffee, and wedges of Havarti cheese and a blue-green veined cheese called Danish Blue.

"What's the blue part?" he asked.

"Mold," she said.

He never understood moldy cheese. It tasted terrible. But, like the two Lutheran sisters in the film, he did not say a negative word. After all, mold gave the world penicillin.

She served the cheese with a silver-handled cheese plane that she had bought, and he ate everything with a smile. Danes, he thought, must be big people if they ate like this at the start of every day.

At the end of the meal, she said, "You're unusually quiet. Anything wrong? You don't like the food?"

"No, no. It's very good. I don't eat most of this stuff normally, and it's all great. I wish I had it all the time."

"So why do you look so sad?" she said.

"Maybe it's that Danish movie we saw."

"But it was so uplifting."

"How could that military guy leave his true love just like that? For what?"

"That's life," said Kara. "I mean really, this world isn't American movies where everything ends happily. You get your pleasure where you can and move on."

That made Gunnar look away. He could feel his eyes puddle, and, goddamn it, this was all so silly. He knew she'd be leaving, and what had he expected? She was right. It was nice, and that was that. She had her career; he had his. Maybe they could meet in thirty-one years and eat quail and cheese.

She took his hand.

"I really like you, Gunnar, so don't think otherwise."

"I was just wishing I had this breakfast all the time — with you."

"I'm not leaving for four days."

"You know what I mean."

"We'll have e-mail. We can attach photos easily."

"Whoopee."

"What do you want?" said Kara.

He thought of the general in the movie and how he had settled for a standard career, and Gunnar said, "What if I don't take the usual career path? What if I found my way to Denmark?"

"And do what?"

"Maybe teach English."

"But you're a scientist." She looked surprised. "You'd do that for me?"

He nodded.

"But Denmark isn't Wisconsin," she said. "You might get lost there."

"You're always saying how I should travel. Maybe I could find a job in science."

Her head cocked as if considering the prospect. "That's true." Her eyes glowed with the possibility. "I told you about that research center outside of Roskilde. It's called Risø and has a lot of physicists. I don't know what they do, though."

"I'll look into it, how's that? I figure if you want me there, I can find a way."

Her smile grew, and she started nodding eagerly. "This could work. That would be smashing!" she said. "My parents would really love you, too."

Over the next few days, Gunnar did research. Risø was the national laboratory for Denmark and was under the guidance of the Ministry of Science, Technology, and Innovation. In the 50s, it was designed to be the research center for nuclear power, but in the 70s, Danish voters banned nuclear power as a source of electricity, so the center became focused on the study of atoms, following in the footsteps of Danish physicist Niels Bohr, whose work in the structure of atoms earned him the Nobel Prize in 1922.

Gunnar learned Risø had been a facility in addition to, and in relationship with, the Niels Bohr Institute (NBI) in Copenhagen, which was a part of the University of Copenhagen. Risø and NBI, however, parted their relationship in the mid-1990's, and Risø had shut down its reactor. While Risø had no program in cold atoms, NBI did.

NBI had pursued research into fusion for years, but now it was particularly interested in cold atoms, with various groups exploring such applications as superconductivity and quantum computing. As Gunnar read a list of recent visiting professors, he recognized the name of an acquaintance from the University of Chicago. Gunnar immediately called the man and learned how to approach the Niels Bohr Institute. Gunnar then told Kara of a possibility with NBI.

"I love you, Gunnar," she said. "I'm sorry, but I never meant for this to happen."

He choked for a second. Was she calling it off? He couldn't even speak. He steadied himself with his arm, even though they were sitting at his kitchen table.

"Are you all right?" she asked.

"What do you mean you didn't mean? What?"

"I didn't mean to fall in love, but I'm glad I did. You're so wonderful. You're smart, you're handsome. How did I get so lucky? I can't believe you're coming. When, do you think?"

"Oh, man," he said, catching his breath. "Anyway, I'll have to finish this semester, but my sabbatical is in the spring. This couldn't be better timing. If NBI or another organization can pay my travel and living expenses, then it'll all fall in place. My friend says the Carlsberg Foundation may help pay, and if I teach a class at the University of Copenhagen, I can make even more money." It was a commitment of at least eight months.

"I am so happy! I can't believe this," she said. "My flat can hold both of us, if you don't mind a cat," she said.

"Frederick, your cat. I love cats." He'd never had a cat.

Four days later, in the two and a quarter hour drive to O'Hare Airport, Kara explained she'd buy him a bicycle unless he required a Vespa. "Most people bicycle around town. It's a different way of life, but you'll love it. You can lock it up at the train station. Oh, I love you, Gunnar Gunderson!" She kissed him on his cheek and neck as he drove.

"I love you!" he said.

She would lift into the sky on SAS Airlines at 7 p.m. She had to switch in Amsterdam, and she'd arrive in Copenhagen at 1:20 p.m. the next day, which would be early morning in Madison.

Gunnar pulled up to the curb of the International Terminal by the SAS sign. "I'm going to drop you off here since I can't go to the gate with you."

After he pulled her large wheeled bag from the trunk, they kissed long and hard at the curb, then, fighting tears, she merely said, "Bye," and hurried off. He stood there in shock. It had happened too quickly. She wasn't going to look back? He mumbled to himself, "Look at me, look at me, look."

And she did. She waved, and, as if remembering something, she reached in her jacket pocket and glanced at a piece of paper. She ran back. "I forgot to give this to you!" she said.

"What is it?"

"My e-mail address."

"I forgot to give you mine!"

"Just e-mail me," she said, wiping a tear. "Then I'll have yours."

With a quick peck, as if more would freeze her, she was off.

He stood there motionless until a policeman came up and stood in front of his car. "Is this yours, buddy?"

Gunnar looked over and tried to make sense of this metal object resting on four tires.

"If it's not yours," the policeman said, "Then it's getting towed. Terrorist precautions."

What did the man's words mean?

The policeman lifted up his walkie-talkie. "Yeah, I have a tow in front of SAS," said the man.

"Oh! No, it's mine." Gunnar ran quickly to his car, leapt in, and started it. As he took off, he could see the tow truck in the rear-view mirror just turning into the terminal area.

On the drive home, his phone rang, and he knew it was Kara. "I love you!" he said happily into it.

"You're funny," said Ursula. "Well, at least that tells me you're still up for a dinner."

A car honked hard at Gunnar as he straddled lanes, and he jerked the car back. His heart raced. He hadn't thought of Ursula for days.

"Did I catch you driving?" she said.

"Yes, sorry about that. Bad drivers around here."

"I'm back and just wanted to say hi."

"How's your Dad?"

"He's better, thanks. His doctor inserted a stent, and Dad gave my nursing skills a good test — he's a tough cookie."

As she spoke, he was trying to figure out how to bring up to her that things had changed. He couldn't date Ursula now, no matter what Carl thought. His heart didn't work that way. Besides, she may still have Jeff, and his plan to woo her away now vanished.

"So when are you free for dinner?" she asked.

He'd tell her at dinner, he decided — best to do it face-to-face. "Tonight?"

"Tonight would be great. Any kind of food you like in particular?"

"Steak," he said without thinking.

"I'm rather fond of Monty's Steak House — kind of old-fashioned but special. Want to meet there?"

The same place he'd first taken Kara? "I'm trying to wean myself off steak, though," he said, wanting to keep Monty's sacred. "Eating fish is supposed to be good. Fish oil and all." He'd be eating a lot of fish in Denmark, so best get used to it.

"I love sushi," she said.

Sushi? He could never bring himself to try raw fish. He could barely stomach the fried stuff. Still, the point of tonight wasn't about eating. "Sushi's wonderful," he said. "Do you have a place?"

"How about Wasabi, right near the university? You probably know it."

"Wasabi is great," he said, figuring he'd find it in the Yellow Pages. "How's seven?"

"Seven p.m. it is at Wasabi. See you there."

Once he arrived home and had stared at the bat on his calendar, Gunnar calculated that seven hours separated Madison from Roskilde. She'd land in about another six hours. Was Kara thinking about him? Her parents would be picking her up. Would she talk about him a lot and explain the love of her life would be coming soon to live with her? Did her parents like America or Americans? Thanks to Iraq, maybe they would detest him. But Kara would explain he's different and that he made her happy. He reached in his pocket and pulled out the piece of paper with her e-mail address: Reddream@sol.dk.

He stared at her handwriting, very different from an American's. It had more curves to it somehow. The small letter "e" had its straight line at an angle. Something as simple as lettering appeared so foreign. That was Kara: similar but very different from anyone he'd known. He would write her tomorrow. Right now, he had to prepare to meet Ursula.

------------→

"You can't sit at the sushi bar until your party is here," said the rather tall hostess at Wasabi.

"I'm sure she'll show up soon," said Gunnar, sitting near the front door, checking his watch. The woman smiled, but Gunnar could see that the only two open spaces at the sushi bar were now going to the couple behind him. Ursula was already fifteen minutes late. From the little he knew of her, this was unlike her. He called her cell phone. No answer. Now he was worried.

Did Ursula stand him up? Perhaps he'd misread her completely, and she was paying him back for what happened at ScurryDate. No, she'd understood what had happened and she'd been upbeat during the last two calls.

How long should he sit there? A half hour? He guessed he should give her at least forty-five minutes — at that point he'd accept the humiliation.

He scratched his hands. He realized this was another thing he didn't like about dating: not knowing the other person's habits and personality. Then again, this wasn't a date, just a meeting to explain his situation.

His cell phone vibrated. He pulled it out of his pocket. The number didn't look familiar. Maybe it was Ursula.

"Hello?" he said, turning into the wall, hoping he wasn't angering anyone nearby by talking on his cell.

"This is AT&T with a collect call from Ursula Nordstrom. Will you accept?"

"Yes. I'll accept," he said, worried.

"Gunnar?" he heard.

"Ursula, where are you?"

"I'm sooo sorry," she said. "This is a bit embarrassing."

Gunnar could hear sirens in the background. She must be on a city street.

"Where are you?" he asked.

"I'm at a gas station."

"You ran out of gas?"

"No, I filled up yesterday just for tonight," she said. "I didn't want anything to go wrong this evening. Then I ran over a nail or something on University. A tire blew. Oh, God, I'm sooo sorry." He could tell she was feeling bad.

"No, it's, ah — what? Another half hour? Don't worry, I'll wait." The sirens were getting louder. "Are you okay?"

"Oh, shit," he heard her say under her breath. "I'll have to talk fast because they've sent a fire truck and a paramedic unit for me. How silly, I'm just — "

"Are you okay?" Now he was getting concerned.

"Don't laugh or hate me," she said. "But I was going to be there early — I'm always early. When I was on the side of the road, I tried calling you on my cell phone, but the battery died. I couldn't even call Triple A. Luckily, a nice policeman came by and called a tow truck, which took me to this gas station. Once the gas station guy was putting on a new tire, it looked like I'd still make it there on time."

"But why a paramedic?" he asked. Was she diabetic or something?

"That's the point. I tried calling you on a payphone to give you a heads up. But the recorded voice said I needed to put in another quarter. I didn't have more change, so I hit the change return button. I couldn't find the hole for the change. I was looking everywhere. I found a hole on the side of the phone and — "

Gunnar could hear some laughing in the background and Ursula said, muffled, "It's not funny!"

"No, ma'am, it's not," said a man's voice, then more laughter.

"Anyway," said Ursula into the phone, "I'm sorry, Gunnar, but my finger is caught in some strange hole here on the side of the phone, and when I couldn't get it out, I called the operator, who called 911. Then I called the collect operator. I'm so sorry, and if you don't want to see me tonight, I fully understand. I'm normally not a klutz in the least, but — "

Gunnar felt like laughing, but he controlled it. "No, no, I'll wait for you. Don't be silly."

A half hour later, they were together at the sushi bar, low seats before a black counter and a refrigerated display of raw fish. Ursula's index finger, wrapped tightly in gauze, pointed straight, constantly catching Gunnar's eye as if she were perpetually indicating something. In addition, her yellow blouse had what looked to be a streak of oil. The paramedics used some sort of grease, some of which had spilled on her blouse.

"I don't want to embarrass you," Ursula told Gunnar. "So we can go whenever you want."

Despite the grease, she radiated elegance. With black satin pants, high heels, and her long, dark blond hair tonight filled with waves and volume, she had dressed to impress — she was gorgeous — yet she was more concerned about him than herself.

"Don't be silly. You've been traumatized enough for one evening," said Gunnar.

"Hai," said the sushi chef, extending a plate of orange fish eggs wrapped in a tight blanket of seaweed.

"Hai," said Ursula in return.

As Ursula slipped one set of fish eggs into her mouth, Gunnar said, "You're more adventurous than I am."

She pointed to his cucumber sushi. "You're not a sushi eater, are you?"

"What makes you say that?" He fumbled with the chopsticks in his hand to make them work as easily as Ursula's.

"Let's just say I notice things. Let me suggest some fish I know you'll like."

"I doubt there's anything here like that."

"I absolutely promise you it's not fishy tasting and, in fact, it'll blow your mind. I promise."

"Promise?" he echoed.

She nodded and ordered halibut. The chef set to work. Gunnar and Ursula watched him, and soon he presented Gunnar with two pieces on a square white plate. The fish, also white, had squiggles of green and red on top, along with some sort of clear sauce.

As if seeing his concern, Ursula said, "It's an extremely light fish, and it has a citrus sauce to give it a little zing. Here."

She lifted a piece to his mouth with her chopsticks. He opened his mouth and closed his eyes. He tasted rice at first, then a subtle tanginess. The texture of the fish was different than he expected, a bit like linguine al dente.

"I'm surprised," he admitted. He took the other piece himself with his chopsticks. He remembered how, now —

after all the Japanese food with Allison. "I'm eating raw fish," he said, amazed.

"Yes," she said, "And I'm impressed, too, by how persistent you've been with me. I appreciate it."

"Oh?" he said, realizing he'd better get started. "While you've been gone, an opportunity came up for my sabbatical next year. Because I earned tenure, I also get a sabbatical."

"That's when you don't have to work but are paid?"

"Or you work elsewhere to stretch yourself. It looks like I may go to Denmark."

"That's fantastic!" she said. "I'm instantly envious."

"The Danes are big into physics, and I was even asked a few years ago to speak at a conference there."

"When would you go?"

"It's still up in the air, but it could be as soon as December."

"Wow. And for how long?"

"I could be gone up to a year."

She nodded. "That must be exciting for you," she said.

He nodded. "Yes." It looked as if she understood. She was smart. If he wasn't going to be around in a few months, no point in getting serious.

For the next forty minutes, he and Ursula talked about innocuous things: a love of outdoors and the lakes, about the joy of using a car wash in the winter, and about nursing. For a few years, she'd been an LVN, working part-time in a nursing home, but being a manager of a restaurant paid more. Now she was training to be an RN. "Soon I'll be interning at a hospital, and I'll just have to drop the restaurant. I've saved enough money to do it."

"Is Jeff in the medical field, too?"

"We're taking a break from each other."

"So..."

"So I find you interesting."

His heart skipped a beat. Didn't she understand Denmark? He'd better be more explicit. Facing the raw fish, he realized he needed to speak now. "You're interesting, too. And easygoing, kind, a great sense of humor, good-looking — "

"Really?"

"Yes. And you'll clearly make a great nurse."

"Are you proposing? I'm confused. We hardly know each other."

"Ursula." He paused. "No, it's not a proposal. In some ways, I wished we'd gone out two weeks ago as intended."

She frowned. "What?"

"Funny how things happen, how the totally unexpected can occur — like your dad's heart attack."

She sensed it now. "Hold it — something more happened in the last two weeks besides the sabbatical?"

"It wasn't wrong that you've come back into my life. You're a wonderful person. I think we'll make great friends."

"*Friends?*"

"The thing is, the truth is, after you left, I happened to step on someone's toes — a Danish woman who was visiting. Kara."

"Kara?" she asked as if it were a word like "supermodel." Her blue eyes started to glisten.

"Things happened rather quickly, and I'm going to be moving to Denmark at the end of the year — yes, with a job, and to live with her, too."

"That fast?" Ursula said, a tear now falling. It was definitely a tear, and Gunnar felt horrible.

"I wanted to tell you in person," he said, "not on the phone — after your dad's heart attack and all."

Ursula looked away as if that would help her regain control. She wiped her eyes. "I feel silly, as silly as with my finger in a phone," she said. "You've been a perfect gentleman, and it's not as if we're an item. Sorry that I thought you were proposing. Thank you for the nice evening. I hope it works out well with you in Denmark."

Instinctively, he pulled her in to hug her. His nose was right in her dark blond hair, and he could smell apples. "Thank you," he said. "You'll find someone special because, honestly, you're a good person. I'm sorry if I misled you. I only do one relationship at a time."

Ursula pulled away. "That's admirable. I'm pissed, but that's admirable. However, fuck friendship." She stood and walked out the door, not looking back.

Gunnar sat for a little bit, paid the bill, and then left. As he drove home, he saw that, despite his best intentions, he'd hurt Ursula. He felt bad.

At home, Gunnar brought up a blank e-mail screen and wrote:

Dear, dear Kara,
I miss you! Thank you for your email address, and now you have mine. What is your phone number? I've meant to ask that, too. International rates are cheap, I understand.

Oh, I miss your laughter, your smiles, the snuggling and cuddling and your coffee and so much more. Do you realize how much you've changed my life? I feel like I'm in one of those old movie laboratories — Dr. Frankenstein's lab — and things have come alive. Electric arcs are everywhere. I'm buzzing.

In this world full of hurt, it can't be wrong that we met. I feel the power of it being right.

I love you,
Gunnar

CHAPTER TWELVE

"IT SEEMS EINSTEIN WAS DOUBLY WRONG WHEN HE SAID, GOD DOES NOT PLAY DICE. NOT ONLY DOES GOD DEFINITELY PLAY DICE, BUT HE SOMETIMES CONFUSES US BY THROWING THEM WHERE THEY CAN'T BE SEEN."

— PHYSICIST STEPHEN HAWKING

Three and a half months later, Gunnar watched the airplane's wing flaps move, and he nodded, tension and worry superseding the exhaustion he'd felt earlier from his more than fifteen-hour trip. He'd been able to nap off and on after he'd switched planes in Newark, but when the sun rose while over the Atlantic, anxiety took over. He pondered the physics of aerodynamics. It always worked. The Airbus A330, the largest twinjet in the world, was an amazing set of systems. Each of the two engines was fueled independently. There were dozens of hydraulic systems. There was an oxygen system, a fire-extinguisher system, as well as other emergency systems. Computers oversaw everything, including the commands by the pilot so that the pilot, for instance, could not turn the plane in a dangerous or acrobatic position, such as upside down. By statistics alone, this airplane was a safer place to be than any automobile.

The plane landed so smoothly that Gunnar didn't know the moment he was back on solid earth. He was in a row by himself; he could make a remark to no one. He stared out the window. A brown grassy field lay beyond the runway, no snow anywhere, and past the field stood short, barren trees, perhaps birch. This far north, he'd expected snow. Madison had already a few feet on the ground, and the lack of snow here seemed strange. It threw him.

An announcement came, first in Danish, he assumed, then in English. "Please remain in your seat until the plane has come to a complete stop, and the 'fasten seat belt' sign has been turned off. The local time is 2:05 p.m. Thank you for flying SAS Airlines, and please join us again."

Gunnar tensed, having shifted from guarded optimism to deep nervousness. He had arrived. She'd be there. She had to be. Still, his stomach knotted. Over the last month, he had started to doubt what she said or wrote — she was always so brief. He recalled her last words by phone: "It'll be a great experience for you." Did she mean it like some sort of state fair ride? "Come experience the Wisconsin State Fair," he thought as the plane taxied toward his future. He then realized the word "experience" suggested a limit. Did this trip have a limit? His sabbatical did, so he'd have to make some tough decisions in about three or four months if he were to stay beyond the summer. Staying longer would mean giving up his tenure, a goal which he had spent the last decade achieving. Was love worth this?

Maybe she'd come back with him to Wisconsin. She loved America. Would they have to marry for her to live there? Sure, why not. Maybe this trip he'd get engaged. Wouldn't his sister love that?

Then again, maybe he'd stay. The physics research at Niels Bohr looked to be awesome, and perhaps a life in Denmark with Kara would be extraordinary. As he gazed out his window and saw the silvery terminal get closer, he pictured Kara's face. She was in that building now, just beyond customs, and he bet she was wondering about her future with him, too. Was he coming for a visit or for life?

That's a big question neither of them had ever verbalized. He figured they were in love, so why worry? Go with the flow.

The plane came to a complete stop, and a friendly "ding" emphasized the fact. Everyone stood, and most people he heard were not speaking English, so it had to be Danish. Then again, he discerned just behind him the sing-song of Swedish. He turned. An elderly couple spoke his grandfather's tongue. The woman brushed some crumbs from her husband's winter coat and said something, perhaps, "You're a handsome man, and I'm proud to be with you." Maybe in another forty years, this would be Kara and him.

A businessman one row ahead seemed to be speaking Danish to a colleague. What business did these Danes have in Chicago? Ham imports? Or maybe cookies. The Danish businessmen laughed about something — maybe how funny it was that the poor Americans loved Danish cookies and ham.

Gunnar opened the overhead bin and pulled down his laptop computer and shoulder bag. He'd been permitted to bring only twenty kilograms — forty-four pounds — in his luggage, so he stuffed many of his extras into this shoulder bag, things like a framed photo of his mother and sister, extra underwear (he might be gone for a while, after all) and several heavy books. He opened the bag and pulled from the top his 35mm camera. He hadn't gone digital yet. Negatives in sleeves seemed a better system for storage versus CD-ROMs. After all, his first computer used 5¼-inch floppy disks, and if his pictures were on those, where would he be now? Negatives would always exist.

He leaned down to his window, and he raised the camera to his eye. He wanted some sort of photo to show his grandkids some day. "See," he might say. "Here's one of the first things I saw when I landed in the country." He shot the baggage cart approaching the plane.

The plane's door opened, and people slowly moved forward. When it was his aisle's turn, Gunnar strode forward to leave. This was it. If nothing else, he thought, pretend it will go well. In minutes, Kara would surely be hugging him so hard, he'd know he was in the right place.

The walkway from the plane into the terminal was all glass, and Gunnar looked out onto the tarmac up into the light blue sky at the thin white clouds. Just a matter of steps until he'd be with Kara.

As he stepped tentatively into the terminal, he was amazed that the flooring was not carpeting but rather a blond hardwood, elegant in the late afternoon light. The orange sun spilled in from the floor-to-ceiling windows. The shiny polished wood stretched into the distance where the sign "Told/Customs" beckoned. He pulled up his camera again. He photographed the sign. He imagined showing it in the future. "I knew right away how different this place was, yet special," he might say someday.

He felt lighter, surer. After all, such a beautiful airport was a definite sign that all would go well. Some of the windows had a blue tint to them. There were potted trees in large silver urns, as well as a twelve-foot-tall Christmas tree with blinking white lights and a sign, "Glaedelig Jul og godt nytår." Overhead he noticed the lighting wasn't standard florescent light boxes, but rather large inset circles evenly lit. These were the details he had to remember. Perhaps he'd relate them to Kara in bed that night.

As people walked past him speaking in Danish, he felt odd, unsafe. It wasn't natural people didn't speak English. He should have traveled when he was younger, when such abnormality might have been fun. Now he missed the bubble of the plane where English was at least expected. But soon he'd have the bubble of Kara.

He stepped down the moving escalator, and a number of stores came into view. The wide hallway stretched far. It was a long indoor mall. As he walked, looking for another customs sign, he noticed stores selling such things as glassware, Royal Copenhagen porcelain, chocolate, cheese, luggage, and more. He came to Whisky World — Tax Free. Ah, yes. That's why the stores were there. Tax-free. He'd overheard on the plane an English couple talk about Denmark's high taxes — that automobiles were taxed something like 100% because Denmark had no auto industry. "Cars, boats, liquor, cigarettes — all the great things have high taxes," the woman had said. Her husband replied, "It'd be hard to live for long in Denmark." Ah, yes, but they didn't have Kara.

Then he realized. He'd been so worried about seeing Kara, where was the small gift box? He felt the pockets of his jacket. Shit! He pictured its exact location. The heart-shaped earrings that he'd bought at Macy's were right where he wrapped them at the last minute: on the dining room table. The renters, a young couple both in physics, would puzzle that one. He had to get Kara something and quickly.

What did she drink? Wine. He popped into Whiskey World and found the wines. He didn't know anything about wines. Maybe he should buy several — one of them would probably be great.

"How many bottles can I bring in?" he said, speaking slowly to a woman behind the counter. Well-dressed in a blouse and skirt, the fortyish woman looked as if she worked in a boutique rather than a liquor store.

"You may bring in one liter of spirits untaxed or two liters of wine," she said in a graceful British accent.

"Do you have California wines?" he asked.

"Of course."

"Red wine from Sonoma?"

She brought him to the red wine section, and she looked carefully at a few of the labels. She smiled, "Here's one from St. Francis Vineyard," she said.

Gunnar, however, spotted something familiar: the gold-edge white label of the Kenwood Russian River Pinot Noir. She'd instantly recognize it and remember their great first night together. This was kismet that he'd forgotten his other gift. This was meant to be, just like they were. He laughed at his good luck. "I'll take two bottles," he said, handing her his credit card.

She wrapped the bottles in tissue and put them in a strong-handled bag.

"Which way to customs?" he asked. She pointed left, and he ran. After all, Kara was waiting. Did she have a car? Or would they be hauling his bags on buses and trains? There were a lot of things he didn't know about her. Soon he would.

He turned into customs. A stern-looking man behind a counter took his declarations notice and his blue American passport. The man shot him a look that felt like a laser ray. Did the man hate him for the American involvement in Iraq?

"Goo-na Goon-dason," said the man, pronouncing his name. While the articulation was the same as Kara's, it didn't have the delight she gave it. "Purpose of your visit?" he asked.

"Pleasure. I assume it's pleasure, I mean — Well, and I'll be working at the Niels Bohr Institute as a visiting professor for a semester."

The man flipped to the back of his passport and looked extremely irritated. Apparently it didn't contain what he was looking for.

"So where is your permit to work? It's supposed to be here."

Gunnar reached inside his jacket pocket for the envelope. He handed it to the man, who then nodded, stapled the permit at the back of his passport, and stamped his passport.

Once past, the next room was baggage claim.

Gunnar found his single large bag spinning on the carousel. He wheeled it to the line of people exiting, and when a man pointed Gunnar down a hallway, he was expecting his luggage to be thoroughly inspected now. He was an American, after all. Humiliate him. Would there be remarks about George Bush or Cowboy Diplomacy? Rather, Gunnar found himself approaching a huge wall of expectant faces, people clearly waiting for others. That was it? He'd made it through security? He looked back. No guard was waving him back.

All the people standing and waiting in front of him looked so white and sweatered. Most faces looked similar to those in Wisconsin: bold yet blanched. There were a few happy jumping-up-and-down kids who yelled something like "Foe-ah!"

Kara, Kara, Kara. There was no Kara. Gunnar strolled past the initial group, and now those waiting were thinning out. Was she running late?

And then Gunnar saw the long red hair and Kara's face, placid as Mona Lisa's. She casually leaned against a post just under a sign that said "Udgang," and an arrow pointed up. She waved a little.

"Kara" he yelled. "It's you!" He ran to her, and she stood a little taller, waiting. Gunnar noticed at the last second she wasn't holding her arms out like women did in romantic films. Kara simply opened up one arm. He swept in and gave her a big embrace, but she only hugged him with the one arm. She didn't seem to be yearning. In that moment, he froze. Light came to a stop. His throat constricted.

He pulled back and looked at her. She smiled. Maybe he was being too sensitive. Hope returned. Her smile seemed appropriately wide.

"It's good to see you, Gunnar."

CHAPTER THIRTEEN

"WAVES EMITTED BY A MOVING OBJECT AS RECEIVED BY AN OBSERVER WILL BE BLUESHIFTED (COMPRESSED) IF APPROACHING, REDSHIFTED (ELONGATED) IF RECEDING. IT OCCURS BOTH IN SOUND AS WELL AS ELECTROMAGNETIC PHENOMENA, ALTHOUGH IT TAKES ON DIFFERENT FORMS IN EACH. AN EXAMPLE IS THE SOUND A TRAIN MAKES AS IT APPROACHES AND PASSES A STATIC OBSERVER BY THE TRACKS."

— THE DOPPLER EFFECT

Gunnar held out his gift, the wine: two bottles in a single bag.

As she opened it, he noticed she wore jeans and a sweatshirt with a substantial drawing of five green pine trees whose roots burrowed into a brown rectangle. Words in English on her shirt proclaimed, "SOIL: We Can't Grow Without It." He glanced to his gray slacks, black shirt, and navy sports jacket. He'd agonized for days what to wear. Apparently she hadn't.

She appraised one bottle, not seeming to recognize the significance of the label. "Very fine," she said. She placed the bottle back into the bag without looking at the other to see if it were different. She said nothing more as she pointed toward where they'd be walking and proceeded to do so.

Stunned, Gunnar remained frozen for a second, thinking maybe he should remind her of Monty's, but she was already five or six steps ahead. He grabbed all his luggage and lurched forward. His camera swung around his neck, bonking into his side as he raced. Once at her side, he wondered if he should hold her hand. Except, he didn't have a free hand. Should he ask her to carry something? It would be awkward, especially since she seemed distracted, looking into her bulky leather bag of a purse for something. He assumed she was looking for car keys.

"Did you drive?" he asked.

"Yes, I'm parked in a place where I probably shouldn't be, so..."

She walked fast, and he was starting to feel discombobulated. With jet lag, his worry, his lack of sleep, and now the stunning revelation with the wine, a sense of nausea was rising. Even though it was midafternoon in Copenhagen, it was just after seven a.m., Madison time. His body was confused. His breathing, in fact, was straining. Perhaps when they arrived at her place — his new place — the joy of it all would make him feel better.

"I have to stop a second," he finally said as they were almost at the door.

She turned and looked at him fully. "I'm sorry. Give me your shoulder bag, or what's that?"

"My laptop."

"I'll take both," she said.

As he handed them to her, he added, "Ah. You like the wine, right? I hear wine and liquor is very expensive here."

"Oh yes, thank you. I'm sorry. My mind's not on straight. That's very kind of you. My friend Peder likes wine, too. We should say *skol* to your arrival."

"Peder?"

"I told you about him. He's the new *skoleinspektør*."

"He inspects people toasting?" His head was spinning. Was she joking?

"*Skole* — school. He's the principal."

"Ah. Your boss."

"I suppose so."

He couldn't think. Was Peder her boss or her friend? Or did friend mean boss here? This language thing was hard when he couldn't focus well. "I should change some money, I think," he said. "I heard I get a better exchange rate here. Euros, right?"

"Actually, the Danes didn't approve the Euro. We still use Danish kroner."

"I thought Denmark was in the Common Market."

"We are. We just didn't want to go with their money — but I'm sure we will eventually." She found her keys. "Didn't you bring your ATM card? You can get money from any ATM machine — better rates than the kiosks."

"An ATM card?" he said. "I didn't think my bank was over here."

"It's not, but ATM cards work all over the world. Why didn't you ask me?"

"I'm sorry. I should've." Was that the right thing to say?

She looked at him oddly. "There's a kiosk over there where you can change your money. Leave your stuff here."

He nodded and walked over, looking back. She was rummaging in her bag again. This time she pulled out a cell phone. She started to use it when she saw him looking, and she gestured for him to move ahead. She began talking into the phone very efficiently, as if talking with a bill collector.

He exchanged a hundred-dollar traveler's check. He had brought a lot of traveler's checks. He had meant to talk with his personal banker back home, and maybe he would've learned about ATM machines then, but when time became short, he opted for changing a few thousand dollars into traveler's checks. Soon, the Niels Bohr Institute would be paying him, so perhaps he'd open a new account and get an ATM card then.

When the woman behind the thick glass at the kiosk handed him the conversion, saying, "Glaedelig Jul,"he was stunned by the color of Denmark's paper money — the bills differed from each other in color and size but shared in common the words *Danmarks Nationalbank*. One note was bright orange, another dark brown. There were pictures on them, too. One had a duck, another a fish, and a third had a centaur-Viking man.

He found himself breathing funny as if he were panicking. Was it just system overload — too many changes at once? Or was he afraid? Afraid of what? He was with the woman he loved. *Calm, be calm,* he told himself. He'd heard the term "culture shock," and he figured he was in it.

He noticed that Kara was now nodding as she spoke into the phone. Wasn't she happy to see him? Maybe he was just tired.

When he joined up with her, she was putting her phone away. "Everything okay?" he said.

"Yes. I was telling my parents you've arrived."

"Oh. Wonderful," he said. He was important after all.

Her car, a very small red Toyota, was in the lot, but it was parked haphazardly in a baggage cart return zone. Amazingly, there was no ticket. Gunnar said, "Nice."

"It's not mine. It's my parents."

He meant the lack of a ticket, but he nodded. God, he was tired. If he could only get to his new home, he could take a nap, and then this would all be so less surreal.

"They let me borrow it," she continued. "I want a car, but cars are extremely expensive in Denmark. I'm saving up to buy a house. Most single people have neither."

"Maybe we'll buy both, eh?"

She smiled and said nothing.

Kara opened the trunk and put his bags in.

"Please," she said. "The doors are unlocked."

Gunnar opened the passenger door. Once they were both belted in, he said, "Where's the snow?"

"It hardly ever snows in Copenhagen. If it does, it melts. It rarely gets colder than zero. Our winters hang around zero."

She backed the car out. Zero. That's right, he reminded himself. Denmark used centigrade, so zero was thirty-two, the freezing point of water. Zero all the time.

"I like snow," said Gunnar.

"This isn't the country for it," she said. "We're surrounded by the sea."

She put the car in first gear using a clutch, he noted. A small car and manual transmission — and all the cars in the lot looked small. Times seemed tougher here than back home. "With houses and cars so expensive here, I guess the cost of living is better in America."

"Hardly. Everyone here has healthcare. If you lose your job here, you have wonderful unemployment. There's great education for all. These things have priorities."

He nodded again, looking around.

Next thing he knew, they were on a highway out of the airport. The pavement had a light reddish tone. Why wasn't it white concrete? The speed limit sign said 100. Then he realized it was kilometers per hour. He didn't like all these differences. It threw him off. Another sign had the word "Fabrik." It looked like a factory of some sort. Every day was going to be like this?

Kara was saying something, but he found himself nodding, not really understanding. Was she talking Danish?

"Gunnar? Okay?"

"What?"

"I'm sorry," she said.

"For what?"

"Weren't you listening?"

He shook his head. "Jet lag, I guess."

"I said you're staying with my parents."

"What? Is something wrong?"

"Peder and I live together now."

He blinked twice. He must have heard wrong. He must be misunderstanding.

"I'm not clear," he said. He glanced out the window. Everything was a blur. "Why do we want your boss as a roommate?"

"You're staying with my parents."

"Why?"

"I've living with Peder."

"Peder is your lover? Your boss? I changed my whole life to come over. Did I do something wrong?"

"No. Peder moved in three weeks ago. We're in love."

He had to concentrate. What could he say? "But Christmas is in a week."

Her face was more angled and sharp than he remembered. She focused on the road and didn't glance at him at all.

"My parents have a room for you," she said.

The car hummed.

"These things happen," she said.

The car turned.

"I didn't intend for it to happen," she said.

Gunnar stared at his hands and saw how he was bleeding. He must have just scratched them very hard. He looked at her again and spoke: "Did I do or say something wrong?"

"Peder and I have a lot in common."

"And you and I don't?"

"You're a lovely person." Now she looked at him. "But I've known you only a couple weeks."

"I moved heaven and earth to get here. I risked my career."

"The Niels Bohr Institute sounds like a step up to me."

"How could you do this to me!"

"I couldn't very well tell you about this with all your plans you set up. You might have done something stupid. You'll see. Traveling is a good thing. You'll love Danmark. And it's not like you don't have a place to stay. My parents are very *venskabelige* — friendly.Ingeborg and Fritz."

There were many more buildings around the highway now, many with wreaths, Christmas trees, and strings of white lights. They must be in Copenhagen proper. A sign said M21. That must be the name of the road.

"Why didn't you tell me in advance?" he said, trying not to yell.

"You were writing me how you had renters, how you had your job set up at Niels Bohr, how — "

"It wasn't like we were strangers. We kept in constant contact."

"Peder and I…. He's a lovely man, as wonderful as you. Things just happened. I was very confused at the time — I didn't do this lightly… but he's Danish."

This is how Ursula must have felt when he told her about Kara. Was this karma? Did the world really work on karma?

The hum of the car burrowed into him. People whom he told how he was going to Denmark for Kara had always look astounded as if he were a bit crazy. They were right. His sister was right. Why was everyone else right? Why didn't he know about love? He had thought *he* was the one who knew. To do it right, you have to give up something, like a throne. He might not know history, but he knew King Edward gave up his throne to marry Mrs. Simpson. Didn't that one turn out well? Actually, he didn't know.

"Remember when you were riding your bike up a hill and were thinking of me? You said you loved me. You were riding, thinking of me, and feeling flushed all over."

"Girlish of me, I guess."

A gas station zipped by. A Shell station. At least that was familiar.

Soon a large stand of new-looking buildings, like condominiums, came into view, and the sun was very low through them. It would be dark soon.

Neither of them said anything for minutes. They veered through another interchange, and a sign for an exit said Høje-Taastrup. Kara spoke of a younger brother, Henrik, home from military service, who could show Gunnar some of the town, Roskilde. Her words became a stream that he could not completely follow. She said Roskilde was a grand old town with a fjord, and kings and queens buried in a cathedral built in the middle ages, and *kilde,* a Danish word for a natural source of water, a spring, *kilde.* The town was Ro's*kilde,* King Ro, King Ro's *kilde,* though King Harald Bluetooth was probably the actual founder, and Gunnar would have a comfortable room.

Before he knew it, they were turning off the highway into Roskilde, and the night was darkening. Best he could tell, Denmark was flat like Iowa. As they approached the town, brightly lit twin spires of a red brick cathedral dominated the town. She pointed and pronounced "*Rawskilla domkierka.*" A sign with an arrow soon said, *Roskilde Domkirke.*

They drove through the town, which seemed like Santa Claus Lane for its quaint narrow streets and holiday lights and wreaths everywhere. Main street curved in a slow arc. White Christmas lights blinked in many windows, as did the occasional lit Christmas tree. It was almost Christmas. 'Twas the season to be jolly.

The buildings joined together, two and three stories tall, in muted colors: ocher, brown, and standard red brick. "These buildings are very old," said Kara. "You can't just knock them down as you do in the states. Danish people like their history."

Gunnar felt himself shaking his head. His breathing was becoming shallow again. Calm, calm, he told himself. This was about survival now. How could he be here? What would his life be like now? He imagined himself like a toad. He was a dying toad under a dark log.

It occurred to him at that moment: look for a hotel. But the stores were streaming by too fast, and nothing looked hotel-like. Was the word "hotel" the same in Danish? He noticed a café, with the word "Internet" on the window, but no hotels. He was too tired to deal with this.

"So, you're what — just dropping me off?" he said.

"I'll stay for dinner with you. I told Peder he was on his own tonight."

"I'd hate to get between you two lovebirds," he said.

"You don't have to be *sarkastisk*.

"Sarcastic?"

"Yes. I knew this would be tough for you, but you're a very good person, so I'm trying to help you. You can stay with my parents until you find other housing. You may want to live in Copenhagen, closer to your job."

"I don't read Danish. How am I to find — "

"We'll figure it out."

"And what about my orthodontist? I found one here in Roskilde. If I move to Copenhagen, he's here."

"Why don't I kick Peder out and have you move in so you'll be close to your orthodontist?"

"*Sarkastisk?*" he said.

"Yes. Don't be crazy right now. You may not believe me, but I'm trying to make this as easy as possible. I want you to like Denmark."

"I already know that."

It was now deep black night, even though it was just after four p.m. They pulled onto a street of small brick homes, snowless and with dark lawns, and Kara expertly parallel parked on the street under a streetlight.

"We're here," she said.

He stared at the two-story house with dormer windows at the top. This was where he was being dumped.

She opened her door, walked around to his side, and stood there, as if pondering whether she should open it for him. As she started reaching, he pulled on the door handle urgently, as if he could prove he knew how it worked. Once outside, he noticed that is was rather chilly.

"This is *femten Dronning Margrethesvej* — fifteen Queen Margaret's Road," she said, with her breath visible. He stood there, waiting for the next instructions. She looked at him as if he were an amputee; he only needed the right prosthetic. "It's important that you learn how to say it because if you don't want to walk everywhere, you will need to tell a taxi driver the address. It could be *very* important. Try saying it. Fem-ten."

"Fem-ten," said Gunnar, helplessly.

"Drone-ing."

"Drone-ing."

"Ma-gray-tahs-vie."

"Ma-gray-tahs-vie."

"*Femten Dronning Margrethesvej.*"

"Femten, bemptem, hempten," he said. He noticed his breath did not burst out like hers. It had less heat. It struggled to become vapor.

"You'll get it," she said. "You'll do fine."

She moved to the trunk. The click of it opening sounded like a scalpel falling on tile.

CHAPTER FOURTEEN

"NO TWO IDENTICAL FERMIONS IN A SYSTEM, SUCH AS ELECTRONS IN AN ATOM, CAN HAVE AN IDENTICAL SET OF QUANTUM NUMBERS. THIS IS TO SAY NO TWO ELECTRONS IN AN ATOM CAN BE AT THE SAME TIME IN THE SAME STATE OR CONFIGURATION."

— PAULI EXCLUSION PRINCIPLE

At the front door, which was not flat but ornately carved, Kara inserted a key into the lock. At that moment, the door opened, and two short, fair-skinned people presented themselves, smiling widely like characters from a cake. "I'm Ingeborg," said Kara's mother, a woman with blond hair whose dark brown sweater featured patterns of snowflakes and reindeer. "Ya, *jeg er Fritz!*" said her father, his hair red like Kara's, but thin and parted to one side. "I am Fritz."

"You must be Gunnar," said Ingeborg in what Gunnar was now hearing as a Danish accent, and she stepped out to shake his hand. Gunnar nodded, thinking how he must be Gunnar. Be Gunnar now.

"Nice to meet you," he said and shook her hand. He shook Fritz's, too. It felt surreal to Gunnar — not a dream but a nightmare. They had to know he'd just been dumped.

"My mother knows a lot of English," Kara said, "but my father not so much."

"Most Danes," said Ingeborg, "learn English starting in the fifth grade. But if you don't use it often, it goes away. My husband manages a large printing *fabrik*, and he never uses English."

"Ya, *fabrik*," said Fritz.

"I am a nurse," said Ingeborg.

"I just met a nurse in Wisconsin," said Gunnar, not knowing what else to say. "Intensive care."

"Very interesting," said Ingeborg. "Nurses are all over the world."

It looked like she meant it, but Gunnar felt like they were in a conversational language class where meaning was secondary to interaction. Christ, how did he get here? His life might be far different this very second if he hadn't stepped on Kara's toes. Was life about finding one's big mistake in order to be crushed?

"And what kind of nurse are you?" asked Gunnar, adding to the script.

"Emergency room," she said. "I'm sure it's quite different here than in America, however. Guns aren't allowed in Denmark, so we don't have the kind of violence you do."

"America's not the Wild West," said Gunnar. "People in Wisconsin don't walk around with guns."

"Columbine," she responded. With that one word, which brought back two boys killing their fellow students, he was even more depressed. He also realized Danes knew more about America than most Americans knew about Denmark. He just nodded.

Fritz looked useless at this point, so he said something to Kara that sounded like "Yelpa die." Yelp or die? Gunnar was doing all he could not to yelp or die. Fritz moved past them and took Gunnar's bags. Ah. Fritz was helping. He then said something like, "Skivvies to Mel."

"Ya, skivvies to Mel," Ingeborg repeated with a big smile, rubbing her hands together as if Mel was going to give them a show. Maybe Mel was her brother.

"Where's your brother?" Gunnar said to Kara.

"He's off with some friends, but you'll meet him in the morning."

"His name's Mel?"

"No, Henrik. 'Mel' is the word for food. It's spelled m-a-d," Kara said, "They've made dinner. Shall we eat? *Skal vi ha' mad?*"

Gunnar nodded. He was going mad himself, but here it meant food. And love meant living with your lover's parents. As they walked into the house, he looked at Kara, still trying to fathom her. This was the same woman he had made love to on the kitchen counter. How could she betray him?

"Okay?" said Kara to Gunnar.

Of course it wasn't okay. He and Kara should be snuggling and laughing and loving, two people celebrating the end of their apartness, and now he was more apart than he could have ever imagined. Maybe he would die here.

"*Dagligstue,*" said Fritz, indicating the living room as he moved through it to the stairs with Gunnar's wheeled suitcase. A Christmas tree stood in the corner, lit not with strings of colored lights but with live burning candles in holders hooked on branches. Was he moving into a fire trap? So be it. He could go out in a blaze.

As they continued through the room, blue porcelain plates encircled the walls at head height — apparently their formal china was mounted on the wall. Odd. Other than that, the dark wood and the stuffed leather chairs made it look like they lived well and formally. Fritz started walking up the stairs, so Gunnar followed with Kara behind him.

"Come down soon," said Ingeborg in English, heading into the dining room.

Still on the stairs, Kara looked at her father and said something in rapid Danish, and her father nodded, as if sensing hopelessness, and spoke in a Danish that sounded slow and philosophical, Kierkegaard with a suitcase. With two more interchanges, and Fritz looking at Gunnar sadly, they reached a hallway and turned into a room.

Fritz now sounded more upbeat, and pointed to a little snow globe on the window ledge, saying, "*Den lille havfrue.*" Fritz picked it up, turned it upside down, and snow started falling on a mermaid on a rock. Ah — the Little Mermaid. Should he be happy Disney made it there? He then remembered that Denmark's Hans Christian Andersen had written the original story, which ended with the mermaid not getting the prince, but dying and becoming sea foam before she turned into an eternal soul. His mother had read him Andersen stories at bedtime. Her favorite was "The Little Match Girl," where a little homeless girl warms herself in winter with matches before she succumbs to the cold and dies. He realized those two stories should have been a big clue to this culture. In death comes relief.

"Nice," said Gunnar.

Fritz said something at length in a very sweet tone to Kara as if recalling a memory. Kara smiled and laughed, saying, "*Nej! Det var ingenting.*"

"*Det var vidunderligt.*"

Then they both laughed. Were they laughing at him now? What a jerk he was to have come all the way here. Gunnar could only shake his head thinking about where he'd gone wrong. Where had his hypothesis faltered? He had been willing and open for love to happen. If a man loved a woman, and she loved you, then...? He recalled Kara's e-mails had become extremely short over the last month. They had always been short, but she was down to mere sentences with more Danish in them than usual; he should have realized there'd been a change. He remembered thinking at one point that all he had to do was get to Denmark and all would be well. How wrong he was.

"Bathroom?" Gunnar said to Fritz, miming the washing of his hands. He'd rather avoid Kara. Each word from her was a knife wound.

"Down the hall to your right," said Kara.

Gunnar grimaced, but he said, "Thanks," and left.

The bathroom was chilly. The water took a while to get warm. As he waited, Gunnar peered out the window. Under a street light, a young woman in a thick sweater walked a

CHRISTOPHER MEEKS · 167

white dog. The scene didn't look that different from Wisconsin. It sure felt different.

He noticed the medicine cabinet. He opened it. The same stuff: perfume bottles, an underarm deodorant stick, nail clippers, and mouthwash, but most had a lot of Danish writing on it that included the extra letters Å, Æ, and Ø. The toothpaste had the bold name of Zendium, which sounded powerful enough to clean tile. Something like aspirin had the name Panodil on it. There was one other pill bottle, a prescription to Fritz Tornsen: "Zopiklone 7,5mg."He shook it, then opened it up. There were at least fifty of the white pills. One handful.

And then he heard the call for dinner.

-------------->

They sat at the dark wood table in high-backed chairs in the dining room.

Gunnar was so tired and depressed, he knew he was operating with mostly nods and weak smiles. Couldn't they just let him go to bed?

In front of each person sat an empty plate, and on the plate, painted in the center, was a windmill in blue. The silverware was heavy. This was what his mother would call the good guest stuff.

Ingeborg and Fritz walked in with two steaming bowls of food apiece and placed them on the table before him.

"Are you hungry?" Ingeborg said.

Frankly, he would have been fine with a dry cracker, but he sensed Kara's parents had gone overboard to soften the blow.

"I'm, ah… Well, I suppose I could use a… Thanks."

Ingeborg smiled deeply as she sat down, satisfied it was all working so well. "So. Kara tells me you're a physicist."

"Yes."

"And you'll be working at the Niels Bohr Institute."

"Yes."

"Niels Bohr was one of our finest scientists."

"I studied him when I was a younger man," said Gunnar. "I found his research on the constitution of the atomic nuclei, and of their transmutations and disintegrations, quite interesting." Why did he say "younger?" Was that to suggest he was an older man, so, ipso facto, wasn't their daughter lucky she squeaked out of a relationship with this old fool? As he looked at their faces, however, he could see they understood little of what he had just said because they had the same pretend smile he probably had most of the time.

"Help yourself," said Ingeborg, and all bowls were before him. One looked like beef stew. He liked that, so he took a few major chunks. Then there was a long, green vegetable, steamed, that looked like a fat green onion — white on the bottom, transitioning into green ribbons on the top.

"Looks interesting," said Gunnar as diplomatically as he could. "What is it?"

"Porrer," said Ingeborg.

"In English?"

"Porrer?" she said as a question to Kara.

Kara shrugged and said, "Porrer."

Ingeborg pulled a book off a nearby bookshelf, then flipped pages. Gunnar could see it was a dictionary. "It's called a leek," she said. "Do you like leeks?"

"Can't say I've ever had one." Why did everything have to be so different?

"Porrer," said Fritz definitively. "Wery good."

Gunnar looked at his other choices. Deep red beets in one bowl. Another held what looked liked sardines in chunks.

"I'm sorry, what's this?"

"That's herring, and we can make you some *nye kartofler* — new potatoes — if you like. Oh! I forgot one plate."

She hurried into the kitchen and returned with a plate with a whole fish on it. It appeared to have been simply sautéed in butter. The fish had two eyes on one side of its head, a malformed fish.

"It's called *rødspætte*, which means red spots," said Kara.

"It's a flounder with red spots on it," said Ingeborg.

Gunnar stared at the two eyes.

"The two eyes on one side of the head," Ingeborg said, "are because the fish lays on the bottom of the sea and one of the eyes changes from one side to the other after a while."

He never had food look at him before, much less mutant food. He looked up to see Kara, Ingeborg, and Fritz gazing at him, too. It was like the time a car hit him from behind on the freeway. He and the young offender pulled to the side, and the young man's radiator shot steam into the air. Cars on the freeway slowed to a crawl to stare. All those eyes searched for death. The eyes asked could it happen to them? Would one day they be on the side of the road? These eyes at the table, too, wanted to see was there a dead body? They saw the victim of a hit-and-run relationship.

"Fish?" asked Ingeborg.

"The beef will do fine," said Gunnar, "and I'll try a porrer and a beet. I ate on the plane twice, so I don't have much appetite." He was coping as best he could, a failed lover masking as an American. Exhaustion swept over him like a wind from the north.

They seemed to be watching whether he'd like the food. He took a bite of the beef. In that instant, he realized it wasn't beef but the sour taste of liver. Liver was a food he detested, perhaps because all the liver did was filter the blood's impurities.

Fritz then took a bite, too.

"Lee-wa," said Fritz. "Wery good."

And Gunnar felt his eyes swell with tears. Fritz's grin became a blur. Ingeborg and Kara became mere spots. Gunnar couldn't believe his body was now betraying him. First Kara, now himself. He didn't have to be so fucking pathetic. He turned and shut his eyes and gritted his teeth. He was not going to blubber. How absolutely revolting. He felt his chest tighten and release, tighten and release. He was sniffling. He could only shake his head.

"I'm sorry," he said. "I'm just so tired. It's best if I ... you know."

"Kara?" said Ingeborg. "Can you show Gunnar his bed?"

"*Ja, undskyld,*" said Kara in what sounded like an apology. "*Jeg kan ikke gøre for det, men...*" and soon her father was talking, and all three quickly conversed in a swell of Danish. Gunnar stood. He would find his room. He felt someone attach to his arm, and he looked to see Kara, gazing compassionately.

"I'm sorry, Gunnar, for everything," she said. "With a little sleep, maybe it will be better."

He nodded. "Yes, I just need sleep."

He followed her up to his room. She fluffed the covers. He didn't see any top sheet.

"This is a nice cozy comforter. In Denmark, the sheet is around the comforter. It makes more sense, no?"

No. Nothing made sense. Kara left him with a nod. He opened his bag and stirred around the inside for his toiletry case, but then decided his teeth could rot for all he cared. He pulled off his clothes except his plaid boxer shorts, and he crawled into bed. It was firmer than he liked, but the comforter felt okay. The room and his mind seemed to whirl, though, and he felt as if the bed were one big black hole. It was sucking him in. He noticed that, in closing his eyes, things slowed. Things became simple:

Beds are good.

Comforters are good.

Kara is bad.

Love sucks.

Denmark sucks.

Sleep is good.

Sleep, sleep. Blessed sleep.

CHAPTER FIFTEEN

"NO SYSTEM CAN REACH ABSOLUTE
ZERO. WHILE THE ENTROPY OF A PURE
PERFECT CRYSTAL OF
      AN ELEMENT AT THE ABSOLUTE
      ZERO OF TEMPERATURE IS ZERO,
ENTROPY CANNOT BE REDUCED TO
ZERO BY FINITE MEANS (AS PER THE
SECOND LAW). THUS ABSOLUTE ZERO
CANNOT BE REACHED."

— THIRD LAW OF THERMODYNAMICS

Gunnar opened his eyes at the smell of coffee. For a brief moment, everything was fine. The deep earthy smell made him think he was home. As the early morning light revealed his surroundings, though, he was baffled. Then he remembered. Shit.

He pulled one arm out from the comforter, and the crisp air made him yank it back under. Nearby, a cherry wood desk had little on it and no envelopes in its honeycombed shelf.

Next to it, two bookcases of the same wood held many books. On top of both cases sat a number of dolls — not Barbies or a plastic kind, but larger, with exquisite porcelain faces, blue eyes, and red hair like Kara's. This must be Kara's childhood bedroom, he realized. This is where she'd planned her future, had her hopes. This is where in high school she had decided to become an exchange student and spend her senior year in Wisconsin. What would it have taken for her to miss that? Or what would it have taken for him to avoid stepping on her toes? Through what untwist of fate would it have taken to have dodged his present misery?

On the floor, his pants and shirt lay not crumpled but stretched out in a way that looked like the person inside had just vanished. His suitcase was open, and the insides looked rifled, distressed. He remembered looking for his toiletries. He'd use them now.

He sat up. He couldn't see his breath, but it was ridiculously cold. It occurred to him that Denmark produced almost no oil, had no nuclear power plants, and was too flat for hydroelectric power. Energy would be extremely expensive here. No wonder the furnace was off. Why, he wondered, could he figure this stuff out and not have a clue to Kara?

A clock radio next to his bed said it was after nine. That had to be wrong because he'd never slept past seven. The light always woke him up. Then he remembered he was so much farther north that the sun would come up later.

He pulled on the clothes from the floor, grabbed fresh socks and a sweater from his suitcase, and glanced out the window. A suburban street with houses made mostly of brick looked different enough that he felt he was in Sartre country. No exit. He seized his black toiletry bag, opened the door to the hallway, and paused, listening. No sounds. Ingeborg and Fritz both worked. Maybe they left him a note of what to eat and do. How about a note of what to think and feel?

**Things to Think About in a Foreign Land
Without Your Love**

- Windmills are a good source of energy for a flat country on the ocean.
- Brick houses are sturdy in the wind.
- How the fuck did I get here?
- Can I get her back?
- Can I get a Danish in Denmark or is it called something else here?

He found the bathroom and peed. He washed his face, brushed his teeth, combed his hair. These things he knew how to do.

As he walked down the stairs, he heard movement somewhere. "Hello?" he said. "Anyone here?"

An unfamiliar male voice said, "Down here. In the kitchen." It had a Danish accent.

Gunnar hesitated. He really didn't want to talk with anyone right now. What choice did he have? He walked past the clean dining room table into the kitchen. A thin young man, longish brown hair, smiled shyly. He wore a tight long-sleeved knit top and wiped the counter under his white coffee cup like a waiter at a diner. "I was wondering if you might get up," said the young man. "*Kaffe?*" he said raising his cup.

"Ah… sure," said Gunnar. The young man poured coffee from a Mr. Coffee pot into another white cup and offered it. Gunnar sipped. It was bitter and dark. Would nothing be right here?

"Cream and sugar?" said the young man, pointing to the counter left of him.

"Yes. Thanks." Gunnar stepped over, spooned sugar from a crystal bowl and poured the cream from a white creamer shaped as a cow. The liquid spilled from its mouth, vomiting into his cup.

"I'm Henrik, Kara's brother. You must be feeling *rå,* I imagine? Raw, uncooked? Is that the right words? English not was my best subject."

"You're doing fine," said Gunnar. Gunnar looked at Henrik more closely and saw a resemblance to Kara. The eyes and nose were similar. He was much younger, though, about twenty-five.

"Nice to meet you, Goona'," pronounced Henrik, and he held out his hand. Gunnar shook it, even if wishing the young man would go away.

"I'm sorry I wasn't here when you arrived yesterday," said Henrik. "I knew what Kara had planned, and I felt *slet* — bad, yes?"

"Thank you."

"You were expecting to live with her, and here you are."

"Yep," said Gunnar. The room was lit by modern, small-headed track lights, pointed to make pools. The floor was the same wood as the dining room — not tile.

"She only told me the truth the other day."

"What did she say before that?"

"She told me a friend from America was coming to work, that's all. At Niels Bohr?"

The information jolted Gunnar. She hadn't told her brother immediately about him when she had returned from America? He had told everyone about her.

"Then a few days ago, she asked for my thoughts. She said you might be expecting to live with her when you came, and I said, 'But what about Peder?' and she said that was the problem."

Gunnar nodded. They each sipped their coffee.

"I asked her how you had the idea you'd live with her," continued Henrik, "and she told me about your relationship. That you were a very nice person. She said you were smart. She didn't know what to do."

"Calling me would have been helpful."

"I said that!" he said proudly, "but she said you might not come, and she felt horrible she might be ruining things for you."

"They're ruined."

"I thought so. I've never understood my sister."

Henrik motioned toward the small round kitchen table. Gunnar sat.

"I thought I'd show you the town today. It's not so bad here," said Henrik.

"Day One," said Gunnar. "My first full day post-Kara."

"Ya. Day One."

"I was thinking I should probably find a hotel."

"*Nej*. My advice is you stay here at least a few days — or a whole month. My parents are nice, and it wasn't your fault Kara met someone else."

"It's awkward."

"Hotels are very expensive. You won't see Kara, so it'll be okay."

Except that didn't seem okay. Gunnar wanted to see her. Maybe she'd change her mind.

"Believe me," said Henrik, "You're better off without her. My sister can be very demanding. Anyway, there's a lot to get used to, so I thought I'd be your guide."

"Did Kara put you up to this?"

"Put up?" asked Henrik. "Oh, you mean asked? No, but I thought I should help you. My parents are off working, so they liked the idea, too."

Gunnar nodded.

Henrik seemed pleased. "Kara's American family paid for Kara when she was an exchange student, so my parents feel this is returning the favor. I say stay here and let me show you around."

"Okay," Gunnar said. "May I shower first?"

"Of course, take your time. Upstairs, *til højre*." Gunnar nodded, not knowing what Henrik had said exactly, but Gunnar knew where the bathroom was.

-------------→

The warm shower shot into his skin, needle-like at first but soon radiating heat throughout his body. His wilted bones seemed to strengthen like a plant in a vase given fresh water. Even so, his mind still felt slow.

The enclosed stall felt safe. There, he considered what he should do. Options. What were his options? Two came immediately: Find an apartment near the Institute in Copenhagen, or turn around and go back to America. The latter, he couldn't. He couldn't tell anyone back home what had happened. He didn't want to be a failure in two countries. In fact, in a day or two, he'd e-mail his mother and basically say all was fine. Perhaps he could say that because

Roskilde was far from the Institute, he'd be getting a place downtown. Did Copenhageners say "downtown?"

He had his contact at the Institute, a professor named Bent Herskind, who headed up the group Gunnar was joining. Gunnar would call Bent, and maybe Bent or someone else might recommend a place to rent. Post-docs and visiting faculty came as regularly as rain, after all.

Methodically, Gunnar washed using a bar of soap that had grit in it. How interesting — how practical. All soap should have sand. The roughness really made his skin red, but the feel of it reminded him that his body had boundaries. He was real in this surreal place.

He stayed in the shower until the water went cold. He then stayed naked in the steamy room as he shaved — the very opposite of what he did in America, but something told him he needed to be doing things differently here if he were to survive. Even minor changes would be good.

He wiped the haze from the medicine cabinet mirror to shave. He stared at his face. He tried to figure out what Kara had once found in his face and found no more. He could only shake his head.

He opened the medicine cabinet and noted the contents again. It looked familiar, which pleased him. He closed the cabinet.

By the time he was ready, it was nearly eleven. The sun was low in the sky, and Gunnar felt bad that he had kept Henrik waiting. Time here seemed to happen faster.

He rushed down the stairs. Henrik, still in the kitchen, drank beer out of a green bottle, reading the newspaper.

"I'm sorry I took so long. I'm still on the foggy side," said Gunnar.

"That's okay. I don't have a job right now, so I am not feeling... running?"

"Rushed?"

"Yes. Let me take you to my favorite lunch spot, *Killians Hus*,'Killian's House.' I can teach you how to order and things."

"Okay," said Gunnar.

Gunnar returned upstairs for his ski jacket, ski hat, scarf, and gloves, preparing for the worst. When he returned downstairs, he found Henrik had only pulled on a lined black leather coat and nothing else. Henrik laughed. "It's not that cold outside, my friend. Maybe only five degrees."

"That's Celsius, I imagine," said Gunnar, "which means it's above freezing."

Henrik nodded.

Once they were outside, Gunnar noticed it was rather mild for winter. That's right, he remembered. It's zero here. No snow on the ground. He had to get used to being zero.

Henrik carried his green beer bottle while they walked into town. Gunnar couldn't tell if Denmark didn't have a law against drinking in public, or whether Henrik simply didn't care. They walked past modest houses.

"So what do you normally do for a living, Henrik?"

"I don't know yet," he said.

"Oh?"

"I studied architecture in school, but I don't like the idea of sitting in a room all day. Not after Afghanistan."

"Afghanistan?"

"I just left the army. I was part of the NATO troops there."

"You wanted to go to there?"

"Every man in Danmark has to serve in the military. It's the law. Afghanistan was just my luck. At least I didn't get Iraq."

"Denmark's in Iraq? I thought it was just the U.S. and England."

"No. And I have to say the few Americans I've come to know really don't know much about other countries."

"It's true," said Gunnar. "I'm sorry."

"There are twenty-six countries in NATO, and I think sixteen of them are in Iraq. Denmark is there."

"Did you see action in Afghanistan?"

Henrik grimaced, and then took a swig of his beer. "Unfortunately, yes," he said. "It's a pretty country in its own way, very dry and hot at times, but when you're shot at and your friends are hit...." Henrik let it trail off.

"I see," said Gunnar.

"One time, I was with some Afghan soldiers, and one down the line stepped on the wrong spot, a land mine. His feet and chunks of both legs became..." He moved all his fingers as if trying to describe what he saw.

"A mist?" Gunnar offered.

"Ya. I fell to the ground from the big bang, and I saw blood coming right out of his..." He pointed to his knee then hacked at it.

"A stump? Stumps?"

"Ya. And he was screaming..."

They walked a few more steps and Henrik finished his beer. "I couldn't do anything — I was just stopped."

"What happened to him?"

"He died."

Henrik stepped up his pace now, as if not wanting to speak more, and Gunnar considered what other things Henrik might have seen or experienced.

They were now approaching a park. A pond lay ahead.

Gunnar looked down to his own legs. At least he had his legs. At least he hadn't been in war. So did the experience of war supersede other pain? Was Gunnar's pain minor compared to Henrik's?

"I'm sorry," said Gunnar.

"For what?" said Henrik.

"For what you had to go through."

"It's not your fault." Henrik wiped his nose with his black jacket sleeve.

They walked on in silence, two bent-headed men with the low sun making their shadows long.

Trees and a wide brown lawn lay ahead. It must be a park, and Henrik ran a few steps ahead as if he spotted something.

"Look at the ducks!" said Henrik.

Henrik galloped ahead. Two white ducks with orange beaks swam and created a wave pattern on the otherwise still surface of a pond. The mere sight of the birds seemed something to see and celebrate. Gunnar ran, too. And the long grass around the pond saluted.

--------------->

"Een grown Tuborg," tried Gunnar at their table at Killians Hus, an Irish pub with tables covered in red-and-white checkerboard tablecloths.

Henrik laughed. "You're close, my friend. The Danish R's are soft and the G is nearly silent in this case, so it's 'Tuboa.' And 'beer' is 'ul,' so you will be saying, 'een ul; grun tuboa'." Henrik wrote it on a napkin, and it looked far different than it sounded: *en øl; grøn Tuborg.*

"One beer, green Tuborg? And how do you say please?"

"We really don't use just one word for please. We might say, *vaersågod at* or *jeg vil gerne have,* but most people say "one beer, green Tuborg.""

"'Een ul; grun tuboa'.""

"Perfect! That will get you through most of your troubles in Danmark."

The place was dominated by the dark wood bar, behind which were beveled mirrors, rows and shelves of different bottles with pouring spouts, and an Asian bartender, who was speaking what seemed to be fluent Danish. The man reminded Gunnar of the sushi restaurant he'd been to with Ursula. He smiled thinking of how she'd caught her finger in a pay phone. Wonder how she was.

Gunnar went up to the bar and said, "*En øl; grøn Tuborg.*" The man nodded, thinking nothing of it, and reached below the bar. He produced one thick glass and a green-bottled Tuborg. "*Ti kroner,*" said the bartender. "Ten crowns."

"Ah," said Gunnar, and gave him a ten-kroner bill and also gave him two single krone coins as a tip.

"*Ja, tak,*" said the bartender with a smile.

As Gunnar carried the beer and glass back, he noticed both were room temperature, as had been his first beer. "Beer here isn't cold, is it?" said Gunnar, sitting.

"Cold?" said Henrik. "Why would you want cold øl?"

"It's always cold in America."

"Isn't that odd?" Henrik was on his third beer to Gunnar's second, and they had the remains of cold open sandwiches on their plates. The sandwiches hadn't been very Irish, but rather a piece of dark, thick pumpernickel bread with, in Gunnar's case, a slice of roast beef and cucumber on top. The menu featured fish and chips, Irish beef stew, barbecued ribs — things he'd feel comfortable with, but Henrik said he was buying lunch — "after all what you'd been through." Henrik had suggested *smørrebrød med leverpostej,* but Gunnar learned that was liverpaste. Why all the liver? Gunnar went with the safer roast beef. The food was fine. He didn't feel very hungry anyway.

As he finished his second beer, Gunnar began to feel relief — better than he imagined he could feel one day after what Kara had done — may she rot in hell.

A young woman, tall, very thin, with black kinky hair, placed her arm around Henrik's shoulders and said, "There ya be! I was just thinking of you, and poof, you're here!" She had a clear Irish accent. "Who's your friend?" She looked at Gunnar and gave a wink.

"Gunnar, this is Kathleen. She works here. Kathleen, Gunnar."

She had pretty green eyes.

"Nice ta meet ya, Gooner," she said with a hard R, holding out her hand.

"Nice to meet you, too. Have you worked here long?" he said. Her baggy red t-shirt said, "Lifeguard. Catalina Island." She must travel a lot.

"Two years, but I'm off fer the day." She sat on Henrik's lap as if they were intimate friends. Kathleen appeared to be in her late twenties.

As Gunnar thought about it, he realized he'd never met an actual Irish person before. He'd seen Irish characters in movies, knew where Ireland was in relation to England, and certainly heard about the IRA and what Clinton had done to help stop the violence. Still, this was his first Irish lass. "I guess because it's an Irish pub, you were able to get a work permit?" he said.

She moved to her own stool and looked at him as if it were an odd question. "Denmark's in the Common Market. I could work in Spain if I wanted. And you're not very Danish, are ya?"

"Gunnar's a physicist from America," said Henrik.

"Ah. Workin' at Risø, are ya?"

"Actually, at the Niels Bohr Institute downtown."

Kathleen laughed and poked Henrik. "I like that word, 'downtown.' That's very American." Back to Gunnar: "You mean Copenhagen, then?"

Gunnar nodded. "I'm from Wisconsin."

"Ballix," said Kathleen. "I'd have no idea where that is."

"In the middle, below the Great Lakes."

"It's a shame I don't know more about America, but I don't like that president a yours, Mr. George W. Bush. I do know that."

"He's religious and conservative. That's why some people voted for him — not that such criteria are for me."

"Look what religion did for Northern Ireland. I don't trust religion," she said.

They ordered three beers, *tre øl; grøn Tuborg,* and then Gunnar noticed that the warmness didn't bother him.

Kathleen turned to Henrik and whispered, "Would ya happen ta have a little smoke?"

"*Nej.*" It sounded like "nigh" and clearly meant no.

She whispered in Henrik's ear and then laughed. He smiled but again said, "*Nej.*"

"Please?" She placed a hand on Henrik's shoulder. Kara might have done something like that last summer, then might stroke Gunnar's hair. Kara had been so friendly, so open.

"I have a guest," said Henrik.

She turned to Gunnar. "Would ya like goin' on a wee journey with us?"

"Christiania is no wee journey," said Henrik.

"Just an afternoon. I'll pay all the fares." She looked at Gunnar, hoping for a positive answer.

"What's Christiania?" he asked.

"A very interesting place," she said. "I think it was in the early eighties — "

"The seventies," said Henrik.

"Yeah. In the early seventies, a bunch a hippies overran an abandoned military base in Copenhagen and renamed it Christiania, a free state. It's been a kind of experiment in living that's worked for all these years. It's mostly young people living in the old small houses and the brick barracks, and there are no cars. It's one big commune, and the people are very friendly."

"You like friendly," laughed Henrik, giving the side of her butt a sociable slap.

"They have daycare for kids, a lake, lots of trees. You'd like the place," she told Gunnar.

"Doesn't sound like my thing," said Gunnar.

"Christiania's on all the tours," she said. "It costs thirty crowns on the Arthur Frommer tour. With us, it's free."

"I don't know." What was his other option? Return to Henrik's parents' house and be by himself?

"A guaranteed delight," she said, again winking.

"It's an interesting place," said Henrik.

"Just come as a tourist, that's all. Aren't you open for new things?" she said.

He nodded. Sure. He needed new things.

--------------➤

As they waited with several other people on one of two platforms at the Roskilde station, Gunnar saw he was the only one wearing a bright-colored ski jacket. Did no one ski here? Everyone except Kathleen wore dark-colored jackets or full-length coats that went to their knees. Kathleen had a white coat and a silk scarf as well as a small black purse around her shoulder. He was the only one with real color, making him stand out like a clownfish in a seabed of kelp. He'd rather be invisible.

As he stared down at the railroad tracks, Gunnar wondered how many times Kara had stood on the same platform. Probably hundreds.

Across the tracks on the other platform, a couple held hands. The young woman had straight blond hair and ruddy cheeks. Her boyfriend was chatting on his cell phone, then finished. She said something to him as if expecting an answer. He kissed her cheek, and she responded by kissing him passionately back. Then the train came, cutting off the view.

The train that stopped at Roskilde station was not like any trains he'd seen in America. There was no locomotive, just passenger cars. The front car had a big curvy window for the train operator. The train wasn't boxy looking, but rather rounded, painted silver and black and emblazoned with the letters DSB. It worked off an overhead electric line, electrons once again helping mankind. The train hummed to a soft stop right on the exact minute when it was supposed to arrive. Things worked the way they were supposed to. And the wheels didn't squeak.

A single door in each of the several cars opened simultaneously with a slight hiss, and a stair silently slid out at each door for people to step up. The passengers were drawn like magnets to metal.

Upon entering the train, Gunnar noted the high-backed, armchair-like seats covered in black. On each side of the aisle, a set of two seats faced another set of two, thus making groups of four seats. Henrik and Kathleen sat side-by-side in one group, and Gunnar joined them. Within a minute, the train quietly started and quickly sped to highway speed, though when they came close to a highway, Gunnar noted they traveled slightly faster than the cars. Shortly after that, they entered a forest then zoomed past a modern apartment complex and through a station. This was an express train.

"I'm thirsty, how about you?" said Henrik.

"Sure," said Gunnar.

"Why not?" said Kathleen.

"Follow me," said Henrik.

The three of them walked into the next car, only slightly jostled by the movement of train. They came to a mini-bar, featuring snacks, sodas, and beer. Most people there were drinking beer. *"Tre Tuborg,"* said Henrik to the server, and soon they had plastic cups with covers. Swaying here and there, they returned to their original seats.

The alcohol and the speed of the train made Gunnar feel more lightheaded than before, but he realized he liked the sense of rushing — much better than the low-level nausea and emptiness he'd had since yesterday.

"This is a great way to travel," said Gunnar.

Kathleen smiled and nodded and raised her glass in a toast. "May the saddest day of your future be no worse than the happiest day of your past," she said.

"That's lovely," said Gunnar. "Cheers."

Kathleen elbowed Henrik, who seemed lost in thought looking through the window.

"Ya," said Henrik, pulling on a half-smile. "*Skol.*"

Another station whisked by where a lot of people stood on the platform. Ninety natural elements to the world, thought Gunnar, but they were all arranged a bit differently here. The houses and buildings looked more square. The leafless trees looked starker.

Twenty-six minutes from when they boarded the train, they pulled into Copenhagen's main train station, which felt grand, substantial and bustling. Multiple trains stood at multiple platforms disgorging and ingesting people. As they sauntered down the platform toward the main building, Gunnar noted the station's name was København H.

"Koben-haven H?" he tried to pronounce.

"Koopen-how," Henrik corrected.

"The separate H is for *Hovedbanegården*," she said with her hard Irish accent. "That translates ta 'head train building'."

"The central station," said Henrik.

"Interesting," said Gunnar.

"Yah, interestin'," said Kathleen, laughing.

Was she mocking him? She winked as he looked at her. She was enjoying herself.

"Gooner," she said, "How come ya live in Roskilde if you work here?"

As they walked up a slight ramp, he stumbled. Perhaps he shouldn't have had another beer. "I'm staying with Henrik's family right now."

"Friend of the family, are ya?"

"I guess."

Kathleen looked confused.

Henrik said, "He met my sister in America. He's staying with us until he can find a place to his liking near here."

"Ah, that's nice," she said with a smile.

Gunnar left it at that. He didn't want to explain he'd loved Henrik's sister, who dumped him.

They went up an escalator to a giant decorated Christmas tree, through a crowded meeting area where there were stations of clerks selling tickets, and out through the front doors, where the day was now gray and chilly. Across the street stood a long, high wall, over which were the tops of numerous, thick trees. Perhaps on the other side was an arboretum. A turnstile within the wall showed an exit.

"What's over there?" asked Gunnar.

"Tivoli!" said Kathleen. "It's an amusement park, over 160 years old. It's very elegant, filled with great restaurants and gardens. The fireworks at New Year's are fabulous, I'm told."

"It's a summer place," said Henrik, "but they open it up for the three weeks before Christmas and through the holidays."

Looking at Gunnar, Kathleen said, "Maybe we should come here some time."

Was she inviting him? Was she attracted to him? Wasn't she Henrik's lover? He studied her form. Her face and limbs were much more angular than Kara's, perhaps because Kathleen was so thin. Even her boots had tiny, sharp heels. Still, she seemed like one big smile.

Across from Tivoli, and across the wide boulevard, Copenhagen's buildings were no taller than six stories, big brick buildings of an old design and connected as one. Tall steeples were visible nearby. The area was as monumental as around Madison's capitol building, but darker. The place seemed old and historic. The only thing that took away from the grandness was a single sign that said Burger King.

A few blocks later, they approached a bus area that appeared to be a major stop, right across from a large open plaza with a huge Christmas tree.

"The bus is here! Let's hurry!" said Kathleen, dashing ahead of them. As they ran after her, Gunnar asked Henrik, "Is she your girlfriend?"

"I wish," said Henrik. "But she's a complicated one."

"Aren't you the complicated one?"

Henrik laughed. "You're right."

They ran the remaining half block and leapt aboard an orange bus. Once they were on, Henrik and Kathleen sat in one seat, and Gunnar took the empty one behind them. All the buildings they passed looked old. In Madison, really old buildings usually were bashed down. Henrik pointed out the window to the large block-wide brown building by the open plaza. The building had two small spires and a large clock tower on top. "That's the *Rådhus*, City Hall. That big statue there — " He pointed to a huge statue of a sitting man wearing a big top hat and holding a book and a cane. A little girl about three years old was sitting in his lap, and her young parents were taking her picture. "That's Hans Christian Andersen — a famous Danish writer."

"I know his fairy tales," said Gunnar.

"Next year," said Henrik, "Crown Prince Frederik and his fiancée, Mary Donaldson, will have a reception there."

"Oh, they're truly a lovely couple," said Kathleen. "She's Australian, and they fell madly in love at the Olympics in Sydney."

"Talk about fairy tales."

"Ah! Don't be so cynical," she said, hitting Henrik on the arm. "Some people can truly love." She turned to Gunnar. "Prince Frederik was in Australia with the Danish sailin' team, and he met Mary at a bar right after the opening ceremonies."

Kathleen looked off as if imagining it could happen to her. It struck Gunnar that she and he had just met at a bar.

Kathleen turned to him to speak. "How long ya been here, then?"

"Just a day."

"A day! You been ta Denmark before?"

"No. First time out of America."

"Wow! It must be like what? So different, no?"

"I'm a stranger in a strange land."

"Eww, I *love* that book," said Kathleen. "Robert Heinlein. I also adore the American author Kurt Vonnegut — you read him?"

"I mostly read scientific papers about what happens to atoms as they approach absolute zero. They start to slow down. They turn into a new form of matter."

"You're pretty smart."

"Not really. I'm feeling rather dumb — perhaps one of the dumbest people in the world right now."

"Don't be gettin' hard on yerself now. I don't know why you're so downcast, but I'm thinkin' it's his sister." She pointed to Henrik with her thumb.

"You're smart yourself."

"I didn't come here only for the work. The Danes can be so lovin' but, aye, mysterious! Like the one who left me. I was so darn naïve. I'm smarter now."

"So no boyfriend?"

She smiled. "I'm not rushin' it."

When they bounced off the bus, they walked a few blocks until they confronted another walled area like Tivoli. Where the wall made shade, dirty piles of snow stood — so it must snow sometimes, he realized, and this was what was left by snowplows from the last snow removal. At an entrance, a large wooden sign on two tall poles proclaimed "Christiania." There were also two Christmas trees with candy canes hanging and the sign, *Glaedelig Jul og godt nytår*. He couldn't picture having a merry Christmas or a good new year. If he were a poster, he'd be smeared in dirt.

"It's kind of like a giant park with buildings," Henrik said as they approached. "It used to be a naval fort from the 18th century."

They wordlessly walked through the gate, and once they did, the first few buildings were covered in posters for rock bands, for upcoming movies, and for other cultural events. There was also graffiti everywhere — some of it artistic, most of it ugly. "Travis," said one scrawl. Another building had the spray-painted words, "Den Kosmiske Kirke."

As they turned a corner, a tarmac-like area, all asphalt, was covered with piles of junk, mostly wood that looked like it had been ripped out in a remodeling project. The larger buildings were made of a dingy brown brick, aged as if in a coal-burning town. Some buildings had dormer windows at the top and red tile roofs. Other structures were Quonset huts.

They came to an area where people in kiosks were selling something.

"Oh, good!" said Kathleen, and she ran ahead of them.

"Kathleen thinks of this place as Santa Clausland," said Henrik.

"Why?"

Henrik didn't answer but caught up with Kathleen. Gunnar followed, and he watched them pore over a display of what at first appeared to be thin chunks of brownies that varied in shades from tan to a deep brown. The pieces were laid out carefully on red velvet. A man with long gray hair and brown stained teeth oversaw the activity with a grin. Signs in mostly English, with prices, were near each chunk. "Super Ryger, 60," said one. "Standard, 40," said another. "X-Treme, 90," said a third, among a dozen such blocks.

"What's this?" asked Gunnar.

"Hash. Many types. I like Moroccan best," said Henrik.

Gunnar was stunned. How did he not understand they were going to buy drugs? This was an outrage. He also noticed elsewhere on the table clear jars of light green clumps marked "Buds, 10 each."

"I'm going to wait over there," said Gunnar, pointing to an oil can that appeared to be burning something inside it.

"Gooner, don't be afraid," said Kathleen. "It's legal here."

"Not legal like Amsterdam," said Henrik. "But it's allowed to happen."

"When did a nice Irish girl like you do stuff like this?" said Gunnar.

"Don't be daft," she said. "It's everywhere in the world, and it's pretty minor when it comes to sins. Believe me, the Pope has bigger worries."

"I thought you said this was a tourist area," he told her.

"Quite so," said the long-haired proprietor, a man in his fifties. "This area has over a thousand visitors a day. Tourists from all over the world."

"Can't we just get a beer?" said Gunnar.

"Try the Moonfisher Café around the corner," said the man.

"I'll take two grams of the standard," Kathleen said to the proprietor. "Standard is plenty strong. And give me two of the really green buds, too. " The man took a pre-wrapped chunk in aluminum foil and dropped it in a small plastic bag, to which he added two buds. She pulled out a 100-kroner note and swapped it for the bag.

As he waited, Gunnar thought that, sure, destiny was an unscientific concept, but maybe it existed and brought him here. After all, he felt the way most physicists must have felt when Einstein came up with his relativity theory, showing gravity could bend light and time could slow or speed up.

Einstein himself was thrown with new parts of quantum physics, such as Heisenberg's Uncertainty Principle, which he didn't buy — so maybe there was destiny.

"*Tusind tak*," said the man to Kathleen. "*Kom igen.*"

"I'm partial to a Tuborg," said Henrik. "Let's try that café."

Kathleen looked at Gunnar with a sparkle in her eyes. "You okay, Gooner?"

"I guess."

She took his arm, and he knew: destiny.

"Oh, *et øjeblik*," said Henrik. "I see one of my mates." Henrik dashed over to two men chatting by their bicycles. Henrik soon was shaking the hand of one and being introduced to the other. That left Kathleen and Gunnar standing by themselves.

"So this wasn't so much a tour but a trip to get a fix," said Gunnar as a statement.

"A *fix*, you're tellin' me? Have you never smoked hash or pot?"

"I don't need foreign substances in my system."

"And what about the beer ya been drinkin'? And isn't food a foreign substance, too?"

"You know what I mean."

"Smokin' this might make you feel better considerin' your lot right now."

"The 'lot' I'm in will take care of itself." He looked off to a large stand of trees. He noticed a small house built within it. In the summer, the house would probably be hidden by the foliage. That would be nice.

Gunnar felt Kathleen's hand move from his arm to his shoulder. "I'm not tryin' to make ya feel worse," she said. "I moved here for a man. We didn't plan on livin' together or nothin', but I moved here figurin' we'd go together like whiskey n' water. I couldn't see it, but we were wrong for each other. So it goes."

"Yes, but Kara and I *were* right for each other. She warmed me."

"Sometimes the coal runs out."

He looked at her, and she looked right back. Her eyes were not afraid to see.

"Have you ever heard of the Danish chap goes by the name of Kierkegaard?" she said.

Gunnar nodded. "Yes, I know the philosopher. Dead, actually."

"Yeah? Anyway, after things didn't work out for me in the love department, I was very sad. Didn't want to work, but I had to. I was kinda stuck. Some fella in the pub told me about Kierkegaard after he saw me mopin' around, and I learned somethin'. I'll tell ya what Kierkegaard said: 'The most painful state of being is remembering the future, particularly one you can never have.' Now how true is that?"

Gunnar had to look away as he felt as if he were falling. It was only a quick flash, but this truth was like a pair of glasses focused into his soul. Since yesterday, with nearly every heartbeat, he had imagined his life with Kara that he would not have. There would be no shopping with her — no selecting cereals or meats. No making the bed together. No playing with her cat Frederik on his lap while Kara made him hot chocolate. Moments selected like a winning racehorse had vanished from the track.

"What do I know about love in this land of the free?" she said. "Where I grew up, the Church was everything, and even lustful thoughts sent ya to the local priest for piety. I'd do my Hail Mary's and feel better. Ma said keep my legs always tight, and don't lead the boys to your box, and I did my best, but boys don't need much to get 'em goin'."

Gunnar just nodded, not sure where this was going.

"Point is," she said, "we each grow up with certain expectations about love. Mine were wrong. How about yours?"

"I didn't grow up with religion, and, frankly, I was rather open and honest with Kara. My only expectation was that if you do right for a person, they do right back."

"That's love? Doin' right?"

"I'm not always good with words."

"And how did you expect her to be good with words with English as her second language?"

"Let's not talk about it, okay?" Why was she busting his chops? He looked up to see Henrik was on his way back, thankfully.

When he looked back at Kathleen, she touched his shoulder again and said, "Everything will be okay. It's okay. Okay?"

"Okay."

Henrik approached saying, "Both those fellows were in Afghanistan. My friend says after he returned to Danmark, he was arguing with everyone — his parents, his teachers at the university, and even his girlfriend, who left him. So he moved here to Christiania. He really likes the place. He works at the daycare center, and he shares a flat with five others, and they're like a family. Two different women are having his babies, he says." Henrik shook his head in amazement, then with a big smile said, "Maybe I should move here."

"You could use a change," said Kathleen.

"And Kathleen, you like coming here," said Henrik, "so it's not like I wouldn't see you."

"You gonna do it?" she asked.

"Their flat has a space. He invited me. Don't know, though. How about a beer?"

"Yes," said Gunnar, who noticed the sun nearing the horizon. Sunset would come soon.

The Moonfisher Café looked to be in what had been a mess hall. The building was long with giant arched windows. Its sign featured a long-nosed witch fishing from a moon's crescent. Outside the front door stood a half dozen new baby carriages — apparently they weren't permitted inside.

They entered through the tall door. Inside was spacious. Round metal tables and matching aluminum chairs filled the main room, and many of the tables had lit candles. A couple of side rooms were visible through tall archways. The place could hold hundreds. A stone-covered floor gave the sense of a patio. The air had a sweet smell, like licorice.

"Sit here, and I'll get us a few øl," said Henrik. Gunnar and Kathleen sat near one of the paned windows.

Gunnar peered at the people around him, all younger people in sweaters, some of which could use a washing. "Christiania feels like a college that gave up on offering classes," said Gunnar. "It feels like a legion of losers." He looked at the long-haired man in a gray coat at the next table. The man wore a silly grin. Gunnar added, "I suppose it's appropriate I'm here."

"I like the spirit in Christiania," said Kathleen. "Denmark may have a liberal image — and it's certainly different from Ireland — but Danish society can be strict. Everyone is expected to go to some kind of schooling. Even after degrees, people are encouraged to better themselves. If you don't fit in, like Henrik, where do you go? Now that I think about it, Christiania's needed. It's okay to be different here."

Henrik soon returned with a tray that carried six beers, a green apple, a large orange, two bananas and some small open-faced sandwiches on dark dense pumpernickel bread.

"What's all this?" said Kathleen.

"I got a variety of fruit and smørrebrød for snacks. No chips here."

"I mean all the beer."

"We have two apiece, two types, so I don't have to get in that line again," he explained. Henrik held up a festive looking bottle, Tuborg Julebryg, which pictured a drawing of a Tuborg truck driving in a night sky of falling snow. "This is Tuborg's Christmas beer, very fine."

"They make a special beer for Christmas?" said Gunnar.

"Don't they do that in America?" said Henrik.

"No," said Gunnar, taking a sandwich with little potatoes on it. He was hungry.

"And the other beer — " Henrik lifted a bottle with a Carlsberg label that featured a large elephant, "is simply called Elephant beer. Also very fine."

"Oh, yeah," said Kathleen. She lifted her Elephant beer and raised it in a toast. "May the sun always shine warm on your windowpane."

Gunnar laughed. "My windowpane is busted — but when the new one comes in, may it be bulletproof." He raised his Elephant and clicked it against Kathleen's and Henrik's bottles.

By the time Gunnar finished the beer and more of the food, the sun shining on the nearby windowpanes had vanished. Even so, he was feeling fine, if not more lightheaded than ever. "What does the Danish word S-O-V-E mean?"

"*Sove*," said Henrik. He pronounced it "so-vay." "It means 'sleep.' Why?"

"It was on a sign I saw today. *Sove*. I propose another toast," he said, raising his Christmas bottle. "To uncertainty. Heisenberg said there are things we can't know, and it's true."

"Are you talking about Heisenberg's uncertainty principle?" said Henrik.

"Yes, you know it?"

"Here in Danmark, there was a famous meeting in World War Two with Niels Bohr and his German friend Werner Heisenberg, who was working with the Nazis. We're taught it in history with the uncertainty principle."

"What's the uncertainty principle?" asked Kathleen. She looked at Gunnar.

"It's one of my lectures," said Gunnar. "Basically, there's Newton's physics, which can describe how the moon goes around the earth, and there's quantum mechanics, the physics of the very small." Gunnar held up the large orange and green apple. "We know where the moon is and how fast it's going." He moved the apple around the orange. "We know exactly what time the moon will appear any given night because we know its position. The same thing can't be done with electrons. Heisenberg said while it appears that an electron swirling around a proton is like the moon around the earth, different forces are at work, atomic forces, and we cannot know at the same time where something is and how fast it is moving. We can't predict where an electron will be."

"What if you could look and measure?" she said.

"You can't. Measuring would change it, and near absolute zero, a single atom seems to be in two and more places at once. This is what I'll be researching here — absolute zero, a temperature that can never be reached. An atom will always have movement. It can never attain complete stillness. There are certainties in the uncertain."

"You're an amazing man, Gooner."

"Thank you."

"Here's an Irish toast just for ya." She held her glass high. "May those who love us, love us. And those that don't love us, may God turn their hearts. And if He doesn't turn their hearts, may he turn their ankles, so we'll know them by their limping.'"

"Cheers!" said Gunnar. "And may Kara limp." They clinked bottles.

"And now I have a proposal for Kathleen," said Henrik. "Why don't you fire up your purchase."

"A splendid idea. But I don't have me pipe."

"I can make a pipe," said Henrik. He grabbed the apple, and from his pants pocket, he produced a Swiss Army knife. Using the thin blade, he carved a pencil-sized hole halfway into the apple. Turning the apple ninety degrees, he carved a bigger hole, more like a funnel, wider at the top. "Got it," said Henrik. He put the smaller hole to his mouth and sucked. He drew air. "See," he said. "A pipe."

"What about a bowl?" said Kathleen.

"Give me the hash."

Kathleen brought out her plastic bag and handed it to Henrik. The two pieces of hash were covered in foil. Henrik opened the foil from one, carefully withdrew the dark chunk of hash, and then flattened the foil. He jammed the foil into the larger hole of the apple. From his knife, he withdrew the ivory toothpick and poked holes in the foil.

"First time I've ever seen anyone use the toothpick," said Kathleen.

Henrik took one of the buds from the bag and, rolling it between thumb and forefinger, broke up the bud into tiny tobacco-sized pieces into the bowl of his apple pipe. Using his knife blade, he shaved tiny strips of hash, dropping them on top of the bud.

"Virgins first," he said to Kathleen.

"I'm no virgin!" she said with a smile, happily taking the apple pipe. Henrik withdrew a lighter from his pocket and lit the mixture while Kathleen inhaled. The bowl soon became a giant red glowing ember, and Kathleen yanked her mouth from the pipe and coughed hard, expelling thick white smoke.

"Yeah, that looks fun," said Gunnar, shaking his head, drinking his Christmas beer.

"It has a wonderful apple taste!" said Kathleen. "It's the best." She offered the pipe to Gunnar.

"No thanks," he said.

"*Nej tak*," said Henrik. He'd pronounced it "nigh tuck." "That's how you say it in Danish, *nej tak*." Henrik grinned. "We'll make you an honorary Dane yet."

"Tuck" said Gunnar.

Henrik took the pipe from Kathleen, lit the mixture again, but inhaled more slowly than she had. He seemed to be an expert. He held his breath several seconds, then exhaled. "Very fine," he said with a broad smile. "I like Christiania."

Gunnar watched them each smoke another round. He looked at his watch and realized he was having a hard time focusing. The beer was stronger than he thought.

"Got someplace to go?" asked Henrik.

"I wish!" said Gunnar. He noticed Kathleen grinning at him. She must really like him. He smiled back. But wasn't he supposed to be sad about Kara? This beer was like a force field, pushing all bad thoughts away. He liked Danish beer. He liked Kathleen. He bet she was the passionate sort in bed.

"The world isn't such a bad place," said Kathleen.

"It can be okay," said Gunnar.

"Gunnar," said Henrik. "This isn't heroin or anything. It's more like... how would you describe hash, Kathleen?"

"Like petting kittens."

"Ya," he said laughing. "Like the fun you have with a kitten or a puppy. You just feel good. It's a small change for the better. Don't you want to feel better, Gunnar?"

"It opens you up to your own thoughts and emotions," said Kathleen. "You're not afraid of that, are you?"

Gunnar was feeling good. What had he had against ever trying it? He couldn't remember. He pulled the apple to his face.

"Suck in slowly," said Henrik, applying the flame from his lighter, and Gunnar inhaled. As a teenager, he'd once stolen a few cigarettes from his mother, and he tried to smoke them by himself in the woods. He found it harsh, and he had coughed hard. This smoke was not as bad.

Henrik withdrew the flame. "Not too much at once," he said. "Hold it in... Good. Now exhale." Gunnar did. He, too, could sense an apple taste. He looked around. He didn't feel that different. "Let me try again," he said.

Henrik looked pleased. "Let me refresh the bowl a little." He broke in a little more bud, scraped in a few more shavings of hash. The flame met the bowl, and Gunnar inhaled. He blew out the white smoke.

"How're ya feelin'?" said Kathleen. She said it rather sensuously.

"Just fine," said Gunnar, and Kathleen and Henrik laughed.

Someone behind him said the word *nej* again, which reminded him of the Japanese word *hai,* which reminded him of Ursula at the sushi bar in Madison. He and Ursula had said *hai* continually to the sushi chef with each fabulous plate. That was a great night. It wasn't as if he dumped her. Things just didn't start.

"I've always been the dumpee," Gunnar then said aloud.

"Really?" said Kathleen.

"I can't remember leaving anyone — after having a relationship, you know? Do I wear people out?"

"Don't think about such things," said Kathleen.

"Ya, think about kittens," said Henrik with a grin.

By the time he finished his beer, and after a few more hits, nature called. When Gunnar stood, he could feel his head pound, and everything became checkerboards. His knees felt weak. He thought he might pass out, and he fell back into his chair.

"You okay?" said Henrik.

"I just have to catch my breath," said Gunnar, and Kathleen laughed.

She said, "Yes, because you're now warped."

Henrik said, "Warped? Like a board? I love Irish expressions."

"Now don't go twistin' hay," said Kathleen, laughing.

"I just have to go the bathroom," said Gunnar, and that made them laugh, too. His bladder was not to be laughed at. Why were they making fun of him?

Gunnar stood, and this time he was okay. He walked toward the bathroom as if he knew where it was, when he realized he knew nothing. He knew not where he was going, nor the word for bathroom. He peered around for anything bathroom like. He could hear Kathleen and Henrik laugh more.

Gunnar noticed a man wiping a table clean with a rag, and he had a plastic bin of dirty dishes. He clearly worked there. "Excuse me," said Gunnar. "Bathroom?" The man looked at him oddly, so Gunnar repeated it more slowly. "Bath-room? I need a bathroom?" He said it as a question. Go declarative. "I *need* a bathroom."

"Yes, yes," said the man. "The water closet. It's down that hallway there."

Gunnar walked and pondered why a closet would have water. Who named it that? It suggested he would open the door and a wall of water would come crashing out. Now that he thought of it, there were never baths in public bathrooms. Maybe that's why some places called them restrooms, but did one really rest in them? A bedroom was a restroom.

Gunnar found two doors, one marked "Herrer," the other was marked "Damer." That one must be for dames, he thought, and this one for Herr Gunderson. He was rewarded when a man, perhaps fifty years old and well-dressed, exited the "Herrer" and looked at Gunnar strangely. Did the man know? Gunnar looked back, and the man still gazed at him. The man must know how Kara left him. The man nodded as if finding it amazing that someone came overseas to be dumped.

Thankfully, no one was in the bathroom when Gunnar entered, and it looked normal. Toilet. Sink. Toilet paper. Gunnar lifted the lid and peed. He kept peeing. Wouldn't it stop? Was he draining out all his liquid and soon he'd be a wizened skeleton on the floor holding his penis. Gunnar laughed. That would show Kara. She caused all his vital fluids to leak out. He would die.

But the stream soon stopped and Gunnar considered how amazing the human body was. It worked on autopilot. The liver and kidneys took out the bad stuff, leaving in the good stuff, the nutrients and glucose. His heart still pumped, his liver still lived, even if he felt he was dying. "I'm dyin'," he verbalized as Kathleen might say. Maybe his purpose in coming here was to find Kathleen. He and Kathleen. Kathleen and he.

As he exited the bathroom, a woman was leaving the "Damer." A beautiful dame in a red sweater with no reindeer. She was rather big breasted, and he smiled. She shook her head and lunged ahead. Whoops — she'd seem him staring. Where was he? Right. The Moonfisher Café. And Kathleen was waiting.

As he walked closer to the table, there was a commingling of colors. Kathleen's white coat seemed unnaturally close to Henrik's black leather jacket. Henrik was kissing Kathleen passionately, their chairs having moved closer together since he'd left. That's why Henrik bought so much beer — to get Gunnar to pee and leave so Henrik could kiss Kathleen. They seemed to sense his approach, and they pulled apart.

"There ya be, Gooner," said Kathleen.

What, she thought of him as a goofball?

Henrik laughed. Henrik thought he was a goofball, too, a sentimental American loser.

Gunnar aimed for the front door and ran. Two young men coming through the door looked at Gunnar with a smile. They, too, knew about Kara. Here was the American who was shot down by the Danish girl. The dumb American. He's from Wisconsin, no wonder. His head's in the electrons.

Gunnar looked right and left into the night. Which way. Left. He sped past three people chatting around a burning oil drum. "Gunnar!" he heard Kathleen say, but he kept running. To his amazement, he soon saw the front gate. He dashed through it. Left or right? Right. The world was bifurcated. Yes, no. One, zero. Left, right? It was also dialectic. To be or not to be? He took a right. The bus had to be there. "Gunnar!" he heard again, this time Henrik's voice, closer. Gunnar looked behind him. Henrik and Kathleen were pumping their arms and legs toward him. Their steps hammered on the asphalt.

Gunnar moved his own legs and arms as fast as he could, but as he tried to cut across the road, his foot hit something slippery. Ice? But ice was his friend. Ice was nice. Ice couldn't harm him in Denmark, too. Et tu, iciclé? He felt himself fall, and he skidded sideways down the curb. He was a luge racing down a mountain's ice tunnel. He was Bob the sled. He was a bum in a gutter. His cheek felt the ice. He felt cold.

"Gooner, you all right?"

Soon Kathleen and Henrik were at his side.

"Move something," Henrik commanded, and Gunnar moved his arms and legs. Henrik and Kathleen pulled him up, and he was now standing.

"Why'd you run?" asked Kathleen.

"Wasn't it time to go?" he asked.

"Did we upset you?" said Henrik.

"Of course not," said Gunnar. "Love is, you know, love. I was just lost for a moment, that's all."

"It's time we return to Roskilde," said Henrik. "This way."

"*Femten,*" mumbled Gunnar. "*Dronning Margrethesvej.*"

Kathleen took Gunnar's arm. Gunnar felt it wasn't so much out of any affection, but to make sure he wouldn't run again. After a few blocks, the sense of Kathleen there showed Gunnar what he was missing from Kara. Kara was on Peder's arm. Kathleen was for Henrik. It just wasn't fair.

As he sat on the train, wedged between Kathleen and the window that reflected the bright interior lights and his dark face, Gunnar felt the train accelerate into the blackness. Soon the gentle rocking motion pulled at him like his mother, long ago rocking him to sleep. For *sove*. He only needed to sleep. He closed his eyes. The train jerked to the right, and he felt his head smack against the window. "Ah!" he yelled, his eyes snapping open.

"You okay, love?" said Kathleen, concerned. Henrik, however, looked at him as if Gunnar had purposely hit his head, a man deranged.

"The train did it!" said Gunnar.

"I didn't feel anything," said Henrik. Other people from other rows stared at him as if he were a car accident.

"Shit," said Gunnar, rubbing his head. "It hurts."

He must have fallen asleep on the train soon after that because he next heard Kathleen's voice say, "He's melted. We got to drag him out, I guess." Once he was on his feet again, Gunnar looked up to see people again looking at him.

"I can do it!" he told Henrik and Kathleen, but as he stepped out of the train in Roskilde, he fell. He thought he might throw up. His stomach was queasy. He was thinking he'd had too much beer and too little to eat that day.

Henrik and Kathleen again pulled him up.

"Oh, man," said Gunnar. "What's happening to me?"

Outside the station, Henrik flagged a cab over.

"We're not walking?" said Gunnar.

"Don't be dense," said Kathleen.

Gunnar felt himself being guided into the cab.

"I'll have it drop us off first," said Henrik to Kathleen. "Then you, if that's okay."

"Yeah. Poor Gooner," she said.

Gooner only shook his head, which now throbbed. He was like a spot. Out, damned spot. He tried to get out of the cab just as Henrik was getting in.

"Just sit, Gunnar. A few more minutes."

"I'm sorry," Gunnar said. "It's just jetlag."

"I'm sure of it," said Kathleen. "Flyin' can take it out of ya."

Yes. It was taken out of him.

As they both helped him into the house, Gunnar's stomach was still feeling delicate as if the least fast motion might make him throw up. He only needed to be alone, and then everything would be okay. He wouldn't be a bother anymore.

He noticed everything downstairs was dark. Ingeborg and Fritz must be asleep.

"I'll use the bathroom," said Gunnar.

"Please do," said Henrik.

"Good night, then," said Kathleen, and she embraced Gunnar, kissed him on the cheek. Then she kissed Henrik fully on the mouth. Henrik was too young for her — didn't she see that?

"Bye," said Kathleen.

"Yeah, bye," said Gunnar, walking up the stairs, not looking back.

Upstairs in his room, Gunnar noticed on the desk in the room a photograph album. The way it lay suggested it had been looked at recently, probably before he had arrived home last night. As drained as he was, he sat at the desk, imagining how Kara had probably sat often at this very desk in high school, doing homework. He opened the album. On the first page were pictures of a cute red-haired girl about the age of seven. Kara. Her hair was cut about half way to her shoulders, and she had bangs and the same smile she had years later. The eyes had a similar twinkle. Damn, she was cute. One pose was before a door, downstairs. Another had her laughing as she was jumping on a bed. Gunnar turned and looked at the bed that he was using now. It was the same bed in the photo, with the same needlepoint of a house on the wall.

He turned the page. There she was, age ten, holding proudly a newborn baby — her brother, Henrik. The next page held a full-page black-and-white formal portrait of the brother and sister together. Kara was in a white dress with bands of a floral design running vertically. Her brother, age two, in a dark shirt and dark shorts, sat on her lap. Their smiles were clones of each other.

A few pages later, in half-page prints, Kara was a teenager in color, wearing a purple leotard top, clipped in the middle, accentuating her breasts. There were a few photos of her with long, shiny hair, freckled summer skin, and a delicate gauzy top, gazing unselfconsciously into the camera.

As a graduating senior in a blue robe and mortarboard, she laughed with her brother, now seven, at her side. On the next page, she kissed a boyfriend in a carefree embrace. In another photo, another boyfriend with a beard hugged her. A third boyfriend — now she appeared college age — stood holding her affectionately on a city street.

On the last page, filled edge to edge, was a recent picture. Kara embraced an older man in his early forties. Peder. This was the asshole. Gray in his hair, the man wore a suit and looked like an administrator. Kara wore a dress. This was a formal picture of some sort — an engagement photo? No! He held his head. Fuck, fuck, fuck.

Gunnar looked back at the picture. Kara and Peder stood next to a wall that featured the head of perhaps a Norse god with wavy hair. The god's head spewed water from its mouth — it was a fountain — and over the head was a word partly obscured by Kara's body. He could read "Magle." If this were a Norse god, he hoped it cursed them.

Yet peace and happiness seemed to radiate from Kara. Her face glowed, the face that had given Gunnar scores of kisses. She wore a necklace made of tiny decorative stones splashed with little jars of French's mustard, yellow and red. Gunnar touched the necklace, the gift he had given her.

Gunnar slammed the book shut. He felt like screaming and running out of the house and jumping in front of the first bus he'd see. Fuck. Could he sleep now? It'd be impossible.

In the bathroom, which again seemed cold to him, he splashed his face with tepid water. He gazed at himself in the mirror. His face had stubble. While he had showered and shaved in the morning, it didn't look that way. One cheek appeared scratched. His thick hair on his head went every which way as if he'd just woken up. He was a bum from a gutter. No wonder he was so alone. Take him away from this place.

He opened the medicine cabinet. The bottle of pills was there still on the second shelf. He picked them up and looked at the label. Among the crazy Danish words, the last sentence said, "Et tablet for sove. He shook out one, swallowed it. Good. Would that be enough for sove? Two. He swallowed it. Then twenty stared at him in his palm. Sove. Yes. Sove.

He swallowed.

He closed the medicine cabinet.

He stared at his face.

He just needed to be away for a bit, that's all.

The pills were there in his stomach.

That's all he needed, right?

But maybe... Maybe this wasn't a good idea.

The realization of what he'd done made him rush to the toilet. He just needed to throw up, and his fast move, in fact, was making him gag. His fast move, however, made him dizzy, too, and before he could open the toilet, he felt himself fall back. Falling. Falling. Gone.

CHAPTER SIXTEEN

"CHAOS IS THE LAW OF NATURE. ORDER IS THE DREAM OF MAN."

— HENRY B. ADAMS

He heard voices.

He felt himself being lifted into a car, which, he realized, was a hearse. He was dead.

A man in a dark coat and a stethoscope around his neck said something in Danish, which may as well have been mumbles from Mars.

"What?" said Gunnar, being slid into the car. There were built-in cabinets with drawers next to him. What kind of hearse was this?

Ingeborg appeared next to him.

"You've fallen and hit your head," she said. "I woke up when I heard a bang. It's lucky I'm a light sleeper."

"Lucky?" he said.

She held up the pill bottle. "Did you take these?" she asked.

"Sove."

"How many did you take?"

Although he was fuzzy, he knew not to answer this one.

"How many?" she said again.

"One for *sove*."

"There are none left in the bottle. Did you take them all?"

"I have a headache," he said and rested his head again.

The man with the stethoscope then spoke rapidly in Danish to Ingeborg, and she turned back to Gunnar. "You vomited with a lot of food, so he can't tell. Did you take them all?"

"No," he knew enough to say.

The doors closed with Ingeborg and the man still next to him. Gunnar turned his head, and outside the window, in the swirl of red lights that swept from above, he could see faces, neighbor's faces, faces that gawked and gaped as if having witnessed someone who had stood on the train tracks, letting the train bear right down on him.

The ambulance lurched forward, and the siren began to wail the way it did in a foreign movie, bee-doooo, bee-doooo, and he felt perhaps he was in a foreign film, something Bergman.

They screamed into the night.

Bee-dooo. Bee-dooo.

--------------→

Gunnar awoke in a strange semi-dark and heard nothing, as if his ears didn't work. Then came a ding and the sounds of an elevator door opening. A woman said something like "Dau." Low chatter.

He realized he was staring at his soundless heart monitor. Ba bump, ba bump, ba bump should be echoing. On the screen, his heart appeared perfectly normal when it clearly wasn't. His center was smashed and ripped and torn in two. Delilah had seared his Samson. Mothra had crushed the hero. Oh, why didn't this machine reflect the depressions greater than the rises? Sometimes science didn't understand things.

A dot in the corner above the door was descending. His floaters must be back. A few years before, when he spent so much time at his white board doing calculations, he'd see the occasional black dot or two floating around. His eye doctor said not to worry, that it was "actually tiny clumps of gel inside the vitreous, the clear jelly-like fluid that fills the inside of your eye. Most people get them." As he now stared at the dot more, he realized it wasn't floating randomly but sliding down steadily. It was a solitary spider. How did such an alien arrive in this sterile land? Why would it want to be here?

As he watched it approach the floor, he wondered how much string was inside of a spider. It must feel incredibly empty by the time it reached the bottom. The moment it landed, it started to walk. The door swung open, and a white shoe unwittingly stepped on it as the lights came on.

"Go' morn," said a smiling nurse entering his hospital room in the morning, carrying a breakfast tray. Godzilla. She had to be around fifty, with gray shoulder-length hair. She placed the tray on the bedside rolling table.

"Rise and shine," she said. "I used to tell my English patients when I lived in London, 'Rise and shine.'"

Christ, Mary Poppins. Nothing was shining, Gunnar thought. Everything outside the windows looked dull, including the leafless trees and the tan and red bricks of the buildings across the drive, but he sat up in bed anyway, and he felt a tightness around his head. His hand found his head was wrapped in something.

"You might not remember," said the nurse, "but the back of your head got shaved a little, and you have eight stitches."

He nodded. He didn't think he could feel worse than after Kara gave him the news, but he now did.

"The English always liked a good breakfast," she said.

"I'm American."

"Then you must not be used to good health care."

She indicated for him to sit up, and when he did, she rolled the table up to him and pulled stainless steel covers from the plates. He saw he had a hardboiled egg in a holder, cut-up fruit, toast, pats of butter, small round potatoes with a cream sauce, and a strange meat, which looked like pastrami but with a rind.

"What's that?" he said, pointing to the thing.

"*Stegt flæsk med persillesovs*. It's fried pork, like thick bacon. It comes with potatoes and a parsley sauce. We have very good cooks."

"I'm not hungry," he said. Only then, in talking, did he feel how dry his mouth was. He skipped the glass of orange juice but sipped from the glass of water, and he swirled the wetness around his Sahara.

She placed the covers back on the food, then wrote something in a small notebook that she pulled from her pocket.

"What are you writing?" he asked.

"You're under observation."

"I'm feeling better."

"Are you?" she said. "You've been up at least twenty minutes, and you haven't asked for anything."

"How do you know I was up?"

"I could tell."

"Will I be checked out today?"

"That's up to the doctor."

"I want to be checked out."

"You're under suicide watch."

"I wasn't trying to kill myself, for crying out loud. I slipped in the bathroom — not my fault I was taken to Christiana, and — " He would just leave it at that.

"Christiana." She wrote that in her notebook.

"I'm sure they know about that. I was told it's a tourist spot, and I've never had hashish in my life until yesterday."

"It's not my business why you tried to kill yourself. That's for the *psykiater*."

"So I have to see a psychiatrist?" He lifted the cover off of one plate, the bacon-and-potato one, and with a fork he took in a big mouthful. "Umm. Yummy," he said. "Write that in your book. I'm eating. And enjoying it. I'm perfectly fine."

She wrote.

"So how long am I under observation?"

"That's for the *psykiater*."

"When do I see him or her?"

"After you're done eating."

He ate more quickly. The nurse smiled and left. He then popped out of bed and hurried to the closet. His clothes weren't in there. Maybe they thought he'd take his belt and hang himself. He was wearing red print pajamas, and he surely couldn't go out on the street that way. He noticed the camera above the door. It wasn't as if he could have dressed and left anyway. And where would he go?

Fuck. All right, he moved back to the bed.

He began to think how great it would be to be near absolute zero. All his atoms would be no longer individual but interconnected, indivisible, eerily indefinable. In the ultra-cold, atoms started showing wave-like properties. Solids became wave packets, very long and overlapping. Protons, neutrons, electrons, seemed to slide over each other like anchovies in the sea. All became one big quantum system and superfluid. Friction ceased to exist. Atoms were no longer points in space but everywhere at once. Matter became God. He wanted to be there.

Research was the closest thing to that state. When researching, he forgot about himself. He needed to research.

So how to get out of the hospital? He plunged himself into this mess, he told himself, and he'd yank himself out. This was his low point, he thought, and it couldn't get worse. Once out, he'd call Bent at the Institute and start his job early.

An hour later, still in his pajamas but with a robe, his nurse directed him into Dr. Dag Jensen's office, which had big windows and looked out at mostly homes and trees. In the background, Gunnar could make out the two steeples of Roskilde's *domkirke*.

"Dr. Gundarson," said the tall man in the white coat, indicating the chair.

"Dr. Jensen," said Gunnar, pronouncing it correctly, "Yensen," as his nurse had.

"I heard a little of what happened from both Ingeborg Tornsen and her son Henrik this morning. It's clear you have reasons to be depressed."

"Well, that... you know." He seemed to choke. He knew Kara would come up, and he meant to say something a little upbeat such as every dog has his day, but the mere mention of what happened brought up such emotion, he couldn't talk.

"People use the word 'depression' as if it's akin to some horrible disease," said Dr. Jensen, "but it's perfectly normal. Now that I've heard about Kara, the better word to use is 'grief,' or *sorg* in Danish. You've lost an important relationship, and you're grieving. It's like death"

"Yes." It came out more like a squeak.

"However, taking too many pills is not the way — "

"I slipped is all." There, his voice was working again. "They didn't find any pills in my vomit."

"Actually, they have now."

Gunnar sighed. "Listen, I didn't try to kill myself — certainly not intentionally. I'm fine. A good sleep helped."

"You're not fine, and you probably won't be for a while," said Jensen. "Grief is not a common cold. Your problems are compounded by not knowing the culture, the language, or anybody other than Kara, and it's gray and dark this time of year. You may be sensitive to seasonal affective disorder."

"Send me to Jamaica."

"All of Denmark could use that," he said with a smile. "No budget. In the meantime, we don't want you curing yourself in an extreme way."

"I won't. I'd like to leave to get to work."

"You're lucky that Roskilde has one of the country's top extended-care facilities, St. Hans Mental Health Centre."

"Extended care? Hold on a sec."

"You didn't come to this hospital voluntarily, and so now we have the responsibility."

"What are you talking about?"

"St. Hans is better set up for your needs. It's perhaps one of the best institutions of its kind in the world. It's a beautiful campus overlooking Roskilde fiord. The staff respects each patient's personal integrity. You'll have conversation therapy, environment therapy, physical training — "

"Please, I can't." He felt as if he were falling again. He held his head.

"It's not necessarily months. It may be just weeks before you're using the word *can* again. You'll be *canning* all over the place." He grinned.

The smile pissed off Gunnar, and he felt a surge of anger, energy. The vertigo disappeared. "Maybe Ingeborg didn't explain, but I'm a physicist."

"Yes, she said that."

"I'm here to work at the Niels Bohr Institute. My job starts there in two weeks — or right away if I choose."

Dr. Jensen flipped through a clipboard on his desk. "I didn't know that. It's not here."

"What happened to me was an unfortunate incident, but it's imperative I get back to my research."

"The reality is that you might not."

"So if Einstein happened to be here after he was so depressed over his wife, you'd have locked him up? Or Kierkegaard — he was Danish, wasn't he?"

"What about SørenKierkegaard?"

"He was obsessed over a woman. She played a crucial part in his developing a philosophy and theology. He courted her for a couple of years, persuaded her father for her hand in marriage, then freaked out."

"Yes, Regine Olsen."

"His philosophy revolved around his relationship to her, his whole notion of faith. If this place was around then, we'd never have had his philosophy."

Dr. Jensen sat up straighter, amused. "And you're saying you're equal to Einstein and Kierkegaard?"

"I *can* do things at Niels Bohr. I *can* do a lot there. The Institute doesn't take just anyone."

"The Niels Bohr Institute is impressive. Bohr was a brilliant man."

"And he could piss people off, too, but we have quantum mechanics thanks to him."

The doctor nodded. "What will you do there?"

"I study the very cold: absolute zero. Atoms change when they get near absolute zero. They lose their identity and become a whole new state of matter." Gunnar quickly explained Bose-Einstein condensates, the pure strangeness and awesomeness of its state, predicted in 1925 by Satyendra Nath Boseand Albert Einstein, but only first created in a lab in 1995. Which atoms or compounds could reach this state was still being discovered. Gunnar covered the competition he'd been in in Wisconsin trying to use strontium, and what he hoped to be doing with compounds there in Denmark. All the while, Dr. Jensen looked impressed, nodding, saying "uh huh" occasionally, and simply listening.

"I have a real opportunity here to work with some of the best minds in Denmark," said Gunnar, "and we can discover things that make a difference. It'll change our lives."

"Interesting," said Dr. Jensen.

"It is," said Gunnar.

"So you're saying what happened yesterday was just an anomaly, truly an accident."

"Yes, absolutely."

"And you're feeling better?"

"Much better."

"From my experience, the truly brilliant are on the edge. I'm going to take a chance." Dr. Jensen smiled, then signed a piece of paper. "Please call me, though, day or night, if you're feeling low. Here's my card. I'd like to be your friend in Denmark. I'd like to say I knew Gunnar Gunderson when."

For Gunnar, it felt like the trees beyond the windows glowed brilliantly, sunspots in the morning.

Gunnar was back at Kara's parents' house within the hour.

CHAPTER SEVENTEEN

"TRADITIONAL SCIENTIFIC METHOD HAS ALWAYS BEEN, AT THE VERY BEST, 20-20 HINDSIGHT. IT'S GOOD FOR SEEING WHERE YOU'VE BEEN. IT'S GOOD FOR TESTING THE TRUTH OF WHAT YOU THINK YOU KNOW, BUT IT CAN'T TELL YOU WHERE YOU OUGHT TO GO."

— ROBERT M. PIRSIG

When Gunnar arrived back at the house, no one was there, but he had a key that Kara had given him the first day. The first thing he noticed was a smell that seemed like bread — warm, friendly bread. Weird.

He didn't want to be around when Ingeborg and Fritz returned from work — he couldn't face them yet — so Gunnar grabbed a pen from the jar on the counter and scrawled a note on the back of a Danske Andelskassers Bank envelope that he found in the trash under the sink. Good to see that Europeans put trash under the sink, too.

"Dear Ingeborg and Fritz" he wrote when the ink ran out. The next two pens didn't work at all. There must be some sort of universal force field in jars that caused pens worldwide not to work. He wrote his note using a colored pencil with a sky blue lead. He said he was feeling better, that the psychiatrist had given his approval, and that he was going out to do many errands. He'd be back late that night. Perhaps he'd see them in the morning.

Would they wonder whether there really were late-night errands? Not his concern. He liked that word, "concern," and wrote, "Thank you for your concern. I'm sorry for the disruption I caused. I'm sorry I haven't been myself, but I'm feeling much better. Perhaps I can see you in the morning for breakfast." The main thing he needed was the space of a day where he could recharge and figure out his life anew. He didn't need people questioning him.

He unwrapped the bandage on his head and, using a hand mirror with the mirror above the sink, saw that he didn't have a lot of hair cut away in the back of his head. In fact, a baseball cap that he brought should cover it up. He showered, changed his clothes, then walked into town.

On the way in, he paused every now and then to look at things such as the gnarl of a tree root, the arc of a street light, and the red roofs of the neighborhood. There were a lot of red-tiled roofs here, so different from Madison. And the clouds — a puffy one looked like Cher, big lips and all. He'd catch himself staring and remind himself he wanted to find the Internet café that he'd spotted the day he arrived when Kara was driving. He sensed he was thinking differently, but he didn't know what that meant. He should get a move on.

He walked past a building labeled *Roskilde Bibliotekerne,* which looked a lot like a library. He remembered *biblioteca,* library, from his high school Spanish, so this was probably a library, and it likely had computers. However, he'd have to get a library card and seek help from someone speaking English and people would stare and wonder why he was so sad-looking because he felt sad, damn it, so he'd better go to the Internet café where, he hoped, it wasn't so big and bright. He sped up his pace and soon found the café.

He thought it'd be like a Starbucks with a few tables having a laptop computer to rent. Instead, the place looked more like a computer store, or perhaps a TV shop, because of all its flat-screen monitors in rows. Three rows of wooden tables on which stood the monitors trisected the narrow shop. Only a few people were at screens, all of them wearing headphones and sitting in ergonomic chairs. Maybe they were mostly interested in music or watching video. Was the Icelandic singer Bjork popular here? Did she still wear the strange Swan dress as she had a couple years ago to the Academy Awards?

Bjork? What's happening to his head? He just needed to check his email and write his mother.

Dominating the room was a counter that featured a cash register, thermos towers of coffee, an espresso maker, and a tall Nordic woman. Nordic was her essence: blond hair that cascaded to her breasts, a strong chin with a small cleft, pink cheeks, and eyes that snapped in their blueness. In her mid-twenties, she had a bemused and observant look that older people had after they had discovered the ironies of life. He felt uncomfortable as if his misery and his life history were a radio broadcast before her. He tried to find some imperfection in her but couldn't. "Dau," she said. That word again. It must mean hello.

"Hi. I'm sorry, I'm new in this country," said Gunnar, "and I just need to email. You speak English?"

"Of course."

"How does this work?"

"I'm happy to show you," she said. "You're American?"

"Yes."

"It's by the hour. Would you like anything to eat or drink first?"

"*Nej tak*," he said using what he'd learned the previous day.

She looked pleased. He imagined her as if she were a Wisconsin native, and he had met her in Madison. There she'd probably be driving a very old Volvo, would make wry comments about cheerleaders, and would sarcastically quote George Bush — "Some folks look at me and see a certain swagger, which in Texas is called 'walking.'" And she'd love brushing her hair naked. She must look beautiful naked.

"How long have you lived here?" she asked.

"This is my third day."

"Sightseeing?"

"I'm a physicist," he said. "I'll be researching and teaching in Copenhagen for at least six months."

"Impressive," she said.

He admitted to himself he enjoyed this flirtation, but he really needed to get to his email. Under the glass near him on a pastry shelf was what looked to be a Danish with what looked to be whipped cream oozing from the center. "Is that a Danish — or what I think of as a Danish?"

"I don't know what you think."

"Oh, that's a problem."

She laughed. "Actually, I do know what you think, and yes, these are Danishes, what we call *wienerbrod,* which means 'Vienna bread.' Danishes are Austrian."

"I wouldn't mind one of those."

"Mind? Oh, you mean you want to buy one?"

"Yes, please."

Using tongs, she lifted it onto a plate for him. "And would you like an hour of Internet?"

"Half hour?" he asked.

She gave him the price for the *wienerbrod* and the computer, and he paid. As she rang him up, he took his first bite of the Danish and discovered an extremely light, delicate, buttery crust that could become flour snowflakes with each bite. On the throne of the pastry sat a vanilla pudding and lemon gel.

He said, "Wow. This is much lighter than we get in Wisconsin. It's fluffy like a croissant — but with sugar."

"We have deliveries twice a day. Fresh." She said the last word as if it held more meaning. He didn't know what. She shook her head and handed him a ticket with a number and letter code on it and explained he could choose any computer. The screen would then ask for his code, and he needed to type it in. If he needed more time, just come back for another code. He wouldn't lose anything onscreen.

"Thanks," he said, holding up the pastry.

"*Selv tak,*" she said, and he moved off, choosing a computer in a row where no one else was.

He quickly logged onto the computer, then into his e-mail. There was business from UW's physics department, and messages from his mother and his sister. He clicked on the one from his sister first.

```
hey bro —
i asked Mom where u been lately and she said u were in
denmark. already? shit. it's hard to imagine u getting your
rocks off to a danish babe in the land of danish babes but
hey I guess u r human 2 even if it hasnt always seemed that
way. u kinda seemed lika worker B but worker Bs need honey 2.

work here sucks but nothing new. love the new house and car.
now gotta find a new guy. shit. 1 breaks your heart but ima
fool i guess. gotta run. right me if u can.
luv your sis
```

Gunnar rarely received e-mails from his sister, but when he did, he was always amazed she was from the same generation as he. Here was a woman who had received her master's degree in library and information science and wrote e-mails like she was twelve. She once told him, though, she loved chat rooms and that one develops shorthand in order to write quickly in a chat room. She said chat rooms helped her unwind. Was it possible her husband Brad felt partly abandoned by Patty's obsession with her computer? As in nature, when a vacuum was created, something had to fill it. He found someone else.

Gunnar considered waiting a few days to write his sister back, but then again, he would love another note back.

```
Patty —

It was great to get your note. Denmark is so similar yet
dissimilar to Wisconsin that my head is spinning. In some
ways, I feel like I can't wake up. Nothing prepared me for
the differences. Everything feels tidy and clean. And dark.
The sun doesn't rise until around 8:45, and it sets before
```

4:00 — deep dark by 4:30. There's no snow. How can winter
this far north have no snow? I'm living in a conundrum.

I'm at an Internet café in Roskilde. I'm still getting used
to things.

More when I have more news.
 — Gunnar

    There. He didn't give too much away. He clicked on the
message from his mother. She wrote:

My dear adventurous son —

Your trip to Denmark remains surprising to me, but I'm also
happy for you for a few reasons. I've often worried that
you'd become too wrapped up in your work. After all, atoms
have been cold since before the Big Bang, so why should you
worry about them now? They do well on their own. You'd become
isolated down in Madison, so I'm pleased you're off seeing
the world.

As I sit here wondering where you are and what you're doing,
I do worry that in some ways I never prepared you enough for
relationships. I'm not saying you'll be marrying Kara anytime
soon, but still, if you're living with her, I'm feeling as if
I should have given you some wise words about women. Now I'm
thinking you're probably learning more than I can teach you.
Here are a few tips anyway:

1. Always open the car door for Kara. Such a small
    kindness works the world over. In some ways, I bemoan
    the advent of remote door locks on new cars because
    the kindness is usurped by remote.

2. At restaurants, let her sit first. Help her into her
    chair. Your father was a master of that.

3. Cook for Kara once in a while. You've gotten good at
    cooking for yourself, so just double the ingredients.

You might learn how to cook at least one gourmet meal. Your dad cooked an amazing chicken marsala.

4. Flowers. Buy her flowers once in a while. I know you. You think that flowers grow for free so why should you buy any? Water flows freely, too, but I see you buy Aquafina for yourself. Women like flowers. Buying on a whim is perfectly fine. If you ever (or I should say WHEN YOU) get into an argument, buy her flowers. It works.

That should get you started. I'm thinking that you haven't always adapted well to change, so I hope this journey of yours is turning out all right. If not, feel free to return to Wisconsin. You are not alone. You never have to cut off your ear.

Love, your mother.

Gunnar was shaking after he read her last paragraph. Did she assume he'd fail? Had he revealed things about Kara that he hadn't seen? What did she mean he didn't adapt well to change? And did she think he could cut off his ear? As he thought about that, though, he'd almost done worse with the pills. He always thought Van Gogh's ear cutting had to do with a prostitute, but what did he know? The point was, Gunnar could identify with an extreme feeling.

Still, his mother's note, long and sensitive, reflected more than he had expected. He wished he could reply in kind, but he couldn't tell her what had happened. He wasn't about to fly home a failure, either. He had to deal with this on his own.

Dear Mom:

Your wonderful email arrived just fine in Denmark. I received a great note from Patty, too, so it's good to hear from my family.

The flight was long and the jet lag has been tremendous, so I apologize if this note is too short or any of this sounds disjointed or abnormal.

He pondered what he'd write next. We're all like Ted Kennedy at some point, he thought. We all have our Chappaquiddicks. He continued:

Kara is fine at home, happy to have her man at her side.

This wasn't a lie, he thought.

I'm getting used to all the changes, the lack of sun, and the lack of snow. Though I'm farther north than you, the daily temperature is just above freezing (so far, at any rate). I have a month before I start at the Niels Bohr Institute, but I will call them today or tomorrow. I'm eager to move ahead.

Anyway, take care.
Love, Gunnar

Gunnar reread the letter, and then sent it. He was ready to go. He stood, and the woman at the counter said, "So soon? Did everything work for you?"

"Yes," he said. "I guess I didn't have as much to say as I thought."

"Are you enjoying Danmark?"

"*Enjoy* may not be the right word. Let's say every day here is packed full." He pointed toward the computer he used. "I guess I've jumped another hurdle."

"Really?"

Maybe she meant it in a Woody Allen way — that he was babbling and she was due back on Planet Earth. Thinking about this added to his sense depletion and enervation. So he said nothing.

She smiled. "I mean, have you had helpful hurdles?"

"I'd love to say yes. But I worry."

"About what?"

"That I've learned nothing."

Without apparent thought, she touched his hand with her pointer finger like God giving life to Adam on the Sistine Chapel, and he felt a rush, not an electric shock but more elastic, more gravity-breaking, more like he was matter becoming a Bose-Einstein condensate, frictionless and fluid. He thought he'd crash right to the floor.

She grabbed him firmly on his forearm. That steadied him. "Are you okay?"

"Yes. Thanks." His balance returned. "You're an angel."

"Would you like some *kaffe?* No charge."

He knew this was the point he should ask her name and how late she worked, or would she like to go out to dinner, and maybe he'd get to see her brush her hair naked in the morning. He realized, though, starting another affair now wasn't the thing. Nothing would ever be casual for him. If he had a choice, he'd rather be back in Madison and find someone like Ursula. He didn't have to be Galvani's frog leg responding to electric current. This woman, as beautiful as she was, needed someone else.

"No, no, I have to go. Thank you."

"I hope you come back," she said.

"Thanks."

With that, he left. He went to the library and found a section of English books, and he chose a nice thick one, *Of Human Bondage,* nice catchy title. Somerset Maugham. He wasn't much for reading novels ever, but he'd always meant to read the classics. He had a lot of free time now, and it was one of those classics. He flipped open to a random page, and started reading. He wasn't a read-the-first-paragraph person to see if he liked a book. He always chose randomly, and he flipped to near the end of the book. He read:

> Philip did not surrender himself willingly to the passion that consumed him. He knew that all things human are transitory and therefore that it must cease one day or another. He looked forward to that day with eager longing. Love was like a parasite in the heart, nourishing a hateful existence on his life's blood.

How true that was! He looked around him to see if anyone was staring at him. Nope.

After reading a few chapters, he went to the front counter and asked for an. He gave his address — *Femtem Dronning Margrethesvej* — and he checked the book out. He read more in the library, had dinner by himself at an Italian café, drank a few Tuborgs at Killians Hus, and read some more. The story was about an orphaned English lad, Philip Carey, a sensitive guy with a clubbed foot in the late 1800's, raised by a religious aunt and uncle. Philip yearns for adventure, and at eighteen pursues a career as an artist in Paris. He returns to England to study something more practical, medicine, and falls for an alluring waitress, Mildred, who works at a teashop. It's a doomed love affair to which Gunnar could completely relate. Mildred barely gives Philip a glance, which hooks Philip more.

By then it was late enough, and Kara's parents should be in bed, so he walked back to the house.

- - - - - - - - - - - - - →

In the morning from Kara's childhood bedroom, Gunnar heard the voices mention his name, and that had him listen carefully. They seemed to be in the hallway. He tried to make sense of the gutteral sounds.

"*Skal vi vække Gunnar for at han kan få middag?*" said Ingeborg.

"*Ja, men Gunnar er træt,*" said Fritz. "*Han er helt knust over Kara.*"

There was that word again, *Kara*. The name held so much power over him still, making him feel as meaningless as a shoe in an alley. He could hear her parents walk down the stairs. His eyes had adjusted to the darkness, and he could see the light under the door. The hands of his watch glowed enough to show him that it was just after 7:30 a.m. He stared up in the darkness and thought, "Please make today easier than the last few days." He wondered who was he saying this to? Why couldn't his brain get back to research or something else besides his plight?

He flicked on the light, and even getting part way out of bed, he sensed his room was chilly again — but not as bad as yesterday. He stared at the light on the ceiling, a domed fixture with alabaster glass. This was the light that Kara had had as a child. This light formed her, shone on her daily until she was twenty. Now it radiated on him. They had something in common. They had many things in common, really.

He counted to three, then bolted out of the bed and pulled on a robe before his warmth radiated away. He showered quickly and hurried downstairs. He wanted to greet them before they left for work.

Ingeborg, in a dark blouse and black pants, was moving food from the kitchen to the table, a breakfast as Kara had once made him: ham, orange juice, dark bread on a plate, yogurt in a bowl, blueberries in a cup, and two soft-boiled eggs in their shells but with their tops off and standing in porcelain holders — and he knew there was more coming. Everything, though, was for two people. Ingeborg's smile looked forced, but she said, "Ah. *Godt.* Sit, sit, please. I was hoping we'd see you. I have food in case you did." She pointed to the head of the table, indicating his spot.

"Thanks." He sat. This was going to be an awkward breakfast.

Fritz came out moments later wearing a sweater vest and khaki slacks, carrying two cereal bowls and a cereal box of something called *Ymerdrys*. He looked truly surprised to see Gunnar. "Goot morning," he said in his limited English. "I am wery happy to see you."

Gunnar nodded. "I'm sorry about what happened. I'm sure you're both wondering about me, and I assure you that everything was an accident. Thank you for your help."

"You're welcome," said Ingeborg.

"I feel so embarrassed about what happened. I'm not a traveler, clearly, and I just wasn't myself."

Fritz looked puzzled and said something to Ingeborg, who then must have translated for Fritz. He nodded. "*Spise*," he said. "Eat."

"Don't worry," said Ingeborg. "Start with an egg, and we'll settle down in a few minutes here and hear more."

More? thought Gunnar. What more is there to say?

More food came: a variety of jams and cheeses, granola, and herring. The yogurt was much thinner than the American variety, so it could be drunk from a glass, and Gunnar particularly liked the sweet and tart jam with the name *tuttebær*. "What's the name of this fruit in English?" he asked.

"Lingonberry," she said. "It's *Svensk*. Swedish. The little red berries grow in Sweden."

Fritz nodded. "*Tuttebær*. Wery good."

They all ate and no one was talking. Fritz and Ingeborg would smile if he made eye contact, yet the noise of chewing and the clinks of their forks against china were the only sounds in the room. It was as if they wanted him to speak when he felt ready.

"Kara cooked for me once like this," said Gunnar, "and I thought, who could eat this much food every morning?" Ingeborg frowned, and he realized it must sound like a criticism. "*I mean*," he said in emphasis, "that the food is so good, what a great way to start each day. This is really special for me, and I thank you for it."

"You're welcome," said Ingeborg, "but you don't have to keep thanking us for everything. You didn't come to Denmark to eat with two old people like us, and I realize how disappointed you must be."

"Disappointment's a good word," said Gunnar.

"Kara is our only daughter, and we've been proud of her."

Fritz was nodding as if he understood this.

"She's was easy to fall in love with," said Gunnar.

"Yes, and she's probably easy to hate, too, right now, and I certainly can't fault you if you do. She does mean well, and we're so sorry this happened."

"It's not your fault."

"Fritz and I would like to help in any way we can. It's not as if we have other daughters or ..." She seemed to search for the right words. "We know no one who can fill your heart, but you have your job to go to soon, yes?"

"In a month it starts, although if I could use your phone this morning, I'll call the Institute and see if they can use me sooner."

"It's in the kitchen, and use it anytime you would like."

Fritz spoke in Danish to Ingeborg urgently and she responded to him warily. He spoke quickly back, using his hands in a pushing motion.

"Fritz wants to know — and I'm not sure how to say this delicately — but he wants to know that you won't kill yourself. He doesn't like blood." She smiled as if to say that's what he said, but don't take it wrongly.

Gunnar glanced to Fritz, who looked back with curiosity.

"Tell him I don't like blood, either. I promise I won't kill myself."

"No?"

"I have a big job to do in Denmark — to discover the universe and why we're here. I know one place the universe isn't. It's not with Kara."

Ingerborg translated for Fritz, who then nodded.

Fritz placed his hands flat on the table and started speaking. Ingeborg said, "My husband has a small story, if you don't mind listening through me."

"Oh?"

Fritz spoke more, and Ingeborg would translate every few sentences. "After I graduated from the gymnasium," said Ingeborg for Fritz, "What you call high school — I wanted to travel the world and also screw my girlfriend Halla as much as I could. This was 1970, and I had very long hair past my shoulders. You wouldn't know it from my gray hair now. I convinced Halla that we should hitchhike to Oslo, Norway. She agreed, and my mother made me a batch of my favorite food, *frikadeller*, Danish meatballs. I had a big baggie of them in my backpack.

"The first part of the trip was so good because we were picked up by a young man in his very old Volvo. The car was a classic, a 122S from 1959, and it made big blue smoke behind us. Of course, nowadays we'd call it pollution, but then it seemed funny. The young man had good hash, too. Yes, I smoked it then, it was the seventies, and when he let us off, we were laughing and had our thumbs out. Soon a fancy Mercedes stopped, and a Norwegian boat captain picked us up. We zipped to Oslo, driving past amazing sites of stark mountains and deep fiords — not flat like Denmark.

We arrived at dinner time. He took us to dinner at his hotel, the Continental in Oslo.

"Everything was expensive then — still is — so we were thankful for the five-star experience. We said good-bye and searched for a room. Halla seemed sad. All we could afford was a room in the Salvation Army Hotel. It was a dreary little thing, dingy walls, and two twin beds. I yanked off my clothes and pulled off Halla's, and we made love, but it wasn't very good. Afterwards, Halla said she needed to go out to a drug store and she'd go alone. When she came back, she told me she was leaving me for the Norwegian boat captain who she just went and saw. He wanted to take her to Ibiza in Spain, and so she left me.

"This is to say, I know your sadness. I know what it feels like to feel a failure. I considered the next morning of killing myself, jumping off a mountain. Of course, that meant getting a train and going to the mountains, which seemed like a lot of work, so I walked around Oslo, drinking beer, getting drunk, and eating meatballs, which I threw up. I stumbled across a place called Vigeland Park. It's an art park filled with sculptures by Gustav Vigeland, hundreds of them in granite and bronze showing the circle of life. I came to a sculpture of a little baby crying, and next to it, watching it, was a young woman crying and crying."

At this point, Ingeborg was getting teary-eyed and said, "I know that park." Fritz patted her hand before speaking again, and she translated.

"I asked the young woman if I could help her, and she said no, that her young nephew had died from cancer that year, and this sculpture reminded her of him. She said she never wanted to have children, so she would never have to experience such a loss again in her life.

"She sensed I was sad, too, and I told her of Halla and the boat captain, and then she asked if I would go with her to the Edvard Munch museum. I never went to museums for anything, but this young woman seemed so honest to me, so understanding, and what did I have to do that day? So I went with her. You ask me, Edvard Munch was a miserable man, not like Vigeland who seems to have loved life. However, Munch had some giant canvases with a sun bursting in brightness. They seemed extraordinary to me. The young woman smiled and was so happy I liked it, and she hugged me. I felt so happy right there. I was wishing that moment would just last."

Ingeborg paused to wipe tears, while Fritz continued in a very happy voice, wiping his own eyes. He said, "And it pretty much has. I've been happy with her ever since. We had children, too, Kara and Henrik."

"You're that woman?" Gunnar said to Ingeborg, amazed.

She nodded. Fritz and Ingeborg hugged each other as best they could across the table.

"Thank you," said Gunnar. "Thank you both. That helps."

CHAPTER EIGHTEEN

"... IF WE DO DISCOVER A COMPLETE THEORY, IT SHOULD IN TIME BE UNDERSTANDABLE IN BROAD PRINCIPLE BY EVERYONE, NOT JUST A FEW SCIENTISTS. THEN WE SHALL ALL, PHILOSOPHERS, SCIENTISTS, AND JUST ORDINARY PEOPLE, BE ABLE TO TAKE PART IN THE DISCUSSION OF THE QUESTION OF WHY IT IS THAT WE AND THE UNIVERSE EXIST."

— PHYSICIST STEPHEN HAWKING

Gunnar used the phone in the Tornsen's kitchen to call Bent, his new boss. The other end was answered with *"Det er Bent."*
"Bent, this is Gunnar Gunnarson. I'm in Denmark now."
"Professor Gunderson?" said Bent.
"Yes?" Gunnar wondered if perhaps they weren't on a first-name basis as he had assumed, and Gunnar had made a mistake.
"This is incredible!" said Bent enthusiastically in an American accent. "You're in Copenhagen?" Bent had studied

in America and received all his degrees there, and it showed in his accent — more American than most Danes.

"Roskilde, actually."

"Fantastic, Gunnar. You don't know what this means. Do you have a line to God or something?"

"What?"

The man was laughing at this point. "Your call couldn't come at a better time. I can use you."

"That's why I'm calling, hoping I can get started sooner than intended."

"How soon can you come?"

"Today — right away if you want."

"Yes, please do. How about in a couple of hours?"

"What's happening?"

"I'm being pulled into a meeting right now, but I can count on you, yes?"

"Yes, but count on what? Where should I meet you?"

"Meet me at Copenhagen's main train station at eleven. I'll explain everything then, and I'll take you to an early lunch." And he hung up. *Where* at the train station would they meet? It was a big place as he'd seen.

After the call, the Tornsens were leaving for work, and Gunnar explained how he'd be going into Copenhagen to see his new boss. "Change your clothes if you want, brush your teeth, and we'll take you to the station," said Ingeborg.

He hurried. They dropped him off at the station and wished him luck. The next train for Copenhagen would get him to the capital at eleven. Bent knew his schedules.

On the train ride in, something like ash, lots of ash, streaked by the window, and Gunnar realized it was snow, wonderful, sanctified snow. He loved how it shot by the windows as streaks, but further out, it was coming down slowly like a mother's wishes on her newborn child. The snow felt magical, as if the laws of the universe were back in action here.

Gunnar contemplated why Bent needed him in such a hurry. Was his team near a breakthrough and they needed Gunnar's expertise? But what expertise was that that he had that they didn't have?

The group that he was joining had a unique, perhaps impossible goal. It had to do with the way particles were divided into two groups: bosons and fermions. All atoms were made up of particles. Most people had heard of the major particles: electrons, protons, and neutrons. These were fermions. Then there were smaller particles: photons, neutrinos, and quarks. They were bosons. The world was simple — bosons and fermions. It all related to how the particles rotated. Bosons spun one way, fermions another.

The spin created very different properties. Bosons were social entities, gregariously joining each other like Southern Baptists linking arms to belt out a gospel hymn. Bosons worked together. If one boson went one way, other bosons were happy to follow. An ensemble of photons in the same state constituted what was called a laser beam.

Fermions, however, were loners. Fermions repelled each other. Thus, it was impossible to get a group of fermions together into a beam like a laser.

An atom itself could be considered "fermionic" or "bosonic" depending on the makeup of its parts. An atom containing an even number of fermions was considered bosonic, an odd number, fermionic. Only bosonic atoms had been turned into Bose-Einstein condensates. Gunnar's group would try to create the first fermionic condensate.

Explorations into the ultracold would tell more about the properties of fermions and bosons because near absolute zero things slowed down so much, people could "read" them better. Gunnar was ready to jump in, but he didn't have any special knowledge on fermions. This made him more nervous about why Bent needed to see him.

As he hurtled toward the capital, he thought about Bent. The eminent scientist had graduated high school in 1965, studied physics at Purdue University, and received his doctorate from Harvard, after which he did post-doctoral work in Copenhagen. In Denmark, he worked closely with Aage Bohr, Niels' son, also a physicist and Nobel Laureate. Bent's interest in atomic structure led him to work in the ultracold. Bent knew as much or more than Gunnar. Did Gunnar oversell himself in some way? He had no answer.

The snow came down so thickly, it looked like fog in the distance, and the white stuff was sticking on the ground now. The dusting made everything beautiful like powdered sugar on a doughnut. The train slowed, and more and more sets of tracks divided off from one another. They were approaching the main station. Soon a shadow enveloped the train, and they were now inside a building, stopping. Gunnar decided that once off the train, he'd go upstairs to the main lobby and stand near the Christmas tree that he remembered. Maybe Bent could find him there. He'd sent Bent his photo, but did he look like that photo anymore? That had been another person, a person in love with Kara.

At the top of the escalator, a tall man with rich gray hair, half glasses, fabulous posture, and who wore a coat and tie looked a lot like Robert Oppenheimer, the physicist who helped create the first atomic bomb. He waved and smiled in delight at Gunnar immediately.

"Professor Herskind?"

"Gunnar! Please, call me Bent."

Gunnar stepped off the escalator and they shook hands warmly. The man grinned and patted Gunnar on the back. He was more outgoing than anyone else he'd met in Denmark.

"You're right on time," said Bent. He stood slightly taller than Gunnar, and, for a man in his sixties, Bent had no extra weight and didn't look the least bit like his name. "Great to finally meet you, Gunnar."

"You, too, Bent." Gunnar waited for the right moment to ask why Bent needed him today, but his new boss pointed to a side door and said "Shall we?" Gunnar followed him out the door. Once on the street, they walked side-by-side.

"I'm so excited to have you on our new team," said Bent. "You'll love it here."

Gunnar doubted that but said, "Yes, it's a lovely city."

"A week after the New Year, I'll be gathering all the research teams to have a strategy meeting."

"So what's happening today?"

"Oh, yes. I'll get to that when we sit down."

"Will I be meeting with my team?"

"You're an eager reindeer, aren't you?"

"I'm here to help."

Bent stretched out his hands to point to the urban landscape before them. "All these people we see on the street now? In a couple more days, it'll look like a neutron bomb had gone off — all the buildings will still be here but hardly any people. One thing about Denmark, Christmas is a big deal. We have not one day of Christmas, but two — three if you count Christmas Eve Day. After Christmas, everyone's off on their winter travels — some to the sun in Spain or Africa."

"I haven't seen the sun yet."

"The number of hours of outright sunshine in December here averages something like forty — a little more than an hour a day."

Gunnar stopped and looked straight up, letting the snow fall on his face. So what if the sun was obscured — it was snowing right on him as if a bag of the stuff had been ripped open just for him. He was in a snow globe. Cool feathers fell on his face.

When Gunnar brought his head back to level, Bent was grinning. "So you like the snow."

"I do. I never thought about it before — like a favorite food you don't think about until you can't have it."

"What food can't you have?"

"Like about everything I know."

Bent laughed. "I was trying to think of a good place to eat. I see the brasserie at the Hotel Imperial ahead. It makes American things. Does that sound okay?"

"Lovely," said Gunnar.

The hotel was one of the few modern-looking buildings in the area and appeared to take up most of a city block. The brasserie's windows faced the street, and a number of people inside looked happy and warm.

When they walked in, a hostess seated them immediately.

Once seated, Bent said, "Now I can ask my favor." He gave a big smile. "I have an exciting proposition for you. As you may know, I'm in the middle of hosting a major ultracold conference that ends tomorrow."

"I didn't know that."

"Oh, ya, a big deal. Well, as you know, the ultracold is really hot now. We've had a great turnout. Late this afternoon, my keynote speaker was going to talk to a gathering of graduate students and visitors, but a family emergency in Finland came up. When you called, I knew you'd be my savior. Your stature — as an American physicist in the field — you'll be perfect."

Gunnar's heart jolted. "Speaking?" he said.

"It's stuff you can do off the top of your head. After all, you'll be teaching the 'Games With Quantum Gases' class in the spring, so all you really need to do is introduce that and talk about your work with strontium and how you'll be exploring fermionic condensates."

"I haven't made up my syllabus for the class yet," he said in a panic, his voice cracking exactly as it used to do when he first started teaching. He'd never expected to teach — he thought he'd always be a pure research scientist — but the offer at UW included teaching. It had taken him two years to not pause in front of his classroom's door and prepare mentally before walking in. Now he felt worse than then. "I was going to design my class over the Christmas break."

Bent smiled. "Your colleagues all told me of your brilliance in teaching. You know this stuff, don't worry, I promise. You'll be doing me a huge favor."

Gunnar felt as if he might throw up, and his breathing became labored. He held up his hand as if to suggest indigestion or something. He couldn't throw up in front of his new boss, but how could he talk Bent out of this?

"Are you okay?" said Bent, leaning closer.

"I — Let me — "

"I know you just got here. I wouldn't have asked if it wasn't an emergency."

Gunnar nodded and concentrated. He liked the man and didn't want to disappoint. Yet if Gunnar had this reaction just in front of Bent, what would he be like in front of a lot of people? He willed himself to calm down. "It's ..." said Gunnar. "It just caught me by surprise like my whole visit so far. I didn't tell you — in fact I didn't expect to have to tell you — but I've been thrown a few times in just a couple of days."

"Thrown?" He looked concerned.

"My girlfriend that I flew over here for is living with another guy. She's having me stay with her parents."

"Oh, my."

"On top of that, I had some sort of strange drug reaction, maybe an allergy," he said to steer away from the drug overdose, "and I was ambulanced to a hospital and nearly died. That was yesterday."

"Oh, no," he said. "I should just cancel the whole thing. After all, hmm ..." Bent stared into the distance as if figuring out options.

"You'd do that?" said Gunnar, relief sweeping over him.

"Of course. I can't even believe you're here now — but you looked so happy outside in the snow."

Gunnar looked at the window again, at the snow still coming down, now thick on the sidewalk. It looked great. Two boys around eight made snowballs with their bare hands and threw them at each other at the same moment.

"Maybe I should do your presentation," Gunnar said. "What the hell. Everything about my trip's been crazy. I may as well keep it up." He couldn't believe he was saying it, but the snow was a sign, as was Bent's willingness to cancel. Things just had to get better.

"Really? You can do it?"

Gunnar nodded. Bent look pleased, and he turned to his menu. So did Gunnar, but everything was in Danish. "Do you think they have any real sandwiches here?" said Gunnar, "With two pieces of bread?"

"That can be done," said Bent. "What would you like?"

"A BLT. I could use that now."

When their lunches came, Bent also had a BLT on toasted sourdough. "I'd forgotten about these. I loved them in America."

"Best sandwich in the world."

Bent talked about when he lived in West Lafayette, going to Purdue where he got his first degree. He'd liked America a lot and seemed to know all things Purdue. An earlier alumnus, John McNamara, was one of the original M's in M & M candies. The first astronaut on the moon, Neil Armstrong, and the last astronaut on the moon, Eugene Cernan, were both Purdue graduates. "And I really liked the snow there in Indiana, too," he said.

"A love of snow we have in common," said Gunnar.

"Tell me about nearly dying yesterday," said Bent. "Did you see the light-at-the-end-of-the-tunnel thing?"

"I didn't. I was dreaming that I was just a brain, no body at all. I was floating in a mist in outer space. It was very lonely, I have to say. I'd have to stare at the Big Dipper for eons."

"That's amazing," said Bent, now thoroughly captivated. "*Fantastisk!*"

"Fantastic?"

"How lucky you got to experience that and come back. Hamlet — a Dane, you know — said no one comes back to explain, but you did. He spent a whole play contemplating it, and one trip to Denmark and — bang — you're an expert. Maybe you can work that into your speech tomorrow."

"On physics?"

"Physicists want to know about death. Doesn't everybody? Isn't that in part why we're investigating Bose-Einstein condensates, to understand the universe, to understand if there's purpose, a design to everything?"

"Really?" He thought about it. "No. I'm not into condensates to see if there's life after death. I'm sure there's not."

"All the more reason to talk about what happened to you and your relation to physics."

"I don't know what my relation to anything is anymore," Gunnar confessed, feeling its truth.

"Sorry to focus on *Hamlet,* but his castle is just up the road in Helsingør, which Shakespeare called Elsinor, and we Danes all know the story well. It took Hamlet's being poisoned to realize death is about nothingness. 'The rest is silence,' says Hamlet. That means you have to live in the moment. That's also what Heidegger was trying to say."

"The German philosopher?"

"Yes. Everything's philosophy. Even physics."

Gunnar liked this guy.

"After lunch, I'll show you your new lab," said Bent. "Give you some keys and have someone take you on a tour of the place. Then I'll come get you about four p.m., so you can talk a half-hour later," said Bent.

"Bring it on," said Gunnar, ready to punch destiny in the eyeballs.

CHAPTER NINETEEN

"CHAOS IS INHERENT IN ALL
COMPOUNDED THINGS. STRIVE ON WITH
DILIGENCE."

— BUDDHA

As they walked to the Institute, Bent gave Gunnar a short, fast tour of old Copenhagen. They strode to the Strøget, a winding walking street full of shops and cafes, which looked Christmasy in the snow with snow-booted people. "It's Europe's longest walking street at 1,111 meters long," said Bent. "I love that number. Many of these buildings are from the 17th Century, when King Christian the Fourth went on a building rampage constructing in the Dutch Renaissance style. Also, we're within the walls of the original fort built in the twelfth century."

The man had facts. Bent probably did this many times before, meeting visitors at the station and whisking them to the Institute. Gunnar would say, "Oh" and "Interesting" to at least appear he was listening.

As Bent talked, Gunnar watched shop owners shovel or sweep away the snow. Where they did, the brick underneath was shiny and wet. It was as if the snow wasn't clear what to be: fluffy and white or just water.

The colorful window displays drew shoppers. Gunnar and Bent passed windows of sweaters, lingerie, crystal, china plates like the ones on the walls at the Tornsens', and many Christmas decorations for trees. They passed narrow cafes and chocolate shops. Bent pointed to a small restaurant, Det Lille Apotek. "The name means 'The Little Drugstore', and it's Copenhagen's oldest bar and restaurant, in operation since 1720 — it was a pharmacy before that."

At this point, Gunnar felt deeply anxious. At first, he thought it was because of the presentation, but he quickly worked out in his head what he'd tell his audience. He'd begin with some first day remarks that he created for his Atomic and Quantum Physics II class and then talk about his research. He always had a lot to say about that. Still, the anxiety didn't go away.

They passed a small church where a man was walking behind a snow blower that threw a huge white arch of snow. Gunnar then knew why he was anxious. He was like that man: alone, lonely, and focused on his work. It occurred to Gunnar he'd never looked at another person and thought "lonely," but what was different was the lump that sat in Gunnar's throat. The lump was often in his throat lately. Sometimes his whole chest cavity was that very thing, a separateness that wouldn't go away. Although he'd lived alone in Madison, he'd never felt particularly lonely before. He had yearnings, yes, but not feeling isolated or forlorn.

Lonely wasn't good. He didn't want Denmark to be about loneliness, yet each step he took with Bent talking, he felt lonelier. Maybe he was just a brain floating in mist. What a god-awful way to live.

This reminded him of a lunch in the University Club, a place open to university faculty and staff. One Friday, tables were scarce and he sat with a man his age who introduced himself as Pete, a biological anthropologist. Gunnar asked him what the heck was that, what was he researching? Pete said, "Love as a phenomenon in the brain."

"Where else would it be a phenomenon?" Gunnar had said without thinking.

Pete held his forefinger aloft. "Most people spend their lives looking for love, but do they really examine what it is? That's what I'm doing."

Gunnar had thought it was a waste of grant money, but to be friendly he asked, "So what happens to a brain in love?"

Pete grinned. "When you're in love, dopamine floods the primitive lizard-part of your brain. Then there's the testosterone receptors in your hypothalamus, and the norepinephrine that's produced, which helps you focus the good effects of the dopamine on the object of your love. That is, you look at the person you love, and your brain rewards you with feeling great."

"It's all chemicals?"

"Neurons in specific regions of your brain light up first, depending on the kind of love you're feeling: lust, attachment, or romance. We've broken love down into those three different types: lust, attachment, and romance. Each type stimulates a different part of the brain. We can look at your brain activity and see what type of love you have."

"So you're saying," said Gunnar, "first comes brain activity, then brain chemistry."

"Exactly," said Pete. "The neurons, once stimulated, call forth your brain chemistry."

Gunnar nodded and ate his meatball sandwich. He always loved meeting other scientists. What they did among the ninety natural elements always stood in contrast to his work.

"For instance, with lust," said Pete, "the caudate part of your brain — the area for cravings and habits like bike riding — is all astir."

"Sex is akin to riding a bike?"

"We don't know why, other than once you learn, you don't forget." The man held a straight face for a second, then laughed. "That's the best we can figure it. It seems strange to us, too. Lust also lights up the hypothalamus and amygdala areas of the brain.

"Romance looks very different from lust in brain scans," Pete continued. "When you can only think of that person, where she could be God as far as you're concerned, you stimulate the ventral tegmental area in the midbrain. That area produces dopamine, a powerful neurotransmitter that affects pleasure and motivation. The more dopamine, the better you feel. It's new love.

"The last kind, attachment, is associated with prairie voles, field rodents from the Midwest that mate for life. There's nothing more faithful than a prairie vole."

"It's the Midwest — they're Lutheran," Gunnar had said.

Pete laughed. "People who find attachment are monogamous and like it. When there's strong attachment, the ventral pallidum part of your brain is alive."

"That part of my brain is wizened, then," said Gunnar. He said it then as a joke, but now he felt it was probably real. Here he was in a foreign country, and he didn't know anyone — Kara was the closest, and she was not available. Lust, romance, and attachment were all falling fast. This was his true science of love.

"People pine for love, people kill for love, they live for love, they die for love," Pete had said. He told him of a study at the college where students were asked about love, with two of the questions being, "Have you ever been rejected by someone who you truly loved?" and "Have you ever dumped someone who deeply loved you?" Ninety-five percent of the people said yes to both. "That shows almost no one makes it through unscathed."

So Gunnar was scathed, now, was that it? Pete had explained that rejection still lit up parts of the brain associated with romance and attachment — perhaps rejection made a person more focused than ever.

"Why do you study love?" Gunnar had asked him. "Isn't that something best left for the English majors?"

"With no disrespect to your cold atoms or English majors," said Pete, "but the science of love may well be the only thing worth studying. Romantic love is perhaps the most addictive substance on earth. Haven't you ever thought of someone so much, she's camping in your head? You can't eat, you can't breathe?"

Yes, thought Gunnar now. And you can't walk well or listen to your boss give a travelogue. Kara had pitched her tent in his brain for months, and now she wouldn't leave. What was he supposed to do? He wished he knew more from

Pete. Gunnar had to be more than a few bundles of neurons that were probably dying on their vines as he walked. He had to be more than what he wasn't.

Bent paused in front of a display of Holmegaard glassware that featured a thick heavy bottom. Each glass had slightly angled sides like a cooling tower for a nuclear power plant, and a curvy top lip. "One thing about us Danes is that modern design of even the simplest things — glasses — can be art. We make it a part of everyday life, so we can enjoy something a little extra."

Gunnar wished he could enjoy something a little extra, but all he had was the emptiness and anxiety that was as sharp as the bells of the Salvation Army Santa ringing across the street in front of a department store.

Soon they passed a brick cylindrical building that Bent explained was part of the University of Copenhagen. "The *Rundetårn*, the Round Tower, with the oldest functioning observatory and planetarium in Europe — built by Christian the Fourth in 1642." It looked like a Holmegaard glass without the lip at the top. "It's attached to Trinity Church, which was also a big project by Christian the Fourth."

They passed a big castle in a park — Christian the Fourth's summer castle — and crossed a street dividing two rectangular lakes with reeds near the lakeshore. The lake was frozen, which told him that it was below freezing here more than he'd been led to believe.

Kara, Kara, Kara, why can't you be my stara?

Soon they were at the small cluster of red-tiled buildings, three- and four-stories tall, that made up the Niels Bohr Institute. Gunnar knew its history — that it was part of the University of Copenhagen unifying four of the physical sciences, exploring the smallest sub-atomic particles to stars and planets. "We have ten research groups," said Bent, "Twelve science centers, and 710 physics students, eighty-five of whom are going for their Ph.D."

Bent looked at his watch. "Mercy. Let me show you your new lab, and I have a key for you."

Gunnar looked at his own watch. "Actually, if you can park me in front of a computer and give me a flash drive, I'll spend the time making a Powerpoint presentation for my speech."

"Ya, ya. Easily arranged."

"Is there a projector where I'm talking?"

"Oh, yes."

Bent took him inside and introduced him to his administrative assistant, Kirsten, a young woman with a lot of enthusiasm. She found a flash drive and took him to an empty desk with a computer.

Over the next hour, Gunnar plunged in, finding photos on the Internet and from his own spot on UW's network, to create a Powerpoint slide show that seemed to order itself. So much fell into place, and he felt relieved. He was inspired not to use the introduction to his most advanced class, but rather, his most basic class, the one for nonmajors. The Powerpoint would keep him on track and focused. He was so single-minded on the project that he didn't hear people had entered the room. "We found you at last," came a familiar voice. Gunnar turned to see the grinning faces of his former research partners, Harry and Carl.

"What the hell?" said Gunnar, confused. But his heart lifted.

"Happy to see you, too," said Carl.

"No, I mean — "

"Travel funds," said Carl. "It's a big conference."

"A last minute deal," said Harry. "After our research crashed and finals were done, we looked at what to do next. Here was this conference."

"Except could you make yourself more difficult to find?" said Carl. "Didn't you get our emails?"

"No."

"And you didn't give your mother Kara's phone or address? How's that possible?"

"I was in such a hurry, and she didn't ask. I only learned her parents' phone number today." Gunnar looked down. The deep darkness he'd felt only yesterday came crashing back. He was such a failure. How could he tell them? "Listen," he said. "Things aren't working out with Kara."

"What do you mean?" said Carl. "Are you arguing? That's just part of couplehood. My first year with Jolene was probably the worst. The thing is not to always try to be right, as you can do."

"Kara's living with another guy."

Harry and Carl both looked stunned.

"So where are you staying?" said Harry.

"Kara's parents," said Gunnar.

Carl looked even more perplexed. "Kara's living with a guy, and you're living with her parents?"

"Yikes," said Harry.

"You're probably regretting you ever met me," said Gunnar. "I fucked up everything — first our research and now my whole life. All for Kara. I'm the most pathetic person in Denmark."

"No you're not," said Carl. "That crazy Danish group Abba is."

"Abba's Swedish," said Harry. "And can't you see Gunnar's upset?"

"I'm sorry," said Carl, looking it. "I'm just trying to take your mind off of things."

"Good idea." Harry pulled out a brochure from his back pocket for the Museum Erotica Copenhagen. It had a naked woman seductively leaning against the lap of Hans Christian Andersen on the statue that Gunnar had seen next to City Hall — the same lap where a three-year-old had been sitting. "Maybe this will take your mind off of things," said Harry. He opened the brochure to show Gunnar wax sculptures of naked women and a photo of Marilyn Monroe in a slinky dress singing to President Kennedy. Apparently the museum now owned the dress.

"It isn't going to do it for me," said Gunnar. "I'm sorry you guys came all this way to see me."

"How about we go get a drink?" said Carl.

"I can't. I'm speaking in an hour to a bunch of grad students and others at the conference."

Carl and Harry, like synchronized swimmers, looked at their watches in tandem. They each nodded.

"How about you give us a tour of the place," said Harry. "I always wanted to see where Niel's Bohr worked."

"I don't know anything," said Gunnar. "They just gave me a key to my lab and a room number, but I haven't even been there yet."

"Let's go see it," said Carl, smiling, ever the optimist.

"All right," said Gunnar. "Let me make sure my Powerpoint is saved on the flash drive."

After he checked, they went downstairs and, following the door numbers, took a few big turns and ended up in a back hallway. They found the right door. Gunnar's key opened it. He flicked on the lights.

Gunnar's eyes quickly flicked over the table-top equipment that nonscientists might think was a futuristic car engine — lots of tubes and wires. After a few moments, all three of them gave their own version of a gasp of pleasure. It was similar to what they'd had in Madison, yet each element was in a different spot and there was more of it. The two squarish glass magneto-optical traps, or MOTs, were where the gaseous atoms entered a high vacuum state. With lasers and magnets, the atoms would be cooled within a few millionths of absolute zero — but the atoms needed to be even colder for BECs.

Outside of the MOTs were the diode lasers, and nearby, an array of coils for a quadrupole magnetic field. The coils themselves heated up, so the coils each needed to be cooled by water from clear plastic tubing. The final destination of the atoms was the Time-Orbiting-Potential trap, or TOP, where the quadrupole field would bring the atoms to within a few billionths of absolute zero, when BECs were formed. Gunnar hoped to do it with fermionic molecules — which would create a whole new state of matter, different from Bose-Einstein condensates.

"I don't see how you're going to make fermionic condensates," said Harry. "I just don't think you can cool fermions as cold as bosons."

"I agree," said Carl. "How can fermions be evaporative cooled if fermions don't collide with each other?"

Gunnar nodded. "As I was making a Powerpoint just before you came, I had a crazy idea."

"What's that?" said Harry.

"Look here." Gunnar pointed to the two MOTs. "What if we cooled bosons in one MOT and fermions in the other. Then what if we then bring the two together, so that the bosons act as a kind of refrigerant to the fermions."

Carl gasped the way Archimedes must have when first understanding water displacement in a full bathtub. "That's brilliant," said Carl. "The bosons won't mind colliding with the fermions, so you'll have evaporative cooling."

"Exactly, but we'd have to rig this thing a bit differently to have a third MOT."

Harry looked at his watch. "Let's try it. It's yours to use, right?"

"I suppose," said Gunnar. "If nothing else, I'll get a feel for this equipment. I've got forty-five minutes until I have to leave." He then cackled and started flipping switches, turning on the lasers and magnets. Harry, meanwhile, found a third MOT and was happy to add it.

Carl looked over the choices of gases they had. "What element should we use, Gunnar?

"I was thinking lithium. Lithium-7 is a boson and lithium-6 is a fermion. Because they have the same configuration of electrons, they'll be chemically identical."

Harry laughed. "Man, we've missed working with you."

All three were so focused, they worked efficiently and mostly silently, like doctors performing microsurgery. The time went quickly. With only a few minutes left, they were ready to try it. The two lithium clouds cooled in the MOT. "I'm going to combine them now," said Gunnar, and when he did, the temperature meters showed it was working. The cloud was condensing and getting colder.

"All right — the final step, said Gunnar," nudging the cloud into the last chamber, the last trap. Their eyes went to screens. Their monitors, for what seemed a mere second, showed a condensate.

"You did it — you fucking did it!" cried Harry. "You created a fermionic condensate."

But it was gone.

"Well, we did, but I didn't record it." He looked at the time. "Are you sure we did it?"

"It was so fast," said Carl. "Let's try it again."

"Shit, I've got to go," said Gunnar, looking at the time.

"Man, you're going to be a hero world-wide," said Harry.

"We've got to recreate it and record everything. I'm not sure we actually did it," said Gunnar. Want to try it again later?"

"We can't. We have a flight tonight," said Carl. "But it was your idea. We were just your friends."

"Just my friends? No. You're more than that. You've brought me back."

Like bosons, they collided in a group hug, and Gunnar felt the best he had in months.

"We'll always have Copenhagen," said Harry.

They rushed out of there. They found Bent outside the door of the auditorium where Gunnar would speak.

"Did you see your lab?" Bent said.

"Oh, yeah," said Gunnar and grabbed his hand. "It's incredible. Thank you for everything. Let me introduce you to my friends and research partners from Wisconsin, Harry Boril and Carl Andresen."

"I know these guys," said Bent. "They've been here before. It was you who hasn't traveled."

"Ah," said Gunnar.

"Let me go introduce you to the audience, and then you can speak. Do you have a flash drive for your Powerpoint?"

"Yes," said Gunnar, handing it over. Bent whispered to the person next to him, gave her the flash drive, and she ran into the auditorium.

"We think he made a fermionic condensate just now" said Harry to Bent.

"What?"

"I'll explain later," said Gunnar.

Another assistant pulled on Bent's sleeve. "Go on in and make your introduction now. They're waiting."

"Oh, yes, yes."

Bent spoke into the microphone, but Gunnar wasn't listening. Instead, he concentrated on not being nervous. Too much had happened that day, and he found himself hyperventilating. He only paid attention to his breathing, willing himself to slow down. He thought of the first words he'd say and the first slide he'd use. He was in the zone.

Bent's assistant tapped Gunnar on the shoulder. "Go on in. Here's a remote to advance your slides. The projector is on, and your first slide is showing."

"Thank you," he said, and then Gunnar heard the applause. Gunnar walked on stage. The spotlights were on the center part of the stage in the small amphitheatre, and on the screen at the back of the stage was the title of his speech. It said, "Bosons, Fermions, Bose-Einstein, and Us." Bent grinned.

When Gunnar stood in the light, the people in the seats were at best silhouettes. He could see Harry and Carl's forms in the front row, which took away some of the shakiness he felt in his legs.

"Good afternoon, and thank you for coming to this, despite the change in speakers," said Gunnar. "Thank you, Dr. Herskind, for inviting me. I'm Gunnar Gunderson, a name which might make you think I'm from here, but the truth is, I was born and raised in Wisconsin and have never traveled to another country until now. Forgive me if I seem out of my element. In many ways I am."

He glanced to his note card and the pause was all he needed. He put the card into his back pocket, holding only his remote slide changer.

"On the first day of my introductory course for undergraduate non-majors, I tell them that according to one perhaps-crackpot wave theory in physics, basic matter first forms as two competing swirls." He clicked a slide that showed two connected rings, perpendicular to each other.

"I tell them, according to this theory, that one loop is electric — the male loop — and the other is magnetic and female. The male loop tries to be free, and it wants to grab onto as many different female loops as possible." People laughed, just as his undergraduates had.

"The universe is about duality, about sex. This comes from Dr. Chaim Tejman's unified field theory, which of course isn't proven and few people buy. Yet for a couple of years, his acquaintance Karol Wojtyla, who later became Pope John Paul the Second, spoke to Tejman's physics students on philosophy and religion. The future pope discussed his notion of souls predating anyone's birth and how souls are immortal. Tejman considers souls much like matter — that they cannot be created or destroyed, but that they transform from one state to another and back again when you are born and when you die. It'd be nice to think that, but my own influences show our beings to be a complex mix of electrical charges and brain chemistry."

The few faces he could see, including his friends looked rapt. This wasn't the usual speech.

"I will agree with Tejman that the creation of our universe is sophisticated beyond our wildest imagination. All of you are probably familiar with Bose-Einstein condensates, so you know the universe is odd. Matter near absolute zero settles into wavelike energy packets, and it appears that atoms can appear in two and more places at once. It does not follow Newtonian physics at all. This is worth exploring. Does it relate to our souls or sex? Give me a few more months in Denmark, and maybe I'll know more."

With the claps, he knew he was on the right path. Keep pushing.

"I nearly died a few nights ago — a bad reaction to something I ate." He wasn't lying. He'd eaten pills. "And it certainly has me thinking about what I do with Bose-Einstein condensates — BECs."

He clicked on his remote and brought up a slide of what looked like three multicolored stalagmites, phalluses colored in a spectrum that went from blue to green to yellow. The slide was marked "Rb-87."

"BECs were predicted by Einstein in 1925, but were only realized in 1995 in laboratories at JILA in Boulder and at MIT in Boston. This slide of rubidium is their proof of a condensate — that atoms suddenly march in lockstep and become superfluid."

His next slide looked similar, but instead of stalagmites, they looked like hamburgers in the same colors.

"The original BECs were held in place by a quadrupole magnetic field for up to a thousand seconds. Soon researchers wanted to spin these BECs to see if vortices could be created, and, if so, it might tell a lot about superfluidity. We've been able to do so using laser rotation. This slide shows sodium atoms set in motion, creating a BEC sixty micrometers wide and forming a regular lattice of vortices."

The next slide was captioned "Bosons and Fermions Near Absolute Zero." The screen was divided into two, one marked "Bosons" and the other marked "Fermions" and each side had what looked to be spectrographs of something at three different nanokelvin temperatures.

"These are pictures of ultracold lithium atom clouds, produced by physicists at Rice University. Lithium has two stable isotopes — one bosonic, the other fermionic. As you know, we can divide the world as we know it into two parts, bosons and fermions, and the differences have to do with spin and their very identities. At the simplest level, bosons are subatomic particles like photons, and they can occupy the same space together. Fermions cannot. We can think of fermions as people. No two people can sit in the exact same spot at the same time. However, bosons can.

"What I'll be doing in Copenhagen over the next six months or more is exploring fermionic condensates, seeing if we can coax a fermion gas into a similar state as a BEC. What will it mean if we can?"

He hit his remote control and brought up a picture of himself with Kara sitting on a picnic blanket on a lawn.

"The way I'm thinking of it these days is say you fall in love. How do you know it's love? You feel in love, so does that count? She says she loves you, and you say you love her, does that count?"

He clicked the remote, and a slide showed Kara under a sheet, smiling. "There are other readings you take that suggest you're in love, and it feels like the center of the universe to you. You must be in love."

The next slide showed him smiling wide.

"We want our lovers to be bosons — atoms that work together, doing the same things. In fact, we want to be one unit, inseparable from each other. But more and more people seem to be fermions — separate units, loners, inherently repelling each other."

He clicked the remote, and a middle-aged man and woman, their faces close to each other's, were locked in anger. "You worry that while new love is indeed bosonic, the more you're together, you get fermionic. You don't want to be like this at all — bitter, resentful, lonely."

He clicked, and a slide showed Kara and him holding hands. "These two states, love/not love are supposedly mutually exclusive, but those in a long marriage can attest these two feelings happen at the same time."

A few chuckles and gasps showed he still had their attention.

"Same with BECs. They seem to be waves, but also particles. We quantum physicists want to know so much. We want to know the true nature of atoms, both bosons and fermions, and figure out what they might do for us. We scientists are also part of a very real world, too. We want to know love and know how to create it, keep it, measure it, hold it to ourselves. We want to know about death, and will we continue somehow? We want to know about *thinking* itself. What happens to our thinking when we die? What can we do with our thinking now? Can science help mankind? Can we stop global warming and overpopulation? Can we stop hate and killing, or will we just invent more gadgets to entertain ourselves till extinction?"

He clicked once more, which gave a totally white screen. Its reflection poured onto the audience, letting him see the people at last. Some looked sad. Some looked deep in thought. He didn't mean to bum anyone out, but no one was laughing anymore. In total, they looked stunned.

"I'm trying to understand the design of the smallest thing, the atom, and perhaps if I can understand that, then I can understand ordinary things like why every pen in my jar on my desk doesn't write. Why do I keep misplacing my cell phone, yet I know the integer spin of strontium atoms. Why do I know that falling in love is fun, but keeping it is something else."

He turned to Bent, whom he saw in the front row. "Bent today gave me a fine tour of Copenhagen, but before that, he was intrigued that I may have died yesterday and come back to life. I do feel I've done that, and I'm seeing things differently. You suggested, Bent, that I bring up the topic in this speech. I hope you liked it."

With that, he stopped. The audience appeared dumbfounded. Harry and Carl in the front row looked dumbfounded — but then their faces changed to grins, and they were the first to clap — good to have friends — and others joined in. People even stood to give him an ovation. He bowed and left.

CHAPTER TWENTY

"A SHIP IS SAFE IN HARBOR, BUT THAT'S NOT WHAT SHIPS ARE FOR."

— WILLIAM SHEDD

On the train back to Roskilde, totally dark outside even though it was just after five, Gunnar found himself staring out the window. He noticed how he could concentrate on an object, such as a lighted apartment building, and it'd be sharp for a second before it passed from view. Otherwise, he could gaze without focus, and everything was a blur of lights as if he was going down a funhouse slide. He loved this. He loved that he could take trains. He truly felt lucky.

He looked around at his fellow passengers. A young woman read what appeared to be a Danish novel. A teenage couple shared an earbud each from the cord of an MP3 player, smiling at each other. He could tell from the way their heads bounced together in rhythm that they were listening to music. An older woman slept. A young man in front of him spoke softly into a cell phone, finished up, and folded the phone away. This was a great way to travel. It was just a great day.

It occurred to him that Kara's parents might be wondering if he'd be there for dinner. They were probably wondering, too, how it'd gone with Bent. He tapped the young man in front of him on the shoulder, and the kid said "Ya?" and turned around.

"I'm a visitor and I was wondering," said Gunnar, "if I might borrow your cell phone for a moment? I need to call to Roskilde to say I'm arriving soon."

"Ya, sure," said the young man, handing his flip phone over.

Gunnar dialed the eight numbers that he'd only learned that morning. "*Det er Ingeborg,*" came Kara's mother's familiar voice.

"Hi, it's Gunnar," he said. "I'm on the Roskilde train. I'd love to join you for dinner, if it's not too late."

"Oh, *godt,* Gunnar, I — Yes — I'm not sure how to say this." She sounded awkward.

"What? Is something wrong?" The young man whose phone he borrowed, turned around again, curious.

"Your sister called," said Ingeborg.

"My sister?" He remembered he'd given Patty Kara's number. Kara must have then told Patty where he was living. Patty and his mother would now know.

"Apparently," said Ingeborg, "your mother's been in a car accident. She's alive, your sister said, but in the hospital. Why don't I come with the car to pick you up at the station?"

"One second." He tapped the young man on the shoulder again. "Can this phone call the United States? I'll gladly pay you for it. It's an emergency."

"Do you know the country and state codes?"

"Codes?"

"I can help you," said the young man.

Gunnar held his index finger up to say to one second and put the phone to his ear again. "Ingeborg? I can use this phone to call my sister. Don't worry about picking me up, I'll take a taxi — but thank you."

"We'll have dinner for you," she said, "and we can help you make arrangements if you need a flight or need to make more calls or anything."

"Thank you," he said. "See you soon."

"*Velbekomme.*"

The young man knew the code for America and punched in all the other numbers Gunnar gave him. The young man handed the phone back, and Gunnar could hear it ringing. His sister answered.

"Patty, it's me in Denmark," said Gunnar. "I'm on a train and I just heard about Mom. What kind of accident? Is she okay?"

Patty started crying.

"What? She didn't die, did she?"

"Mom's in a coma," she squeaked out. "On life support."

"Oh, God. How did this happen?"

"Mom and her friend Lorelei took a trip to the Minnesota Zoo."

"They drove to Minneapolis?"

"It's not that far away. You know how she likes wolverines."

"Wolverines?"

"Yes. They saw them, had a good time, and were returning when they were coming off the off-ramp on I-90. Mom'd been driving for like five hours. It was dark, and a wolverine just darted out from nowhere."

"But there aren't any wolverines in Madison. They're arctic creatures."

"It could've been a dog or whatever. Who cares, Gunnar. Mom cranked her wheel sharp while hitting the brakes, and they flipped. She's in a coma."

"God…" Gunnar could see the well-lit Roskilde cathedral, its two spires shooting heavenward. "Roskilde. Roskilde," said a male voice over the speakers and Gunnar could feel the train slow down.

"Patty, I'm going to get the first plane I can. I'll call you back when I know more."

"Okay," said Patty. "I love you."

"I love you, too."

When Gunnar stepped out of the train, his mind whirled at what he'd have to do. Kara's parents would help him get a flight and probably take him to the airport tonight or tomorrow morning. He'd have to call Bent, tell him he'd be back way before the semester started. It wasn't critical to call

Bent, but still if something came up over the next week or two, Bent should know he wouldn't be around. Gunnar would have to be back before the semester started — no time to recreate the fermionic condensate until his return.

He needed a taxi. There were always a few standing out front. Before he stepped outside, an odd thought hit him: were there Danish wolverines? If his mother came out of a coma, she'd surely like a stuffed toy one, right? He should assume she'd wake up. His expectation could help her wake up. If she were still in a coma, he could talk in her ear. Mom, wake up, he'd say. I have a wolverine for you.

When Gunnar stepped out of the train station and stood at the top of the steps under the big arch, there were no taxis. He glanced up the street and down. Nothing. However, a few blocks away the cathedral stood swathed in light.

There was absolutely no logic in his hurrying toward the cathedral, but he moved as if the very life of his mother depended on it. He knew it made no sense, but when he was a teenager, after his father was in the hospital with a heart attack, Gunnar hadn't prayed for his father because Gunnar hadn't believed in that stuff, and his dad died. He'd never whipped himself over it, but still — what if Gunnar had prayed? The agnostic in him told him it would've been as effective as milking a unicorn — but part of him had always wondered.

Gunnar had hurried into the hospital then, and as he walked toward the room number he'd been given, his mother stood just outside his father's hospital room. Her expression said everything. She took Gunnar's hands and said, "I'm sorry. He passed."

"When?"

"About two hours ago."

"I'm sorry. I just got the message."

She let him go into the room by himself. His dad lay frozen in the bed under a sheet, head slightly tilted back, and his mouth an "oh" like the Edvard Munch painting of the skeletal guy screaming at the orange-white sky. Seeing Dad not moving in that "oh" showed Dad's last moments weren't great.

"Dad, Dad, Dad," he whispered to the body. "I'm sorry I didn't make it here on time." Gunnar and his friends had been drinking at the quarry. When they'd driven back to his friend's house, his friend's mother told him about the hospital.

Gunnar touched his father's face and was surprised. It was still warm. Gunnar pulled back the sheet to see his father wore a green hospital gown, and his father's chest was exposed. Gunnar placed his palm on his father's chest, and that, too, was still warm, as if his heart had been a hot engine still radiating heat. All the anger Gunnar had seemed to evaporate then and there. His dad had kept some warmth for him.

Now, however, Gunnar had the strange sense the cathedral had been lit for him and he had this chance. Please, dear universal life force, if there was one. Let her live. As he quickened his pace, he considered was he being a hypocrite? Fuck it. Who cares? Not stepping on cracks or knocking on wood never hurt anything. So what's a cathedral?

He kept looking up at the spires for direction. He was getting closer. As he marched on the narrow sidewalk down one side street, the people in front of him seemed to sense his mission, and they moved to give him room.

At the next intersection, he took a right, and the huge gothic church, all brick with twin towers rising high from the modest buildings of the town, stood before him, bathed in light, its arched wooden doorway closed. Of course it'd be closed — it was a winter evening. As he approached the door, however, he came to the posted hours: 10 a.m. to 4 p.m., and the cost of admission was 25 kroner. Was this a cruel trick? Was this to show how stupid his thinking was?

Two things happened right then. First, it started to snow again. Large flakes settled into the light like baby fingernails floating, and then Bach's Tocata and Fugue in D minor burst from inside the church. He knew this piece from Allison, practicing over and over again after she'd bought a Yamaha electronic keyboard and took lessons. It could be no accident he knew the piece. The cathedral's powerful organ built to a loud crescendo as if God had ordered it, and then the door opened. Gunnar hurried over and a man pulling on gloves smiled and spoke in Danish to him.

"I'm sorry," said Gunnar, "I don't understand."

"Ah, the Rasmussen memorial? You must be the cousin from America."

"Yes, one of them," said Gunnar.

"Welcome," said the man, indicating the door. Gunnar entered.

Gunnar entered and was immediately stunned by the high vaulted ceilings, white walls, the slate floor, and the grand main aisle that led to the huge altarpiece, intricate and elegant. A man in a fancy robe with a tunic stood at the lectern. He must be the minister or priest or whatever Lutherans had. People sat in the pews. A table near him had some brochures or something, and one small stack had the word "English" on a label beneath it. He picked one up, assuming it'd explain the Rassmussen service, and he sat in a pew toward the back.

He read, "Built in the 12th and 13th centuries, this was Scandinavia's first Gothic cathedral to be built of brick, and it encouraged the spread of this style throughout northern Europe. The cathedral has been the mausoleum of the Danish royal family since the 15th century." Ah. The brochure was for the tourists.

Gunnar thought about how people had been sitting in these pews for over seven hundred years. In Madison, the oldest church was not even a hundred fifty, and it burned up a few years ago — gone. The oldest gathering place he'd go to regularly was a pancake house, fifty-four years old. The original owners were still alive. This place — how many sermons have been spoken? Weddings held? Eulogies given? How many people have streamed through? He felt humbled.

He looked down the main aisle again to soak in the arches, the large fluted pipes of the pipe organ, and some of the intricate gold-leafed carvings around the pipes. He felt then a surge of hope. This was the place to be. Dear God, I'll call you God, save the life of my mother.

The man who'd let him in was now talking to the priest, then pointing to Gunnar.

"*Godt,*" said the priest into his microphone. "I understand Herr Vinter's young cousin Leonard has arrived from America. Would you mind standing, Leonard?"

Everyone turned to look at Gunnar. He didn't know what else to do. He stood.

"We are ready for your words, if you are."

Tears came to his eyes — he couldn't control it — and he said, "Excuse me a moment," and he turned and hurried for the front door. Just as he reached for the knob, it burst open, hitting him. "Oh, I'm so sorry," said the young man entering in a bright ski jacket. This must be the real cousin, Gunnar realized, so he said, "No problem. They're waiting for you to speak."

"Thank you," said the young man who then hurried past.

Once outside the cathedral, Gunnar looked up again at the spires, and he felt dizzy, and, reorienting himself, he hurried down the side road that should take him to the station. All he could think about was his mother in a similar hospital and hospital bed as his father had been and maybe she was gasping for breath and her face would be an "oh." The flight over had been something like seventeen hours. Could she hold on for that long? He had so much to do.

At the sound of splashing water, he realized he'd been walking down a hill. There had been no hill on the way to the cathedral. The splashing sound was from a fountain lit by a street light, and under the falling snow, he looked at the fountain nestled into a wall. Water poured out from a large head of a lion — no, it was a man with wavy hair. Perhaps he was a Norse god.

In an instant, he was struck: he had seen this in a picture. — of Kara. Peder had held her here. The word over the figure's head had been partly obscured then, but now it was fully visible: "Maglekilde." What did it mean?

Across the street, a small two-story building in gray was wedged among a lot of trees. They were apartments because there were three front doors, and in one of the larger upper story windows he could see a couch. One of the doors, which had a light on over it, now opened. A woman with red hair emerged. She was in a dark coat like most Danes and had a little dog on a leash.

"Gunnar, what are you doing here?"

"Kara?"

"Did my mother give you the address?"

He sensed her anger. He should be the one outraged. In fact, his body tensed, ready for a fight. The peace he'd had only moments earlier vanished. He should not give in. He was the better person. He pointed to the fountain's head and said, "What is this, a lion or a god?"

"It's Neptune. Roskilde is a town of many springs, and this one's the largest.

"This is where you live with Peder?"

She nodded.

"Perhaps I can buy you a drink," he said, letting his resentment flow. "And you can throw it in my face."

"I was honest with you. Really, we were both rather naïve."

"We were in love," Gunnar blurted.

"In lust, perhaps. It'd been nearly a year for me, and I'm guessing as long for you."

"Love isn't just sex."

"No, but sex can fool people."

"I gotta go," he said. "Point me the way to the train station."

She pointed up the hill. "I'll walk with you a little," she said. "So why are you here?"

"I needed to see the cathedral."

"It's closed at this time."

"So I learned."

"How did you end up at my place?"

"Everything is an accident. Our whole lives are — fuck. This whole thing..." How could he put it into words? "You really did a number on me."

"I'm sorry. I hadn't planned on falling for Peder. It was unexpected."

"How were you even open to that?"

"The heart has its own reasons," she said.

"And those reasons make no sense."

"Do they ever?"

He blinked. Maybe she had a point. "So how is it? How's living with Peder?"

"Godt."

"Just godt?" He could hear anger in his own voice.

"You want to hear about our sex life or what movies we see? Or would you like to hear we argue once in a while?"

He said nothing. His stomach lurched. He thought he'd been over her, but then here she was, walking next to him, very real. He stared at her dog, a Yorkie, which was walking fast on its little legs, not inquisitive at all.

"I suppose I should let you hate me and leave it at that," she said, "but you weren't innocent in all this, you see? When I think of your e-mails, how *romantisk* they were. Maybe I just wanted to believe in that."

"You're blaming *me*?"

"You fooled yourself. Your e-mail to me was always about what you were doing and planning."

"And you were supposed to tell me what you were doing and planning."

"I couldn't tell you that I met someone and I had doubts about us. I didn't know things would go the way they would with Peder." She looked at him bitterly. "You were planning your sabbatical. I couldn't ruin your sabbatical!"

"No, just ruin my life!"

She spun on her heel, giving him an angry glare, and stomped away from him. At first he was stunned, then he sprang for her. She started running, too, but he caught up with her and grabbed her shoulder.

"You killed me," he shouted.

"No, I didn't!" she shouted back. "You're perfectly alive."

They were each breathing harder from their run and their feelings.

"I'm sorry," she said. "I'm sorry, I'm sorry. Okay?"

He shook his head.

She frowned.

Then he nodded. "You're right. I suppose I wasn't the most adept of lovers — at least in terms of understanding what you wanted. You're right. I didn't ask things. I guess I just expected." He looked up the hill at the spires. "Also, I suppose I didn't ask because I didn't want to hear any wrong answers."

"Yes?" she said.

"I'm sorry."

"You're sorry?" she said, surprised.

"I am. When it comes down to it, you've helped me. This has all made me see what I want — what I still want. Yes, I love being a scientist, but I also need love. Is that wrong?"

"No," she said.

"Okay," he said. They stood before each other like dazed boxers.

"My mother's been in a car accident. I'm about to fly back to Wisconsin."

"Oh, Gunnar. I'm so sorry."

They reached for each other. They hugged. She then walked with him to the station where there were now two taxis. He hugged Kara once more, bent into a taxi, and gave the address that he knew so well. "Femten Dronning Margrethesvej."

CHAPTER TWENTY-ONE

"AN EXPERT IS A PERSON WHO HAS
MADE ALL THE MISTAKES THAT CAN BE
MADE IN A VERY NARROW FIELD."

— NIELS BOHR

On the plane, Gunnar found himself wedged between an older ruddy-faced man whose hands shook — perhaps he had Parkinson's — and a large woman who nervously kept glancing around the plane as if looking for terrorists or signs the plane was breaking up. Her hands like clamps squeezed both arms of her seat, thus leaving nowhere for Gunnar to rest his right elbow. Instead, he tucked both arms close to him underneath a blanket. He felt cold.

Using Ingeborg's help, they had booked the first flight they could out of Copenhagen to Chicago, which had been for the early morning — and he could get only a middle seat because the flight was nearly full. It also cost him double what his original roundtrip fare had been because he wasn't willing to save $500 by waiting another day. He had to get home quickly.

Gunnar stared out the plane's window at the puffy columned clouds, golden with deep shadows in the early morning light. He pictured the physics of a sliding SUV. Its specific gravity was clearly too high, allowing for its easy ability to fall over, and with its large mass and high velocity at the time of the flip, its momentum was colossal. Momentum equals mass times velocity. While some people thought more steel equals more safety, the truth is that other physics were involved.

"*Kaffe?* Coffee?" a voice said, and Gunnar realized he was being spoken to. A petite flight attendant was already handing the ruddy-faced man next to Gunnar a coffee, and Gunnar watched the man concentrate on trying to keep his shake under control. Gunnar cringed. That hot coffee would surely soon shake all over Gunnar. "No thank you," said Gunnar to the young woman.

"Yes, thank you," said the nervous woman next to Gunnar.

Great, Gunnar thought. Let's get an already edgy woman more nervous with coffee, and she could spill it on him, too. He could be burned in stereo.

"Excuse me," said Gunnar, standing, leaving his blanket rumpled on the seat. "I have to use the lavatory."

"Can you wait until the coffee cart passes?" asked the stewardess.

"I can't," said Gunnar. He wanted to add, "Not with you passing out scalding hot stimulants to my seatmates," but he held his tongue. The stewardess pulled the cart forward, allowing the ruddy-faced man to, with a quivering hand, remove his seatbelt and stand. The man's other hand, however, wasn't steady enough, and a wave of hot coffee blurped onto the coffee cart.

"*Undskyld*," said the man to the stewardess, and she responded in rapid Danish, indicating she had plenty more coffee. How wonderful. Gunnar better hide in the head for twenty minutes.

In the lavatory, he sat on the toilet and covered his eyes. What was the point of a person learning so much and then, through death, it disappeared forever? If an atom never stopped moving, why did people have to? He needed her.

His mother's words from her last note returned. *This world is rarely easy.* True. Look at his time in Denmark. Look at his seatmates. The poor gentleman had to shake through each day, and the woman by the window could barely stay in her skin. Why did the world throb with so much difficulty and pain?

He wondered how Patty was doing. He had called her back once he'd secured a flight, and she said she'd pick him up at the airport. His plane would land around three-thirty. With a cracking voice, she had added, "Mom just won't wake up. They won't call it a coma, but she responds to little. They say she shows 'flexion to pain,' which is good. But I think she's dying."

Please no.

Please no.

When Gunnar returned to his seat, his seatmates no longer had their coffee. He also noticed his blanket was now neatly folded. The woman noticed him looking and said, "I'm sorry, but I accidentally spilled my coffee on your blanket."

"Me, too," said the man. "The flight attendant got you another blanket."

"Lucky you weren't here," said the woman.

"Yes, lucky," said Gunnar, taking his seat. He again stared out the window.

After a while, the man said with an accent, "I've always thought the top side of clouds are special, like the far side of the moon. From below, clouds can look so gray, but up here, they are what? God's hopes turned into pillows."

Gunnar looked at the clouds again, then at the man anew. He had to be deep into his sixties, and with the white light reflecting off the clouds, the man's face was soft. His thin white hair revealed a hint of sand color in parts. Gunnar tried to imagine him younger, with thicker all-blond hair, with steady hands, and minus the large potbelly. One of the man's fingers pointed at the clouds, hand quivering, yet he smiled. It was the smile of youth and hope.

"I like it up here," he said.

"Those clouds *are* pretty," said the woman.

"You know," said Gunnar. "I wish I could see that."

---------------→

Gunnar drove Patty's car because she had asked him to. "I'm afraid," she said. "I just don't like driving."

The sun would soon be setting, and Gunnar knew the roads would be getting slicker. Here, leaving O'Hare Airport, there were no clouds, just the darkening sky. Gunnar drove quickly, but he kept aware of the conditions. The physics of friction were still at work.

Patty was dressed all in black, and he had on his bright red ski jacket. He pictured their mother in a green hospital gown beneath a thin sheet, struggling to maintain her tiny hold on this world. She was in intensive care at Meriter Hospital, near the university.

"You have to be prepared, Gunnar," said Patty. "She's getting worse. She has a respirator tube down her throat, electrodes on her skin, something on her finger, and the monitors are beeping away. Yet she just lies there. It's all mechanical sounding."

"The body sometimes slows down to heal itself."

"Mr. Optimist." He shot her a look, but she had a small smile. "I like that about you," she said.

"Thanks."

"Though I thought Kara had knocked the optimism out of you."

"Well..." He stared off at nothing. Patty was right. He had changed. He wanted his mother to be better, but maybe that would not happen.

She looked at him as if hearing his thoughts. "Yes," she said. "Life often sucks."

"I'm trying for hope."

They drove silently for a long time when Patty spoke again. "Does Mom have a will?"

"Why would you think of such a thing now?" he said.

"Do you know what a mess it can be if she doesn't have one? We'll have to go into probate court. Plus her accounts will be frozen, yet some bills will go on, like her mortgage. Do you have extra money to be paying things for her?"

"I'm sure the court will — "

"And even if she has a will, there'll be a lot of details, such as the cable has to be shut off, magazine subscriptions cancelled, her house cleaned and sold."

"Patty."

"And who will get stuck with all the details? You'll be off in Denmark, no doubt, so it'll be me. Death is a lot of details."

"Patty!"

"I'm the one who's always lived near Mom and had to bring her chicken soup when she's been sick or help her with her rose garden, etcetera, etcetera, while you've always lived far away. Denmark far enough for you?"

He squealed into the Meriter Hospital parking garage, a brand new structure for a brand new hospital, and he leaped out of the car, walking quickly, putting some distance between him and his sister. He walked as if he knew exactly where his mother was. His legs were stiff. All the sitting he did all day made them feel as if they belonged to someone who needed a walker.

"Gunnar, you're going the wrong direction. It's after five, so we have to check in at the Emergency Room," said Patty. "This way." He had a brief flash of his own visit to the emergency room in Denmark. He didn't particularly want to go into an emergency room again.

He turned and caught up with Patty, but stayed just far enough behind so he wouldn't have to converse anymore. Patty stopped to wait for him.

"And someone's got to deal with the insurance company, too. Her car is totaled, so when it's replaced, I want her new car."

"You already have a new car," he said as they left the parking garage and approached the entrance that had a cantilevered concrete overhang. "And if the car's totaled, she'll probably just get a check, and if she's... Nevermind, I refuse to talk about this."

"That's because you know I'll be there to sweep up the mess."

"First things first, Patty." He tried to push out his anger, but his words sounded controlled. He was so worn out, he couldn't even have a good fight. He said, "She's still alive. There's a logical order to all of this. Mom has to get better. If not, if she passes — "

"Dies, you mean."

"Then we'll get a lawyer to help us," he said.

"We'll need a Fond du Lac lawyer, so we'll —

"You are so goddamn spoiled, so plainly insensitive, I can't even believe you're my sister!" Now his anger flowed. "Your mother is what? Just a burden? She helped you with your divorce, with your new house, with your new car, and you still don't have enough? For what? Will you have happiness if you have more things? You want her to die so you'll have more?"

Gunnar saw his outburst had its effect. Patty held herself, and her face was frozen in the rictus of sorrow, tears silently slipping from each eye as her body wracked in pain. This surprised him. She stared at Gunnar as if he'd just shot her. "I'm sorry," she said. "I just needed to talk is all. I just needed someone to listen. I'd give up everything if Mom can only live. I'll make a deal with the devil."

Gunnar felt his own eyes well up, and he hugged Patty, hugged her as if everything would be better. She responded in kind.

At last they pulled back. "I guess we should see her," he said.

"I'm afraid."

"We'll go together."

She took his hand. "Okay," she said.

In the elevator, which they had to themselves, Gunnar looked at his sister and realized that her talking about a will, while peppered with selfishness, was Patty's way of dealing with worry. It was as if, in being bitchy, she would defuse the possibilities. As he considered that, he worried, in fact, what would happen to Patty without their mother? Patty and Mom were close. Patty saw and talked with her often — certainly more than he did. He'd been with Patty when Patty might dial up Mom on the cell phone to tell her about something funny she just saw or a story she just heard. Mom and Patty were plugged into each other in a way he wasn't. Each had a wry sense of humor he didn't have, and it was their way to communicate. Could he help his sister if Mom died?

Patty knew the way, and he followed.

They had to wait for an ICU nurse to let them in and lead them to their mother's room. As they waited, Patty said, "She's in Room B."

"Okay," he said. "What happened to Mom's friend Lorelei?"

"I thought I told you. She was released right away. They treated her for shock. She has a broken rib and is black and blue, but otherwise she's all right."

"Good," said Gunnar.

As they stood there, Patty looked down at the floor, and Gunnar considered all Patty had been through herself, what with the betrayal by her husband, the divorce, the sadness, and more. He may have felt unfairly squeezed by love, but so had Patty. Wasn't it just a part of living?

"So are you dating?" The moment he said it, he realized maybe it wasn't a good subject for now, but she looked up with a small smile.

"Didn't Mom tell you?"

"What?"

"I met a guy named Rick — a chef. In fact, sometimes I wonder how I lucked out. He's easy-going, makes me laugh."

"Laughing's good."

"Yep."

"And he cooks well?"

She laughed. "Yes, he does. Sometimes I think maybe I don't deserve him. I'll ruin him."

"Don't say that. You're a good person, Patty."

"Really?"

He nodded and pulled her in for another hug. If he kept this up, they might actually come to like each other.

A door opened, and a nurse with a mixture of dark and gray hair, who in a flash reminded him of one of his high school English teachers, said, "You came to see Mrs. Gunderson?"

Gunnar's heart surged. Was the nurse going to say Mom died? Was this it — a stranger telling him his life as he knew it was over?

"She's in Room B," said the nurse and motioned them in. They paused at the nursing station, a square island, where the nurse took a call. Just underneath the clean counters were tiny TVs showing continuing EKG info and something marked "pulse oximeter," as well as computer monitors with various other data, overseen by nurses in chairs, watching things the way security guards kept attention on parking garage views from hidden cameras.

A beeping sound punctuated the air — an emergency? — and the nurse held up her hand for Gunnar and Patty to stay as she swung around the counter to see on a monitor what the alert was. Was his mother dying that very second? Gunnar instinctively ran into Room B, disobeying the nurse. He wasn't prepared for what he saw.

There was Audrey sitting perfectly fine up in bed, alert and as regal as one could be in a hospital gown. She was also smoking a cigarette.

"Gunnar. Patty," she said surprised.

"Mom!" said Gunnar. "You're awake."

"I hope so. I hope I'm not dreaming."

He gawked as if witnessing desktop fusion. Had Patty exaggerated? No, the accident had happened. This was the ICU, after all.

"Where's the respiratory tube, the monitors and things?" said Patty.

"I woke up a few hours ago."

Gunnar laughed and rushed over and hugged her, rocking her back and forth.

"Nice to see you, too," said Audrey and motioned Patty over. She pulled Patty in for a group hug.

"You're here," he said, feeling his arms around his mother, her real breathing body, her atoms still in the same place. Today she was still here, and that was everything.

"Great to be back," said Audrey. "I'm a lucky woman to still have you both."

"You're smoking," said Gunnar.

"And you're not in Denmark," she said.

"Of course not. You were in a near-fatal accident."

"So you won't mind my one little vice," she said.

"Of course we do!" said Patty, taking the cigarette from her mother. "There's oxygen here. You want to blow this whole place up?"

"Oxygen itself isn't flammable," said Gunnar. "It's not — "

"We don't need a chemistry lesson now," said Patty, stubbing the cigarette out on the remnants of red Jell-O on her mother's dinner tray. Apparently Audrey had even been eating. "Mom shouldn't be smoking in ICU."

At that moment, the nurse, a husky short woman with gray hair, walked in, seeing Patty with the cigarette stub. "Ah," said the nurse to Audrey. "The alarm was a change in your EKG. Your heart rate went up — and your pulse-ox showed a substantial decrease in your oh-two sat."

"What?" said Audrey.

"You were smoking, Mrs. Gunderson. You're breaking strict rules. So many patients are on oxygen; don't you know smoking here is a fire hazard?"

Patty shot Gunnar a look of vindication.

"Celebrating is all," said Audrey. "Scotch and soda isn't on your snack list."

"Neither are Marlboros."

"Marie, these are my children, Patty and Gunnar." Audrey turned to her children. "And this is my ever-efficient and lovely nurse, Marie."

"Nice to meet you," said Patty and Gunnar in tandem.

"A pleasure to meet you," said Marie. "And, Mrs. Gunderson, you'll be moved out of here within the hour, now that your situation has happily changed."

"Can I get checked out?"

"Not at night. Your doctor will let you know in the morning, but my guess is you'll be here at least half a day for observation. You've had a severe head trauma."

"I feel perfectly fine."

"Please listen to the experts, Mother," said Patty.

"I suppose so," said Audrey.

Gunnar and Patty chatted for the next hour and accompanied their mother to her new room. Once Audrey was settled, they left, and Gunnar jogged the remaining few steps into the elevator, which seemed to be waiting for them. He punched the button for the first floor.

"I thought..." said Patty haltingly, "that I'd never see her again. Talking and laughing."

Gunnar realized she was crying, and, without thinking, he gathered her into his arms.

"Yeah, amazing," he said. "I'm not a fan of surprises, but this was a good one." He rocked, happy to be with his sister.

The elevator slowed, and the doors opened to the sixth floor. "Pediatrics," a sign proclaimed on the wall across the empty space, and then a blue-uniformed nurse entered, holding a thick dark coat in her arms, apparently ready to go home. She glanced at Gunnar holding Patty, then turned like a good elevator passenger to stare at the closing doors.

Gunnar felt instantly dizzy, and his heart raced. Was he seeing right? The nurse's dark blond hair was parted in the middle. A practical cut — she'd cut her hair. Her profile as she stared blankly ahead looked as he remembered. "Ursula?" he said.

The woman looked at him, evaluating. She went from his face to noting how he was hugging Patty, and instinctively, he let go of his sister. Ursula took a slight step back as she said, "Gunderson?"

"Ursula, what're you doing here?"

She pointed to herself in her nurse's uniform.

"I mean," he said, "I thought you worked somewhere else."

"No. Here. Tonight in pediatrics ICU. I thought you were in Denmark." She looked aghast as if he were Hamlet's ghost.

"Yes, I am." He realized. "I mean, not now, but — "

"Is this Kara?"

Patty guffawed, wiping a tear with her finger, then holding out her hand. "I'm Gunnar's sister, Patty. Our mom's here in the hospital."

"I'm sorry to hear," Ursula said, shaking Patty's hand. "I'm Ursula Nordstrom."

"Mom had been in a car accident and in a coma," said Gunnar. "I had to fly back."

The doors opened to the ground floor, and they stepped out.

"She's doing pretty well now, actually," Gunnar added as they stood in the lobby.

"Thank goodness," Ursula said, nodding earnestly. "Well, nice running into — "

"So you two dated?" said Patty.

"Not really," said Ursula, taking a moment as if to find the right words. "Gunnar met a Danish hottie. Was that right, Gunnar?"

Gunnar coughed. "Hot can be debated, I suppose."

"So Gunnar and I," said Ursula, "have had a few good conversations. That's about it." She said it dismissively.

Gunnar could feel his face flush. Ursula was right to look pissed. He had had her interest, and he had selected wrong.

"So are you still Eight-Minute Dating?" asked Gunnar.

She looked at Gunnar, caught off guard. "Me? No. I mean, I tried it once more, and it worked! Yes, quite well. I met Jonathan, and we're kinda regular."

"Oh." His heart sank. What had he expected — that she'd been waiting for him?

"And how's Kara?" she said.

He stared at the floor for a second, realizing how pathetic he was. What else could he say but, "Kara's good. And Denmark's wonderful." He could see his sister screw her face. There was no point, however, in explaining a complicated situation to Ursula. Best to keep things simple. It was obvious Ursula had her own life.

Still, Ursula, despite her attitude, radiated such innocent sexiness as she stared at her shoes, he imagined what could have been. He could have been happily involved with her now if he hadn't gone for Door Number One, Kara. How could it have been different, though? Kara had grabbed him heart-and-soul. Ursula might have done so under different circumstances, but he'd gone with the truth he'd known at the time. He shouldn't be regretful.

"Good, good," said Ursula. Her cell phone buzzed, and she opened it, listened, and said, "I'll be right there." She turned to Gunnar. "I'm sorry, I've got to go back, but it's nice to see you again, Gunnar. So you'll be returning to Denmark?"

"I imagine so. Classes start soon." When he'd booked his flight to America, he'd made it round-trip in a week because the price was nearly the same as one-way, and one week would give him only a day to prepare for his first classes. However, if his mother hadn't been improving, or there'd been a funeral involved, he could have changed the date of return. He'd have to return no matter what to get his things and close out his apartment if he had to quit NBI.

Ursula nodded as if disappointed. Did he see that correctly? "Take care then," she said, and she pushed the elevator button for up. The doors opened. He watched her walk in. She turned and glanced up.

He waved. "Take care," he said, meaning it.

She nodded, still looking astounded, and she added a small smile. She looked so good, like an ad for Dove soap: blond hair against perfect skin and a bright face.

A moment after the doors shut, Patty said, "Ursula seemed attracted to you. I never met Kara, but Ursula — "

"She's involved. You heard her. She has a boyfriend."

"I could tell she liked you."

"Really? Except, if she wanted to see me, she wouldn't have told me about her boyfriend. That's a woman's way to say no thanks."

"I suppose you're right. Let's get to the hotel."

Because Gunnar had rented his house out for a six-month minimum, Patty had booked Gunnar and herself a suite at the Holiday Inn on the Westside, not far from his house and near Houlihan's. When they checked in, the desk clerk mentioned the room came with two complimentary drinks at the bar in the lobby. "I could use a drink," Gunnar said. After they dropped off their luggage in their room, they returned downstairs. With its coffee tables, stuffed couches, and large potted plants, the lobby bar felt elegant. "Very European," he told Patty as he sipped his orange juice and vodka.

"I wouldn't know," said Patty.

"When did the Holiday Inn become so cosmopolitan? When we were kids on those road trips with Mom and Dad, the Holiday Inn was always so cheap."

"People want more these days."

They had a quiet dinner at George's Chop House, which was attached to the hotel, and they watched a movie with Tom Hanks on HBO. The hotel had a tropical-looking indoor swimming pool with a long, curved water slide, worthy of a water park, but Gunnar didn't feel like swimming. His mind buzzed about possibilities. His mother was alive, and he wanted to get her to Denmark for a visit as soon as her energy returned. He'd take her to museums and others places he hadn't been to — time to get to know Copenhagen. As he drifted finally toward sleep, he pictured, however,

Ursula in the elevator glancing up and how maybe she really liked seeing him. Her final smile said so.

-------------→

The next morning, he lay in his bed thinking about his mother, Patty, Kara, and Ursula. They each had surprised him in significant ways. Freud's famous quote came to mind: "Despite my thirty years of research into the feminine soul, I have not been able to answer the great question that has never been answered: what does a woman want?" Gunnar had always assumed Freud wasn't a true scientist. Now he realized Freud was onto something.

Kara certainly had shown him that people's behavior could be, in part, random. Patty, too, had astonished him yesterday with her reaction to his outburst when he called her selfish. He had no idea Patty had felt that much. She was as unpredictable and breathtaking as the next meteor entering the atmosphere.

His mother was a force to herself. It was as if her personality pushed her out of a coma.

And then there was Ursula. Her jitteriness around him and that smile at the end — maybe she cared. How amazing was it that they met again? Was it meant to be? Mathematicians, though, said coincidences really weren't amazing. Professor J.E. Littlewood created Littlewood's Law: "Individuals can expect a miracle to happen to them at the rate of about one per month." So, too, she was a nurse in a hospital, and there were only so many hospitals in Madison. It wasn't that farfetched.

So what did seeing her again mean? Leave it to people to take random events and want meaning. But he was attracted to her. Was it too late to show her he was interested? What if they went to Ireland together someday?

Things to do in Ireland with Ursula

- Laugh in an emerald field
- Have sex in that same field. On top of clover.
- What if she became pregnant in that field? If it's a girl, name her Shannon. If it's a boy, name it after her father.
- Listen. Always be a good listener. Especially in pubs in Ireland.

With a sigh, he decided he'd better get on with the day and that he should inquire at the hotel's front desk about a computer. He needed to create the syllabus for his Danish course, "Games with Quantum Gases." Bent had suggested the title. It would match his ongoing research with several graduate students' interest in the field. Gunnar certainly wasn't doing well in games with people, so maybe he'd do better with gases.

By the time he dressed and went into the common living room, his sister was just entering from the hallway.

"We've got to get going," she said. "I called the hospital, and they'll be releasing Mom this morning."

"Should we have breakfast first?"

"You missed it, lazybones. I just had it. You can grab something at the hospital."

Patty drove. She was no longer worried about driving.

"I'm planning to stay with Mom," said Patty. "She'll undoubtedly be on low power for a while. Do you want to stay with us, or will you be getting back to Denmark sooner?"

"I'll stay with you until I have to go back."

At the hospital, they found their mother in her room. Her doctor would be releasing her within the hour. She hadn't dressed yet. Patty said she'd help her. "While Gunnar was in bed this morning, Mom, I went to a nearby mall and got you a new dress and underwear." Patty was more sensitive and adept than he'd ever seen her. Excellent. Interesting.

Before Gunnar went down to breakfast, he returned to the Newborn ICU where he asked for Ursula Nordstrom. He learned she wouldn't be in that day. She would return to her usual 7 a.m to 3 p.m. shift tomorrow.

The hospital cafeteria was much like the one at the student union at the university. One grabbed a tray and slid it down stainless steel rails to move past various offerings, starting with dessert first. Dessert for breakfast? Gunnar selected a slice of chocolate cake. If he couldn't find love, at least there was chocolate. He also grabbed a breakfast burrito and a carton of milk.

As he sat at a table in a corner and sliced into his burrito with a plastic knife, he noticed two nurses, late twenties, early thirties, sitting nearby with a third woman in street clothes. One nurse, Hispanic looking, had beautiful high cheekbones and dark hair knotted in a bun. Even from where he sat, he could tell she used heavy blue eye shadow. The other nurse had short black hair. The woman in street clothes, a tan turtleneck and jeans, had short dark blond hair parted in the middle.

"Ursula?" he said. No one turned around. Maybe he didn't say it loud enough. "Ursula" he tried again, but there was no movement. He'd say it even louder if he could be sure it was her. He stared at the back of her head. Turn around. Turn around.

But nothing happened. Was he just inventing her, was that it? What if it was Ursula? If only she turned around. Turn around.

She turned to look out the window. It was enough of her face for him to confirm.

"Ursula!" he cried.

All three women turned, as well as people at other tables.

"Gunderson?" said Ursula. "How's your Mom?"

"Ah...." He was so stunned and happy, nothing else came to mind at the moment. "Mom's doing well, thanks," he said across the room.

She excused herself to her friends and approached his table without her tray. He was at a round table with chairs. He stood and pulled out a seat for her. She waved it off saying, "Thank you, but I only have a minute. I came in to give my friend a gift on her break. It's her birthday." Gunnar looked over and saw both nurses looking curiously at them, even pleased. The dark-haired woman had a box with crushed wrapping paper next to it. The box's largest letters said, "Panini Grill."

"Have a seat for just a minute then," he said, still offering the chair.

"Actually, I've got to — "

"Just for a minute?" he said. "After all I've been through with my mother, I've been at wit's end."

She paused. "Okay," she said. "A minute." She looked over at her friends, one of whom gave an okay sign.

"We call ourselves 'The Wild Bunch,' she said with a laugh. "It's not like we're *wild,* but we have a good time. We help each other."

Gunnar looked back over, and both women turned to pretend they weren't watching. Why were they watching?

"Is it usual for someone — my Mom — to be released so soon after a coma?" Gunnar said, returning to his own chair.

"Maybe they didn't consider it a coma, per se, according to the Glasgow Coma Score. Whatever she had, you'll have to watch her closely."

"Ah," he said. "Good."

She pointed to his tray. "I see we both have the breakfast burrito. We're samers."

"Yes?" he said.

"Anyway, blunt head traumas can be tricky."

"I hear," he said. "So you have a boyfriend." It was a statement.

"Yes." She looked down, scratching at a stuck particle on the table. He watched her index finger, the one that had been stuck in the payphone. It looked delicate, gentle.

"And you have a girlfriend," she said, "I'd better get back to my friends. Nice seeing you again."

He could feel his throat begin to clamp shut, but he forced out his breath to say, "Actually, I don't have a girlfriend. I was stupid to go over there, especially after I met you. When I got to Denmark, she was living with another guy. I'm a fool. I only wish I'd have kept going out with you. I'm sorry."

He couldn't tell what to read from Ursula's astonished face — whether there was some hope in there or whether she was looking at him merely like some demented man who lived in a boiler room and played with rats.

"I'm sorry," she said. "I've got to go."

"When your friends have to go back to work, want to come back over?" he tried. "I'm not rushing away."

"I'll think about it," she said.

He watched Ursula return to her friends, who huddled closer together as Ursula began whispering, no doubt. The birthday girl looked over his way.

A few minutes later, the three women stood, and Ursula hugged each woman, mentioning something about breakfast. "See you tomorrow," each nurse said while hugging, each glancing at Gunnar, evaluating him, then whispering in Ursula's ear. Were they encouraging Ursula to talk with him? Maybe they didn't like her boyfriend?

Ursula strode back over, a black purse over her shoulder. Again Gunnar stood and offered her a chair.

"You're such a gentleman," said Ursula sitting. "That's nice. And I'm sorry to hear what happened to you in Denmark."

He nodded. "Your friends seem to care for you."

"True."

"I mean the way they kept looking at me as if making sure I was all right."

"We help each other."

"You'd think they'd be upset — you know, for your boyfriend's sake — talking with a strange man and all."

"Oh. Well." She looked like a teenager caught smoking in the bathroom. "I have to say: I made up all that stuff about a boyfriend. I didn't want to come off like a loser. I mean, you had Kara. Who am I but a single nurse working with babies or dying people."

"Not always dying."

"No, thank god," she said. "So about Kara. She was living with another guy?"

He told her all the details of arriving with nervousness and hope, and told of the initial clues. "And then she said she was living with a guy named Peder."

Ursula laughed. "You're kidding."

"I'm not."

"So what did you do? I mean, you moved all the way there for her."

"I've been living with her parents."

Ursula laughed again, and he smiled. She was right — it was funny. With some distance, he could see the humor.

"Yep," he said. "And then I ended up with her brother and an Irish girl going to a hippie part of town where, to my surprise, they bought hashish. I was so low, I smoked some and got paranoid and even more depressed until I was running away from them. Then, whoosh, I slipped on some ice and slid like a frozen banana down the gutter. I think that had to be my lowest moment." He wouldn't mention the sleeping pills now. That was the worst.

"You've had an adventure."

They spent the next hour talking. He asked about her father, who continued to do well, post-heart attack.

She asked him what he's still doing in Denmark, and he explained how he's locked into researching and teaching there through the summer. "I'm trying to make the best of things," he said. "I'll get a place in Copenhagen, and Denmark's not so bad. I look forward to teaching there."

"When do you have to go back?"

"Less than a week."

"So you'll be around for a few more days?" She looked hopeful.

He grimaced. "Actually, we're checking Mom out soon and going to Fond du Lac."

"That's too bad," she said. "And I've got a dental appointment this morning and a physical this afternoon."

Those weren't things to accompany her on. She was basically saying this was it. Fate could be cruel. His mother entered the cafeteria dressed in a pleasing navy blue dress, and she peered around, Patty at her side. When they saw he was with Ursula, Patty smiled, and Gunnar could read her lips. She said, "Told you so."

They all chatted with Ursula for another five minutes, but it felt generalized, the way talking to a distant aunt did — the cold weather, the adept hospital staff, the joys of a new year, until Ursula looked at her watch. "Mercy," she said. "Time to go. Nice to meet you all."

"Nice to meet you again," said Patty. She raised her right hand, palm out with her ring finger and middle finger spread to form a V-shape. "Live long and prosper."

Ursula frowned, then smiled. "Thanks — I guess."

"That's what Mr. Spock does," said Gunnar. "It's the Vulcan greeting — sort of like *Aloha*."

"Funny," said Ursula.

"A pleasure to meet you," said Audrey, unashamed. "I sure hope Santa brought you everything you wanted."

"Nearly. You're a fun family," said Ursula. Gunnar saw it: a mere glance his way by Ursula before she said, "Best to you all in this new year." And they all shook hands. Gunnar felt Patty's elbow. He wasn't sure what the elbow meant other than he should do something. He blurted out, "Would it be okay if I wrote you? From Denmark?"

"Oh. Sure. Send me postcards. I like foreign countries." Ursula opened her purse, pulled out her checkbook, and ripped off the last page, a deposit slip. "Here's my address," she said. She lived in Middleton, just a short jog northwest of the university. "Maybe I'll see you in eight months?" she added.

"Slightly less," said Gunnar.

And then she was gone.

"She's nice," said Audrey.

"Yes," said Gunnar. "Have you been released?"

"Yes. Checked out and wheelchaired to the car where we've put my stuff already. We came to find you."

They walked out of the cafeteria and down the hall. "Eight months is a long time," said Patty.

"Slightly less," said Gunnar.

"A lot of things happen in that time," said Audrey.

"If I were sick," added Patty, "I'd like Ursula as a nurse. She seems compassionate. How long's Ursula been a nurse?"

"I don't know. Five years, I think."

"I liked her when I met her at the baby shower," said Audrey.

"That's right — we met her there." Gunnar scratched his hands. His old nervousness was coming back because Ursula was gone. That was that.

Once at the car in the parking garage, Gunnar opened the right passenger door for his mother. "What would you like to do tonight, Mom?" he asked.

"I have a good yarn of a book, *Shogun* by James Clavell. It'll keep me occupied for a while."

Gunnar nodded, thinking how she loved to read. "What's it about?" he asked.

"Love in Japan in the early seventeenth century. It's mostly about acting versus observing."

"It is?" said Patty. "I thought it's about the exploitation of Asia by the Portuguese and English."

"Depends what you focus on," said Audrey. "Anyway, I have to stay in bed mostly for the next week. Not a lot for you to do with me," said Audrey.

"I flew all the way here for you," said Gunnar.

"I appreciate that," said Audrey. "I'm low power, so perhaps you can keep yourself entertained while you're here?"

An idea chipped away at Gunnar. "So you wouldn't mind if I stayed another day or two in Madison — to catch up with my colleagues at the university?"

"That's a good idea," said Audrey, smiling slyly, Gunnar noted.

"I'm fine with that," said Patty.

He would stay another night at the Holiday Inn. Patty dropped him off at the Dane County regional airport, which was on the way to Fond du Lac, so that he could rent a car.

As he left Patty, she shouted "Hey!" and gave him a thumbs-up. That was all he needed.

CHAPTER TWENTY-TWO

"IN ALL CHAOS THERE IS A COSMOS."

— CARL JUNG

Gunnar set his bedside alarm for five a.m. He figured if Ursula started her shift at seven, she probably had breakfast in the cafeteria sometime after six. After all, he heard her mention breakfast to her girlfriends.

Five a.m. came far too quickly. It was mighty dark. Going back to sleep beckoned, and he considered the likelihood of Ursula not being in the cafeteria. After all, he had not made any arrangements with her. Would he kick himself years later if he slept in? Was getting up and going stupid?

He pulled on his sweats. As he left his room and took the elevator down, every fiber of his body said go back to bed, get under those warm covers, sleep is good. The moment he walked outside and the frigid air hit him like a semi, he jerked awake. He jogged around the Holiday Inn twice in the cold air to further set his system in motion. He showered, dressed, brushed his teeth, and carefully packed because he didn't know if he might stay in town another night. At a few minutes before six, he stepped downstairs. He noticed the gift shop was opening and a flower vendor was delivering flowers, white ones, pinks ones and more. He didn't know flowers. Still, if he was going to surprise Ursula, he may as well go all the way.

"Are you open?" asked Gunnar to the salesclerk, a strong-armed woman with gray hair who looked like she grew up milking cows.

"Why not?" said the woman.

"Can you help me with a bouquet? I don't know what to buy."

"What's the occasion?"

"I don't know if it's a category. It's 'Hello, I'm Still in Town, You're Nice'."

"Ah, a kind of 'I'd Like to Know You Better'."

"Exactly."

"Not too overwhelming but pretty, right? How about one red rose surrounded by an array of complementary colors?"

"I'm in your hands," Gunnar said, and he bought the bouquet. When the woman read his credit card, she said, "Gunderson, as in the funeral home?"

"I hope not," he said. "I'm not related at all."

Gunnar arrived at ten after six. The cafeteria was a sea of green surgical uniforms and whites. Gunnar scanned the area. No Ursula. He stood in line to buy another breakfast burrito when he spotted the dark-haired nurse, Ursula's friend. She noticed Gunnar, too, and looked amazed. Gunnar pulled out of line and dashed to her.

"Hi, I'm — "

"Gunnar Gunderson, I know. A name you can't forget. My name's Yuka."

He shook her hand thankfully, as if she were an emissary to the Pope. "Is Ursula coming this morning?"

Yuka said nothing, but simply looked to her right. Ursula approached in her uniform, ready for work, and in seeing Gunnar, she nearly dropped her tray. "Is your mother back in the hospital?"

He extended the bouquet. "No, she's fine. I thought you should start the day right."

At first Ursula looked at the flowers warily, but when she glanced at him and back to the bouquet, she smiled. "Gunnar Gunderson, what are you doing?"

Yuka laughed seeing her friend's reaction and said, "Put your tray down and take the flowers."

"Oh, right," said Ursula, placing her tray on the nearest table and taking the gift. "I'm ... stunned. Thank you," she said to Gunnar.

He resisted saying what his students would say, "No problem." Instead he went with the more direct, "You're welcome."

"So your mother's okay?" Ursula asked.

"Yes. She and my sister went to Fond du Lac. Mom has to stay in bed."

"You got up this early? For me?" She still looked astounded.

Gunnar turned to Yuka and said, "Mind if I borrow your friend for just a little bit?"

"Hell, I gotta work all day with her. You can have her."

Ursula stuck out her tongue at her friend, adding "Thanks."

Gunnar now saw the other nurse approach with her tray. In seeing Gunnar, she said, "Well, well, well."

"Hello," said Gunnar.

"I'm Luna."

"If you don't mind, Luna, I'm going to dine with Ursula for a bit."

"Dine away."

The next forty-five minutes went quickly. He and Ursula covered a lot of ground, mostly about each other's work — new territory for them. At one point, he realized he was enjoying himself. His anxiety had fallen away. But how was he doing it? He was only working on instinct. It's what helped him in science, and maybe it was working here.

"It seems in your job," said Ursula, "that you have to be so patient and persistent at what you do. Right? You analyze data for years just to understand a moment?"

"If even then. But I like the fact that nature does this stuff. It's there for the taking."

"Physics is just whizzing around us, isn't it?"

She understood.

"What you do with cold atoms makes me think of other small things most people don't think about, like dust mites in our carpets or, say, viruses waiting on doorknobs or in salad bars."

"Yeah. Maybe that's why I stay away from salad."

"What I remember from high school physics was curved space. You ever think about what else is happening, and you just don't notice?"

He nodded. "I don't see a lot of things," he said with a sigh.

"What is it you create again?"

"Bose-Einstein condensates."

"I love the sound of that. Better than, say, 'Nurse, pass the evacuation tube'."

He laughed, then noticed people starting to get up — the start of a new shift — and realized he had to make a move. "Would you like to go out tonight, Ursula?"

"Don't you have to go to Fond du Lac?"

"Maybe in a day or two. And, yes, I have to go back to Denmark soon, but I just didn't want to wait a chunk of a year to see you again."

"You're very kind, but — "

"Oh, no," he said, already anticipating her rejection. Had he misread her?

"No, I was going to say I have to go home first and shower, and I live in Middleton."

"I'm at the Holiday Inn nearby. I was thinking the hotel has a nice restaurant, George's Chop House."

"I like that place a lot."

"So I can pick you up?"

"Of course, Gunderson."

"How about six p.m.?"

"Perfect."

That evening, as they strolled into George's Chop House, he held open the door for her. She nodded, noticing.

For dinner, she went for the chicken picata, while he opted for a blackened filet mignon stuffed with garlic. Afterwards, when she saw the water slide at the hotel's indoor pool, she said, "Doesn't that look like fun? I wish they had things like that when I was a kid."

"It's never too late."

"Sometime I'll try it with you."

"Right now," he said.

"I don't have a suit."

"Yes, you do," and he took her a few steps to the gift shop, where he offered to buy her a swimsuit. "I have to buy one for myself, anyway," he said.

"No. You bought me dinner, so I'm buying the suits. If you refuse, I won't go."

"Really?"

She nodded.

"Okay then. I defer to you."

The same farmhouse woman who was there at six a.m. was still working. "Hello, Mr. Gunderson," the lady said.

Ursula nodded, impressed.

"You have long hours," said Gunnar.

"Just covering an extra shift," said the lady.

Ursula bought the suits, and they slid down the slide with mostly five-to-ten-year-olds.

"Wrap your legs around me," she said once at the top. "We can be a train."

"What's your brother's name?"

"Charles, why?"

"I realized you never told me."

"You're freaking me out, Gunderson. I like this new you."

He pondered whether to ask her to spend the night, but they hadn't even kissed yet.

Ursula said, "I hate to be a spoil-sport, but I have to be at work early. I feel like Cinderella, but I have to dash." The clock near the pool entrance said it was just after nine.

"May I bring you a glass slipper tomorrow?"

"You want to do something tomorrow night, you mean?"

He nodded.

They dressed in his room after swimming — she using his bathroom and he quickly changing by the bed. At her car, a black Honda Accord, his stomach wrenched. He wanted to kiss her but... Don't think, he told himself. Act. He moved in, and she smiled, ready. Their lips finally met, and she responded as eagerly as he. Their tongues touched. She laughed as if relieved of the tension, and so did he.

"Thanks for the evening," she said. "And thanks for the flowers. You make me feel special."

"Because you are." They kissed again.

"What're we going to do tomorrow?" she asked.

"A surprise. I'll call you."

"My cell number's on the deposit slip. Still have it?"

"Absolutely."

He had no idea what they would do the next day. How could he top dinner and a water slide? As he drove home, he found himself smiling still. Was he being obsessive-compulsive with Ursula? What was he expecting? Maybe he shouldn't analyze so much. Yes, but this is what got him in trouble with Kara. Then again, Ursula was from his culture. There were subtle things at work here, variables he couldn't identify.

The next day, because Ursula worked until three, he popped into the physics department to say hello. The secretaries were surprised to see him. As he was leaving, a poster told him that that night the Madison Metro School District planetarium was having a show for the public, "The Stargazer." The poster stated, "Dr. James Kaler shares his excitement about the fast-moving field of stellar evolution. Nichelle Nichols (Uhura from the original *Star Trek*) and Dr. Kaler narrate this personal look at gravity, light, and the spectrum and how they help us, and scientists of the past, to decipher the lifestyles of the stars." That sounded like a great second date. He called Ursula on her cell phone and told her about it. "Would you like to go?"

"Sure. It sounds fun."

He picked her up at the hospital after her shift. At the planetarium, as the lights were going down, he leaned over and kissed her. They missed the entire sequence about the Milky Way.

She rearranged her schedule so that she worked only two more days in the week, and they saw each other every day, with his mother's blessing. Gunnar chatted with his mother a couple times each day. Each morning, the salesclerk at the Holiday Inn happily sold him a bouquet.

One day he suggested to Ursula the Elvehjem Museum of Art, a modern four-story building on the University of Wisconsin campus.

"Really?" Ursula had said when he proposed the place. "You don't seem like an art museum kind of guy."

"Maybe I'm becoming my mother. She loves museums."

They didn't say much at first in the museum, other than agree to go to the fourth floor first where there was the 20th Century American and European art. They nodded at the red broomstick-looking sculpture on a stand entitled "Red Monument to Lost Dirigible" that first greeted them. They wandered to the closest windowless beige wall where they nodded at an abstract painting with a lot of red and blue. They passed several other pieces to which they did not react. Then they came across what looked to be an actual dark-haired young woman sitting on a piece of marble, nude. She didn't move.

"Superrealism," said Ursula.

Gunnar walked very close, at which point he could see it was like an incredibly detailed mannequin.

They walked around it. The seated woman was looking at her feet as if, post-bath, she were contemplating whether to apply athlete's foot cream or not. Then it struck Gunnar: she looked a lot like the Little Mermaid on the rock in Copenhagen, just naked and finless. Did that make it art? He went to read the plaque.

"This says," said Gunnar, "that it's a polyvinyl casting with mixed media by John DeAndrea. It says he's best known for his castings of nudes, which he paints and adds hair to, to look real." He frowned. "It's not like he sculpted it. He hired a model and cast her the way my orthodontist casts my teeth. Are my teeth art?"

"Once they're finished straightening," said Ursula.

"Yes, but this DeAndrea guy's just a technician."

"I like it." Ursula moved around the woman more. "So what if it's casting? He's the one to cast it — to make her sit this way, to paint her so real."

"Isn't art about interpreting? There's no interpretation here."

"How can you say that?" she said, with some emphasis. "I suppose photography isn't art because there's no painting involved, and it's just being a technician to click a camera."

"Frankly, I don't see why museums buy photographs."

"I can't believe you!"

"What?"

"Does this surprise you, this piece?"

"Yes, of course, but only because — "

"There you have it!" she said. "It's done its job. It surprised you. It's made us talk. Maybe those other pieces aren't art because we didn't feel anything for them."

Maybe she was right.

"I like art that celebrates life," she said, "and how can you celebrate more than showing a beautiful naked person?"

"All right, then. I don't mind beautiful naked people." He looked at her directly as he said it and wiggled his eyebrows up and down.

She laughed. "Make me blush."

They skied at Cascade Mountain near Portage that Saturday and planned to spend the next day at his mother's house. Cascade was just forty-five minutes north of Madison, and Fond du Lac was still much further east. Ursula turned out to be a better skier than he was. He could tell a lot about a person skiing — whether she was a loner or not, aggressive or not, full of fear or not. Ursula had no fear, even taking small jumps with glee, but she never went out of sight. Rather, she skied either to the side of him or just in front or behind.

At lunch, she said, "I realize you've checked out of the hotel, and you want to take the Fond du Lac shuttle to your Mom's house, but — how can I say this? You're more than welcome to take the couch at my house."

"Really?" he said, wondering if she actually meant the couch.

"I don't think we should sleep with each other yet, though — not that I'm not attracted to you."

"Oh," he said, his mind racing, trying to figure out what she really meant. Did she want to just be friends? But they were kissing all the time, and more than that. He was ready — but then again, thanks to Kara perhaps, he felt disheartened. Anxiety hung over him like a vulture in a tree, and he sensed depression was around the corner. He guessed pure misery was ready to drop on him like a frozen ball of waste from a passing jet plane.

He tried to fathom the dialectics of this. When he was with Ursula, the excitement of it all made him feel he could slice down armies of gladiators if they were in his way, but now that doubt danced in, he worried. Were he and Ursula rushing things? Were they love junkies needing a fix? And what would being in Denmark be like after this? He could already guess he'd worry that someone else would come along for her. Yet he could not break his commitment to NBI. Everyone there had been good to him, and it was his career on the line. The months would go quickly — if they didn't push for a whole year.

What if he and Ursula had sex? Could the result be any worse than he knew separation would be? He was having difficulties sleeping at night, in fact, thinking of this very thing.

"I — I kind of know maybe what you're feeling," he said.

"Well, you're going away for many months, and if we sleep together, I know me," she said. "I'll get obsessed, wishing I were there with you. I'll be thinking about you as I fall asleep, when I wake up — at work as I'm filling out forms. It's that whole long distance thing. Maybe if we don't sleep together...."

"I think you're right," he said, and at a stop sign, they kissed on that.

Her condominium was cute — very feminine — with an open floor plan. The living room, dining room, and kitchen were together under a vaulted ceiling that had a skylight. A large cloth rainbow hung from a tall living room wall. Her dark wood dining room table had bright red place mats. The walls, couch, and love seat were white. The furniture was awash in pillows.

That night, even though the queen-size sofa bed was comfortable, he couldn't sleep. He thought about Ursula beyond the bedroom door. With the moon peeking through the skylight, he could see the outlines of her picture frames on the walls. Standing in his underwear and a t-shirt, he turned on a light to look more closely. There were pictures of what seemed to be her family — her brother, mother, father, aunts, uncles, he guessed, and one of her skiing in fine form.

He managed to fall asleep. He was awakened by a kiss. He peered right into Ursula's perky face. "Hello," she said, in pink pajamas, morning light hitting the wall from the skylight. "You looked so peaceful sleeping, but I couldn't resist." He pulled her close and kissed her again. They took off each other's clothes as the passion swept over them.

At first, finding each other naked, they were giggling like little kids. Her skin was pink and beautiful, punctuated here and there with moles a little larger than a freckle, giving a sense of how the rest of her skin was so pure. Her breasts were not large but wide and smooth, like an athletic model's. The perfect size.

He and Ursula massaged each other, their hands going over each other's bodies like Vikings discovering Vinland. When he finally followed the lines of her legs, reaching the blond and trimmed pinnacle — interesting, Ursula trimmed, too — he found her moist. She was better than art. As he massaged the right little spot, her back started to arch, and she was breathing harder. As he moved his body closer, his erection pounding, she rolled away. He involuntarily gasped.

"I'm sorry," she said. "I don't have any birth control."

He condemned himself for not asking. He had considered asking, but everything was rolling along, and he even thought if she became pregnant, it was meant to be. Now that she brought the subject up, he could only say, "I don't have anything, either."

She laughed. "We said we'd wait."

"Yes, we did, and I can do so."

"I can wait, too — I hope," she said, looking at his face more closely.

"Me, too," he repeated, as if willing himself.

For Gunnar, dressing came with difficulty. Even a shower didn't take away the need. But Ursula was right. Once he was away, he'd be glad they hadn't slept together.

Sunday they spent fully in Fond du Lac, where they had turkey burgers for lunch. Ursula volunteered to cook dinner, so he and Ursula shopped for the makings of Chicken Kiev. That evening, alone with his mother in the kitchen as Ursula and Patty were preparing the table, Gunnar asked, "How're you feeling, Mom?"

"You keep asking me. I'm having a great time."

"We don't want to wear you out."

"I'm fine. I'll tell you when I'm otherwise. I'm not shy."

"Okay. So... would you mind if Ursula and I spent the night? Ursula would need her own room."

"Gunnar, dear. You can have a room together if you like."

"Actually, we haven't slept together yet. She thought the whole thing with my being away through the summer in Denmark — well, she doesn't want to rush things."

"Wow. Sensible girl. I don't believe it for a second, but you can have two rooms."

At dinner, after they trashed the war in Iraq and the sureness of more terrorism in America, Audrey said, "Speaking of tragedies, Ursula, I've always wondered how nurses do what they do. You must see people die."

Ursula nodded and said, "That's still the hardest part of my job, seeing people go. When I first started, I cried often, and I thought I couldn't continue. Now I see death is natural. We've got to enjoy the time we have."

"Here, here," said Audrey, raising her glass.

"Yeah," said Patty. "If we're lucky, we work forty-five years, then die."

"You guys are all morbid!" said Gunnar.

"You either laugh or you cry," said Audrey. She lifted her glass higher. "May we enjoy the days we have."

"Cheers," said the women.

"*Skol*," said Gunnar.

Ursula and Gunnar each dressed for bed in their separate rooms, having kissed and said good-night, but fifteen minutes later, in the dark, Gunnar found Ursula tiptoeing toward his room as he was headed for hers. They laughed, keeping their voices low. No point in letting his mother know she was right.

They chose Ursula's room.

They took off each other's clothes and found their passion was bringing them toward consummation.

"I forgot to buy condoms," she said.

"I thought we weren't going to have sex. I didn't get any either."

"You didn't?"

"And I'm not going to ask my mother."

Ursula giggled at that one.

"I don't know how we're doing it," she said, "but we have to keep celibate. If we can get through this night and tomorrow, it'll be worth it."

"Yeah," said Gunnar, not believing it either.

They fell asleep holding each other. They awoke at the same time, spooned together, Gunnar up front.

"This feels so natural," said Gunnar.

"It does," said Ursula.

Their hands again traced each other. With fingers and oral stimulation, they satisfied each other.

"It's not really sex," said Ursula afterwards.

"No," said Gunnar. "Clinton didn't have sex with Monica Lewinsky, either."

Ursula tickled him until he cried uncle.

Monday afternoon, Ursula had to work, but Tuesday she was off and would take Gunnar to the airport that evening. Hence, Monday night was their last full night together, and Tuesday was their last day.

On Monday morning, Gunnar said his good-byes to his mother and Patty. "Will you visit me in Demark?" he asked his mother.

"I won't promise anything, but that sounds nice," she said.

"I love you, Mom."

"I love you, too. Keep on loving."

Monday evening started with a dance recital. Ursula's niece, age thirteen, was passionate about dance and had been in Madison's Pavlova Academy of Dance, explained Ursula. The recital was a major presentation for parents and friends, to which Ursula had committed months earlier. "I'm sorry," she said. "You probably think this is the lamest thing for your last night here, but you'll get to meet my brother and sister-in-law."

"If it was to watch you whittle, I'd go," said Gunnar. He didn't exactly relish little girls tap-dancing their way across a stage singing "Me and My Shadow" or whatever, but he would go.

During the day while Ursula worked, he walked from her condo to a drugstore where he bought a small box of condoms. Ribbed for her pleasure. At least this time he and she would have another option.

As Ursula drove them to the recital, Gunnar recalled how he had vowed to himself that his next relationship — this one — would be nothing but clear communication. Now he realized in his and Ursula's silence how much went unsaid. Some things were easier to avoid in hopes of the right moment, even if the right moment might not come. He wanted to talk about sex, his fears and needs, and hers — the very things he knew he avoided with Kara. With only one night left, would they or wouldn't they? But it wasn't just a deed. He knew their souls would meld. Then again, he'd had sex with Kara, and that didn't work. He didn't want to ruin this. With Ursula, their life together just had to work. It had to. It had to. It had to.

They arrived to the recital a little late. The recital room was long and narrow, with mirrors on the side where the audience sat on two rows of benches. The other side had a double railing installed at waist height against the plain yellow wall. Overhead, air conditioning ductwork was exposed. Ursula waved to someone who looked much like her, same hair but shorter. Ursula's brother, Charles, who wore a professor-like brown cardigan, enthusiastically waved back and smiled. He winked at Gunnar.

Ms. Vera Pavlova, artistic director, introduced the show. Vera was in her mid-forties, thin, wearing a tight top, a colorful skirt, and flats. With a Russian accent, she said, "These young men and women that you will see are most devoted to their art. After a full day of regular school, they come here and work out for three hours. Then they go home around seven to eat and focus on their homework."

Gunnar could see he wasn't in what he'd consider Wisconsin anymore. Dancing seemed like a rare art — one he didn't expect from a dairy state.

"To make a career in dancing's tough," she said. "But there is nothing like it, no? Watch the beauty of these dancers."

Ursula elbowed him as the first group of dancers entered, seven junior high school girls wearing black heeled shoes, black pants, and black Lycra tops. "The rather womanly girl is my niece, Brittany," said Ursula. Brittany wasn't thin like Vera, but rather short and bell-shaped.

"She's thirteen?"

"Yes."

Vera continued, "The evening is broken into six parts: jazz, modern, character, mime, historical dance, and ballet. What's the difference between jazz and modern, you might ask? Modern is what I call a rebellion — breaking rules and finding a new way of moving. Anyway, enjoy."

The first song, a jazz piece, he recognized from one of the few jazz albums he had: Charlie Haden and Pat Metheny's *Beyond the Missouri Sky*. It was the last song, "Spiritual." Haden's bass and Metheny's guitar rose slowly, and the dancers, so young but individually expressive, flowed as if not bound by bones, creating something he'd never seen before in dance: movement with emotion. They were seven eagles looking for their own piece of the sky, but the song, the emotion, pulled them together until they were in tandem, seven sets of arms and legs, looking as if they were improvising but acting as one unit, one mind. In fact, in a flash, he realized they were like atoms coming together as one in a Bose-Einstein condensate.

He looked around. Did no one else see? The movement was all quantum mechanics.

Brittany, despite not having a traditional dancer's body, was flawless and light on her feet. The next modern pieces he didn't get — it looked like chaos — but the mime pieces were funny. Then the character pieces gave a sense of real people with different personalities. The ballet pieces were taut, exacting, and while the dancers seemingly operated without effort, he noticed each of them soon radiated with sweat, beads like dandelion dew. He was in their thrall, the dancers, instruments to grace.

--------------->

As they'd returned in her car to her condo from the dance concert — he was driving — Ursula had said, "What do you think of Brittany — isn't she something?"

"I was swept away by her," he said. "I didn't think someone of her, you know, size would be so graceful."

"Are you calling her fat?"

"No, not at all."

"Oh, right. She's not one of those anorexic ballet-dancer types, the kind all women are supposed to be."

"I didn't mean that — "

"I'm sure you didn't mind her big breasts," Ursula added, "but those hips...."

"She has nice hips. I'm not calling her — "

"You were looking at her hips? Or her breasts?"

"She's a dancer — what am I supposed to look at?"

"She's thirteen, Gunnar."

"I wasn't looking at her that way. I don't find her attractive."

"You don't? She's ugly?"

"Are we having an argument?"

Ursula shook her head. "I'm sorry," she said. "But I realized that thirteen is perhaps the last moment of childhood for a lot of girls. Any second now she'll be worrying about boys, about men, and whether or not she'll put out, whether she'll be liked for herself or just as an object."

"Put out?" said Gunnar, wondering if Ursula was seeing her own situation. Was this about putting out instead of love? Maybe he had misread Ursula. Maybe this was a window into her true thoughts.

She continued, "Brittany's probably already worrying whether or not she'll find her Prince Charming to save her from — what? — from a life of spinsterhood?"

"At least she's not a boy," said Gunnar.

"Boys have it easy. Seduce and conquer."

"Are you kidding? Boys have it worse. At thirteen, eighth grade, I remember it well. Most of the girls had developed physically, and boys, they're all geeky and awkward. I was geeky and awkward."

"Not you," she said.

Was she being sarcastic or merely teasing? He couldn't tell. Did she find him geeky and awkward now? He gave up and continued. "I remember asking God to stop the pubic hair that was growing on me."

"You're kidding," she said.

"No. I wondered, 'Why the pubic hair? Why did my penis have to grow?' It was as if I was becoming a freak. I didn't quite get how important a penis would be. And I remember looking at the girls, seeing that they now had breasts, but I had never seen a real naked breast before, not even my sister's or mother's, and neither had told me about sex. I remember feeling like such an outsider. Girls had all the power."

"But they don't," she said.

"I don't see that."

At the stoplight, Ursula stared at him as if he were a stranger. "I'm puzzled."

"Me, too," he said, but he couldn't put his finger on what bothered him most — that they were arguing about nothing or that he couldn't figure out what they were really discussing. Maybe there should be a scientific name for what they were doing, something he might call Gunderson's Certainty Principle. If you're involved with someone, it's certain you'll be confused.

The light went green.

---------------→

When they had reached her condo, he had hoped the argument in the car was over, but as Ursula ushered him in, she said, "I'm not clear how women have power. Men usually make the first moves — whether it's in office politics or in sex."

"The first-move rule is a joke," he said, walking in. "The first-move rule is one of those weird ones you sense around eighth grade, right? Men are supposed to make the first move, but only after the woman makes some sort of indication it's okay. Maybe she flirts. Maybe she gets into, as they say, 'Something more comfortable.' Women really have the power. Women can be outright sexual if they want, and it's okay, and if they say no, it's no. Men being sexual is just simply taken for granted. They'd have sex with a knothole in a tree."

She laughed. "Would you?"

"My point is women get to control sex. They are goddesses, and they rule men."

Ursula gave a long and astounded laugh. "You've got to be kidding. Women have to fit into a mold. Look at most magazine covers if you don't believe me."

This statement brought back his uncomfortable moments with Marshelle, the tall woman he had met briefly when speed dating. In fact, it was dawning on Gunnar that this evening wasn't going to turn out well — all after an amazing week. He sighed. What does a woman want?

"Women have to look a certain way, or men don't pay any attention to them," she said.

"Yes, but attention of a certain sort, no? Objectification? You want it both ways, it seems to me. To be an object and not an object."

"Big boobs. That's not me," she replied.

"Don't you see?" he said, feeling but not understanding a sudden adrenaline rush. "I look at you like you're an amazing new phenomenon. I'd always thought people were predictable, but you're not. With you, I'm in shock and awe, and that's a good thing. Even if I don't understand your inner workings, I'm fascinated. You're a strike of lightning, zapping me to my core. You're beautiful, smart, funny. You're not a magazine cover. You're someone real, someone I've touched — and you touch me."

"Wow," she said. She looked as if she'd just witnessed a supernova in her back yard. "You affect me, too."

"And I'm not talking just physically, which, by the way, is nice. If a soul is twenty-one grams, you have it all."

"It is nice," she said, and she took his hand.

"See," he said. "You made the first move."

She shook her head surely, smiling. "Uh uh. You spoke your feelings. Truthful feelings. That's the first move."

"It is — or was?" he said. "Good for me." And he leaned in and kissed her. She returned his contact with passion. Next thing he knew, they were going down to the floor.

--------------→

When he and Ursula had stripped each other of clothes and found themselves excited and eager, the foreplay creating an unstoppable need, he eagerly reached for his pants, searching for the condoms he knew were there. Ursula, meanwhile, grabbed for the drawer in the side table next to the couch. They found themselves each holding foil packs of condoms.

"How about we try mine first, then yours next?" said Ursula.

"Wow," said Gunnar. "There's a lot of optimism in that statement."

She fumbled trying to take the condom out of her pack. She threw it aside and pulled him on top of her, guiding his penis not inside her but right against her happy spot.

"Do you mind if we try this kind of foreplay first?" she said.

"Mind?"

"I just want to feel the real you for a bit."

He came to understand that as he lay atop her and pressed down, much as he did as a kid in bed at night pressing his penis against the mattress, he was touching, even teasing, her clitoris. She gave a quick "oh!" every time he moved. It felt remarkably good to him, too.

He had to stop, not wanting to reach climax yet. He also wanted entrance. Being inside her seemed important, as if he could be closer to her soul. He opened his condom pack. She reached for and pulled the rubbery disc out.

"Lie flat," she whispered, and she slipped it on him. She straddled him and guided him in. Her movements were slow, rocking up and down, and soon his movements matched hers. The way she moved reminded Gunnar of the dancers in sync, each seeming to sense each other and move as if one mind.

Gunnar could see Ursula's eyes starting to glisten, as if near tears, and the magic of that amazed him.

None of this was making sense. It was just imagery, and her movement was as if God, any God, Zeus, Odin, Diana, created all of the universe for these very seconds of swaying.

"It's okay," she said as if she heard his thoughts. In seeing her look at him so lovingly, to his surprise, his own eyes watered.

"It's okay," she said again.

He nodded, tears coming more truly. "I love you," he called, and then he realized his timing. Was this too soon to say "love?" Was this a mistake? Was he going too fast? Would he lose her? Yet he hadn't known he'd say this. It was just what came out.

"Yes," she said. "And I love you."

--------------->

The next day, Gunnar had to go to the airport for Copenhagen, but he and Ursula made love again. They made it last even longer than the evening before. He started thinking of it as tantric sex, something he'd heard on an HBO commercial for *Real Sex*. He couldn't tell how long they went, many minutes or many hours. Time and space became relative.

They weren't crying this time, but laughing. As they lay together, legs intertwined afterwards, Ursula said, "I'll miss you."

"I'll miss you, too."

He felt his eyes water, and he had to turn away. He had the feeling as if someone had just stepped on his grave. What if this were it, the end of his relationship, just as it had been with Kara? He and Ursula were happy and optimistic, but what if he had some strange destiny thing going on, always to be in long-distance relationships that failed? What if, in fact, he created these long distance relationships that failed? His subconscious self was the controller. An observer, a scientist, would notice these things about him and create a hypothesis: "Gunnar Gunderson cannot exist in a relationship for long — he's a fermion — and thus he fashions temporary relationships separated by distance."

"What's wrong?" said Ursula.

His heart pounded. "Nothing," he said, trying to mean it.

"You just look so... deep in thought."

"Nope," he said. "Just enjoying the moment."

She smiled. "Me, too," she said.

On the way to the airport, night descended like a smothering pillow, and as he sensed this might be the end of them, he couldn't help but think he was witness to his own undoing. Thoughts are always one's undoing, weren't they?

"You'll wait for me, right?" he said.

"I love you," she said.

CHAPTER TWENTY-THREE

"THE PRESSURE APPLIED TO A FLUID
CONFINED IN A CONTAINER IS
TRANSMITTED UNDIMINISHED
THROUGHOUT THE FLUID AND ACTS IN
ALL DIRECTIONS."

— PASCAL'S PRINCIPLE

There are immutable laws, Gunnar Gunderson thought as Ursula pulled up to the curb of the International Terminal by the SAS sign. A long line came out from the door, and a dark-skinned TSA officer in black pants and unzipped coat showing the blue shirt and badge underneath, watched over the line. This is where he had dropped Kara off, which was the beginning of the end of their relationship. Now he was leaving Ursula to go to the same place.

He turned to face Ursula, and she seemed near tears. "I haven't looked forward to this moment," he said.

"It's like you're a soldier going off to war," she said, "but this isn't a war. This is just, you know, life. We have to be practical."

There it was again: practicality, a word Kara had used. His stomach lurched, and he felt as if he were plummeting from a mountaintop. With a mere gesture, however — Ursula smiling — that sensation stopped, replaced by such a rush of hope, it could be a horse rushing over a ridge. He leaned in, and they kissed long and hard, and it felt different from moments earlier. This kiss said hang on.

"We didn't talk about this," said Gunnar, "but what about vacations? Do you have one coming up anytime soon?"

"I'm just starting a job. I won't get one for a year."

"Maybe a long weekend. You might trade shifts, right? And I'll get you a ticket for a long weekend, say four days. Come to Denmark. Stay with me. It's a great country."

"I love the idea," she said, but she was blinking hard as if to stave off tears. "I can probably work my schedule that way, and it could work."

"It could work." He nodded. He exited the car. The moment he did, he heard, "Hey, Professor" from somewhere in the line. The TSA officer waved at him. "Professor Gunderson, Josh Stevens. I took your physics for non-majors a few years ago — a great class." The kid beamed, making Gunnar feel like a rock star.

"Thank you," Gunnar said, getting his bag from the car and wondering is this where a college degree got someone these days? "Did you graduate?" he asked.

"Not yet. This is a part-time job for me. They're using a lot of college students these days. It couldn't be better."

Gunnar remembered the kid. He always sat up front and asked great questions. "Nice seeing you, Josh." Ursula was now out of the car at his side. She looked very sad, the way he felt.

"Maybe in a month or two you could come?" he said.

"Yes. That's not so long. You can wait, can't you?" she said.

Could he wait? Yes, yes, but so much of him said if he left now, that's it, things will happen. She may meet someone else, or she stops missing him, or he's forced to stay in Denmark for some reason. A thousand things could happen. Say good-bye to her forever.

"I tell my introductory students about certain laws of physics," Gunnar said, taking her hands. "They are the rules except when it comes to quantum physics, especially at absolute zero, when things change. I talk about Werner Heisenberg's Uncertainty Principle. We cannot know, for instance, where an electron is at the same time we know how fast it is moving."

"What are you saying?"

"I love you, and I hate the uncertainty and I wish I didn't have to go right now."

"The way I look at it," she said, "Is that the sooner you go, the sooner you'll come back. So go." She looked down at the ground, as if not looking at him, he'd believe it.

"Why is it everything in me says for me not to go?" Gunnar pulled her closer.

"Sweetie, we know this isn't the way our lives work. We're sensible, no-nonsense people. We can't help that — but it's also our greatest strength. I believe in you. I believe in us." She kissed him tenderly again.

He sighed, glanced at Josh the TSA officer, and strode to the line.

"Show your boarding passes, please," said Josh to everyone in line — or maybe just to him because he did not have his boarding pass out. He unzipped the outside of his bag and retrieved his boarding pass. He was ready. The line started moving quickly. Ursula stood by the car, watching. She couldn't leave it or it'd be towed. He waved as she waved, and then he was inside the terminal between two velvet ropes that guided the line. Ahead was a checkpoint with a young female TSA officer checking that everyone who walked past her had a boarding pass. She appeared to be in her early twenties — probably a college student with a boyfriend and no thought of traveling to another country and being away from him. Young people seemed as if they understood love better than people his age. It was careers. Careers made you more dumb when it came to relationships. He was feeling sick. This wasn't right. Every electron in his body seemed to bellow out not to leave. He felt superglued to the spot. Yet his right foot took the next step toward the young woman.

Just as it was nearing his turn, he heard, "Gunnar!"

He turned to see Ursula running toward him.

"Your car!" was the first words out of his mouth. A fraction of a second later, he knew he should have said "Ursula!" or "Yea!" He was too damn practical, but she said, "It's okay. Your friend Josh is looking at it.

He wanted to kiss her right then and there, but he noticed the TSA officer and nearly everyone in line looking at him. He stepped out of line, grabbed Ursula's hand, and pulled her fast into a sitting area over where there was a line of giant square gray posts that held up the ceiling. He pulled her close behind a post where no one could see them, and they kissed as if they'd been gone months. He realized they must of have been groaning when he looked up to see a bespectacled man, a traveler with his cell phone out and pocketing it. The man said, "Sorry. I thought someone was being mugged or something."

"Sorry," Ursula said to Gunnar. "I had to see you one more time."

The man hurried off, embarrassed.

Everything right then made sense, and the words just came to Gunnar. "I've always believed in science and the scientific method but in these last months, I've come to understand that there's scientific thinking, and there's creative thinking."

"Yeah?" said Ursula.

"It's the creative side that lets us love. Science and love don't intertwine easily — fermions and bosons. I'm thinking we have to think creatively here. I don't want to dash off."

Her eyes looked hopeful, but she also looked puzzled.

"How can we think creatively right now when people are expecting you in Denmark?"

"I can't leave."

"But you don't have a house or a job, and you have responsibilities in Copenhagen. I have responsibilities here."

"Yes, we're responsible people. We've both studied science because it explains things — but it doesn't explain how we feel — or at least how I feel."

"Or how I feel, too."

"And it doesn't explain how we got together or the chemistry we have. I hate to admit it, but I have to rely on instinct. The way artists do. The way creative thinkers do. My friend Jeet in theatre knows this, and I finally get it. We have to be true to us. You with me?"

"Continue."

"So I don't have a house, and I'm not sure what I'm going to do, but I'm going to fake it, okay?"

"Really?" she said.

"So I shouldn't go. I can't go."

She stood there, blinking.

He said, "Right?"

"Of course not, you asshole. Let's get back in the car."

As they exited, Josh stood at the car and smiled. "So things worked out," he said, pointing to Ursula. "You explained the universe to me, Professor. I'm glad to see it's still all in order. It's absolutely something."

Gunnar said, "Thank you."

"You're welcome," said Josh.

"The white zone is for loading and unloading of bags only," said the speakers above. Gunnar and Ursula loaded Gunnar's bag.

ACKNOWLEDGEMENTS

A project like this book, where the protagonist is in a profession far different than the author, can require a great deal of research — and in this case, it did. I am utterly thankful for the scientists who sent me research, advised me, or looked parts of this over, including: Nils O. Anderson, director of the Niels Bohr Institute; Mark Saffman, Physics, University of Wisconsin; Emil Sidky, Physics, University of Chicago; David Goulet, Mathematics, California Institute of Technology; Tim Roberts, Raytheon; and Sidney Nagel, Physics, University of Chicago.

Also, I deeply thank those who read early drafts of the book in whole or parts, adding their own sense and sensibility. In particular, thank you to Ann Pibel, Roberta Lawrence, Peter Seed, Daniel Will-Harris, Keri DuLaney, Dee Edler, Molly Headley, Stewart Lindh, Michael J. Moore, Jim Jennewein, Kelly Hewins, Kristen Tsetsi, Kevin Kilpatrick, Vibeke Sorensen, Elisabeth Young, Barbara Young, the late Marie Franco, my nephew Eric Meeks, my father George Meeks, and my late mother Sidney Wear. The first draft of a novel isn't necessarily compelling, so it takes a handful of people to dance through the words and tell the author what's good and what isn't. The people above took me into the critical final stages and helped me marry my vision with what was actually on the page.

Those people who read the earliest and rawest chapters for this book include Jessica Barksdale Inclan, who guided me steadily and well, Maria Maturana, Ishamea Harris, Diane Rosenblum, Norman Nuwash, Katharine Johnson, Richard Ireland, Annamari Lilja, Julie Swayze, Mortimer Adams, Jim Boyle, Molly Bruns, Diane Freiberg, Kristen Osman, Judith Daigle Milan, and Marlene Margulius. It was fun to have a small core group look over my shoulder, as it were, as the story progressed. I felt like Charles Dickens giving weekly installments.

Many thanks, too, to Carol Fuchs for proofreading brilliantly and to Palle Henckel for going over my Danish and all things Danish (as well as English), and, to Dr. Jeremiah Young, Dr. Mark Tarica, Dr. Joseph Cannon, and Beverly Young, R.N., for their medical and dental knowledge.

ABOUT THE AUTHOR

Christopher Meeks has had stories published in several literary journals, and he has two collections of stories, *Months and Seasons* and *The Middle-Aged Man and the Sea*. His novel *The Brightest Moon of the Century* made the list of three book critics' Ten Best Book of 2009. He has had three full-length plays mounted in Los Angeles, and one, *Who Lives?* had been nominated for five Ovation Awards, Los Angeles' top theatre prize. Mr. Meeks teaches English at Santa Monica College, fiction writing at UCLA Extension, and Children's Literature at the Art Center College of Design. Visit his website at:

WWW.CHRISMEEKS.COM

Chrismeeks@gmail.com

READ CHRISTOPHER MEEKS'S OTHER BOOKS, WWW.CHRISMEEKS.COM

THE BRIGHTEST MOON OF THE CENTURY

"Christopher Meeks chronicles one man's path to middle-age and, in doing so, illustrates how choices and circumstances — even those that seem arbitrary and the time — have a way of irrevocably cementing a person's future." — **Cherie Parker,** *Minneapolis Star Tribune*

"This is a moving novel." — **Rachel Durfor,** *Rebecca's Reads*

"Charming and endlessly entertaining." — *Midwest Book Review*

"Throughout it all, Meeks uses Edward's worries and internal dialogue as a focus to show the possibilities found in small moments: in sunrises, in friendships, in apparent disaster. Unpretentious and deeply human, the normalcy and every-man nature of the novel give it power." — **Jennie Blake,** *BookGeeks*

"This is what I love about Meeks: his ability to gauge human-ity, his understanding and acceptance of the strangeness of intricacies of life and personality, and his wonderful sense of compassion for his characters." — **Heather Figearo,** *Raging Bibliomania*

"I have to say I've gone from being an admirer of his work to a full-blown fan bordering on groupie." — **Marc Schuster,** *Small Press Reviews*

"His stance in the echelon of new important American writ-ers seems solidly secure." — **Grady Harp,** *Top Ten Amazon Reviewer*

"Meeks has the talent to carry his quirky characters and their 'find their extraordinary in the everyday' plots into a full-length novel." — **Dawn Rennert, *She's Too Fond of Books***

"[Meeks] gives us characters who are very human and who face many obstacles in life, and then he infuses their stories with hope." — **Wendy Robards, *Caribousmom***

"Within the pages of *Brightest Moon* lies an entertaining saturnalia of authenticity also found in Meeks's short stories (see *Months and Seasons*). He has a knack for making readers believe his characters are real people." — **Diana Raabe, *The Raabe Review***

MONTHS AND SEASONS AND OTHER STORIES:

"For those readers fortunate enough to have read Christopher Meeks's first short story collection, *The Middle-Aged Man and the Sea,* and discovered the idiosyncrasies of Meeks's writing style and content, rest assured that this new collection, *Months and Seasons,* not only will not disappoint, but also it will provide further proof that we have a superior writer of the genre in our presence."
— **Grady Harp, Top Ten Reviewer, Amazon.com**

"The stories in *Months and Seasons* are like potato chips: you can't read just one. Just a few sentences into the first piece, "Dracula Sinks into the Night," I immediately felt at home in the world Meeks has created."
— **Marc Schuster, *Small Press Reviews***

"With this collection, Christopher Meeks proves there is an audience for short stories. His characters are well defined with problems that they can't resolve. There are twelve tales that reveal a lot about our present society. Meeks's stories reminded me of those of John Cheever."
— **Gary Roen, *The Midwest Book Review***

"Full of complete randomness and quirkiness, ingredients I cherish, the stories in this twelve-story collection chronicle the eccentricities of an array of diverse characters, who are dealing with life thrown at them in the only way actually possible: by dealing with their problems, not escaping them."
— **Rachel Durfor,** *Rececca's Reads*

THE MIDDLE-AGED MAN AND THE SEA AND OTHER STORIES:

"A collection that is so stunning...that I could not help but move on to the next story."
— *Entertainment Weekly*

"Poignant and wise, sympathetic to the everyday struggles these characters face."
— *Los Angeles Times*

"These are original, articulate, engaging stories which examine life in America from the unique perspectives of ordinary people searching for their share of the promises held out as part of the American dream. ... *The Middle-Aged Man & The Sea* is highly recommended, highly entertaining, highly rewarding reading."
— *The Midwest Book Review*

"Christopher Meeks bounces onto the literary scene as a vibrant new voice filled with talent and imagination. The Middle-Aged Man and the Sea is one of the finer collections of short stories that will rapidly rise to the top to of the heap of a battery of fine writers of this difficult medium."
— **Grady Harp, Top Ten Reviewer, Amazon.com**

"Mr. Meeks has a wonderfully fun writing style — witty, cynical, and often poignant. His stories are about the stuff of life: love and heartbreak, sickness and death, desires and struggles, spirituality and the search for meaning."
— **Janet Rubin, *Novel Reviews***

"In this collection of short stories, Christopher Meeks examines the small heartbreaks and quiet despair that are so much a part of all of our lives. He does it in language that is resonant, poetic, and precise. Franz Kafka said that a book should be an ice-axe to break the frozen sea within us. This collection is just such a weapon. If you like Raymond Carver,

you'll love Meeks. He may be as good — or better. He de-
serves major recognition."
— **author David Scott Milton** (*Paradise Road*)

"If the publishing and reading world is fair and just, Christopher Meeks is destined to be widely read and deservedly
honored." — **Carolyn Howard-Johnson,** *Myshelf.com*

"Many of these tales have appeared in American literary
journals, but reading them together, you get the full impact
of Meeks's talent, as he takes you in a head-long assault
through ordinary day-to-day life, the mundane under the
microscope and given the once-over through Meeks's careful
eye." — **Susan Tomaselli,** *Dogmatika*

"While Ellis and the other characters in Meeks's stories are in
one way or another, and to varying degrees, 'Californicat-
ed'...they and the stories that contain them are firmly rooted
in this universe where the only magic available to save any
of them is the only kind available to save any of us: self-
awareness and self-discipline."
— **David Reilly,** *Lance Mannion*

Made in the USA
Charleston, SC
23 October 2011